S.A. Montgomery was bor
of Edinburgh. After stı
Edinburgh University, he
for a number of years befoı
high school for almost a decade. He is a keen kayaker and motorcyclist and lives in the Scottish Borders with his two daughters and two cats.

JANUS

BY
S.A. MONTGOMERY

First published on Kindle in 2015
First printed edition 2017

Copyright © S.A. Montgomery 2015

The right of S.A. Montgomery to be identified as the author of this work has been asserted by him in accordance with the Copyright, Designs and Patents Act 1988.

All characters and events in this publication are fictitious and any resemblance to real persons, living or dead, is purely coincidental.

All rights reserved.
No part of this book may be reproduced, stored in a retrieval system, or transmitted, in any form or by any means, nor be otherwise circulated in any form of binding other than that in which it is published and without a similar condition including this condition being imposed on the subsequent publisher.

ISBN 978-1542966153

Cover design © Karen Ward 2015

Acknowledgments

Many thanks to all who have read and commented on *Janus* over the years. The feedback and comments have always been appreciated and I am indebted to those who helped proofread early copies - you know who you are. Many thanks to my brother Mark for keeping me right with road geography around London and to Karen for the wonderful cover.

Any errors which remain are mine...

CONTENTS

PROLOGUE 1
PART I - "NUMBER FOUR" 5
PART II - ALTER EGO 93
PART III - THE HUNT 223
EPILOGUE 361

Foreword

This novel is set just after the turn of millennium, a time not too long ago, yet quite different to today in terms of accessibility of information, computing and the internet.

S.A. Montgomery

PROLOGUE

The preparation had been meticulous: anatomy books read, the finest scalpels ordered, an autopsy attended.

As usual the table was covered with sheets of industrial polythene. This chimpanzee was an adult male. Stretched out on the makeshift operating table it was almost as long as a man.

The scalpel blade pierced just in front of the creature's left ear. The animal flinched. More chloroform was poured onto the cloth and pressed over the chimp's muzzle.

After, the work was surveyed; the removed tissue was a near perfect mask of flesh.

It was time.

He checks around the room: the window is still intact and the box is still behind the door. He crosses to the window and wipes off a stripe of grime. It is raining; heavy black clouds roll slowly over the sky. The streets are shiny, with animated puddles feeding small rivers in the gutters of the road. There is even a small pool developing on top of the bus shelter culminating in a mini waterfall as it escapes from one of the corners.

No one is about and it seems a good time to leave his hideaway. He crosses to the door, checks to see he hasn't left anything, opens the door a crack and manoeuvres to view the hallway. The carpet is waterlogged from a missing pane in the skylight. He listens: nothing but the sound of rain thooping onto the carpet. Bending his arm around the door as he closes it, he pulls the box as near to the back of the door as he can; it was always useful to know if there had been any visitors while you were gone. He moves quickly down the hallway, edging round the mushy carpet, and looks over the railing down into the stairwell. The place is deserted. He descends the two floors and exits into the street and begins his walk to the Plaza in the centre of town. The rain is bouncing off the streets around him.

The Plaza is one of the two main shopping centres in the City. He enters through the glass doors which swish open at his approach. There aren't many people here and those who are stay in the shadows. He steps onto the escalator and looks around as he begins the slow glide to the floor below. There is a lot of visible destruction: broken mirrors, smashed shop windows, fire damage. As he descends, he looks at the devastation sliding past him. Surely it was justified to remove the people who had turned this place into a desolate warzone.

He steps from the escalator. Most of the lights down here are broken. A tube light buzzes and flashes irregularly to his right. He lights a cigarette, the flare from the match revealing his dim reflection in a smoke-darkened shop window in front of him. He sets off along the concourse, his footsteps crunching as he walks over broken glass and the general detritus surrounding him. He walks into the main shopping hall.

The centre is adorned with a fountain containing human statues that appear to be constructing some kind of giant object under the various streams of water. At least that's what it had been before; he had seen pictures. Today it is a stagnant pool of oily black water with chunks of rock jutting from the blackness. A pair of blue legs stand near the centre, the sheared residue of one of the figures.

'Hello,' he shouts, his voice echoing around the cavernous hall. Smoke billows in front of him as his words exhale the smoke from his cigarette.

'Over here.' The voice comes from the left of the pool.

He steps over some debris and moves past the defunct fountain, his feet splashing on the wet floor. Traversing the pool allows him to see that one of the shops has a dim sodium light burning behind a half-closed door. As he moves closer he can hear almost-whispered voices engaged in a heated discussion. He pushes the door fully open. It swings unevenly on its broken hinges.

'You people contacted Mr Janus?'

'Yes, come in.' A bearded man rises from the far side of the room, nervously offering his hand.

The visitor shakes the hand then takes a seat facing the group of about twelve sitting on various bits of office furniture and filing cabinets around the room. He draws on his cigarette.

The bearded man sits by the door, looks around at the others, then levels his gaze: 'Okay. We didn't want to have to contact Mr Janus, but this situation has gone on long enough. The place is in ruins and nobody uses any of the shops here now. We've all lost a fortune and some of us have even gone bust.'

A voice from atop a filing cabinet swears and mutters. The woman's head moves slowly from side to side as it hangs dejectedly.

The bearded man continues, 'I assume you need a picture and the money. £500, wasn't it? We've transferred it into Mr Janus's account. You can check it. It went in this afternoon.' He pauses briefly. 'It's a lot of mon—'

The bearded man trails off when, between draws of his cigarette, the visitor pulls a cell phone from his pocket and presses a quick-dial button. The phone at the other end rings once.

'Confirm £500 deposited this afternoon' he says, before hanging up. The phone gives an electronic click as he returns

it to the inside pocket of his jacket. The bearded man is shuffling in his seat. 'Go on.'

'Er, yes, anyway, it's a lot of money, so we'd like,' he hesitates briefly, 'we'd like it done soon.' He crosses to the desk and opens the top drawer. 'We've put together all the information we could get our hands on. His name is Kane; here's his picture. He seems to hang around the New Town a lot, as far as we can ascertain, and seems to be active mostly between five and nine. We've no idea where he goes when he's not here, although he's usually seen coming from the west side of town. He comes here around eight mostly.'

The visitor looks at the picture. The face bears a startling resemblance to the actor Michael Caine. It doesn't betray any trace of malicious intent, but then why should it? His mobile rings. 'Hello ... yes ... thanks.' He hangs up, the phone again making the small electronic click. 'Okay, your payment is confirmed.'

'So when will it be done?' All the faces in the room are looking at him now, expressions full of anticipation.

'Let's just say that Mr Janus will make sure that Mr Kane won't be troubling you for too much longer.' The visitor stands and walks to the door, picking up the folder the bearded man has been leafing through. 'Just watch the news.'

He walks out into the shopping hall and crunches and splashes past the fountain. As he leaves the whispers begin again and before they fade into the distance he hears a fragment in a whispered voice, ' ... son-of-a-bitch Janus ... thieving scum ... '

He flicks his cigarette butt into the inky black fountain, causing dark ripples to lap at the statue's legs. The wisp of smoke from the extinguished butt hangs in the air as he steps onto the escalator.

PART I - "NUMBER FOUR"

9 September, 8:07pm
The City

Vincent flicks the two locks on the case; the double thud sounds loud in the quiet of the rooftop. Opening the lid he views the two parts of the rifle. He lifts them out and with a quarter turn of the barrel locks them together with a satisfying click. He unclips the scope from the top part of the case and edges to the lip of the roof.

Through the cross-haired orange-tinted scope he can see the first camera team on a rooftop to his left. The producer is pressing an earpiece hard into his ear as he shouts into a walkie-talkie, while the cameraman rehearses the likely camera moves he'll need to get the shot. Beside them the soundman fiddles with knobs on a box attached by a coiled wire to a directional microphone.

Vincent moves the scope to the right. The second crew, similarly populated, is on the second floor of the hotel that overlooks Bushnell Road. The second unit's producer is obviously in conversation with the first unit's, judging by his animated gesticulations and unhappy expression.

A sweep of the scope down to the tree line reveals the two-man mobile unit. The mobile soundman has the traditional boom arm, complete with furry microphone. The cameraman is chatting to a couple of girls, a bulky camera on his shoulder.

Vincent snaps the scope to the rifle and slides forward until the knuckles of his left hand are on the damp edge of the roofing felt. He picks out some targets on the street below. There is no wind right now: the shots will be easy. He locks the scope onto a figure walking from the west. The cross-hairs pause on the man's chest before he zooms in, raising the cross-hairs between the target's eyes. 'Bang, bang. You're dead,' he whispers. He picks out another figure, closer this time, and again concentrates the cross-hairs between the eyes, then eases himself backwards, sits up and waits.

It is twenty minutes before Kane and four cronies begin their unsuspecting walk towards Bushnell Road. Kane has a cocky gait, his trench coat flapping and swinging behind him as he walks, revealing two holstered automatic pistols strapped over his Hawaiian shirt. He looks unconcerned as his gang randomly discharge their weapons into shop fronts at anything that moves.

As the group nears the junction, a speeding car is caught in the destructive hail from the weapons. The video footage shown on the news later that evening will show the driver's head explode onto the windscreen as the bullets tear through his car, the mobile camera catching its veering trajectory as it screeches through the junction, crashing through the fence where it finally barrel-rolls down into the gardens which run along Bushnell Road.

From the rooftop, Vincent watches the group approach.

Five.

He moves the sight across each of them. Another few steps and there will be nowhere to run.

Vincent walks up a staircase onto the sweeping road known as the Mound which connects Bushnell Road to Muzyka Street. As he walks, people watch him, whisper, point, step out of his way. One even pats him on the back. But only one.

He reaches Muzyka Street and begins the short trek up the hill. The street is washed clean by the recent rain, the cobbles shiny on the road. The car tyres make a buzzing sound here as they hurl up and down. He reaches the top of the hill and glances briefly at the view of The City. From here he can see that people are still crowding at the site of the hit. He can't see the red-stained street from here though.

He approaches a magnificent building with an even more magnificent studded oak door. He knocks and almost immediately a metal peephole slides open. A bolt is thrown and the door squeaks open.

'All right, Vincent?' says a beefy-looking man wearing a Trilby hat and dressed in a smart pinstriped suit. He is holding a machine pistol loosely by his leg.

Vincent quickly crosses the uneven flagstones of the courtyard and enters the main hall of the building. In the centre of the room a giant staircase sprouts from the floor and curls its way to the first floor. Plant pots sit on the edges of the individual stairs. He replaces one that has fallen over, brushing the loose dirt over the edge of the staircase; tiny, whispered echoes of sand on stone briefly fill his ears.

Upstairs is a large room. The main wall is adorned with a roaring fire. Various pieces of elaborate furniture carefully placed around the room cast shadows which dance on the walls. One of the walls is entirely made of glass, allowing an uninterrupted view over The City. The blinds have been pulled back and the evening sunlight spills into the room. He places his rifle case by the door and walks to the window.

'So I see we've done some more good today.' The voice comes from behind.

'Yes, Swift, I suppose we have.' Vincent doesn't turn.

'The live feed from City News was pretty good. How did you manage to get three crews?'

'It just kind of worked out that way.' Vincent moves to one of the large sofas in the back of the room and sinks into it, his shoulders slumping forward slightly. 'I just told them it was going to be a Bushnell Road hit and they jumped at the chance. I suppose it's what sells news at the end of the day.'

'Actually, Vincent,' Swift says moving towards the TV, 'it's about the right time for the news. Let's see your handiwork, shall we?' Swift is relishing this. He flicks the large television screen into life. The television's barely-audible high-pitched whine is quickly drowned out by the jingle for the evening news broadcast. Swift increases the volume. The fanfares stop and the newscaster begins - oozing sensationalism.

'At a little after eight fifteen this evening the criminal known as Kane was brutally gunned down, along with four accomplices, by an employee of the mysterious Mr Janus.' The image on the screen shows slow-motion footage of Kane strutting up the middle of the road. The slow-motion gives an almost artistic impression to the scene: Kane's trench coat swinging rhythmically as he walks, his stooges randomly firing weaponry slightly out of focus behind him, the empty shell casings expelled from their pistols slowly arcing and spinning, catching sunlight before bouncing into the blur.

'It is understood that Mr Kane had been holding the Bushnell Plaza to ransom in a campaign of hatred which has wreaked havoc in the buildings and forced a number of businesses to close. Tonight, his reign of violence in The City was brought to an abrupt and brutal close.' The scene now shows the car screeching through the junction and barrel rolling into the gardens. 'The mysterious employee of Mr Janus apparently delivered his shots from atop a West End building, but the speed and accuracy of the shots suggests another gunman may also have been involved'

'Where do they come up with these things?' says Vincent smiling. The screen is now running the moments of the hit in slow motion. Vincent had fired nine shots. He watches on screen as the drama slowly unfolds.

The first to be hit is one of the maniacal pistol-wielding stooges. The top of his hair appears to flip up suddenly in a spray of deep crimson. Over the next couple of slow-motion seconds his eyes glaze over and his knees begin to slowly buckle under him. His gun's rhythmic ejection of casings continues as he commences his sluggish drop to the ground.

The second shot passes through Kane's leg; his bloodied trousers burst backwards causing his trench coat to flip up as the bullet passes through. The first two shots have been fired so close together that none of the other three are even showing expressions of fear on the screen.

The third shot, shown from the second static camera position, hits a second goon in the middle of the chest, throwing him backwards. The first goon has almost hit the floor by this point, his buttocks jarring onto his heels as he falls, bouncing him slightly up again as he journeys downwards. The new camera angle shows it to perfection.

The look of fear on Kane's and the others' faces are showing now, Kane's mixed with agony. He is reaching for his guns as he tries to regain his balance, his leg unable to hold his weight properly. The fourth shot passes through his left wrist. His machine pistol rolls forward as it falls, catching on his trigger finger and causing the newly broken wrist to bend to an obscene angle. He is looking around frantically, trying to see where the shots are coming from. Behind him one of his goons is in the process of lifting a pointing finger and opening his mouth to shout when the fifth bullet slams through his nose, blowing the back of his head out. Vincent remembers this moment: the instant the goon had seen his position, the instant his head was kicked back by the force of the bullet's impact. It had seemed to take longer when it had happened.

The sixth shot spins the final goon off his feet as it hits him in the shoulder; the seventh tears into the back of his head before he reaches the ground.

A wide-angle view now replaces the close-ups. The scene shows four dead goons and Kane, staggering to keep his balance, his left arm pulled tightly in at his side, the machine pistol in his good hand bucking as he instinctively fires, searching for his opponent. It is at this point the eighth bullet hits him, bending him double as it slams into his stomach, simultaneously lifting him backwards off his feet. As the sequence slowly advances he touches down bit by bit: his buttocks, his back and head, and finally his arms, arcing over to hit the ground, his gun bouncing from his grasp as all movement ripples to a stop.

'In this most brutal display of Mr Janus's grip on the City, this latest clean-up appears to have been a warning to all gangster wanabes.' The newscaster pauses. The scene cuts to one of Vincent walking from the doorway of a building, pistol in hand, his rifle case in the other. He walks to the broken form of Kane dragging himself weakly towards his gun. The camera zooms in.

'Kane.' TV Vincent raises his gun as Kane tries to turn to face him. 'Mr Janus doesn't want scum like you in his City.' He pulls the trigger.

'And that warning seems to be: don't get on the wrong side of Mr Janus.'

'That was a bit out there, Vincent, don't you think?' Swift clicks the television off from the sofa. 'Getting a bit feral wouldn't you say?' He nudges Vincent with his elbow before he stands and walks to the fireplace. He picks up one of the stacked logs and throws it into the flames; an explosion of orange sparks dart into the chimney.

Vincent stands and walks out onto the landing. 'Swift.' He is looking into the next room, where three men lie sleeping on reclining chairs. His voice is low as he continues, 'Has Tyler been up at all?'

'Nope.' Swift moves into the room with the figures. 'Unfortunately not.' He stops beside one of the sleeping men and lifts the man's wrist up. As he releases it, it slumps down, the hand opening slightly. Compared to the other two

sleepers Tyler is grey and gaunt, his eye sockets sunken and dark. His cheekbones are pronounced under his thinly stretched skin, and some of his hair, which has fallen out, is lying on the area around his head.

'This isn't good,' Vincent says, lighting a cigarette. He continues, his words half spoken half blown, as he expels the smoke, 'How long has that been now?'

'Seven, eight days, I'm not too sure. He's looking pretty bad though.'

'Yeah, he's not in good shape at all. I'm surprised he's lasted this long. You'd have thought he'd have said something before he went and did this wouldn't you?' He again draws on the cigarette.

'You don't suppose he didn't plan this, do you? Maybe something bad's happened to him.' Swift makes a mock scary wooing noise as he pushes Vincent over Tyler's body. He is laughing as he leaves the room. Vincent draws deeply on the cigarette as he looks at Tyler's slowly wasting form.

'I hope not.' He turns and leaves the room, closing the door behind him.

It is after twelve when Vincent leaves and begins the trek to his safe house. The City is quiet. Most people are asleep, and the minimal international presence won't be up for a few hours yet. The streets are dry now, the moon a beacon in the clear deep blue sky.

The blow is delivered as he walks past the trees at the bottom of the pedestrian area of the City Park. He is on the ground before he can react. A kick to his head renders him almost unconscious, leaving him helpless as he is dragged into the darkness that edges the path.

His aggressor is breathing heavily as he wrestles with the dead weight of his load, the water-logged grass causing him to slip a couple of times before he has dragged Vincent to a wall.

Vincent is dimly aware that his hands are being bound behind him as he sluggishly struggles to get his face out of the mud. His vision is slowly clearing, but not quickly enough for him to free his hands before they are tied. A knee in his back forces the air from his lungs, not helping to rid him of the haze he desperately needs to shake off. The voice, when it comes, is a raspy whisper.

'You will be number four, Janus.' Then a whoosh as a cosh cuts through the air.

Black silence.

He comes round after about two minutes, his vision slowly clearing as he wriggles to get to a sitting position with his back to the wall. He checks his legs and stomach. Thankfully the psycho hasn't cut him.

'What the hell was that about?' he says as he pushes himself to a standing position. His hands are still tied, but by twisting his wrists he eventually manages to work the bindings loose. He staggers down the hill towards the path as the rope drops from his hands. Reaching the relative safety of the light he can see that he is covered in mud and grass stains. He looks up and down the street. Not a soul. Who was that? What had just happened?

He runs across the centre of the park and crosses the road into the street where his safe house is located. Entering a doorway, he waits. For fifteen minutes he stands, motionless, watching, waiting to see that it is safe to sleep.

No one.

Using an alleyway to access the overgrown gardens behind the buildings, he quickly moves to the back door. He scampers up the two flights of stairs then stops, panting on the landing. Again he listens: silence. Crossing the squelchy floor, he pushes the door and to his relief feels the resistance as the box he'd pulled there earlier in the day scrapes over the floor. He pushes it against the door once again before he carefully camouflages himself with rubbish from around the room and slips into sleep.

17 September, 6:08pm
Central London

Stella Robertson stood safely behind the yellow line on the hot stuffy platform at Tottenham Court Road and looked through the strange indoor haze that exists in the London Underground in the evening. She noticed that time had stopped: the next train to Epping was, according to the electronic sign, due in two minutes, but had been for the last five. In London it often seemed that time froze, with minutes becoming endless as she stood with her face pressed into the shoulder of the ignorant businessman who had forced his way onto the crowded eastbound Central Line service—despite the fact there was no visible room for him—and then had the audacity to make space enough to read his *Evening Standard* at the expense of Stella's face room. Rush hour always made her wish she didn't live in the South East.

By Stratford the train and the air were clearing and she was able perch on a seat at the end of her carriage. More of a ledge than a seat, she watched the landscape slip by as she picked at her fingernails. Mile after mile of city blocks slid past, before the view was suddenly replaced by rolling fields. Only the briefest glimpse of a motorway betrayed that this wasn't the real countryside.

Five minutes later she was in Theydon Bois pressing a piece of tissue to a throbbing finger as she covered the two hundred yards to the front door of her flat above a garage and an engraver's at the ultra-cheap end of one of the most exclusive areas in the vicinity. Her rented flat obviously hadn't cost a fraction of the £1,500,000 that the average house in Theydon Bois did; but then her flat had fungus growing on the living room wall and was cold due to the damp that she couldn't get rid of, despite the so-called central heating.

The tip of her left index finger throbbed as she opened the door and walked into her hall. She shivered, bolting the door top and bottom before she picked up her three bits of junk mail and trudged upstairs. It was almost twenty past seven. She'd need to hurry if she was to get something to eat.

She slipped off her coat in the living room and opened the door out to the rooftop. The evening was sunny, the white clouds on the horizon all that was left of the rainy late-summer's day.

'Thomas!" she called. "*Psht! Psht!*" No sign. She called again closing her eyes briefly, feeling the evening sun on her face. The metallic crump of Thomas jumping from the fence onto the bonnet of an old car in the car yard brought a smile to her face as she blinked, opening her eyes. He bounded across, appearing quickly on the roof, meowing as he ran. Stella picked him up and hugged him closely, rubbing his stomach.

'Where have you been? You're soaking.' She placed him back on the floor. He circled her legs as she moved through the kitchen to the bedroom, stopping only briefly to switch on the kettle. She relayed her day to Thomas as she undressed, hanging her work clothes neatly on hangers in the wardrobe before slipping into jogging bottoms and a fleece. Thomas purred and rolled ecstatically on the bed, occasionally finding a few seconds to lick his front paws. Stella rubbed his stomach. 'Who's a good boy?' As the rumble of the boiling kettle increased she gave him a final pat on the head.

The kettle clicked off as Stella opened the fridge and pulled out the cat food. Thomas took up station rubbing himself against her ankles, his ecstatic purrs and circling manoeuvres becoming more pronounced with each passing second. It was always the same and Stella smiled while spooning the food past his head into the bowl trying hard not to get it on his head.

Her own meal came from the freezer, caught a quick view of the inside of the microwave (just long enough to make a quick coffee), then was slopped into a large Ikea bowl. The side dish was a couple of slices of frozen bread defrosted in the toaster, then generously layered with butter. These were dunked into what appeared to be a pasta dish as Stella channel-hopped the *Freeview* television channels.

17 September, 8:53pm
East London

Jarvis Nickleby's face flickered grey as the light emissions from two of his four console monitors flashed dozens of images per second across their grimy screens. His curtains were drawn, as usual, and he was unaware the sun was shining outside his window. His desk was littered with the detritus of various fast food meals: pizzas, burgers, Chinese, fish and chips; and conventional crockery was randomly strewn across the desk, although its general function was to collect ash, the items having long ago served their time as vessels for food.

A single desk lamp assisted the monitor light, reassuringly masking the nicotine staining on the walls, the fingerprints on the monitor power switches, the light switches and around the door frames. The floor was carpeted by ash, house dust and budget brand cigarette butts, which built in number around his bed: a mattress on the floor, a couple of yellowed sheets and a brown tinged pillow his bedclothes. Pinhole sheet burns betrayed Jarvis's bedtime marijuana penchant.

From his beat-up leather armchair Jarvis leaned forward to get a closer look at one of the images on the screen. A swift bit of typing on the keyboard centred the streaming video image on the monitor he was scrutinising. He leaned in closer putting down his smoke. It missed the ashtray, rolling along the desk and under a couple of CD boxes.

'What the fuck?' His eyes narrowed as he concentrated on the image of a bearded man being roughly dragged from a chair in front of his computer. The webcam image was refreshing fairly quickly, so the image was relatively smooth. A dark figure appeared to have a garrotte around the neck of the bearded man who was making gurgling noises while he was being lifted up slightly from his chair. His eyes were bulging as blood began to run from his neck through fingers clawing to pry the garrotte from his neck. The chair flipped backwards and Jarvis's image was suddenly lost.

'Fuck me!' Jarvis's eyes were bulging, goose bumps creeping along his arms.

Despite the lost image, the sound continued: thudding, scraping. The gurgling was also continuing and to Jarvis's ears seemed to be getting wetter. A thrashing kick knocked the camera once again onto the fight, with a sideways picture filling the window: the bearded man was still struggling to free himself from his attacker, looking weaker now. Jarvis was leaning his head to the side for a better view, his greasy ponytail hanging into the scum on his desk.

The image was short-lived and was soon replaced by a view of the computer keyboard and a television set in the corner of the room. A last ditch survival effort from the bearded man knocked the camera to show a now quite blue victim with blood covering his front, waning badly and not putting up much of a fight. The dark figure visibly strained harder at the garrotte, his hands vibrating with the pressure. A subtle crunching sound and the man relaxed.

The on-screen figure grabbed the ankles of the bearded man's corpse, dragging it out of view. The bloodied seat followed, hooked by one of the dead man's arms. All that remained onscreen was an innocent-looking view of a room with a picture on the wall of a country scene at the far side, a garishly coloured sofa on the left and what seemed to be the front door—since it had a letter box—on the right.

Jarvis shakily lit a cigarette and stared at the image. Small boxes of graphical decompression jumped around a dark corner of the image. He turned up his speakers. Twenty minutes passed before the figure again crossed the view of the camera, opened the door and left. It was clear as he walked out into the brightly lit hallway that he was completely dressed in black including gloves and a balaclava. The door shut with a click and Jarvis let go of the breath he didn't know he was holding in a long 'ffff—' sound.

'Oh, wow!' He stared at the screen as he took another cigarette out and unsteadily put it in his mouth. The flame from the match twitched as he drew on the cigarette. 'Fuck me,' he said, his heart pounding. 'Fuck me!'

His fingers raced over the keyboard and a window popped up, numbers and files cascading over the screen. He found the program he was looking for and searched through a list of files on one of his other monitors.

'Gotcha.' He clicked the file and the image of the bearded man sitting in front of his PC popped into the video viewer he had loaded. 'I got it.' He used a small button on the graphics interface to slide the video forward to the end. He had the whole grisly scene on disk. 'This is quality stuff,' he said, the ash from the cigarette in his mouth falling down the front of his yellowed vest. 'Real fuckin' quality.'

17 September, 11:25pm
The City

Vincent looks out over the City. Only the slight shimmer of stars interrupts the blackness of the sky. There is no moon tonight and the yellow streetlamps below give the scene a sepia quality. There aren't a lot of people around, although a few cars are using Bushnell Road as a kind of drag strip while it is quiet. As he watches, a tiny lone figure between the cars drops its arms and two cars race at break-neck speed along the road. The glass dulls the roar of the engines.

He hits the switch that closes the electric blinds and turns on the television. The final second of a City News Special Report appears briefly before the announcer's voice says, 'And now we'll return to this evening's coverage of the drag racing on Bushnell Road.' An annoying commentator appears and gushes with far too much excitement for the events being described.

'Great,' Vincent mutters, 'racing or racing.' He switches off and moves through to the other room.

It is now day fourteen of Tyler's decay and his body looks like it could have come from one of those documentaries where a sarcophagus from an ancient tomb is cracked open to reveal the mummified body inside. Tyler has taken on a flaky, dusty quality. Vincent touches his arm and the grey flesh crumbles and falls into a small pile of dust leaving a hole where the bone of the arm is now clearly visible. It is not a pretty sight. The sleeping bodies of Swift, Wilson and Frank look pictures of health in contrast to the wasted form of Tyler.

Vincent returns to the large room. The clock on the wall reads 11:26pm. Boyd is nearly two and a half hours late. He had phoned in three hours before saying he was on his way, but had not yet materialised.

Looking in on the sleepers once more, Vincent decides he has to go and find Boyd. He goes to the munitions room and grabs a machine pistol, then straps on a bulletproof vest before donning his coat.

Boyd would be coming from down by the docks so Vincent heads down Muzyka Street before crossing to the Bleszinski Walkway that runs down for about half a mile to the docks and the waterfront. The streets are largely deserted, although there are the usual people sleeping on them. Only one car passes him as he walks down the Walkway.

'Hey!' A man's voice shouts from an alleyway. 'You're one of Janus's men aren't you?'

'What of it?' Vincent replies.

'I hear one of your men got shot this evening.'

Vincent moves towards the alley, slowly moving his hand onto the pistol grip of his weapon. 'What do you mean shot?' Vincent is now close enough to see a man crouched in the shadow of a rubbish bin. He isn't armed and looks harmless enough; Vincent relaxes his grip on the machine pistol.

'Dunno,' shrugs the man. 'I just heard his body was down at the docks, all slumped over where he was gunned down. I'm surprised you didn't catch it on the news.'

'Do you know where at the docks?' Vincent's voice sounds concerned

'They said on one of the piers, but I haven't been down. As I said, I only heard rumours, although I saw a news van going down about two hours ago. I take it you're here to whack whoever did it.'

Vincent doesn't reply as he turns and resolutely continues his journey to the docks.

'Give'm hell, man!' the man from the alley shouts.

At the main entrance to the docks Vincent can see the lights from the camera crew over by Pier 4. A small gathering of eight or ten people is around the scene. He makes his way along.

The camera turns to film his approach, the reporter's questions bombarding him as he gets closer. 'Do you know who's behind this killing? Will Mr Janus be putting out a contract on the perpetrators? Does this mean that an even more brutal regime under Janus will be implemented? Are there going to be any knee-jerk retaliation killings?'

The reporter doesn't give any time between questions for Vincent to answer, so he doesn't bother. He moves across to Boyd's crumpled but bulky form. He is lying face down, his right arm under his body. Vincent can't see any blood and notices Boyd does not have a gun in his hand, which considering someone allegedly gunned him down would have been almost guaranteed. He looks around. 'Did any of you people see who did this or what happened?' The news reporter stops his question barrage and began to film the crowd.

A woman speaks up, 'I did. He just crumpled and fell, like you see on the news, you know, like he was shot. I saw it.'

'Did you see who shot him?'

'No, I didn't, I didn't even hear the shot.'

'So what happens now? What will Mr Janus's response be?' The return of the reporter's insistent questions signals to Vincent that there is little point in trying to pursue the conversation with the woman. He lifts Boyd's body and walks back to the gates of the dock. The news crew follow him, the reporter sticking a microphone in his face and firing more questions. Vincent walks on in silence. His only words are to hail the taxi that happens to be sitting across the street.

After carefully placing Boyd in the back seat, Vincent climbs into the front of the cab.

'Just drive,' he tells the driver. The taxi speeds off.

'It's not wonderful when someone kills someone, is it?' says the driver.

'No, it isn't,' Vincent observes that the taxi driver is heading in the right direction, but by little-known back alleys. They are soon on route to Muzyka Street and the safety of the Janus building. They drive in silence along the quiet roads.

They pull up outside the Janus building and Vincent starts to pull Boyd's dead weight from the cab.

'It'll soon be you, you know,' says the driver from the front seat.

'Sorry?' Vincent stops, not quite hearing the driver.

'I said, it'll soon be you.'

'What do you mean?' Vincent barks.

'I'm watching you, number four.' The wheels of the cab screech and Boyd's body tumbles out of the open door knocking Vincent over as the cab roars away. He quickly gets to his feet, manhandles Boyd's corpse onto his shoulder and hurriedly unlocks the main gate, enters, slamming it shut, bolting it quickly.

Heaving the body leaves him panting for breath, and by the time he's reached the sleepers' room and placed Boyd gently onto one of the reclining chairs, he is almost spent.

Only then does he take the time to examine the body. Boyd, he finds, is breathing normally, and a quick examination shows that he has neither a bullet hole on him or any mark indicating he has been attacked. The only wound is the cut on his forehead from falling onto his face. Vincent steps back from the chair. What had happened to Boyd? He looks over at the wasted form of Tyler...

Before returning to his safe house Vincent leaves a note in the hand of each of the sleepers. The note asks them all to meet the following evening. Then he leaves, nervously locking every door as he exits.

**18 September, 11:46am
London, Soho**

Stella sat at her desk in an office building. The dark shadows below her blue eyes revealed a late night and a fitful night's sleep. Her stomach growled. 'Quiet,' she whispered pressing her hand to her her midriff, looking around the office. The roar had gone unnoticed. Eleanor at the other side of the room caught her look around and smiled at her. Stella smiled back, a little embarrassed. She lifted her hand from her stomach in a brief wave, her sweater briefly tugged against the adhesive of the *Elastoplast* on her finger. It was almost lunchtime, so she tidied her desk a little and donned her coat for the short trip to the Prêt-a-Manger on Broadwick Street. It had been a long morning.

As Stella walked she mulled over the morning's events. She had arrived early at the office and had stolen some early morning time while it was quiet to get a few personal emails out. The most prominent was to try to find out what had happened to Niall Davidson the previous evening. It wasn't like Niall to leave Boyd in such an obviously dangerous location, or not to take out any opposition with his usual consummate ease. It also wasn't like Niall not to reply to emails with his usual unprecedented swiftness. He seemed to spend all his time in front of a computer as far as she knew. And she knew he was getting the emails because a delivery receipt was bouncing back by return on each mail. The lack of any reply worried her.

Despite her questions and a need to find answers, her email inbox had only been filled with trivial Flash movies, Cialis and Viagara emails, the usual funny stories that circulate across the Internet between friends, and a blank email from a blank sender with a blank subject – useful.

She stood in line at Prêt, eyeing the salads and sandwiches. She knew she'd been eating a bit too much junk these last weeks so felt compelled to eat a salad. She got her purse out.

'Can I help you, miss?'

'Yes,' Stella smiled. 'A BLT please.' She gave a small shrug. 'And a Coke.' Good eating would have to wait till later. 'Actually, make that a Diet Coke.'

She began the trek back towards Oxford Street, her thoughts returning to Niall. Suddenly her appetite did not feel quite as large as the BLT sub she had just bought. She sighed.

Walking past Marks & Spencer she noticed her image in the video monitors fitted to the ceiling just inside the doors, cunningly placed so shoppers would look directly at the cameras as they entered the store giving the security people a good look at their face. How stupid we humans are, she thought, that such a simple trick could actually work.

'Niall's webcam.' Stella suddenly blurted out.

'Sorry?' The young man looked totally confused.

'Sorry. I was talking to myself.' Stella's face beamed red. 'I'm sorry.' Niall had sent her an email a couple of months back with a link to his freshly new freshly live webcam. She quickened her step, opened her sub and munched as she walked along, a renewed impetus now added to the day.

She arrived back at the office and was glad to see most people were at lunch. She was especially glad to see her boss wasn't at his desk. Her system, which had gone to sleep in her absence, was now displaying a now-dated Matrix screen saver where green typed characters streamed down from the top of the screen in a similar manner to the opening sequence of the movie. As she moved her mouse she was prompted for her password. *T-O-M-C-A-T*, she typed then hit the RETURN button. Her desktop popped into view.

She loaded up her email program and scanned through the folder marked "Inbox". At the bottom of the screen below the list of old emails a small box said "3661 message(s), 2 Unread." She hadn't realised she had so many old messages stored. No wonder that irritating guy from systems kept writing her emails telling her to free up some of her disk space. She clicked the "From" button at the top, putting all the emails into alphabetical order by name, then she scanned down to the "n"s and found Niall's name. There were about sixty emails from Niall; this was going to take a while.

She scanned down the subjects looking for something that might jog her memory as to which of these held the information with the webcam link. After a couple of dead-ends she narrowed her search to emails between six and twelve weeks old. Scanning down she found that there were only ten emails in this smaller group. She began to open them one by one. Nothing about web sites appeared in any. She leaned back in her swivel chair, her fingers drumming on the plastic below the keys of her keyboard.

'Come on, Stella, think.' She opened her Diet Coke, took a sip, then absently wiped some of the spray from the work documents. 'Surely I didn't delete it.' Her eyes again caught the 3661 messages box. 'I don't delete anything.' She leaned back in her chair, frustrated. Where was it?

'Pseudonyms!' She snapped her fingers—dully because of her plaster. 'Email pseudonyms.' She mumbled to herself as she scanned her finger down the list of names. Superdog277. It was an old name Niall had used when Internet gaming had first become a serious proposition around the turn of the century. Nowadays everyone had stupid names, tags, that didn't make any sense but which sounded a bit more in tune with hulking brutes running through post-apocalyptic wastelands in endless death matches involving weapons no normal human being could ever even lift and aim let alone run and jump around with.

There were four emails from Superdog277. She opened them one by one and found the address of the site containing the new webcam. Clicking the link caused a new window to pop up. The screen indicated the page was being loaded, a small bar representing the percentage complete so far quickly filled. The site looked very professional she thought, but then Niall did this as a sideline along with other hardware and software freelance work.

She scanned down the list of options and found the link to the live webcam. She hoped it was online and she'd be able to see if Niall was just being a no-good waster and not returning her emails. She clicked the link.

It took a few seconds to make the connection and a few more for the video window to start streaming the video. She looked at the image. It didn't look to be a static picture as there was a slight boxy effect around the edges of the image, artefacts of the decompression of the live image. Putting on some headphones confirmed her observations; she could hear traffic in the background. Live or not, Niall was nowhere to be seen. The image consisted only of a view of a room with a picture on the far wall, Niall's front door on the right and his sofa on the left hand side.

'Well Niall, I can afford to wait,' she said quietly. 'And when you get back to your desk, I'll give you a piece of my mind.'

'Miss Robertson.' The voice was behind her and she felt her shoulders lift and hunch slightly.

'Yes, Alvin,' she said turning to face him, her headphones getting half-dragged from her ears as the cable caught on the edge of her keyboard. She quickly removed them and smoothed her hair.

There he stood, her boss, Alvin, with his standard aggravated look. Over his shoulder she noticed that most of the other staff were filing back into the office, clip-boards in hand.

'Did you not get the emails about the meeting?'

'No, I don't think I did.' She remembered the two unread emails she had noticed over forty-five minutes before and tried not to visibly show it.

'Uh-huh.' He paused briefly, his eyes rolling upwards. 'Well you've just missed the planning meeting for the next quarter which I emailed you about this morning. In your absence however, you have been volunteered to work the budget details for the new project. You will find your brief in the minutes of the meeting on the server.'

'That's great. Thanks.' She smiled emptily and screamed inwardly: she hated budgeting for advertising projects. Niall would get an earful for this, without a doubt.

18 September, 8:29pm
The City

It is the first time in several months that everyone has been active at the same time. Vincent stands by the window, Swift by his side. Both are smoking cigarettes; wispy smoke hangs in the air around them. Wilson sits on the sofa; Frank stands by the fire, his pose extremely theatrical as he leans against the fireplace, staring into the flames. His face appears animated as the moving flame casts its shimmering light. In the other room lie the sleeping body of Boyd and the decaying corpse of Tyler.

'So Vincent, what's this all about?' Frank doesn't look up from the flames.

'I think it's quite self-evident.' Vincent replies. 'We've got two of our men out of action through there, and if we don't find out why, or what's happened, we're not going to be able to perpetuate the Janus domination because there won't be enough of us to provide the round-the-clock presence it requires. We spoke about this six months ago, and agreed then that no one would just drop out.'

The others murmur agreement.

'So do we know what's happened to either of them?' Frank asks.

No one does.

'Okay, so we know that Boyd was here last night and was fine until about half eight, yes?' continues Frank.

'Yup.'

'Then you found him down at the docks unconscious. And apart from that we know that Tyler hasn't been around for about a fortnight.'

'So do we keep going with just us?' Wilson asks from the sofa, "or do we try and recruit some new blood?'

'I think it's more important to find out what's happened to the other two,' says Vincent blowing smoke out into the centre of the room.

'Agreed.' Frank turns so he is facing into the room. 'Has anyone been in contact with Tyler outside?'

'No, he seemed to keep himself to himself. He is on that emailing list we set up at the start though,' replies Vincent. 'Why don't you try and contact him through that.'

'What about Boyd?' enquires Swift.

Vincent responds: 'I've dropped him some emails, but he wasn't at his desk at all today. I'll sort that side of things out.'

'Okay then,' says Frank, 'I'll try Tyler and you keep trying Boyd. Let's try and get more information over the next couple of days and we'll meet back here Thursday.'

They all agree.

'Hold on, though,' says Vincent moving away from the window and taking a drag on his cigarette. 'While we're all here, have any of you been attacked over the last couple of weeks?'

'How do you mean? Like in gunfights on behalf of Janus?' says Swift. 'Of course, does a bear shit in the—'

'No!' Vincent interrupts, 'I mean odd attacks.' He pauses momentarily. 'The other night someone blackjacked me on the way home, and after tying me up, told me I would be number four.' He looks around the room, eying their expressions. No one says anything for numerous long seconds.

'When was this?' asks Wilson.

'About a week ago on the road through the park. I didn't even see anyone. Not even straight after the attack.'

'Some guy threatened me a couple of weeks back,' offers Wilson sitting forward on the sofa. 'But I figured he was some kind of nut job and just told him to piss off.'

'What about you guys? Swift? Frank?'

'No, nothing.'

'Me neither,' says Swift.

'Also last night, some cab driver who drove me and Boyd back here made some crack about people getting killed, and said it would soon be me.'

'Oh come on,' blurts out Swift. 'Are you suggesting some bogie man's out there trying to get us, and that Tyler and Boyd have been bumped off and that you'll be number four? That's crazy.' His arms are gesticulating throughout the outburst, ash flying from the end of his cigarette.

'Yes,' Frank agrees, 'it does seem a bit far-fetched, don't you think? Besides, Wilson was threatened and he's here.'

'Yes, I suppose,' Vincent agrees.

'Listen, it's more likely they've both just buggered off and haven't said.' Frank continues, 'let's just get in contact with them and find out what's what.'

'Sounds good,' Swift shouts as he moves into the next room. 'Murder and mayhem. Good one.' His voice can be heard raving in the other room as he lies down on his reclining chair. His rantings end only when he goes to sleep.

Vincent chats for a while longer with the other two then leaves, walking mostly in the shadows as he returns to his safe house. The night sky is cloudy.

19 September, 3:11am
Theydon Bois, Essex

Stella sat bolt upright in bed, sweat covering her body. She swung her legs over the side of her bed trying to shake off the feeling of the nightmare she was still fighting her way to consciousness from. Her toes spread as her feet searched out her slippers. Thomas made an irritated mewling sound at the disturbance, then tucked his body into a tight circle, closed his eyes and went back to sleep.

'Great help you are, Thomas,' Stella muttered looking at the cat's bed-hogging position. She pulled her robe from the hook behind the door and walked into the kitchen flicking on the light. Stumbling through into the bathroom she washed her face in cold water to try to waken up more. She could feel the uncomfortable sensation of her heart beating a little bit faster than it normally did as she stared at the bloodshot-eyed reflection in the mirror.

After drying her face she returned to the kitchen. The clock said 3:15am. She shook her head. This was the fourth night of nightmares and the sleep deprivation was killing her. Even worse, the nightmares were getting more vivid each night as she got more anxious about having them, a circular situation she was aware of but was finding hard to break.

She rifled in the fridge and found just enough milk to make some hot chocolate. She'd need to remember to get more milk tomorrow or Thomas would be unbearable. She heated the milk in the pan and generously spooned the hot chocolate mix into a large mug, using twice as much as the box suggested. As the milk in the pan began to hiss she stirred it, waiting until small wisps of steam began to rise, then she poured the milk into her mug and moved the double-dose concoction around with a spoon.

Standing on a chair from the living room, she reached up to the top of the cupboard above the sink where she stashed a packet of cigarettes for just such occasions. Her doctor repeatedly told her not to smoke at all because of her asthma, but she found, strangely, that the cigarettes helped her breathing when she was really stressed. And she was really stressed now, so she took her hot chocolate and her cigarettes and went out onto the roof at the back of her flat.

As she lit up her cigarette, carefully balancing the hot chocolate on the window ledge, she looked out over the old rusting cars that sat in the lot behind the garage beneath her flat. It was a clear night, the brightness of the moon hiding most of the smaller stars that were visible on moonless nights. She cocked her head, observing the way the moonlight made the car graveyard look artistic. She drew deeply on her cigarette, feeling slightly giddy from the oxygen starvation. Before this week, it had been a couple of months since she had felt fazed enough to resort to a smoke. She leaned against the window ledge and looked at the bridge at the far side of the car yard as she supped at her hot chocolate.

A dark figure was walking up the slight incline of the bridge. It suddenly stopped and turned. She couldn't make out whether the figure was facing towards her or away from her, but it had definitely stopped and was doing one of the two. She felt the hair on the back of her neck stand up and the blood rush from her face.

'What on earth?'

Although she had just lit a cigarette, she hadn't put the light on so reckoned the figure would not see her; but her eyes widened as she glanced down at the glowing tip of her cigarette that now seemed to her like a beacon in the darkness. She quickly stubbed it out on the rooftop.

An involuntary cry escaped her lips as a shower of orange embers were blown across the rooftop only burning out near the edge of the roof. The figure on the bridge turned and began to run quickly down the bridge towards the entrance to her street. A dog barked in the distance.

Stella dropped the hot chocolate as she promptly stood up, the mug shattering on the rooftop. The hot drink burned her slippered feet, but she hardly noticed as she hurriedly ran into the flat and with shaking hands bolted the door top and bottom. She ran through to her bedroom and looked out the window. The dark figure was walking purposefully down the street towards her flat.

Stella didn't wait to see what would happen next. She ran through, picked up the phone and dialled 999 while sitting hunched low on the floor by the television set. The phone at the other end rang once, before a voice asked her which emergency service she required.

'Police,' she whispered as loudly as she dared. She was swiftly connected through.

'Hello, can I take you name please?' said the police operator.

'Stella Robertson,' came her shaky reply.

'And your address?' The male voice at the other end sounded friendly and calm, very in control. Stella most definitely did not feel that way.

'Someone is coming to get me in my flat. You need to send someone now.' She could feel her chest tightening as she spoke. Her hand reached for her handbag on the table, rifling the contents out onto the floor until she found her asthma inhaler. She didn't hear what the person at the other end of the phone was saying as she pressed the canister down and deeply inhaled the medicinal-tasting vapour.

Stella was vaguely aware of the voice on the phone telling her they were sending someone right away, and that if she could give her address it would save time.

'7B, Station Approach, Theydon Bois. Near the tube station. Hurry!'

'I'll just stay on the line with you right now, Stella,' the voice was saying. 'Someone's on their way now. They should be with you in a few minutes. Don't worry.'

Stella sat petrified on the floor of her living room, the friendly voice slowing her panic down. Long minutes passed before the squad car arrived. She heard it when it turned into the road at the pub on the corner and drove down towards her flat.

The voice on the other end of the phone told her the police officers had just pulled up outside and that he would hang up now. Stella thanked him and hung up the phone. Her knees felt weak as she walked hazily through to her bedroom and looked out of the window. The police car was sitting directly below, a female police officer was at her door. The officer looked up, smiled and motioned for her to open the door. The male officer was doing a quick sweep of the immediate area, torch in hand.

The female police officer was extremely sympathetic as she took all the details. She had even very kindly made Stella another hot drink. The male officer in the meantime had checked around the area and had walked onto the bridge looking for any clues. His reconnoitre revealed nothing out of the ordinary though, which left Stella feeling more than a little sheepish. She was even beginning to doubt that the figure she had seen was real.

After taking all the details, extremely vague as they were, the officers said their goodnights and Stella saw them out. Thomas, who had made sure he took good advantage of the visitor's stroking skills also took this opportunity to slip out, quickly jumping up onto the wall beside the front door from where he could watch the departing police car.

An extremely embarrassed Stella locked up and went back to bed, where she fell into a fitful sleep where the nightmares returned. When she woke at 8:15am she had overslept by half an hour and would be late for work.

'Shit!'

19 September, 6:03am
East London

Just under two hours before Stella woke up late for work, Jarvis Nickleby was shocked from his slumber by the sound of his front door being smashed in.

'What the fu—'

His head was extremely fuzzy from the soporific effect of the previous night's bedtime joint, and he had only managed to get his body onto one elbow when three uniformed police officers bundled through his living room door, followed a few seconds later by Detective Inspector Jack Stanton, warrants clearly visible in his hand.

'Hello Jarvis. How have you been?' Stanton nodded down at Jarvis.

'All right, Jack, and you?' Jarvis replied, his free hand fumbling across the floor looking for the cigarettes he had dropped there the night before.

'Yes, not too bad, Jarvis, although I have to say I'm never too fond of having to get up in the middle of the night to arrest you.' Stanton slid a cigarette pack across the floor using his well-polished shoe.

'It's a bummer all round, mate. Believe me.' Jarvis opened the packet and lit a slightly bent cigarette as he watched the uniformed officers pull on rubber gloves and begin to shut down his computer equipment.

'You know, Jarvis, you really need to pick the place up a bit.' Stanton lifted a foam burger container between his thumb and forefinger as if a sergeant-major in some military inspection, pulled a face, and then carefully replaced it.

'Yeah, sorry 'bout that, Jack. Maid's on 'oliday, mate. Know what I mean?' Jarvis blew smoke up in the direction of Stanton who stepped out of the way, despite the smoke stalling before it reached his face.

The uniformed officers were already removing cables from the various computer components in readiness to load them into the van that was parked outside.

'By the way, Jack, where's Starsky this morning?'

'Probably tucked up warm in bed, where I should be too.'

'Draw the short straw did you?' Jarvis's laugh quickly degenerated into a convulsive series of phlegmy-sounding coughs. When the coughing subsided he continued, 'Unlucky.'

'Yes it is.' Stanton began to look bored of the conversation. 'Come on now Jarvis. Let's go.' He gave the mattress on the floor a nudge with his foot and Jarvis dragged himself onto the floor and stood up. He was wearing all of his clothes except his shoes which were lying where they had been kicked off in the small hours of the morning beside the door. Jarvis ambled over, making a big deal about moving past one of the officers: his hands up like a surrendering cowboy in a John Wayne movie. He laughed, triggering another bout of coughing as he slid his feet into his heavily worn *Converse*.

'Come on then, Jack,' Jarvis said, grabbing his grubby black leather coat from somewhere in the bed. 'Let's go.' He put it on as he moved towards the door.

'Hold on,' said Stanton. 'Haven't you forgotten something?'

Jarvis turned to see Stanton holding up a pair of handcuffs. He dejectedly turned and put his hands behind his back, where Stanton expertly cuffed them.

'Carry on gentlemen,' said Stanton.

As they walked through the hall Jarvis looked at the smashed door. The door, which had been badly repaired after the last raid was now hanging from its hinges, the rough cut piece of ¾ inch chipboard which had been nailed onto it to replace the glass was lying on the floor. 'Do you fucking people really need to do this every time?'

'If you'd get a real job, Jarvis, we wouldn't need to.'

Stanton directed Jarvis by his upper arm towards one of the squad cars parked outside. Jarvis had never tried to run in the past, and today would doubtless be no different, but it was better not to make a scene. People were peeking at the events from behind curtains at Jarvis being lifted, while for his part Jarvis was shouting abuse at the hidden neighbours. The cracks in the curtains were flicking closed as if the vitriol was some kind of physical projectile to be avoided. A uniformed female officer was holding the car door open.

'Hello, love. You gonna be taking me for a ride?'

The officer did not respond. She just pressed down on Jarvis's head as he climbed into the car to ensure he didn't bump it, then closed the door. He looked up and made a kissing gesture through the window. Two other officers climbed into the car and drove him away.

'Come on,' said Stanton to Lisa Collier, the female officer. 'Let's go and take a look.' They walked back into Jarvis's house. One of the officers in the main room was nearly finished removing all the cabling from the equipment, which he had bundled into a large white plastic evidence bag.

'Do any of you guys know which cables connect which things?' Stanton asked.

The three officers looked at each other. None knew.

'Patrick is not going to be pleased with you boys.'

Lisa was unable to stop her nose screwing up as she looked around the room. 'This is the most disgusting flat I've ever seen. And I mean even worse than some of the flats my male friends stayed in at university.' She pulled on a pair of disposable gloves and began to look at some of the items around the room. 'Do you see the greasy deposits on everything? Like you get in a kitchen on top of the units. This is disgusting.'

Stanton Smiled. 'Right, Lisa. See what you can find.'

The other officers were beginning to shuttle out the various bits of hardware to the blue unmarked police van that had been backed to the end of the path. Meanwhile Lisa began to pick through the rubbish on the floor for anything that might be useful. Sifting through the rubbish she found a small polythene bag with green leafy material inside.

'Sir.' She held up the small bag then dropped it into the small evidence bag Stanton held out in his own gloved hands. Lisa returned to her examination of the floor. There was nothing else but rubbish.

She checked the other two ground floor rooms. Across the hall was the kitchen. Dishes filled the cracked yellowing sink; the kitchen table was covered in tins, packets, plates with rotting food and pans with food which, when the traffic was quiet enough, could be heard to bubble as the microbes produced their waste gases. The door to the fridge sat propped against the wall, the fridge itself acting more as a shelving unit than a fridge since its cabling had been chewed through by the rat that was now rotting behind it. The kitchen was devoid of any useful evidence. Lisa moved on.

She entered the bathroom. Around the floor were old newspapers at various stages of systematic tearing. A small pile of pornographic magazines sat on the cistern beside a sink that had about an inch of stagnant brown water sitting in the bottom, despite the fact that the plug was on the windowsill. The window was blocked by two cardboard boxes pressed into the frame, a temporary solution to the broken pane that had been there for months. Around the bath were four rings at different heights. Apart from telling her more about Jarvis Nickleby as a person, the room was "clean". She returned to the living room.

Stanton was standing by the window. He had pulled back the curtains a little highlighting how ash-covered the carpet actually was. The officers were picking up the last of the computer equipment.

'That's it, sir,' said the officer picking up the last monitor. 'We'll see you back at the station.'

'See you,' Lisa replied, smiling. Stanton was already going through the drawers of the console desk now there was nobody walking back and forth. The drawers were filled with various computer hardware circuit boards. Stanton examined them briefly but had no idea what they did. Most of the drawers were filled with papers and disks. All of it seemed to be just randomly dumped in.

'Come on, let's go. This is a waste of time. There's nothing here but junk.' Stanton snapped one of his gloves off, then pulled the other over the first, trapping the muck inside.

Lisa nodded as she walked back to the door. 'Hold on,' she said. 'Those guys have left a cable.'

She reached down under the desk and grabbed the end of the cable she had spotted below the desk. She tugged at it. 'It seems to be jammed.' She gave it a good jerk, and across the other side of the room the carpet was suddenly pulled back. Lisa and Stanton both looked at each other.

'What have we here?' Stanton said in a quiet voice as he walked over to the upturned carpet edge. The cable ran around the edge of the room and Lisa's pull had dislodged it. He pulled on a fresh set of gloves and began to gently pull up the cable, following it around the room. On the far side it went down under the floorboards. Stanton pulled back the carpet causing both to press their noses and mouths into her shoulders as ash and grime was puffed into the air. The floorboards were loose and Stanton easily lifted two of them out liberating a barely audible whirring sound. Removing a third board allowed him to get his head down into the small area below the floorboards. About fifteen inches from his head he could see a small red LED and below it a flickering green one.

'Well, Constable Collier,' he said as he looked up at Lisa. 'You've been looking for a recommendation to become a detective; I think you might just have found it.'

19 September, 9:34am
London, Soho

Stella rushed into her office looking every bit like she had only had twenty minutes to get ready. The tube had been a bit quieter than it tended to be earlier. But even considering this she hadn't been able to grab enough stuff to take on the tube to salvage a less bedraggled look. Alvin took the opportunity to come over before she could get properly settled down to work. 'I see you've decided to grace us with your company, Miss Robertson.'

'Yes, sorry about that, there was a delay on the tube this morning,' she lied.

'And how is the budgeting going for the Middleton account?' he asked, knowing full well she had had precious little time to work on it.

'Not too bad. I got some of it worked out yesterday afternoon.' She inwardly cringed at this second lie in less than a minute.

'Good, good. So I'll be seeing it by,' he drew her another nightmare, 'Friday?'

'I'll see what I can do.' Three days, she thought. Bugger, bugger, bugger! She waited until Alvin had returned to his desk before she powered up her machine. She loaded up her email expecting to see a reply or two to the eight or so emails she had sent the previous day. She didn't have any. She loaded a browser and selected the bookmark for Niall's webcam page. It took a few seconds to load. She sighed as she was confronted with the same image. 'Where the hell are you Niall?'

She closed both programs and tried to clear her head enough to get on with her budgeting. She could almost feel Alvin's beady, prying eyes making sure she was working.

19 September, 9:45am
London, Metropolitan Police Headquarters

The vanload of computer equipment had already been unloaded into Patrick Bateson's lab by the time he arrived at work. He looked over the numerous monitors and bits of hardware spread over his benches, feeling his anger welling at the sight of the slightly furred-up equipment—although it was only after he found the bag of cabling that he finally cracked.

It had been hidden behind a monitor on the end of one of the benches, and when Patrick opened the bag and tipped the contents onto some free bench space, it looked like a modern artist had recreated a plate of spaghetti out of computer cabling. The Irishman didn't waste any time, immediately picking up the phone and punching in some numbers. When the receiver at the other end was picked up he took a long deep breath, then unleashed his initial volley.

'Who the hell dumped all this shit all round my lab? ... Well put Stevens on the phone ... are you the pillock that's dumped all this crap all over my lab ... I don't care if it's part of a case ... I know it's my job... Don't you get stroppy with me ... Don't you understand that this is like you people finding a whole dinosaur skeleton completely intact, then digging it up with a bloody bulldozer and dumping it in a museum foyer. It's not bloody on ... Did *you* pack the cabling? ... uh-huh ... well what's *his* extension then?' He slammed the phone down, picked it up again and dialled the new number.

'Is that Williams?' he said calmly. 'Ah, good. It's Patrick Bateson here over in Computer Forensics.' His voice sounded friendly and unthreatening. 'I'm just calling about the computer equipment you guys picked up this morning.' He paused again briefly. 'WHAT THE HELL WERE YOU

THINKING DUMPING ALL THE BLOODY CABLING INTO ONE BAG WITHOUT MARKING ANY OF IT? YOU'RE AN ARSEHOLE! YOU HEAR ME? AN ARSEHOLE!' He slammed down the phone before Williams at the other end could even really take in what had happened.

It was in this fizzing state that Jack Stanton found Patrick ten minutes later. When he walked into the lab, Patrick's head had turned so quickly to shoot him a steely glance that a lesser man would have suffered a whiplash.

'Hello, Patrick, and how are you this fine morning?' Stanton asked walking forward with a computer case wrapped in a white evidence bag under his arm.

'Hello, Jack.' Patrick shook his head slightly, as if trying to shake off his mood. 'Are you well?' His face brightened slightly, but only very slightly. 'Did you have any part in this bloody fiasco? Tell me you didn't because then I'd have to start disliking you, and we both know that would be no bloody good, don't we?'

Stanton smiled. He knew Patrick had one of the worst tempers he'd ever seen and was glad he had never been on the receiving end.

'You know I would never deliver stuff to you like this, Patrick. I couldn't afford to get on the wrong side of you.' He placed the wrapped box on the end of a bench. 'I tried to warn them at the time.'

'Yes, well, a couple of them are sitting with burning ears right now, I tell you.' Patrick smiled at the thought of his handiwork. 'Maybe that'll make them think the next time.' He walked over and nodded towards the wrapped computer Stanton had delivered, 'What have you got for me here anyway, Jack?' His tone had lost all its bite in his final question.

'This is the last bit of the system. We found it hidden under the floor boards, sitting on a stack of silica gel packs.'

'Aah, a special one.' Patrick was peaking in through the polythene.

'How long will it take you to get all of this up and running?'

'Considering the shite those cowboys have dumped on me, I really don't know.' He looked around, 'I never understand why you don't bring me to the scene to dismantle the equipment in the first place. At least then I'd know how the thing was originally configured.'

'Yes, I know,' Stanton nodded. 'It was a timing issue. We just had to go.'

'Well, Jack,' Patrick said smiling and leaning in close, 'they'd better sort it out these procedures soon or it'll be more than the uniforms that'll be getting an earful from me if you know what I mean.'

'I don't doubt that for a second, Patrick,' Stanton laughed.

9 September, 12:03pm
London, Metropolitan Police Headquarters

The ashtray on the table in the interview room already had twelve butts in it when Stanton walked in. He waved his hand in a fanning motion in front of his face when the smoke hit his lungs.

'Jeez, Jarvis, when I said they could let you have a cigarette I didn't think you'd try to smoke us out.' He walked over and flicked the switch on the extractor fan, which made a loud buzzing noise as it visibly began to suck the smoke up into a vent.

Jarvis, slumped down in the chair, staring at Stanton. 'I hope you people have been careful with my equipment this time.'

'I'm sure the boys took exceptional care with your stuff. After all, it was plain to see you're a man who likes to keep things nice and proper.'

'Yeah, ha-ha,' Jarvis retorted sarcastically. 'Why am I here this time anyway?'

'We're investigating claims from the Internet Watch Foundation about some of your sites, so we figured you'd be quite happy for us to check through your systems and prove your innocence.'

'How magnanimous of you.'

'We thought so.' Stanton picked up the dirty ashtray and asked the officer outside the door if he could get a clean one. 'So, Jarvis, do you want to tell me anything while we're still conducting "friendly" chats?'

'I haven't done anything.' It was one of Jarvis's catch phrases: "oy-ayn-dun-nuffink".

'I'm sure you haven't,' Stanton said, not quite believing it, 'but our people in the labs will bear that out. Do you fancy a coffee before we start?'

'Yeh. I'll have a tea, milk and three sugars.'
Stanton walked out.

Two floors up, Lisa Collier sat nervously on one of the seats outside Detective Chief Superintendent Mayfield's office. She had been summoned about an hour after their return from the raid on Jarvis's flat.

She fidgeted as she waited, nervous. Her summoning here today was another major step in her career in the Metropolitan Police, and by most standards her rise was nothing short of meteoric. For Lisa though her thoughts were of her father, not of her achievements. It didn't seem to matter what she did, it never quite met the mark that her father kept moving. For him this would be just another achievement that was merely expected – that is if he knew about it.

Lisa's thoughts fell back to when she'd reached her first grade on the cello she had been forced to play as soon as her hands were large enough to go round the neck of the instrument to cover the finger-board. Her father had dismissed it with a "Well, dear, we wouldn't have expected anything less". Her mother had been proud; she was proud of all Lisa's achievements, but she had died in a car accident when Lisa was six, and since then there hadn't been a balancing force for her father's dismissive disposition.

A brief surge of anger washed over her at moments like these because it was still her father she wanted to impress. She had been working on trying to do things for herself since she'd stopped seeing him. But the old habit was proving hard to break. She caught herself and relaxed, her knuckles regaining some colour as she stopped wringing them.

She checked her uniform: relatively neat and tidy, if a little dusty, and smoothed her hair with her hand. Her knees were grimy too from crawling on Jarvis's floor, but there was nothing she could do about that since she hadn't had enough notice to get into a clean uniform.

Maisie, the DCS's middle-aged secretary, appeared, smiled and showed her through to Mayfield's office. He stood as she entered, his big friendly face breaking into a welcoming smile.

'Aah, Lisa, good to see you. Take a seat.' He gestured to the seat in front of his desk. 'Would you like a drink? Tea, coffee?'

Lisa was too nervous to accept a drink. She could see herself spilling hot coffee over herself as her hands nervously began to shake. She held them both firmly in her lap. 'No thank you sir, I'm fine.'

'Thank you, Maisie,' said the DCS as Maisie saw herself out. He sat down opposite Lisa and pulled her file towards him. 'So, Lisa, how are you?'

'I'm just fine, sir.'

'Any problems this morning?'

'No, sir, I think it went pretty well.'

'Detective Inspector Stanton called me this morning saying your services were invaluable today in finding some hidden computer equipment. Good work.'

'Yes, sir. Thank you, sir.'

He opened the file and put on some spectacles that had been sitting on his desk. They sat half way down his nose as he read. 'Good. Uh-huh. So you're looking to become a detective.'

'Yes, sir, I've had an application in for a few months.'

'Uh-huh. Good recommendations I see.' He trailed off. He began leafing through her record. About a minute passed in silence as he read various bits of the file. Lisa tried hard not to fidget. He suddenly snapped the file closed.

'Excellent, Lisa. Excellent.'

She let out a small, barely discernible sigh of relief.

'Yes, Jack Stanton has given you a very high recommendation based on your work with him over the last weeks, and so I'm pleased to say you are being transferred to work along with Jack for the time being in a probationary detective role. You should report to him tomorrow morning.'

Lisa could barely believe her ears.

'Thank you, sir, I won't let you down,' she gushed.

The DCS offered his hand. 'Congratulations, Detective.'

'Thank you, sir' she said, shaking his hand, acutely aware that she was repeating herself. But then what more could she say. She could barely hide her smile from Maisie as she walked out of the DCS's office. Maisie smiled back knowingly and mouthed, 'Congratulations, Lisa.'

19 September, 4:00pm,
London, Metropolitan Police Headquarters

Patrick stood back and looked at the console of computers and monitors he was working with. Setting them up had left his hands slick with a greasy residue, although he was more irritated by the strange way the hardware seemed to be set up. He didn't know who owned this, but they had more than a passing knowledge of hardware and software, and it was stretching him to his limit.

His first breakthrough was in getting the system to boot to a password, it then took him a while to get it to boot on more favourable terms for accessing it. Patrick was in his element when it came to computer problems. He loved the thrill of the chase – and the kill. For most people computers tended to be seen as mysterious boxes, which, if they went wrong, required expert help to fix. For Patrick, though, the basic simplicity of the common computer never escaped him. Every problem could be broken down into simple steps, and eliminating all the small steps, he knew, would lead him to his goal and allow him to see whatever was on a computer. And if all else failed he wasn't scared to get in there with a screwdriver. He knew that he could pull out hard drives and link them directly to his test system. From there he could access anything. Only password-protected files would need some extra work, and he had already written software for that very purpose. But that was some way down the road. He still wanted to get the bloody thing to work without resorting to taking it apart.

It had taken practically all day working solely on the project, but Patrick had finally got all the bits wired together and functioning as something like a computer system, albeit a filthy, bastardised, technological monster of a computer system. In a little over an hour he managed to infiltrate the various front-end passwords and to get to grips with the general system that Jarvis was running, which seemed to be some kind of modified Linux judging by the various software hacks in the registry. Now he was able to view the majority of the files.

He browsed through the directories. There were dozens upon dozens of movie files in a range of formats as well as what appeared to be thousands of image files. He clicked on a file at random. A window popped into place showing a video of three men and two women involved in various acts that could most definitely be considered to be hardcore pornography. 'Bingo,' he said, picking up the phone.

'Could you get me Jack Stanton please ... yes I know he's in an interview. It's in connection with it.'

The person at the other end asked him to wait. He opened another file while he waited: two women (one with a feather boa), a parrot and a man dragging a vat of what appeared to be chocolate appeared on the screen. 'Interesting,' Patrick said to no one in particular.

Some rustling preceded Stanton's voice, 'Patrick, what have you got?'

'Well right now I'm watching a man with a parrot smearing chocolate from a giant vat over a lady in a feather boa.'

'Remarkable,' Stanton said, picturing the absurdity of the image. 'Is there anything other than kinky weird stuff?'

'Well, we've got hardcore video material here that you probably need a license to publish, so I figure this is almost certainly bookable.' He continued while he scanned through a few directories. 'But I'm in the system now, so I thought I should let you know.'

'Thanks Patrick. How long do you think it will take to search through?'

'Well, there are literally thousands of pictures and movie files here, so this is going to take a while, but I'm thinking we'll find quite a bit of incriminating stuff just based on what I've seen already.' The file he had clicked open while he had been talking reinforced this observation.

'Good stuff. What about the computer I brought in, are there files on that?'

Patrick looked across the room to where the computer was still sitting, exactly where Stanton had put it down. He rolled his eyes as he spoke, 'Well, would you bloody believe that, I'd completely forgot about the bastard. Listen, I'll need to get onto it first thing tomorrow morning, I'm on me own here today and I'll need to search this system. Are you able to hold onto your man for now?'

'Sure thing, Patrick. See what you can find first thing though, and give me a bell.'

'Will do.'

20 September, 8:15am,
London, Metropolitan Police Headquarters

Lisa arrived about half an hour earlier than usual and made her way across to Stanton's office. She was both excited and apprehensive: a Detective Constable; she could hardly believe it, and felt strange not wearing her uniform. Her head hurt from the impromptu party thrown by her uniformed colleagues the previous evening, a night that ended at 2:00am in a dingy club in Soho. It wasn't the best way to start a new job, but she'd taken a couple of aspirin and figured she'd just about weather the hangover. Her fists clenched and unclenched involuntarily as she followed signs that would lead her to Stanton's office.

Stanton shared an office with three other detectives judging by the number of desks. Two were chaotic with piles of files and papers, dirty coffee cups and sweet wrappers; the third was neat and ordered. No one was in. She decided to start the coffee machine in the corner to try and spur herself into a more lifelike state.

Stanton marched in just as the water, hissing and gurgling, began to run over the ground coffee. 'Congratulations, by the way.' He offered his hand. 'Good night last night?'

'Thanks. Yes, a bit too good, I think.'

'Your desk is that one over there,' he said motioning over by some filing cabinets. 'Sorry about the mess, you can just move all the files onto the floor by the window. I'm afraid since Andy was transferred we've been using the desk as a bit of a storage area.'

Lisa walked over to her new desk, Stanton's old partner's desk. It was covered in stacks of files. The pin-board on the wall facing her still had newspaper cuttings, which she pulled down as they talked.

'Yes, Mayfield briefed me about you this morning,' Stanton continued. 'You're going to be joining me on this Nickleby thing for now. So we'll be sort of trying each other out for size if you will.'

Lisa was glad: it was nerve-wracking enough starting a new job. At least this way she was going to be working with Stanton who she had known for about a year and got on well with. Plus she knew something of the case from being there when Jarvis had been brought in.

'Great.' She smiled.

'So you'd better get this stuff tidied up just now and we'll head across and interview him again this morning.' Stanton was pouring her a cup of the newly brewed coffee, 'Do you take milk? Sugar?'

'Just milk please', Lisa replied as she carried one of the stacks of files over to the window. The exertion was making her head pound behind her eyes. She tried not to let it show in her face.

'Patrick over at Computer Forensics said he found some illegal porn on the seized computers last night, so we've got a bit more to discuss with Jarvis today.' Stanton put the coffee on Lisa's new desk.

'Thanks,' she said, sipping her coffee.

Stanton picked up one of the stacks and helped her clear the rest of the desk.

'So what about the other computer we found?' Lisa asked.

'You found, you mean, detective.' Stanton smiled at her as he neatly delivered a stack to the floor.

'Yes,' she said, almost managing to suppress a smile.

'He hasn't set it up yet. He's going to get back to us this morning about it.'

The desk was soon cleared and Lisa began to unload the few personal items she had brought in the bag quickly packed at her old job the previous evening. The items made it look a bit more like home, if a little minimalist. No doubt that would change, she thought, looking at the three other messy, busy desks around the office.

Five minutes later, having gulped down the last of her coffee, she and Stanton, two detectives, went down to further interview Jarvis Nickleby. She was smiling as they walked.

In Computer Forensics Patrick Bateson was supping a Costa large latte through its plastic lid while he connected up the computer Stanton had brought in. He had eaten the Danish before he had started working after finding that the muck on his hands from setting up the computers the previous day had been quite difficult to remove. The new piece of hardware wasn't difficult to link in since only one long umbilical cable had connected it into the main system. Patrick unscrewed the back of the case and removed the side to reveal the systems innards. Some kind of makeshift server, he thought.

He booted up the newly added unit and it began its long initiation process. He returned to transferring some of the more lurid movies onto videotape as the machine ran through its initialisation and boot sequence. His hunch the previous evening was being upheld by the large percentage of quite disturbing pornographic files he was finding on the main system's hard disks. He had one hour and fifteen minutes of evidence on tape so far.

Stanton handed Jarvis a cup of coffee with three sugars in it, along with a packet of cigarettes. Lisa stood over by the window.

'Hello, love,' Jarvis sneered.

'Hey!' Stanton barked, slamming his hand down on the table. 'Enough Jarvis. You're in enough trouble without getting on our bad sides this morning. This is Detective Constable Collier, and you *will* be nice.'

To Lisa, Stanton's voice sounded like a Sergeant Major from an old film: very firm, and not to be messed with. She gave a curt nod, a little bit scared of Jarvis, but making sure the rogue emotion didn't spill onto her face. Jarvis apologised, his face looking a bit worried by Stanton's statement and tone. He decided not to say anything until he knew what was being talked about.

'Hardcore porn publication needs a license Jarvis,' Stanton continued in a level voice, 'and my guess is you don't have one.'

Jarvis sighed with relief: maybe they didn't find his server under the floor. He knew he'd not get much for a license violation. He revealed his rotting teeth in a crooked smile as he prepared himself to be as defiant as possible to these two fuckers.

Patrick sat in stunned silence as he watched the drama unfold onscreen. He had managed to bypass the security on the system with a few bits of software from his disk box of tricks, which had allowed him into the variety of web sites that were located on the server. Most had the usual XXX titles, and he'd printed off a few of the pages as evidence. It had been one of the few sites that hadn't contained a lurid title that had made his stomach turn though.

The main part of the site's address was simply "snuff_n_stuff". He had double clicked to open the page, to find there was just one option titled "Garrotte". Perhaps even more disturbing was the small "New!" icon that flashed beside the title. He had clicked the link hoping this wasn't what it suggested. Unfortunately it was, and soon he was viewing the recent murder that had inadvertently been recorded for posterity.

He sat in silence, watched and listened as the onscreen victim was slowly but surely murdered by a man dressed in dark clothes. He strained for any detail that might give a clue to who the perpetrator was, but when the victim was dragged offscreen and nothing but a view of a room filled the screen, he realised there was no clue here. He watched for a further two minutes, noticing that there was about twenty minutes of the video sequence still to run. He used a mouse to grab the bar and slide the video quickly to the next piece of action. He could barely believe it when the dark figure walked towards the door. He backed the sequence up until the figure was just about to enter the scene and watched as the murderer left the room. As the door closed, Patrick realised the hairs on the back of his neck were standing on end. He shivered, ran his hands through his hair, then picked up the phone.

'Get me Jack Stanton,' he demanded in a shaky voice. The person on the other end was telling him Stanton was in an interview. 'Just get him a message immediately to come and see me. And I mean immediately. This thing's just become a murder investigation.'

When the uniformed officer came in and asked to speak to Stanton, Jarvis was feeling pretty good about himself. He thought he'd weathered the storm pretty well over all, they didn't have too much, he could tell by the questions. As a rather more serious-faced Jack Stanton returned with a uniformed officer, though, Jarvis felt a little of his former optimism evaporate.

Stanton said something quietly to Collier, his back to Jarvis. The colour drained from the woman detective's face.

When he finished talking, they both left the interview room leaving the uniformed officer to guard Jarvis, who decided to continue his cocky arrogant attitude by shouting, 'See ya! Do call in later. We'll have another nice cup of tea.' But the change of mood was shaking Jarvis much more than he was letting on—although anyone watching his renewed vigour for cigarettes could probably have guessed this.

**20 September, 10:42am,
London, Soho**

Stella had been becoming increasingly worried about Niall's absence from his computer and the fact that his webcam was always showing the same image. It had been twenty-four hours since she'd checked it, so she decided to see if anything had changed this Thursday morning.

On opening up her browser and connecting to the site, she was shocked to see that there was a pile of mail that had obviously been building over the last few days which was now beginning to appear at the bottom of the door.

'Oh, come on Niall. Where are you?'

She had a sick feeling in her stomach that something bad had happened to him. Maybe he'd had a heart attack, or been knocked down in the street. Her mind raced.

Maybe she should go and report it to the police. But then she remembered her embarrassment the other night and decided she should try to be a little bit less worried about things. She forced herself to think of less dark reasons for Niall's absence.

Maybe he had simply and innocently gone on holiday. But nobody went on holiday and left their computer on like this, her worried self argued. Unless, she thought, he was using the camera as a kind of remote security camera and was checking it just like she had been. But then why had he gone so suddenly without saying anything to anyone? And what about Boyd's collapse?

She had too many questions and too few answers, and a deadline that she would be lucky to meet even if she wasn't so worried. She pushed Niall to the back of her mind and laid out the documents to do with the budget. It was going to be another long day.

She hoped that maybe one of the others had managed to find something more useful than her wild imagination fuelled ideas. She'd find out that night.

20 September, 10:51am, London, Metropolitan Police Headquarters

The three of them sat in silence watching the grisly scene of the bearded man being garrotted. It wasn't often the case that murders were being viewed by detectives.

'And then if I forward it a bit, we have this.' Patrick sat back and they watched the murderer leave the flat.

'So we have nothing on the perpetrator except his rough build and height,' Lisa ventured, 'you know, based on the height of a standard door.'

'Looks that way,' replied Stanton, 'although I think we'll be seeing what Jarvis has to say about this.' Stanton walked over and looked out the window, the sun was shining in a sky filled with white fluffy clouds. 'Get this on tape, Patrick, I'd like to discuss it with Jarvis right away.'

'Already done.'

When the door bumped open, Jarvis was surprised to see Stanton push a trolley holding a television and video player into the room.

'That's big of you, Jack. Are we going to watch a film?' Jarvis's stomach was knotted. He didn't know what was going on here, but worry certainly had its grip on him. Had they found his server?

'You could say that.' Lisa walked in holding a videotape with a large sticker on it that read in black marker pen "Nickleby, Jarvis. Tape 2. Video Evidence" followed by the date. Were they going to show him some of his own porn? He shuffled uneasily in his seat, reaching for the packet of cigarettes. He found it was empty and began to feel a small panic rising inside him. He swallowed as the woman pushed the tape into the machine that Stanton had just plugged in.

The snowy screen was replaced by a typed form with various serial numbers, Jarvis's name and a brief description of the tape contents. Jarvis was still turning white as the image of the bearded man appeared. He suddenly felt very scared: they might think he had something to do with this.

When the bearded man had been dragged from the scene, Stanton forwarded to the murderer leaving the room, then paused the video. 'Who is he Jarvis? We know it's not you because you're too skinny. But we'd like to know who your friend is.'

'My friend? What? How the fuck would I know who that is?'

'Come on Jarvis, you know you're just making this worse for yourself. We found this on the hard disk on the server under your floor.'

Jarvis swallowed hard.

'So don't try and pretend you've never seen it before. Who is he, and when did this happen?'

Jarvis was now feeling very sick at the prospect of not being able to talk his way out of this. They might think he had set this up to encourage more dodgy people to subscribe to his websites.

'Listen,' he started to quickly blurt out what had happened. 'I only happened on this by accident last Monday. I was trawling for porn on various servers, you know, looking for streaming video porn, and this popped onto my screen. I had nothing to do with it. Honest, I was just recording stuff.'

'And withholding evidence of a murder didn't seem a bit morally reprehensible to you, never mind illegal?' Stanton switched off the television.

'Look, I had nothing to do with this, Jack, honest. All I do is intercept streaming video on servers. Little video windows pop up for about ten seconds and if I like what I see

I start to record. I wrote the software myself. I can show you if you like.' Jarvis was so panicked all he could think to do was to keep explaining what he had been doing while professing his innocence for the murder—totally unaware he was incriminating himself in a variety of other crimes.

'That may have been the case at the time, although why I should believe you I have no idea. And unfortunately the fact remains, you have withheld evidence for a murder enquiry and published a snuff movie on the Internet. For all we know you might even be an accessory to the murder itself.' Stanton didn't really believe Jarvis was capable of this sort of thing, and his opportunistic account seemed the most plausible explanation, but he decided to press Jarvis in case he had any further information. Jarvis held his greasy head in his hands. He desperately wanted a cigarette, or better still a joint. Snuff publication and withholding evidence hadn't really occurred to him when he'd decided to put a site up and not tell the police. He suddenly realised it was likely he'd be going to jail.

Stanton and Collier sat in their office, trying to make sense of the strange turn this apparently simple case had taken. It was the first murder investigation Lisa had ever worked on and it was a strange one.

The interview with Jarvis had divulged little more than they had found out in the first five minutes. He'd been using his own software to find and download video porn on the Internet to put on his sites. Patrick said the file in question had been saved at 9:47pm on the Monday evening, which made the actual time of the murder about twenty minutes before at 9:27pm. Lisa doubted many murder investigations had that level of accuracy for the time of death.

Their biggest problem was that they didn't know who the victim was or where the body was. Stanton had first thought of running Jarvis's program again, but the likelihood of the search engine finding the same webcam again was remote, and that was assuming it was still active. And considering the engine was made to move on if it wasn't manually set to record, someone would need to sit and watch the screens until the right camera was found. The chances were too slim to be worth pursuing.

One thing that was beneficial was that they had a picture of the victim, of sorts. Right now they had a police artist trying to draw him. It was not an easy job, and trying to work out what someone would look like without his face contorted by pain and the knowledge he was about to die was causing the young artist more than a little dismay. They planned to broadcast the picture on local news that evening, to try to provoke someone in the general public to come forward with information on any missing person that looked like the victim. But even this they knew was largely futile: they didn't even know whether the murder had occurred locally.

As for the aggressor, they had no indication of his identity. He had been wearing black clothes, gloves and a balaclava. As Lisa had observed earlier, they knew he was between five foot nine and five foot eleven approximately, based on the door frame, and that he was of medium build. Short of that they would need to find the scene and examine it for more clues.

20 September, 6:11pm, Central London

Stella's journey home had been more than the customary rush hour madness. The weather was awful, with large raindrops bouncing off the streets of Central London. Oxford Street had its usual large puddles on the pavements causing untold pedestrian congestion and, as usual, the rain was causing every returning worker to scurry underground to take even the shortest journey by tube, out of the rain. On days like these the amount of water people brought into the warm subway stations made the air humid and clammy. Worse than the stations were the trains themselves, where damp bodies rubbed against each other in enclosed, moist, airless carriages.

Crammed into one of these carriages, Stella was digging frantically in her bag for her inhaler as she found herself struggling for breath. But the heat and stuffiness of the air in the tube mocked her petty attempt to breathe, and it was with a feeling of respiratory panic that she got off the train at Stratford where she stood for many long minutes gulping in the fresher outdoor air.

The next two trains were filled to overflowing with soaking commuters, so she stood and waited on the platform, watching pencil-thick waterfalls running from the edge of the platform roof. She felt frustrated by her ailment. She knew she had to get her supper and sort out Thomas before she logged on, and now she was twenty minutes later than she'd planned and there still wasn't a train.

An Epping train with enough space arrived twelve minutes later. She stood near the door and watched the view slide by. The high-pitched beep that announced the doors were about to close was exceptionally loud where she was, but she figured it was better to be slightly deafened than to be suffocated. In what seemed an age, as is always the case when you are in a rush, the automated female voice finally announced that the next stop was Theydon Bois - and that the train terminated at Epping. She had her ticket ready and was soon through the turnstile on the way to her flat.

She found a very wet Thomas waiting outside.

'You look like you've had a similar day to I have, Thomas.' She reached down and stroked him once along his back. His fur matted down, but his face showed he liked it. He barrelled upstairs as the door scraped over the two bits of junk mail that greeted their arrival. Stella picked the letters up, bolted the door and went upstairs.

She found Thomas on the surface, licking the water from a puddle which covered the surface by the window.

'Thomas! Get down!' The cat scurried, sliding on the surface as he ran to the other room. Stella sighed: she was going to be late because of this rain. She quickly mopped the surface and put a pan under the leak at the windowsill. The flat felt colder than usual, and Thomas, now rubbing his wet fur on her as she prepared his food, didn't help.

She didn't have time to catch any television this evening, and instead found herself wolfing her food down in front of her computer in the living room as she checked her home email account. She had six new mails, five of which were newsletters from sites she'd subscribed to. The sixth was entirely blank, with no sender, subject details or text. Spooning her last mouthful of supper into her mouth, she took her plate to the kitchen, put it in the sink and ran hot soapy water over it and the pan she'd used to prepare the food. She boiled water as she changed out of her work clothes and made a quick cup of instant coffee before she returned to her computer.

She logged on.

Vincent stirs in his haven of rubbish in the safe house. Opening his eyes he can see shards of orange light streaking in through the gaps in the slats that cover the windows. He brushes the layer of disguising rubbish from his body.

The raspy male voice comes from behind him to the left, 'Hello Vincent.'

At her desk in Theydon Bois, Stella's stomach knotted, her face losing its colour. The gooseflesh on her arms made her feel unusually cold.

Vincent turns his head as far as he dares. Was this person armed? His view settles on the door: the box has been pushed back, betraying the intruder's entrance. Turning slightly more, he can see a shady figure in the periphery of his vision. It is sitting, pushed far into the deep shadows in the corner of the room. There isn't enough light to see whether he has a gun or not. Vincent figures he probably does.

Stella swallowed hard then spoke, hoping the fear she felt wouldn't be noticeable.

'So who might you be?' Vincent enquires, a slight tremor to his voice. He is moving himself extremely slowly to view the figure better as he speaks.

'It doesn't matter who I am. Let's just say you can call me ... Grendel.' The shadowy figure doesn't move at all as he speaks.

The increasingly scared Stella racked her brains: Grendel, the name was familiar somehow.

'Strange name,' says Vincent looking at the figure straight on, although the new position is not allowing him to see any more detail. 'So what can I do for you?' Vincent asks as he begins pushing himself up to a better sitting position.

'Uh-uh,' says Grendel, the tone ensures Vincent is quick to carefully lower himself back to where he began. 'Just stay

where you are.' He pauses briefly. 'Oh, not much Stella, not much at all.'

Stella could feel her throat constricting. Who the hell was this, and how did he know her name?

Vincent's face is reflecting Stella's own look of horror as he speaks, 'How do you know who I am?'

'Oh I know lots of things, Stella.' Grendel lights a cigarette, the glow from the match revealing his face: blue eyes, handsome features in a plain sort of way, dark hair flopping over his forehead, 'like I know you shouldn't have called the police the other night. It was most inconvenient for me.'

Stella swallowed hard, her chest and throat feeling extremely tight. 'Who are you, and what do you want?'

'I want you, Stella,' replies Grendel, 'and all your pitiful Janus friends.'

'What?' Vincent says. 'Why? What have we done?' Stella was struggling to breathe as she spoke and it was telling in Vincent's voice.

Grendel suddenly leans forward, venomously spitting his reply. 'That's just it, bitch! You people have no idea what you're doing.' The contorted face visibly calms once again and Grendel sits back into the shadows. He continues, 'Anyway, to business, I just thought you'd like to know your friend Swift won't be coming to the little meeting tonight.'

'What have you done to him?' Vincent wheezes.

'Oh let's just say he's,' Grendel draws out the vowel and the z sound, 'dead.'

Vincent slumps unconscious as Stella cut the power to her system. She stood up quickly, knocking her chair over, one hand pressed to her chest as she staggered towards the kitchen, falling over the coffee table. She pulled open a kitchen drawer, which fell onto the floor spilling its contents. She felt like she was breathing through a pin thickness straw as she pushed a fresh canister into her spare plastic inhaler. The edges of her vision were closing in as she repeatedly depressed the plunger and inhaled.

She had never been as scared in her life as she lay semi-incapacitated on the floor of her kitchen staring up at the ceiling. She hardly noticed the yellowed stains where the rain had soaked in.

20 September, 7:54pm, Theydon Bois

It was a full twenty minutes before the constriction in Stella's chest subsided and she was able to drag herself to her feet. Her heart was still pounding thunderously in her ears as she checked that each window and door in the flat was locked and all the curtains were drawn. Rationally she realised the curtain closing was no real protection, but the child in her clung to the feeling that if she could not be seen that she would be invisible and safe from harm. She shakily filled the kettle and made hot sweet tea to try to steady her nerves; the encounter with Grendel had shaken her almost to breaking point.

As she sat taking regular small sips of the hot tea, she tried to figure out what to do. She couldn't really phone the police because they would think she was a mad woman who was afraid of her own shadow – especially after the other night. She felt a wave of acute embarrassment when she thought of the two officers, but it was quickly dispelled by a feeling of nausea as she felt her stomach almost expel its contents at the thought of the dark figure on the bridge. She had been right to phone the police; the situation had been real. But the police didn't know that, and to call them again would only make them think even less of her.

She had only one choice. She would need to go to the City and check the truth of Grendel's statement. She had to see if Swift was awake. She looked at the clock on the fireplace: it was almost half past eight.

She powered up the computer again, her hands shaking as she sat not quite knowing what she would find. Suddenly, she wondered if Vincent was even still alive.

She logged on.

Vincent opens his eyes and slowly looks around the room. Dim reddish light is all that remains of the day's artificial sun. He looks over his body, breathing a sigh of relief that he is unharmed. The corner where Grendel had sat is now brightly lit by large shards of light. Grendel is nowhere to be seen.

Vincent gets to his feet, brushing off the bits of rubbish clinging to his clothes. As he turns to leave, he wheezes involuntarily at the sight of part of a message scrawled over the wall. He turns to read the whole message. It reads: "YOU WILL BE NUMBER 4, STELLA. IT WILL BE SOON!" The red paint has bled down from each of the graffitied letters.

Stella's breathing quickened as she read. Number four was next if Swift was still asleep.

Vincent quickly pulls open the door, runs across the hallway and launches down the flights of stairs to the street. As he exits onto the street he breaks into a full run, heading towards Muzyka Street and the Janus building.

The streets look different tonight: the people more imposing and the city more threatening. As Vincent arrives at the far side of the park he is puffing audibly from the exertion, but he presses on up the hill towards the street that leads to Muzyka Street.

Less than two minutes later he rounds the corner onto Muzyka Street at a gallop. There is no time to avoid the camera crew who are set up on the corner, pointing their camera up at the Janus building.

'Shit!' yells one of the crew. 'Watch where you're—' He stops abruptly. 'Aren't you one of Janus's men?' Then in true City journalistic style the barrage of questions begins: 'Is it true Mr Janus has been assassinated? Can you shed any light on Mr Janus's more limited visible street presence these last

few days? Is Janus going to be addressing the increasing trend for destructive crime in the City?'

Vincent manages to quickly regain his feet and presses on up to the building, ignoring the questions. There are news crews and people all round the entrance. Vincent slows to walking pace and bustles his way through the people. He doesn't say anything despite the stream of questions and the pleas from some of the City residents for Janus to help them. He finally reaches the studded oak door, unlocks it, and is almost forced through the gap by the pressing bodies. No one is acting as gatekeeper. He swings the door shut against the bodies, the barely audible click letting him know the latch has fallen. He runs to the main door then up the stairs to the sleeping room.

He enters the room.

Swift is lying peacefully asleep on his reclining chair beside Tyler, whose body has now started to collapse in on itself. Large flaky crusts have dropped into the cavity where the chest has started to cave in. In the void the remains of the internal organs are clearly visible. They too are flaky, husk-like.

Vincent crosses over to Swift's sleeping form. Could this possibly be a joke? Please. 'Swift,' Vincent pleads in a loud voice shaking the body.

A voice from the door answers, 'He's not here yet. You guys are slovenly time keepers.' Frank is leaning against the doorpost. 'Did you have any joy contacting Boyd?'

Stella didn't know where to begin. Her chest was tight and her heart was pounding.

'I think Niall, I mean Boyd, is dead.'

'What?' Frank's face is visibly shocked.

'I can't get in contact with him and his webcam keeps showing the same image and the mail's beginning to pile up behind the door.' Vincent stops. *A brief hissing sound accompanied by a deep intake of breath emanates from his lips before he continues,* 'Remember the other day I said someone had attacked me. Well, he was there when I woke up tonight and he said I'd be number four and that Swift was dead.' *Vincent's face is bravely trying not to cry, but Stella is losing that particular battle. Vincent sobs and wheezes:* 'What about Tyler? Did you find him?'

Frank's eyes are looking at the floor. 'No, I didn't get any reply from him. I've been keeping him up to date with everything that's going on, but it's one of those web-based email accounts, so it's pretty hard to track him down.'

'We have to go to the police. Someone is trying to kill us.' *Vincent involuntarily sobs as he continues,* 'And Grendel told me I was next.'

'Who's Grendel?' *Wilson enters from the main room.*

'The person who attacked me; the person who was there when I logged on tonight; the person who said I'd be number four and it would be soon.' *Vincent looks at the three bodies around the room. Boyd's skin has already become papery, his cheekbones are growing prominent, and, as had happened with Tyler before him, some of his hair has fallen out and is lying on the pillow.*

'What? Surely you don't believe someone is trying to bump us all off.' *Wilson walks over to Vincent.* 'No way.'

'How else do you explain this?' *Vincent replies visibly bringing his emotions more into check.*

'Well, they might all just, oh I don't know, they might have decided they didn't want to play any more.'

'Without saying though?' *says Frank.*

'Well it makes more sense than to assume someone is out to kill us all. Doesn't it?' The question suggests Wilson isn't entirely sure. *'So what do we do?'*

'I think Vincent's right, we should go to the police. Although it would make more sense for you to go, Vincent, since you're meant to be next and considering the other three were also from the South East. I mean, I'm based in Manchester and Wilson here is in Scotland. So if something is happening it looks like it's happening down there.'

'Yes,' Vincent says in a quiet and shaky voice. He pauses briefly before continuing. *'He was outside my flat the other night.'*

'Grendel?'

'Yes, well the person who comes here as Grendel.' Stella took a couple of deep breaths. *'I called the police but they couldn't find anything, but tonight he said he had been there.'*

'Shit,' says Wilson. *'That is not good.'*

'I am so scared.' Vincent begins to sob quietly again.

Frank moves forward nearer to Vincent and says in a soothing voice. 'Look, go to the police. Tell them what's happened. They'll be able to find out if any of this is real.' His voice takes on a reassuring quality, *'They'll be able to trace Tyler because they can make people do things that we can't. And they'll find Niall. They'll sort this.'*

20 September, 11:34pm, Theydon Bois

Stella left Vincent at the Janus building. Not because the safe house had been violated, but because she was presently more worried about her own rather than Vincent's well-being. It was getting late so she checked the doors and windows of her flat again and then went online to Niall's website. She knew the address by heart now because she had checked it so frequently over the last days. The image popped onto the screen, the only change was that the mail pile had collapsed and was now barely visible at the bottom of the screen. She printed out a hard copy of the screen.

As she looked at the printout she felt deflated: how could she convince the police that her friend had maybe been murdered when all she had was a picture of his room as evidence? And what would they think of her when she had to admit she had never even met Niall in person, but had only ever got together online? She shuddered at her nightmare, feeling helpless and sure that no one would believe her especially considering she had no real proof.

When she had finished, she switched everything off and again checked the windows and doors. Only then did she go into her bedroom, with the telephone, where she pushed the wardrobe in front of the door and lay down on her bed in a vain attempt to get some sleep.

The fitful night was haunted with nightmares.

She woke at six and decided to abandon her attempts at sleep. A quick shower followed by some coffee and two bites of a slice of toast fuelled her for the trip to the police station. She felt exhausted from lack of sleep and worry. She was number four, and number four's number was up. She walked briskly to the tube station, finding the turnstiles still open from the previous evening. The first trains of the day had already begun and she was soon sitting in the front carriage of a train to Epping. As she looked through the windows towards the back of the train, the empty carriages gave a hall of mirrors effect as the virtual infinite reflection curved and snaked into the distance. Tiredness was not a good companion to fear, and Stella was soon rocking back and forth, breathing deep regular breaths as she waited on the tube's arrival in Epping.

The walk from the station up the hill had been refreshing, and Stella felt safer since she was somewhere she wouldn't normally be. If Grendel *was* looking for her, he would have needed to have been up pretty early to be following her now. She paced the main street for over an hour, waiting for a reasonable time to go into the police station.

At eight o'clock she walked through the door of the station to be met by two male uniformed officers.

'Morning madam, and what can we do for you today?' said the older of the two, a sergeant she guessed from the stripes on his shoulder.

'Hi,' she couldn't help but think that what she was about to say would sound absolutely ridiculous. 'I think someone is going to kill me.'

'Okay,' said the older man slowly looking at the younger, who gave a brief look like *can you believe this one?* 'And why would you think that Miss—?'

'Robertson, Stella.'

'Why would you be thinking that, Miss Robertson? Has someone threatened you?'

'Well kind of.'

'How do you mean kind of?' the younger officer asked, writing Stella's name onto one of the forms he had taken from some shelves behind.

'Well, I play this computer game and one of the people in the game has said he would kill me.'

'Uh-huh,' said the older policeman raising his eyebrows.

Stella realised how crazy it all sounded, but she was here now and decided to persist. After all, she was pretty sure she was in real danger, despite having no concrete evidence to base it on. 'You see, I think three of my friends have been killed, because their characters in the game have died.'

'Characters in the game?' the older officer quizzed, while the junior officer hid a smile.

'Yes, we play a game together with lots of other people online. It's called a Massive Multiplayer Online Role Playing Game.'

'A what?'

'An MMORPG.' The abbreviation didn't help. Stella rolled her eyes. 'It's a kind of virtual world, a virtual online city, where you can do whatever you want to do, and be whoever you want to be. It's called *Alter Ego*.' The young policeman was writing this down, barely suppressing his smile.

'And someone in this virtual city has threatened you; is that what you are saying?'

'Yes. He said I would be number four, and three people have already died.'

The young officer took over, 'And do people usually get killed in this city or is it a peaceful kind of place?'

'Eh, people get killed a lot. It's allowed in the game.'

'I see, but you think someone is going to kill you out of the game?'

'Yes, because I can't get in contact with my friend Niall and he used to play the game, and now his character is dead, because I think he's dead in real life.' Stella was aware that she sounded like she was babbling. None of this was coming out as she wanted it to. She pulled the picture from her handbag and put it on the desk. The older officer picked it up.

'This is a picture of a room, Miss Robertson.' He looked at her over his spectacles, his brow furrowed.

'I know.' She took a deep breath. *He's looking at me like that because this sounds like the ranting of a mad woman. Brilliant.* She tried to organise her thoughts before she continued. 'Niall went missing the other day in the game, and since then he's not been there.' She pointed at the picture. 'That's a picture from his webcam. He's always at his computer. And last night a man calling himself Grendel—'

'Grendel?' said the younger man, the word ejected from his mouth with a laugh.

'Yes! Grendel said that Swift was dead and that I would be number four and that it would be soon.'

'And Swift is?' the older officer enquired.

'Another of the players.'

'The computer game player?'

'Yes.'

'And Swift is also dead?'

'I think so, along with Tyler. Well not Swift and Tyler, but the people who play as them.' It sounded implausible to Stella's ears. She could only imagine how bad it sounded to the policemen.

'And you're going to be next you say,' said the younger man.

'Yes, Grendel said I would be next.'

'And have you ever killed or threatened anyone in this Ego game, Miss Robertson?' asked the older officer.

Stella paused before she replied, 'Well, yes, it can be part of the game.'

'But you think this is different?'

'Yes. He wants to kill people in the real world rather than in the game. Like Niall,' she said, again pointing at the picture. She knew she was losing what little sympathy was going from the older man, and that the younger officer had abandoned her to her fate long before. 'Listen, he was outside my flat the other night, I phoned the police and he said I had interrupted him and it was very inconvenient.' She knew she was blurting, but she hoped her desperation would convince them to believe her. 'A police woman and man had come and scared him off.'

The older officer typed in Stella's details to the computer. A record of the previous callout appeared on screen. He scanned down it, far enough to read that no one had been found at the scene and that the woman was frantic with nerves. The older man's attitude instantaneously transformed into a dismissive rounding-up tone.

'OK, Miss Robertson, I think we've got everything we need here. We've got your address, and we'll make sure we have a look whenever we're passing. Don't you worry about it.'

'I'm not making this up. I know they didn't find anyone the other night, but that doesn't mean Grendel wasn't there. You have to believe me.'

'Oh, I believe you madam,' said the older man holding two forms vertically and tapping them on the desk to line them up, 'and we'll make sure we keep an eye out for cyber stalkers.' The young man couldn't contain the laugh that grunted from his nose as he held his lips tightly together.

Stella stared in disbelief at the two officers. They didn't believe her. They thought she was a lunatic, and now she was beginning to think that too. 'You'll be sorry when they find me dead!' she spat, turning on her heals.

'I'm sure it won't come to that ma'am, I'm sure it won't.'

As Stella walked out of the station the young officer roared with laughter. 'What a nut job,' she heard him say through bouts of laughter.

21 September, 10:56am,
London, Metropolitan Police Headquarters

Lisa Collier had received details of thirty-five calls after the photo fit had been shown on the news the previous evening. She and Stanton had been slowly eliminating the leads over fresh coffee since they had got in this morning. She dialled the final phone number. 'Hello, is that Mrs Davis?'

'You'll have to speak up dear, I'm a bit hard of hearing,' said the elderly female voice on the other end of the phone.

Lisa spoke louder, 'This is Detective Sergeant Collier. You phoned yesterday evening about the photograph shown on the news.'

'Yes,'

'And do you know the person in the photograph.'

'Yes,' said the old woman. 'It's my friend Bill from Uxbridge. I've known him since the war.'

'Okay. And is Bill missing Mrs Davis?'

'Oh no dear, he's housebound. He has problems with his knees.'

'Sorry Mrs Davis, what age is Bill?'

'My pills, dear? Yes, I've taken them.'

'No, sorry, what age is Bill?' Lisa repeated, louder and clearer.

'Oh he'll be about eighty-three dear. I don't know where you got that picture of him for the telly. He's lost most of his hair since that was taken. It must have been taken during the war'

'Okay,' said Lisa politely. 'Thank you very much for your time, Mrs Davis.'

'That's all right dear. Thank you for calling. It's been lovely to speak to you.'

Lisa shook her head as she turned to Stanton, 'Another dead end. That makes it twenty-one hoax calls, twelve missing bearded men who have since turned up, one misdial, and an old lady whose eighty-three-year-old friend Bob appears to have looked like our man in his youth. Some morning's work.'

Stanton smiled from behind his desk, 'I know what you mean. I really don't know where we can get a handle on this: a murder we can watch again and again, that we know the exact time of, yet we have no clue who the victim is or where the body is.'

'I know.' Lisa moved her list to a corner of her desk. 'Did Jarvis tell you anything new this morning?'

'Afraid not. He's scared, but doesn't seem to know any more than he's telling us. He's getting a bit like a broken record with explaining how he came across the video.'

'Did he get charged?'

'Yes, with withholding evidence, illegal publication of pornography and various other copyright and invasion of privacy charges. He'll no doubt be doing a bit of time.'

'Shame he doesn't know anything more. Looks like our bearded friend will need to be put on the shelf until someone sees a stack of milk bottles or a pile of mail.' She pinned a photocopy of the bearded man onto the pinboard behind her desk.

'I guess so.'

Eight hours later and Lisa was at a more prepared gathering to celebrate her new career direction, eating in an expensive Italian restaurant in Soho. The night had been organised by Anne, one of her uniformed colleagues, and she'd done a great job in finding most of the people Lisa had been friendly with when she'd first joined the force. They had all since gone their separate roads after their initial training, and Lisa was the only one who had decided to join the Met. She had figured it would be a boost to her career, and so far she seemed to have been right: Alison worked the main radio hub for a station near Birmingham, Brian was struggling to escape front desk work in Epping, while Fiona was a beat officer in Bristol. Jane was the last of the original group, and she was doing better than the other three. She was in the traffic division, which had been her ambition from the first day she joined the force. As Lisa surveyed the twelve casually dressed police officers round the table, she felt quietly content about her career. She, like Jane, was doing what she had joined up to do, and it felt good.

'You're looking a bit wistful there,' Jane said quietly as she leaned over.

'I was just thinking about when we joined up.'

'Yes, it's been a slog since then. Hasn't it?' Jane's gaze stared into the past in her mind.

'Still, you're driving the big fast police cars you always wanted to, and now I'm a detective like I always wanted to be.' Lisa lifted her glass and Jane, snapping back to the present, clinked glasses and they both drank silently. Lisa looked down at the twenty pound note that Stanton had given her to buy a drink. He had insisted, despite her protestations that it was too much. He had said that because he couldn't make it for a drink that it was only fair, seeing as he was now her new colleague that he should buy her a good drink. She called over a waiter and ordered a cheap bottle of champagne and glasses for everyone. They could all enjoy Stanton's gift.

After the champagne the fine Italian food was consumed, washed down with litres of house wine. The night was good fun, and Lisa was glad to be away from the conundrum of the murder case. The alcohol-fuelled conversation had moved away from catch up and serious talk to a less formal good time, with various people recounting funny stories.

Dave from her old department was recounting his most embarrassing moment, a story the Scot liked like to trawl up for the laughs at gatherings such as these.

'So, anyway, this guy I used to work with turns up at this formal dinner wearing his kilt back to front, you know with the pleats down the front and the flap at the back.' People were already laughing because Dave couldn't keep the smile from his face as he told the story. 'He even had the chain for the sporran through the loops they use to hang it up.' He was shaking his head as he smiled broadly, looking down at the table. 'Anyway, I says to him that he can't wear his kilt like that, and that he'd need to go and sort it out in the bathroom. And he starts looking really panicked, like it had taken him all day to get it on like this. Anyway, to cut a long story short, I said I'd give him a hand being the kind gentleman that I am.' The others were roaring with laughter by now, knowing where this was going. 'So anyway, we get into the toilet and this guy takes off his jacket and sporran and I tell him to just slide the kilt round his body so it's facing the right way. So he starts doing this, and his shirt's getting all dragged round by the kilt.' Dave is pulling his own shirt in demonstration. 'So I say to him that he needs to loosen the buckles more so his shirt won't twist. So he does this, and he's still all over the place. Anyway, at some point he manages to drop the whole kilt on the floor. And we all know how skanky gent's loos can be. So my first instinct is to pick the kilt up quickly since this guy is just standing there with his hands in the air.' Dave takes a swig of his wine. 'So, anyway, there I am, bent down with my hands on the kilt and my head at about crotch height while this bloke's standing there with his hands in the air. For all the world it looked like I'd just taken his kilt down,' Dave paused, picturing the scene in his head. 'And just at this exact point, the boss of the entire company walks in.' Dave sat back in his chair wallowing in the shaking heads and teary laughter. 'Total nightmare,' he said swigging from his wine glass. 'And you know what the moral of the story is, don't you? Don't ever help anyone, ever!' Tears, laughter and wine were flowing freely.

'I had a funny one this morning,' Brian began, seizing the opportunity to jump in while the audience was still hot. 'This woman came in saying someone from a computer game was trying to kill her.' Everyone laughed, more from the contagion of the laughter from Dave's story than from Brian's statement being really funny. 'Turns out she plays this game online where people kill each other, and she's all freaked out because someone is going to kill her. Complete nut job.' He looked around, realising the audience was cooling visibly. His funny anecdote wasn't really of the calibre of Dave's he realised. He pressed on, 'She even pulled out this picture of a room, saying this was evidence that her friend was dead and that she would be next. A picture of a room! Can you believe that?'

'What did it look like?' The jovial atmosphere around the table instantly evaporated at Lisa's serious tone.

'Sorry?' Brian was still forcing a smile as he wondered how this could have all gone so wrong.

'What did the room look like?' Lisa's seriousness was palpable.

'Oh, I don't know, it was just a room.'

'Think, damn it.' She slammed her hand onto the table, all the glasses jumping slightly. 'This is serious.'

'I don't know, a sofa, a door: room things.'

'Garish sofa on the left, door on the right, landscape picture on the far wall.' Lisa described the final scene of the video footage from Jarvis's computer.

'Yes, how do you know tha—' Brian was dumbfounded.

'Which station do you work at right now?'

'Epping, Why? What's this about Lisa?' Brian's mouth was slightly open in amazement at the turn of events.

'I have to go.' Lisa stood and got her things together. 'I'm sorry. I'll try to call you all next week.'

As Lisa left the restaurant Brian asked, 'What was all that about?'

'Dunno,' Dave replied, filling Brian's glass. 'I do not know. Anyway, this other time I was in this club...'

Lisa was on her mobile phone as soon as she left the restaurant. She had been surprised by how serious she had felt, but then she had seen the murder on video and this was the only lead they had. She felt excited as she dialled Stanton's home number. If this lead proved real, they would finally be able to get this case moving.

'Jack. It's Lisa. I'm sorry. I didn't disturb you did I?'

'No. Well not really. I've got a friend round for dinner.' A female voice in the background was asking who was on the phone, and from the rustling sound, it sounded like Stanton was maybe in bed. Lisa waited as he explained the call was about work, his hand cupped over the mouthpiece.

Lisa continued, 'Sorry. The reason I'm calling is that I've just stumbled onto some information that might let us find the scene from the video.'

'Uh-huh. Go on.'

'Apparently a woman came into Epping police station this morning showing a picture of a room, saying that the empty room showed that her friend was dead. The room description is the same as the one in the video.'

'Wow,' Stanton replied, not quite believing their luck. 'We'll need to get onto this first thing tomorrow.'

'Yes, that's what I thought.'

'I'll pick you up tomorrow at half past seven. Sorry, no lie in I'm afraid.'

'That's okay. I'll see you then.'

Lisa walked smiling to the tube station. Luck was really on her side this week: first the hidden computer and now this. She hoped it would last.

PART II - ALTER EGO

22 September, 7:30am, London, Lisa's Flat

Stanton was outside Lisa's flat at 7:30am sharp. It was a sunny morning and Lisa had been up for an hour, excited that they were going to be following up her lead. It took them the best part of an hour to get to the police station in Epping. The old desk sergeant was on duty again. Stanton let Lisa take the lead.

'Good morning, I'm Detective Constable Lisa Collier and this is Detective Inspector Jack Stanton.' Stanton was standing tall beside her; she was glad she had his imposing presence beside her. 'I was wondering if you could help us.' Lisa showed her ID.

'Good morning. Well, I can certainly try.'

'We understand you had a woman in here yesterday with a picture of a room, claiming her friend had been murdered.'

'Yes.' Williams began to type into the computer. 'She was a completely dotty girl. Seemed to think someone from a video game was going to kill her. Quite disturbing really.'

'Has anyone done anything to check if she was in danger?'

'Not since yesterday, but we did respond to a 999 about a possible intruder a few nights ago. We didn't find anyone. We figured yesterday was just more nervousness.'

'Did you get a description of the intruder?'

'Hold on, I'll just check.' He scanned down the screen, 'It just says here he was described as a "dark figure". The officers couldn't find anything, and she seemed extremely strung out. They figured it was just a panic call from a nervous single woman who lives alone.'

'Did she leave the picture with you?'

'Yes, it's in her file.' He looked through the pile of files that had not yet been put into filing cabinets. 'Here it is,

Robertson, Stella.' He handed over the picture of the room. Lisa's heart was pumping: it was the same room. She had stumbled on their only lead in this murder investigation. She fought to maintain her professional composure. As she wrote the address from the front of the file into a small notepad along with directions of how to get to Theydon Bois and the woman's flat.

The car ride took just over ten minutes. It was quarter past nine. They parked opposite the address, outside an Indian restaurant. The flat they were looking at was unusual with its flat roof, perched above the engraver's shop. It looked in desperate need of repair.

They had rung the doorbell three times when Stanton decided to walk around the side of the building. All the front curtains were tightly shut. Maybe there would be more life at the back. He walked to the back of the property. He could see a derelict car yard through the fence behind the property, and the roof section that worked a bit like a balcony, but access was blocked. A cat was sitting staring down at him as he strained to see any signs of habitation. The curtains were closely drawn here too.

'Do you live here?' Stanton said to the cat. The cat looked blankly back

After ten minutes, Lisa decided that perhaps the woman was too scared to answer. She opened the letterbox. 'Hello. Stella. This is Detective Sergeant Collier from CID. I'm here about your picture, the one you took to the police station yesterday.' Stanton was over the street, watching for any movements of the curtains. The upper left window moved back a fraction and he could almost make out the eye peering through. He held up his police identification in the hope she would see it. His plan seemed to work and the curtain opened more. The woman strained to see Lisa at the front door. Stanton told Lisa to step back and show her ID. A few moments later they heard the sound of the bolts being drawn. The door opened. Stella Robertson's eyes were sunken from lack of sleep. Her skin was white and she looked about ready to pass out.

'Do you mind if I open the curtains, Stella? Let a little light in.' Lisa was moving to the window.

'No, that's fine.' Stella was sitting on the sofa, her legs curled under her. She ran her hands through her hair, pulling it into a ponytail that she secured with an elastic she had round her wrist. She played nervously with some rogue loose blond strands with slim fingers that were red and chewed. She spoke slowly, with little emotion due to her lack of sleep.

Stanton began: 'So, Stella, what can you tell us about this picture of the room? Do you know whose house it is, and where it is?'

'No, I'm not sure where it is, but the picture is of Niall Davidson's flat. I've never been there; I've only ever seen it on the web cam.' She got up and switched on the computer.

'The people at the station in Epping said you think Niall is dead. What makes you think that?'

'Well,' Stella didn't know whether these two would be likely to believe what she was about to tell them, but they had come here uninvited this time, which meant at least she wasn't the mad woman who had phoned in a panic again. And the man, something about his manner reassured her; his rugged tough-looking features softened as he spoke in a way that reassured her. She took a deep breath and began. 'I play this online game called *Alter Ego*, where you can be whatever you want in a virtual city. It's in this game that I first began to think something must have happened to Niall.

He plays a character called Boyd, who collapsed for no reason the other night.' She looked at both Stanton and Collier. Neither looked judgemental and both seemed to be seriously absorbing her words. She continued, 'Anyway, Niall's quite serious about the game, so it wouldn't have been like him to just decide to leave his character wherever he fell.'

The computer had now booted and she quickly connected to the live video feed from Niall's camera. 'Here's the web page for his camera. The picture was of this.' She motioned at the screen, which still showed the same image as the picture showed, and little had changed since Jarvis had made his video.

'Can you write down the web address for us?' Lisa asked.

'Sure, I'll just print it out for you.' Stella punched some keys and her printer whirred to life. Seconds later she handed Lisa a sheet of paper that had the address of Niall's web cam. Lisa took the sheet, aware that potentially they could use it to find his address, which would allow them finally to examine the crime scene.

'So what makes you think you're in danger?' Collier folded the paper and put it into her notebook, secured with an elastic band.

'Well, in the game, six of us, including Niall and me - well actually originally four of us - had set up a sort of cooperative to kind of gain an upper hand in the game. And now three of the other five ... well, their game characters are inactive.'

'So their characters don't come into the game any more and you're thinking this might mean something has happened to them?'

'No, your character stays in the game when you leave. It just goes to sleep. It's called a persistent online universe. So their characters are just,' she looked for a different word, 'kind of dormant.'

'Let me get this clear,' Stanton interrupted. 'Do you mean that this city exists somewhere online, right now?'

'In cyberspace,' Stella volunteered.

'Yes, in cyberspace, and your character is in it whether you are there or not?'

'Yes, it just stays there, asleep.'

'Wow,' said Stanton. 'I've never heard of anything like this.' He looked over at Lisa who looked similarly amazed. 'So can your character be killed while you are not even there?'

Stella nodded, 'That's why we set up the Janus group.'

'The Janus group?'

'The cooperative. We noticed that if we played as a team we could run the City. We decided to create a figurehead, Mr Janus, a sort of omnipresent gangster overlord, who didn't exist but who we would all seem to work for. And because we would be doing things apparently on his behalf, he would seem to be online in the City all the time since we worked in sort of shifts.'

'Sorry, run that by me again.' Stanton looked a bit confused.

Stella tried to explain as simply as possible: 'Mr Janus is a pure fiction in the game, a kind of fiction within the fiction if you follow me. He doesn't exist at all. But the same name is always associated with the things that we in the Janus group were doing in the City, and so it began to seem like he was real to the other players. He kind of became real by reputation, and we made sure we used the game's news service to publicise what we were doing, to make sure everyone knew of Mr Janus's reputation.'

'The news service?' Lisa could hardly believe she had never heard of this, but then she had never been into computer games so why should she have? It seemed so complex it almost defied belief.

'Yes, there's a news service, so you can see what's going on around the City. You know, who killed who, and what events are going to happen. That sort of stuff.' Stella returned to what she had been saying: 'Anyway, we use it a lot to get publicity, and in effect, our fictitious leader runs the City. But in reality we, the Janus group run, or rather we ran, the City.'

Jack Stanton looked at the drained, rundown woman in front of him and wondered how she had got into this kind of thing. He would never have taken her for a gangster, not even a virtual one. 'Interesting idea.'

'Thanks,' Stella felt little enthusiasm for their great scheme right now.

'So three of your Janus group are constantly asleep now? Is that right?' Stanton felt he was getting to grips with what was going on.

'Basically.'

'And what makes you think they are dead in the real world?' Stanton stumbled over the last words. He felt strange clarifying the obvious. Until today Stanton's world had always just been the world, now it had become the "real world".

'Grendel, one of the characters in the game, told me he had killed Swift, and then Swift hadn't woken up when I went to check.' Tears were welling in Stella's eyes.

'Grendel?'

'He's the person I think wants to kill me. He told me I would be number four, and three of them are lying there now. And he knows my real name and he said I disturbed him the other night by phoning the police.' Tears were running down her cheeks as she spoke. She sniffed intermittently as her nose began to run.

Lisa walked over and sat down beside Stella, putting her arm round her. 'It'll be all right, Stella. Don't worry.' Stanton offered his handkerchief, which Stella took to wipe her eyes.

'This Grendel's contacted you since the prowler the other night then?' Stanton enquired.

'Yes,' Stella sounded like she had a bad cold. 'He was waiting for me when I went online last night, and he left a message on the wall saying that he would kill me soon.' The words were enunciated in time with the involuntary spasms of Stella's sobs.

Lisa had done what she could to comfort Stella, but she had been uncontrollably sobbing when exhaustion finally got the better of her. The detectives discussed what information they had in the kitchen and Lisa opted to stay until Stella woke up so there would be a friendly face around.

Stanton organised a twenty-four hour watch on Stella's flat from the Epping station: two officers would sit out front in a squad car while a patrol of two would cover the general area, including the bridge. Stanton and Lisa had both agreed that based on the video evidence of Niall Davidson's murder, Stella was in obvious imminent danger. The perpetrator knew where she lived and had her down as the fourth victim.

As Stanton drove to Patrick Bateson's lab he mulled over the other sickening possibility from what Stella had said: they had to assume that the two other inactive characters had real-world counterparts who were probably dead. In the space of twenty-four hours the case had moved from being dead in the water to a multiple murder investigation.

What was desperately needed was to get more information from Stella to find the other victims. But Stanton also figured she was safe for now and that it would be better for her to get some sleep. She was the next planned victim, so if they protected her, they had time to let her sleep.

22 September, 12:22pm,
London, Metropolitan Police Headquarters

'It's a fine thing that you've got me in here this day of rest, Jack,' Patrick said sarcastically as he unlocked the lab door.

'I know, Patrick, and I'm sorry about that. But we've got a pretty good lead on the video murder and we couldn't think of anyone more qualified than you to find us the address.' Stanton grinned.

'Aw, you're a big flatterer, Jack. I actually don't mind you know.' He leaned in close. 'But don't tell anyone. I'd only be at home fiddling with my own computers, so I might as well be here getting overtime. So anyway, what have you got for me?'

Stanton produced the printout Stella had made. 'Here's the Internet address of the web cam that Jarvis recorded the murder on.'

'Yer arse and parsley. Are you serious? How did you get your hands on this?' Patrick took the paper as he tilted his head and half smiled at it in disbelief.

'Lisa had a bit of good fortune,'

'Lisa? Your new partner?'

'Yes, she__'

'I like her. Seems like a really nice lass,' Patrick interrupted.

'Uh-huh.'

'And obviously clever too.' He waved the sheet of paper.

'Indeed.' Stanton smiled at Patrick's ingenuous manner; this was not at all like him. He wasn't aware Patrick had met Lisa, far less that he was interested in her. 'Anyway, she happened on information that found us someone who was missing our victim, and this morning we managed to get her address. So now your part is to find the address of the murder scene from this, so we can go round and sort it out. And the sooner the better, because it's been a while now and the longer it takes, the more nasty the body will be and the less likely it is we'll get any useful evidence from it.'

Patrick screwed up his nose. It was terrible to think that the person they had watched fighting for his life was now a corpse. 'I'll get right onto it, Jack. I can pull in a few favours to get the address for you today. Do you have a mobile number and I'll call you when I get it?'

Stanton gave him his mobile number.

Stella began to emerge from a deep and hazy sleep around one in the afternoon.

'Hi, Stella,' Lisa said gently. 'How are you feeling now?'

'A bit better.' Stella was lying on the sofa, blinking through sleepy eyes.

'Would you like a cup of tea, coffee?'

'A cup of tea would be good. The bags are on the surface by the fridge.'

Lisa went through and made two mugs of tea, putting a tea bag into each mug rather than using a teapot. She smelled the milk from the fridge before she poured it.

Stella was sitting like she had been earlier, curled on the sofa playing with her hair. Her eyes seemed more alert now that she had slept for the longest single period she had experienced in the last four days. Lisa looked at the woman in front of her, aware now Stella was slightly refreshed, how attractive she was: blonde medium-long hair, pretty blue eyes, nice bone structure. She was a little thinner than Lisa's own athletic figure, and paler, but otherwise a similar type to Lisa herself.

'Thanks,' said Stella taking the mug. 'What did you say your name was again?'

'Lisa.'

'Thanks, Lisa. It's really good of you to have stayed. Is the other officer still here too, the guy?'

'No, Jack's gone to sort out some other things so we can go round and check on your friend Niall's flat.'

Stella's hand involuntarily rose, her fingers covering her mouth. 'God, I hope he's all right.'

'We'll go and check just as soon as we have the address.' Lisa paused briefly, weighing up whether Stella could handle being asked more questions. She decided she was in better shape now than before. 'So, Stella, is there anything else you think we need to know about? We will need email addresses, telephone numbers, postal addresses for the other Janus group members if you have them. But anything you feel might be relevant is worth mentioning.'

'I've only got their email addresses. We never met except in *Alter Ego*. There was no point. We could talk face to face there, so there was no need to get together. We use emails to make sure we all know what is going on. I'll give you the addresses. She moved to the computer, which was still quietly humming along after its earlier use. As Stella moved the mouse, the screen came to life showing the feed from Niall's webcam. She closed it down with a sigh. A couple of minutes later the printer fired up again and Lisa was given the email addresses of the other Janus members. 'I can't think of anything else that I haven't already told you.'

'Look, here's my number, you can call me anytime, night or day, if you remember anything or just want to talk.' She scribbled the number on the corner of the paper with the email addresses on it and tore it off, handing it to Stella.

'You're not leaving now are you?' Stella voice was slightly higher than before, the words tumbling from her mouth in the beginnings of panic.

'No, don't worry. I have to wait for Jack to come back. I'll stay until then.'

Stella visibly relaxed and sat deeper into the sofa. 'Good.'

'And we've got officers outside, and two others patrolling round your house. You're going to be okay, Stella.'

'I hope so,' Stella said, cupping the mug with both hands and holding it near her mouth between sips.

'Jack. It's Patrick.'

Stanton looked at his watch: it was half past three. 'Have you got me the address?'

'I surely have, Jack. It's near Shepherd's Bush. Do you have a pen there?'

'I do, hold on.' Stanton cradled his mobile on his shoulder as he got out a small notepad and a pen. 'Go on.'

'It's 16C Hetley Road.'

Stanton arrived back at Stella's forty minutes later. He had arranged for the forensic people to be ready to go when he called. He figured they would all be on site in about an hour's time. He rang Stella's doorbell and Lisa answered the door.

'Lisa.' He glanced up the stair at Stella peering round the doorframe. He raised his hand in a small wave and continued quietly, 'We've got the address for Niall Davidson's flat. We should get on our way.'

'OK. I'll tell Stella. I'll just be a couple of minutes.' Stanton nodded at the officers in the squad car as he returned to his car.

Five minutes later Jack Stanton and Lisa Collier were exiting Stella's road, en route to 16C Hetley Road.

22 September, 4:58pm, London, Shepherd's Bush

There were seven of them altogether: Stanton, Collier, three people from Forensics, one of them a photographer, and two uniformed officers, one of whom was holding a short, heavy-looking battering ram. Everyone but the two uniformed officers was zipped into a disposable paper overall, complete with an elasticated hood. Latex gloves were pulled on and snapped over the cuffs, ensuring no contaminants could get onto the crime scene. Only the wearer's eyes were visible through plastic spectacles, the nose and mouth hidden behind surgeon's masks. They looked like they were from a science fiction movie.

'Ready?' One of the uniformed officers looked at Stanton. Stanton nodded. The officer lined up the ram with the lock, swung it away from the door, then with one big gravity-assisted pendular motion, he slammed it into the door. In the confines of the uncarpeted corridor the thud was deafening, but the splintering accompaniment indicated the brute force was working. It took two more arcs of the ram before the doorframe finally gave. Stanton pushed the door, feeling the resistance of the mail behind it as the door ploughed open. Everyone took a slight backwards step as the room's air wafted out.

'Phew,' said the officer with the ram, covering his nose and mouth. 'I thought this guy had been dead for less than a week.'

'He has,' said Collier through a screwed up nose, although her facemask hid this.

With a pop, the photographer's camera flashed through the door. The rising high-pitched whine of the capacitor charging for the next flash was a haunting sound, made famous in the countless movies where forensic photographers document grisly scenes. Another pop and the two other Forensics men took briefcases out of protective polythene bags and entered the room. One of them immediately began to construct a protective barrier at the door to keep contaminants out of the room. The other followed the photographer who was systematically photographing everything in the room.

As Stanton and Lisa entered, the quiet hum of the computer was evident. Lisa looked at the computer across the room: she could see the small lens of the webcam, the silent witness to the demise of Niall Davidson. From her viewpoint in the doorway a trail of blood was clearly visible. Its dark trail led to another door between the garish sofa and the computer desk. The desk chair was lying on its side, dark blood splashes covering the back.

One of the forensic scientists was scraping samples into a small vial he had taken from his case. He vigilantly labelled the sample before he carefully screwed the top and secured it in his case.

The second forensic investigator was over by the door where the blood trail led. He was taking prints from the door handle and doorframe, ensuring nothing would be smeared or lost when the door was opened.

It was thirty minutes before the second door was opened. The smell of decay was almost overpowering. Stanton swallowed, breathing in shallow breaths as he tried not to inhale the smell of rotten flesh. His mind flashed into his past, causing him to reel. He staggered one tiny step before regaining his balance.

'You okay?' asked Lisa.

Stanton gave a nod and breathed heavily through his nose.

The photographer did not seem fazed by the smell, and pop-whined two shots from the doorway. The body was clearly visible from the doorway as the flash lit the room.

Without the flash the heavily curtained room reduced the prone body to a dark shadow. The photographer continued to photograph the body and room from every conceivable angle.

When Stanton and Lisa finally entered the room, the switches and doorframes both inside and out had been dusted for prints.

'He looks like he's been bludgeoned on the back of his head,' Lisa observed. The injury on the back of Niall's head was encrusted with blood, and bits of dark flesh clung to the wound. 'Why would he bludgeon him when he was obviously dead from the garrotte?'

'I don't know.' Stanton was struggling to hold onto his stomach contents. He looked at the dark patch of dried blood Niall was face down in.

'Look at this.' Collier was pointing at other patches of blood in line with the head of Niall's corpse. 'It looks like he must have moved him.' She was pointing with a pen as she squatted down by the body. 'Look, you can see where the blood from his throat has smeared, then there's the round patch here where his head's been and this patch here. Weird, isn't it?'

'I've got to get a breath of fresh air, Lisa. Sorry.'

'Don't worry.' Lisa couldn't work out whether it was excitement at being at a real-life murder crime scene, or whether she had somehow been desensitised to this sort of thing from watching the plethora of forensic dramas on TV. Whatever it was, she wasn't fazed by this situation. She turned back to the stains on the floor.

Images of mutilated bodies flashed across Stanton's mind causing his stomach to heave as he carefully, but quickly, walked back through to the other room and let himself out of the makeshift plastic door.

'How is it?' one of the uniformed officers asked.

Stanton walked on, clawing at his mask, tearing the paper hood as he pulled it back. The dry retching was subsiding as he finally got down to the street where he stood sucking in deep breaths of uncontaminated air.

It was another forty minutes before the coroner arrived. Stanton was still outside. Collier had told one of the uniforms to tell him that she could deal with this for now. There was no real need for both of them to be there when the body was removed anyway. Stanton was glad. He had seen too many bodies while he had been a detective – and before – each in a different state of disrepair. All of them had made him feel sick to the core. A good detective doesn't need to be good with dead bodies, he told himself.

'Lovely day,' the coroner said politely as he walked up to the door.

'Yes, it is,' said Stanton, not quite enjoying it.

Lisa was still writing down every scrap of information she could observe from the room and the body when the coroner came through the door.

'Hello,' he said politely. 'Lovely day.' He immediately began to take notes.

'Er, yes.' Lisa was quite taken aback by the coroner's politeness, and that despite the scene before him that he could think this was a lovely day. She watched as he looked over his half-moon spectacles and *hmm*-ed and *uh-huh*-ed as he jotted down his initial observations. After a few minutes he asked Lisa to give him a hand to roll the body over onto its back.

'Sure,' said Lisa. She moved in line with the hips of Niall Davidson's corpse and kneeled down.

'On three. One, two, three.' They began to turn the body over. Lisa quickly had the hips perpendicular to the floor. The coroner, holding the shoulders had managed a lesser angle. He visibly strained. A crunching sound was replaced by a squelch as Niall's face suddenly came free from the floor to which it had become encrusted. As it slumped over onto its back the air from the lungs was expelled in a hiss through the teeth, which were clearly visible through the remains of the mutilated face. Lisa scrambled backwards trying to put some distance between her and the body.

'Uh-huh,' said the coroner.

22 September, 7:12pm,
London, Metropolitan Police Headquarters

Back in his office Stanton rolled open his desk drawer. The square bottle of Jack Daniels slid rather than rolled to the front of the drawer. He drew his fingers gently across the cool contoured glass of the bottle, running his fingertip over the bottle top, before he slowly slid the drawer shut again. He closed his eyes and took a deep breath.

Collier walked in and sat down. Her look confirmed to him that she also couldn't quite believe the horror that this case now involved. As they sat, not saying a great deal, the possibility that two other people had been murdered and similarly mutilated was a prominent thought in both of their minds.

'I can't believe he cut off his face.'

'I know,' Stanton replied, his stomach lurching. 'It's twisted. Any idea why?'

Lisa shook her head. 'And why he would bludgeon in the back of his head after he was dead is beyond me too.'

Stanton nodded.

'This mutilation aspect is something I hadn't expected at all when we saw that video,' said Lisa.

'Me neither.' Stanton's face was contorted from his obvious discomfort at the subject matter. 'So do you think there's any relevance to the name of our bad guy in the game? What was it again, Grendor?' He said changing the subject to something he found slightly less distasteful.

'Grendel,' Lisa replied. 'I don't know. The name's really familiar. I'm sure it's from classical mythology or something. I do know I've heard it before, I just can't quite place it right now.'

Stanton turned both his palms up. 'Don't look at me. I've never heard the name in my life before today.'

'I'll find out where it's from, and whether there's any relevance to the mutilation.' Lisa stood and crossed to the coffee machine. 'Do you want a coffee?' she offered.

'No, thanks. I'm heading off soon.'

'So what happens now?' Lisa sat down again, deciding she would have coffee at home later.

'Well, I think for now we need to try and get in contact with the other names Stella gave us. We've got all their email addresses and Patrick's working on their "real world" addresses.'

'How long will that take?'

'Looks like it's going to be Monday before we get them. Patrick gave me an earful about not getting the addresses we had to him as soon as we got them because his contacts won't be in now until first thing Monday morning. He's sending them all an email telling them to phone here as soon as possible with their details. Short of them reading their email and getting back to us though, we'll just need to wait 'til Monday.'

'I'd forgotten too. Sorry. It seemed more important to get to the crime scene.'

'I know. It's not your fault. It's been a hell of day.'

'At least we have the next victim under police protection,' Lisa offered on the more positive side.

'Yes, there is that.' Stanton got up and put on his jacket and coat. 'Anyway, we might as well get out of here and salvage what we can of the weekend. The people on the switchboard have been told to call me when they hear something. I'll call you if they call me.'

23 September, 10:30am, London, Lisa's Flat

Sunday morning came sooner than Lisa Collier had expected. She looked across at her radio alarm. It said 10:30am. She tested the air with a foot, quickly withdrawing it back into the warm cocoon of her duvet when she felt how cold the outside air was. It had been a strange night, the sound of Niall Davidson's face cracking free from the carpet circling through her mind in the small hours of the night. She hadn't so much had nightmares, as long waking periods of reflection on what had happened. She swung her legs over the side of the bed, her toes curled in against the cold as they sought out the slippers beside the bed. She quickly sat up, making her body as small a target as possible for the cold air, then grabbed a towel from the radiator and quickly dashed through and jumped in the shower. As she stood under the hot stream of water, she shivered at the strange way this, her first case, was unfolding.

In the early afternoon, having not heard anything from Stanton, she decided to check out the name Grendel. She definitely knew the name from somewhere, she just wasn't sure from where. She opened her dread cupboard in the hall, which was filled with the junk she had never bothered to unpack when she had moved in over a year ago helped by Rob, her now ex-boyfriend. She sighed, hands on hips as she looked at the stack of boxes. The bottom box was marked in black marker with the words BOOKS: CLASSICS & TRASHY.

'Some classification system.' She smiled as she lifted the first of the four boxes stacked on top to the floor. The box of books was filled to the brim, so she decided it was probably best to just drag it from the cupboard through into the sitting room. Soon she was rifling through her old books, smiling at the horror novels she had once read with such gusto, and feeling a slight tinge of embarrassment at the number of trashy romance novels she had kept.

At the bottom she found what she was looking for: her mythology books. She flicked to the back of a copy of Ovid's *Metamorphoses*, scanning down for Grendel in the index of names. It wasn't there. Flicking through a couple of other classics she was still without an answer.

'Kids' books!' She snapped her fingers. She hurriedly rifled through the hall cupboard again, this time for her children's books. It was a smaller box, and she found it near the back of the cupboard. Almost the whole of the cupboard's contents were now in the hall as she carried the new box back to the other room.

The Legend of Beowulf was near the top of her box of children's books. As Lisa handled the dog-eared book her mind flooded back to her childhood when she had repeatedly read of the heroic exploits of Beowulf as he fought with the monster Grendel, who had been killing Danish warriors from the king's hall as they slept. She slowly leafed through the book looking at the illustrations of the creature, her mind floating somewhere between childhood and the present.

After she had read every page and looked at every picture, she decided to get a translation of Beowulf that wasn't abridged for children. She grabbed her coat, remembered to pick up her mobile, then half climbed over the boxes in the hallway as she made for Oxford Street to find a bookshop.

By ten to five that same Sunday evening, Jack Stanton was wondering why no one had called him yet. He had expected that the other two Janus people would have contacted the switchboard, who in turn would have contacted him. Surely they must have checked their emails by now. He left the

Midget's carburettor on the kitchen table on last week's newspapers, where he had neatly taken it to pieces.

He washed his oily hands in the sink leaving dirty splashes all around it, then picked up the phone. 'Can I speak to Alice, please? It's Jack Stanton here.'

'Sorry, Jack, Alice isn't on today. This is Bill, can I help you at all?'

'Yes, maybe you can. I told Alice that I would be expecting a couple of calls either last night or first thing this morni—'

Bill butted in, 'Yes, there were two calls for you this morning. Would you like the messages?'

'The messages! Why wasn't I called immediately? I told Alice to contact me as soon as these people called.'

'I'm sorry Jack,' said Bill, 'but she didn't—' He paused. 'Sorry Jack, she left a Post-It note on the computer screen before she finished last night. I just didn't notice it. I'm really sorry. Was it important?'

'It…' Stanton stopped. There was no point in grilling Bill; he just hadn't been informed correctly. 'Look Bill, just give me the details and I'll sort this, okay.'

As he hung up the phone, looking at the names, addresses and numbers of the other two Janus members, he was thankful that at least they were guarding Stella. If they hadn't known she was to be Grendel's next victim, this sort of cock-up could have cost one of these faceless names his life.

He wasted no time, and immediately began making calls, having decided to get someone from local forces to go and physically make sure the names on his sheet of paper were all right, and that they would be regularly checked for the duration of this investigation. It took nearly an hour to track down the relevant people to do this, and it was a little after six o'clock when he was finally able to get back to the dismantled carburettor. He took one look at the pieces of metal on the newspapers and decided it could wait until another day.

As he made a sandwich for his dinner, though, he couldn't help but tinker, and soon he was eating an oily sandwich as he cleaned the various parts for reassembly. At quarter past midnight he slid himself out from under the front of the wheel-less Midget. Its immaculate British Racing Green bodywork was propped up on two axle stands at the front and two stacks of planks that he had tied together with some old belts at the back. He felt exhausted as he pulled off his oily overalls. But as he looked at the Midget that had once belonged to his older brother, he smiled. Simon would have been proud of his work. He flipped off the garage light switch.

23 September, 6:22pm, Oxton, Scottish Borders

While Stanton worked on the carburettor in his kitchen in London, a uniformed officer from the Lothian and Borders Police walked down from the main road in the small village of Oxton. He was walking towards a small late eighteenth century cottage where he had been told to check on the resident. The light drizzle glowed as it passed through the beam of his torch, which wagged rhythmically back and forth in front of the stocky Scottish policeman.

He walked down the hill, his torchlight his guide to the little house: there were no streetlights apart from those on the main street, which was now a couple of hundred yards behind him. The sound of a coming vehicle hissing along the wet road made him move onto the grass verge. He nodded and smiled as the woman driver slowed and waved a thank you at his yellow reflective form. He wasn't looking forward to the walk back up the hill to the car as he puffed his way to the front door of the cottage.

Stepping onto the small porch, he flapped his arms to rid himself of some of the water sitting on the surface of his waterproof coat, then looking for the doorbell but not finding one he used the small gargoyle-shaped doorknocker.

He was beginning to wonder if there was anyone home when the sounds of a thrown bolt and a turning key signalled otherwise. He extinguished his torch as the door opened, bathing him in warm yellow light from the tiny hall of the cottage.

'Good evening, sir. I'm Sergeant Dickinson from the Lothian and Borders Police. Are you Andrew Miller?'

A man in his late twenties or early thirties of medium build with short hair smiled broadly from beneath his spectacles. 'Yes, I am. This must be in connection with the email sent from London yesterday I assume.' He had a nondescript south-eastern accent.

'Yes, I'm just here to check you're doing all right, and that you haven't had any problems or uninvited visitors.'

'No, officer, neither.'

'No one's contacted you, or threatened you in any way.'

'No, as you can see, this place is quiet as the grave.'

'You're not wrong there, sir.' Dickinson got out a small notepad. 'I've been asked by Detective Inspector Stanton of the London CID to ask you if you have any further information that may be of relevance from the game itself.' Dickinson's intonation betrayed that he was asking a question about a subject he was not entirely sure about.

Miller leaned against the wall, his hand on his chin, his eyes looking up as he thought. 'Well, I was threatened a couple of weeks back in the game. He told me to piss off.'

'Sorry, who told you this?'

'In the game, I was threatened, by the Grendel guy. Sorry, I mean I told him to piss off,' Miller corrected.

'I see,' said Dickinson, writing down the vague statement. 'So you were threatened in a game by,' he paused while wrote, 'Grendel, and you told him to "piss off", or did you say he told you to piss off?' Dickinson had been only slightly briefed about what this was all about and none of it was making much sense. Games for him had only ever involved silver top hats, cars, dogs and piles of paper money—and of course his favourite: just plain old playing cards and piles of paper money.

'I told *him* to piss off.' Miller clarified.

'Uh-huh. And was there anything else at all?'

'No, I don't think so.' Miller adopted the thinking pose again. 'No. Nothing. Personally I think this has all probably been blown out of proportion.'

'Maybe, sir, but it's always better to be safe than sorry.'

'Indeed.'

'Anyway, we'll check in with you from time to time, just to make sure you're doing okay. Until they get this thing sorted out down in London.'

'Eh, that's okay, actually. I thought it would be better, safer, if I went away up north for a while. I figure if this Grendel guy doesn't know where I am, he won't be able to get to me.'

'I see. So when are you thinking of going, and where do you plan to stay?'

'I was going to go first thing tomorrow to Skye, just to a B&B somewhere. I could do with a holiday and now seems as good a time as any to go, especially considering all of this.'

Dickinson nodded, 'Well I recommend you contact the local police station on Skye, so they know what's going on. They can contact me if they need any details.'

'Great,' Miller said. He paused for a couple of seconds. 'Do you think this is a good idea? You sound a bit unsure, you know, for me to go away.'

'No, I mean yes. It's fine. It probably is a good idea, and it'll keep you out of harm's way for now anyway. Just make sure you get back in contact with us when you get back.'

'Sure thing.'

'All right then, sir. Enjoy your trip.'

'I will. And thanks for calling round, officer.'

'That's no problem at all, sir,' said Dickinson, pulling his collar tight round his neck and switching his torch on as he began the walk back up the hill. Miller watched from the door as the sergeant puffed his way into the night, the torch beam rhythmically scanning his path like a blind man's cane.

When he was about two hundred yards away, Miller closed the door, carefully pulling the bolt across at the top of the door. He went to the kitchen and made himself a cup of tea before climbing the stairs to the small cottage's single attic bedroom. In the centre of the room, with one eye heavily swollen and blood encrusted over the silver tape that was being used to cover his mouth, Andrew Miller was bound to a chair by more silver tape. The white around his good eye was clearly visible, as was the involuntary quaking of his whole body.

Grendel put the cup of tea down on a bedside table after taking a small sip. "Ooh! Hot!" He silently mouthed at Miller, smiling. He then produced Miller's largest kitchen knife, which he had tucked under his arm in the kitchen, and walked over to the terrified Miller who leaned as far away from him as his silver tape bindings allowed.

'I'd forgotten you had told me to piss off,' said Grendel, leaning over to bring his face near to Miller's. His right hand leaned on his knee, the large knife protruding sideways like a blade on a chariot wheel.

Miller began a muffled scream.

24 September, 9:05am,
London, Metropolitan Police Headquarters

Lisa had been in for twenty minutes when Stanton arrived. After hanging his coat and jacket on the old-fashioned wooden coat stand, Stanton sat and turned his chair to face Lisa's direction. 'So, what have we got and what do we need to do?'

Lisa turned her chair a little to face him better, feeling a surge of pride at what she'd managed to find out for this case so far. 'Well, I found out who Grendel was. I was wrong about the whole classics thing. It's actually from an Old English poem called *Beowulf* about Danish warriors and monsters.'

Stanton raised his eyebrows. 'Uh-huh.'

'Yes, Grendel is a monster in the poem who is killed by the hero Beowulf.'

'So how does this help us if Grendel is a monster who is killed by the hero? Does he cut people's faces off?'

Lisa smiled. 'If only it were that simple. I'm really not sure about why our Grendel would have cut off his victim's face. It certainly doesn't seem to have a great deal to do with the Grendel from *Beowulf*. I think the link is that Grendel used to come at night while the warriors of the story slept, then he'd kill them. So in the morning when the warriors got up, they would find some of their fellow warriors had disappeared.' Stanton nodded as Lisa continued, 'So it would seem that our man is comparing himself to the Grendel from *Beowulf* in that he is killing warriors from the game in a similar way. And it's a clumsy connection, because he isn't killing them all while they sleep. From what Stella said, it sounds as if Niall was up and about in the game at the point he was killed.'

'That's true. It does make some sense though. So why is Grendel from the book killing the warriors? Is there any motivation for Grendel's attacks that might give us some clue as to why our Grendel has decided to kill these people?'

'Well Grendel in *Beowulf* seems generally to be an outcast, but apart from that the only thing that is maybe a clue to our Grendel comes from one of the lines where it is describing Grendel when he first appears in the story.' Stella fished her new copy *Beowulf* out of her bag. It had little torn off strips of paper marking certain pages where she had underlined lines she thought might give a clue as to the psychology of the murderer. 'It says, "after night came, Grendel went to survey the tall house" ... blah, blah ... yes, here it is, "then he found therein a band of nobles asleep after the feast: they felt no sorrow, no misery of men."'

'So has our Grendel been aggrieved by his victims in some way?'

'Well, the line suggests that the Grendel in *Beowulf* felt the warriors should have felt these things, you know, felt more empathy for other people. So, I suppose it might be that our Grendel is feeling that his victims should have felt more of the misery of men in some way, or maybe that they aren't aware of the misery they are causing. It's hard to say what it means. We'll need to see if Stella can shed any light on this. It might make more sense to her.'

'Good idea. So how does Grendel kill his victims in Beowulf? There's definitely nothing to give us a clue to the mutilation?'

'No.' She flicked forward a few pages. 'It says "he saw many men in the hall, a band of kinsmen all asleep together, a company of war-men ..."' She scanned down the page, '"he suddenly seized a sleeping man, tore him ravenously, bit into his bone-locks, drank his blood from his veins, swallowed huge morsels; quickly he had eaten all of the lifeless one, feet and hands."' Lisa looked up from the book,

'It doesn't say anything about cutting off faces, or bludgeoning in the backs of heads. Grendel sounds like he literally ripped the warriors to pieces and ate the bits.'

'Lovely,' said Stanton hoping they didn't find any evidence that any part of Niall had been eaten. He didn't know if his stomach would be able to cope with that.

'Anyway, that's all I found out.'

'It's a good start anyway. As you say, we'll need to get over and check with Stella and see if anything from it maybe rings a bell for her.'

'I could go across this afternoon. She should be at home, because I told her she'd be best to not go to work for a few days considering the state she was in.'

'We'll both go across,' Stanton said, figuring there was precious little to go on with this case even now they had found the body. 'We also need to check how Patrick's getting on with the addresses. We can do that before we go.'

'That's fine.'

'See what else you can find from the book just now. I need to check that our two members of the Janus group we know are alive have been checked on and that everything is okay. And I'll give the coroner a phone. The autopsy on Niall Davidson was being done yesterday, so the results should be available this morning.'

'No problem,' said Lisa, getting herself more coffee to drink while she ploughed through more of *Beowulf*.

Stanton's phone calls to the police stations local to the other two surviving Janus group members, Andrew Miller and David Rawling, took much less time than it had the day before, although it still took nearly forty minutes with all the waiting on hold and the time it took to get hold of the officers he had spoken to the previous evening. He was glad to hear that both Miller and Rawling's wellbeing had been physically verified by police officers and that everything was all right with both of them. He was concerned that Miller had decided to go away, figuring it would have been better for him to be somewhere they could easily check on him; but he also understood the logic of not being where a killer may be trying to find you. Stanton had suggested that the officer dealing with Miller, Sergeant Dickinson, should contact the local force on Skye, though, and explain what was going on and tell them to expect Miller. Rawling by contrast had opted to stay put, glad that an officer would check on him every evening until this was all over. He had told the officer who had checked on him that he had only been with the Janus group for a few months and that this was quite concerning overall. The officer said he was dealing with the situation well and that he had offered whatever help he could in the inquiries.

The call to the coroner followed. 'Can I speak to Albert Steadman please?'

'Speaking,' said the voice on the telephone.

'Hello, this is Detective Inspector Jack Stanton here from CID. I'm phoning about the Niall Davidson autopsy and cause of death.'

'Yes, hello, Detective Inspector Stanton, I remember: the weak-stomached one who was standing outside the flat when I arrived the other day.'

'Yup, that would be me. I never had much of a tolerance for bodies,' Stanton said, avoiding his real reasons for his squeamishness. 'And that scene was a bit more than I could stand.'

'It's horses for courses, I always say.'

'Anyway,' Stanton said, moving the conversation on, 'do you have the details?'

'Yes, I do.' Papers shuffled in the background. The scraping of Albert Steadman's tweed sports jacket across his telephone microphone as he struggled to hold the phone with his shoulder made Stanton hold his receiver slightly away from his ear. 'Ah, yes. Here it is. Are you still there?' said Steadman, as if Stanton might have got bored in the ten seconds and hung up.

'Yes, I am,' Stanton replied.

'I'll just read the roundup, and I'll send across the whole report first class tonight.'

'Great.'

Steadman began, the tone and tempo of his voice switching to a reading mode: '"Initial examination of the body of Niall Davidson, which was found face down in the bedroom of his flat, suggested severe non-descript trauma to the back of the head. Observations on turning the body over revealed a deep garrotte wound, which the police video evidence shows was the cause of death. This finding was corroborated by the autopsy, which concluded Mr Davidson's actual cause of death was suffocation caused by a garrotte pulled round the throat from behind. With the body turned over, it was also evident that the victim's face had been removed. The removal operation was initiated post-mortem, with the wounds suggesting the perpetrator undertaking the removal was unskilled in surgical procedures. The autopsy confirmed this assumption and also corrected an original misidentification concerning the trauma to the back of the head. What was originally thought to be a head wound was in fact made up of facial tissue that had been translocated to the back of the head. Follicles with beard hair were found congealed and dried into the hair on the back of the head reflecting this. The state of the face after the translocation of the facial tissue clearly revealed the surgical inexperience, since the face was no longer recognisable as such after its removal. The state of the tissue involved also goes some way to explaining the speed of decomposition and the high level of decomposition of the head area in general considering the short period since death. The sheer amount of flesh removed and the large surface area of the open wound involved appears to have given an ideal site for bacteria to gain access and get to work immediately."' Steadman's voice switched back to normal mode, 'So basically we've got a garrotting, followed by post-mortem mutilation of the body, specifically removal and relocation of the facial tissue.'

'Was there anything about bite marks, or eating the flesh or anything?' Stanton's mind was visualising the gruesome scene as he spoke. It was not enjoyable.

'No, there was no evidence of cannibalism from the autopsy. Should there have been?'

'We're not sure yet. It's just something else the investigation has turned up. If there's no sign of cannibalism though, that can only be for the good. This is grisly enough as it is.'

'Indeed it is. Anyway, I'll get the report in the post to you tonight. And if there's anything you would like to ask about, just give me a call.'

'I will do. Thanks very much for your time.'

'It's no problem at all. Good day, detective.'

Stanton hung up the phone and slumped back into his chair.

'Is everything all right?' Lisa asked from the other side of the room.

'Yes, well as good as it seems to get these days. Niall Davidson didn't have a wound to the back of his head at all. The wound was actually the remains of his face, which was cut off by our obviously surgically inexperienced Grendel and then placed on the back of Niall's head.'

'That would explain the patches of blood beside Niall's body. He must have cut the face off, put the bits on the floor by the head and then rolled Niall over to place the bits on the back of his head.'

Stanton's winced at the visceral image. 'That sounds about right. Why on earth would someone cut off his face and put the bits on the back of his head though?'

Lisa swallowed hard before she spoke. 'Oh my God. Janus. He's recreating the two faces of the Roman god Janus?' She paused then looked at Stanton. 'Grendel has tried to make Niall Davidson look like Janus.'

Stanton shivered visibly. 'Great. This is all we need. I hope he hasn't done this to those other two poor buggers.'

At this thought Lisa stared into a patch of infinity located somewhere on the floor. This new job was definitely enjoyable, but it was also interlaced with aspects that made her reel.

'Come on, Lisa. Let's go and see what Patrick's got and then get on our way to Stella's.'

Patrick blushed slightly as Stanton and Lisa walked through the door of his lab. This was the first time he had actually physically met Lisa. Before this he had only ever seen her from his window which overlooked the squad car bays. He had found out her name through a bit of unofficial hacking of the personnel files, although his general honesty and gentlemanly instincts had only allowed him to look at her name. Patrick was far from a criminal.

'Patrick, this is Detective Constable Lisa Collier.'

Patrick offered his hand to Lisa: 'Hello, Lisa, are you well?'

'I certainly am Patrick. Thank you.' Lisa smiled at Patrick's greeting.

Patrick's eyes lingered a little bit longer than they should on Lisa's, a small smile on his lips. He was a little confused to hear Stanton say, 'Patrick, hello.' Stanton was waving his hand to attract his attention. 'I said how are you getting on with the addresses?'

Patrick looked sheepish and Lisa smiled, also a little embarrassed, but glad of this lighter normality. 'Sorry Jack, don't know where my mind was there.' Patrick snapped back to his usual professionalism. 'I've managed to track down all but two of them, and unfortunately the two I can't find yet are the two others who are dead in this game you talked about. Everyone else uses an email service, and it was just a case of contacting their service providers to get their home details.'

'So we have addresses for Miller and Rawling who phoned in over the weekend, but no addresses for Tyler and Swift?'

'I'm afraid so, Jack. I'll have to keep tapping away at this, but the others are both using anonymous web-based email accounts and it'll take a while to track down their addresses from that. I'm sorry.'

'Don't worry, Patrick,' said Lisa. 'Just keep us informed of the developments.'

'I will do, Lisa.' Patrick's head bobbed up and down in a smiley nod.

'Yes, keep us informed,' Stanton said, feeling a little bit spare. 'And if you get names, fire them to us and we'll check vehicle registrations and whatever else we can think of to try and find these people.'

'I will do, just as soon as I get anything.'

'I can't believe these people are anonymous right down to their email addresses. It's beyond me. Faceless in every sense,' Stanton stated absently.

'That's the Internet for you, Jack. It's where people can be someone else if they want to be.'

'Yes, like Grendel, who wants to be a psychotically murderous mutilator,' Stanton said surprised by the anger he felt.

'It's not because of his anonymity in a computer game that Grendel is a psycho, that's just his outlet. Psychos are psychos whether they're into games, bikes or old-people's coffee mornings. They have to be predisposed to it. And let's face it, he doesn't want to be a murderer in a game, he's murdering in real life.'

'That's true.' Stanton rubbed his face with his hands. This case had torn open memories he had shut away decades before. 'Sorry, it's the state that Niall Davidson was in when we found him. This case is just giving me the creeps. Sorry.' Both Lisa and Patrick looked at him, accepting the reason for the outpouring. 'Anyway, Lisa, let's go.'

Patrick found himself waving as Lisa left. She smiled at the Irishman.

Pulling up outside Stella's flat they found no squad car. Lisa got out of the car and quickly looked up and down the street. There were no officers anywhere. She ran and rang the doorbell. Before Stella would even have had time to answer she was banging on the door and shouting through the letterbox. After about ten seconds an officer opened the door.

'What the hell's all this about?' he said.

'Where's the squad car?' Lisa demanded.

'We're changing shifts, so it's on its way back to the station. The two of us who were patrolling are in here looking after Miss Robertson while the guys swap. This isn't London with a car for each officer you know.'

'That's fine.' Lisa was suddenly very glad everything was all right and that Stella wasn't lying upstairs with her face cut off. 'Sorry, it's just we've seen the handiwork of the man who's threatened Stella.' Lisa went in, squeezing past the officer, followed by Stanton.

'Don't worry about it,' said the officer letting them through. 'We'd usually be out here guarding the flat during the shift change, but the tempting offer of some tea was too much I'm afraid.'

'No problem,' Stanton replied as he moved up the stairs.

Stella looked like a different person having had better sleep the last couple of nights in the knowledge that outside were four officers protecting her, although her eyes were puffy from recent crying.

'You're looking better,' Stanton said.

'Thanks. It's amazing how different you feel after some good sleep.'

'I know.' Lisa figured there was no point in delaying the inevitable: 'Did you hear about Niall?'

Stella sighed, 'Yes, I was told they found his body in his flat.' More tears welled up.

Lisa decided not to go into his injuries at this point unless she had to. 'Yes, that's right. I'm sorry.'

'Thanks,' Stella's voice cracked. 'It's pretty bad. I don't know quite how to feel. I mean I never really knew him that well. I had never met him after all.'

'But you don't need to meet someone to consider them a friend.'

'I know.' Stella sniffed. Stanton passed her his handkerchief.

Stella sniffed and smiled weakly: 'I'm going to have all your hankies.'

'Don't you worry about that, Stella.' Stanton's face gave a reassuring smile. Stella liked this man.

The two officers had finished their tea. 'We'll be heading back outside,' said the officer who had opened the door. 'Thanks for the tea ma'am.'

'No problem,' Stella said collecting the cups and dumping them in the sink. 'Would you two like a cup of anything?' She asked Stanton and Collier. They both declined and the three of them moved through to the sitting room.

'So, Stella, we're having a bit of difficulty tracing Tyler and Swift. Do you have any other details that might be able to help us?' Lisa asked.

'No, I didn't ever learn their real names. Both of them used their game names as email names, and in the game you just call people what they say they are called. It was never relevant because it was only a game.' Stella pulled her legs up under herself as she spoke, fiddling with her hair in what Lisa now recognised as Stella's "scared" posture.

'So they never used any other email addresses or anything at any stage?'

'No, not to my knowledge. I never really had any emails from either of them. Tyler was only in the group for about six weeks before he didn't wake up whenever that was. And Swift was one of those irritating sorts, so I never made any real effort to befriend him. We just cooperated in the game and spoke when we had to. I was only really friendly with Niall and David Rawling, Frank in the game. The others I didn't really know.'

'Okay, Stella. It's all right.' Lisa could see Stella was getting more upset as she mentioned Niall.

As if on cue, Thomas rolled in from the other room, slinked past the two detectives and jumped up onto Stella's lap, where he purred and rolled over to be rubbed. Stella's shoulder's slightly, yet visibly, relaxed as she looked at the bundle of fur on her lap.

Stella continued: 'It was only a game. I don't understand why suddenly I'm sitting here talking to police detectives, with policemen watching my house in case someone comes and kills me. It was only a game.' Stella was fighting hard not to cry, but some tears wouldn't be swallowed back and she ran an index finger under each eye to recapture them. Thomas peddled at her sweatshirt.

'I know it was,' said Lisa gently. 'But we need to try and find out as much as we can, Stella, so we can find out who is after you. And right now the only clues we have about his identity are from the game.'

'I know.' Stella tried to swallow the lump in her throat.

'Does the name Grendel mean anything to you?'

'Apart from being the name of the guy who threatened me, no.'

'So you hadn't encountered the name at all before, either in the game or otherwise?' Stanton interrupted.

'No, I don't think so. If he was in the game before, I never met him.'

Lisa continued, 'Do you know if anyone in the game thought your Janus group was doing things to the detriment of other people in the game?'

'I know from the news that we weren't always popular. But it was a game, no one was really being hurt.'

'Can you think of anyone you may have hurt in the game who might have taken it personally and would be looking for revenge?'

'Oh, I don't know. We did lots of paid hits on lots of people.'

'Sorry?' Stanton interrupted again. 'Paid hits?'

'Yes, people use the game to sell through virtual shops, so there were times when people paid us to assassinate players who were affecting their business.'

'You mean paid in real money?' Stanton couldn't believe this.

'Yes, because it was going to be cheaper for them to pay us to dispose of their problem than it would be to let people destroy their shops.'

'But didn't the people just come back again as other people and do it again? You know, just log in again as some new character and get back at them.'

'Yes, although if you get killed, you can't get back online for a fortnight, although I suppose you could buy another copy of the game and get back on that way, but that would be pretty expensive.'

'Sort of like when you had to count to ten if you got shot when you play soldiers as a kid?' Stanton offered.

'Something like that.'

'So can you think of anyone who you might have assassinated that would maybe want to come after you?'

'No, I can't. It could have been anyone we killed.' Stella paused. 'But also, how could anyone know who we were to be killing us? In the City it was Mr Janus who was apparently masterminding everything. And no one who plays the game knows Janus isn't real, even now. So how could someone have found out who we are in the real world to hunt us down? It doesn't make sense.'

'Good point,' agreed Jack. 'Could someone in the Janus group have let it slip to anyone?'

'I don't think so. We all agreed the only way it could work was if we all kept it as an absolute secret in and out of the game. You guys are the first people I ever spoke to this about.'

'What about Tyler and Frank? Didn't they join later than everyone else?' Stanton asked.

'We didn't let on to them that Janus wasn't real until we knew we could trust them. The system was working fine and we had control of the whole City.'

'Hmm. It doesn't make a lot of sense really, does it?' Stanton mused. 'What about the people who made the game? Surely they would know who everyone was and would have details of all of you and what was going on.'

'I suppose that's possible. But they're surely not allowed to divulge any information under the Data Protection Act.'

'Considering what's going on, I think we'll be able to get the authorisation we need for that, but I think that's something we'll definitely need to check out. Do you have details of the company who make and run this *Alter Ego* game?'

Stella got up and crossed to her bookshelves. She withdrew a DVD-style case. The cover was emblazoned with the title *Alter Ego* along with a photograph of the City. At the bottom of the front of the box it read simply: "Be whoever you want to be." Stanton flipped the box over. It had an 18-certificate logo at the bottom. 'What are all these photographs of on the back? Why have they used actors for shots of the game?'

'They're not photographs and actors, they're screenshots. The game is played in a world that is almost indistinguishable from video.'

'You're kidding?' Stanton wondered when Asteroids had become so obsolete.

'The company's web address is at the bottom. You'll be able to get their telephone numbers from the net.'

Stanton took out his pad and began to write down the details. After he had done this he figured they had to ask the one question both of them had been dreading. 'I'm sorry to ask this, Stella, but did you or any of the other Janus people ever mutilate any bodies in the game?'

Stella's face went pure white at the realisation that something bad had been done to Niall. 'No!' she blurted out. 'Never. What happened to Niall? Did someone do something to him?' Stella jumped to her feet—dumping Thomas unceremoniously onto the floor—and paced, looking at Stanton as her breath began to wheeze. 'What happened to him?' Stella pleaded, grabbing her inhaler from the mantle piece.

'It's all right Stella,' Lisa said. 'We're just checking all the possibilities. Unfortunately Niall was cut during the attack.' Lisa knew this was a gross understatement. But as she watched Stella push the plunger on her inhaler and gasp in the spray, she figured it was the right thing to do. 'We're just wondering if there were ever any mutilations in the game which would give us any clues.'

'No, never!' Stella repeated in a burst of gasps. 'Oh my God! He's going to come and cut me up.' Stella was frantically wheezing as she walked back and forth, Lisa's arm round her shoulders doing little to assuage her fears.

It was an hour later when they finally calmed Stella down enough to leave. Lisa suggested that Stella should come with them to see the game company who had developed *Alter Ego* the next day. More worried than ever for her safety, and now with the added imagination-fuelled fear of being killed with a knife, Stella was only too keen to come along.

25 September, 8:59am,
London, Metropolitan Police Headquarters

The following morning Jack Stanton checked his telephone messages at the office. Richardson from Forensics had left a message saying there was no forensic evidence of the intruder at all at the Davidson scene. All prints, hair samples and blood belonged to the victim.

Stanton felt sorry for Niall. He had obviously been so reclusive that he hadn't even had *anyone* round to leave a trace of his or her existence. Stella was testament to that: she had been one of Niall's closest friends and yet she had never physically met him. Forensics hadn't even been able to find a fibre from Grendel's clothing, and Niall's carpet was unfortunately not the type that would capture a convenient footprint or the tread from a shoe. Basically the scene was devoid of any useful forensic material, which told Stanton one thing: Grendel had been extremely careful to make sure he didn't leave any clues. Stanton recalled the figure leaving the flat on the video. He had been almost as enclosed when he left the flat as Stanton had been when he himself entered dressed in his paper overalls the following Saturday, only Grendel had been dressed in black. Stanton thought it was appropriate: good guys in white, bad guys in black. If only this was a game, he thought.

There were no other messages of note, so Stanton dropped into Patrick's lab.

'Any joy?'

Patrick looked up from the report he was writing and over Stanton's shoulder to see if Lisa was with him. He looked disappointed when he realised she wasn't. 'We're getting there.'

Stanton nodded, 'But still no addresses?'

'No, I'm afraid not. I've got people from the net-based email accounts trawling through old server data to try to find out when the accounts were last used and then they'll need to try to track the route of the connection through the other servers, back to the source. We'll get the addresses, Stanton, assuming they're logging in from a single location. It's just a matter of time.'

'Good stuff, Patrick.' Stanton pulled his notebook from his pocket. 'Could you do me a favour?'

'Sure, what's that?'

'Could you get me the address of this company?' He handed him the web address.

'No probs.' Patrick moved over to his desk in the corner and quickly surfed to the relevant webpage then printed off the screen. 'You know, you really should try to embrace technology more.'

'Yes, I know, but then there'd be no reason to come and see you.'

'Now that wouldn't be so good.' Patrick smiled. 'Where's your other half today?'

'I'm picking her up on the way here.' Stanton shook the sheet of paper. 'Actually where is here?' Stanton looked at the address and breathed a sigh of relief when he found the game developer was only a couple of hours drive away in Warwickshire. 'Yes, there didn't seem much point in us both coming in to the station, so right now she'll be on the tube out to where I'm picking her up.' Stanton looked at his watch. 'Actually, I better get my skates on. Thanks for this,' he said waving the printed page in the air as he walked out of the lab.

'No problem,' said Patrick.

Lisa had been at Stella's flat for a little over an hour when Stanton arrived. Stella was more nervous than she had been when they arrived the day before. A shiver ran down Lisa's spine as she imagined how she would feel if someone was after her to kill and mutilate her with a knife. No wonder Stella was nervous.

They relieved the local uniformed officers and were soon on the road, Stella having restocked Thomas's food bowl, which she'd placed on the rooftop. Theydon Bois was only minutes from London's huge orbital, the M25, and they were soon speeding along the infamous motorway which was miraculously clear all the way to the junction that took them on a large diagonal journey that eventually would join the M6 in a more as-the-crow-flies route to their destination. As the car engine hummed along the busy pipeline to the North, Stanton glanced in his rear-view mirror: Stella's head was lolling around as she slept in the back seat. Stanton was glad he could offer this unfortunate woman some comfort and sleep. He just hoped they would be able to find Grendel before Grendel got to her.

'You know what bothers me most about this case?' he said to Lisa, glancing into the mirror again to see if his words had wakened Stella. She was still sound.

'That it's likely that we have more bodies that we haven't found yet?' Lisa's voice betrayed her own near-sleep experience.

'Well, there is that. But no, I was thinking more about Grendel. We don't have the first clue who he is. I mean, if these guys at this software place can't help us find him, we're going to have to just wait until he tries to attack Stella and catch him there.' His voice lowered. 'Or try to. And I think we're both agreed that isn't the best solution.'

Lisa nodded.

'I mean we have absolutely nothing at this point on our guy: no forensics—'

'The Forensics people found nothing at all at the scene?' Lisa's voice was amazed.

'Absolutely nothing. So we have no forensic evidence, even if we knew who we would try to link to the scene with it,' he added. 'But that's exactly the point, we don't even remotely know who we're looking for. We have no suspect at all. We're protecting someone against what might as well be a bogey-man.' Stanton's frustration was showing, but he kept his voice low so as not to wake Stella.

'I know what you mean.' Lisa thought about the state of Niall's body when they found it. 'We'll just need to hope these people have some means of telling us who Grendel is so we can find him.'

'Let's hope so.'

25 September, 11:41am, Southam, Warwickshire

Stella awoke to the sound of Stanton's door closing. They were in a garage in Southam, a quaint small town in Warwickshire. Stanton was on his way to ask the attendant at a petrol station where they could find Pendicke Street.

'Hi,' Stella said to Lisa through a stretch.

'Aah, back with us in the land of the living.' Lisa winced at the statement considering Stella's life was in danger.

'Uh-huh,' Stella yawned. 'Are we almost there?'

'Well, we're in the right town. Now we've just got to find the right street. Stanton's just checking.'

'I'm actually quite excited about meeting these people. I mean this is my favourite game and I get to meet the people who made it.'

Lisa was glad Stella was finding the bright side of this, although she couldn't really understand why someone like Stella played games in the first place. 'Yes, it should be interesting,' Lisa replied—and hopefully they'll be able to tell us who's trying to kill you, she thought.

Stanton got back into the car. He was already driving when he reached back to pull his seatbelt forward to fasten it. 'It's about half a mile away.' They drove down into the small main street before turning back along Pendicke Street. Stanton drove slowly. 'There it is.' He pulled the car up outside the offices of Binary Cityworks.

'Good morning, I'm Detective Inspector Jack Stanton. We're conducting an investigation and I'm wondering who the best person is to talk to about the *Alter Ego* game.'

The receptionist looked a bit shocked that she was talking to the police. 'I think you'll probably want to speak to Sam Stark. He's the founder of the company and the main developer of *Alter Ego*. Hold on one moment and I'll just check if he can see you.' She dialled into the small switchboard console in front of her. 'It's ringing,' she said. 'You're lucky he's in the office today; he's back and forth to New York all the time these days setting up the new US office. He's a workaholic.' She motioned to the telephone and rolled her eyes to suggest that Mr Stark always took ages to pick up his phone. 'Yes, our Sam works like a sla—Hello, Sam ... I've got three detectives here would like to speak to you about *Alter Ego* ... He says he'll be right through. If you would just take a seat over there.' She pointed to two facing leather sofas over in the corner. The walls around the sofas were covered with awards for *Alter Ego*. In the corner, a television was displaying a news report of a violent clash between police and a rampaging gunman.

'Could you turn this up, please?' Stanton asked the receptionist, concerned that they hadn't heard about this on the news on the way up here.

The receptionist pressed a button on her remote. And the reporter's voice began to increase in volume. '... latest violence marks yet another blow for the people of the City.'

Stanton didn't recognise the part of London the reporter was in.

'It has now been over two weeks since Mr Janus has loosened his grip on the City. And with every punk vying for control, we can only hope that Mr. Janus appears soon to bring the situation back under control.' The reporter looked directly into the lens and said, 'Come back Janus. All is forgiven.'

'No way.' Stanton's mouth was open. 'Not a chance. Is that *Alter Ego*?' He turned towards Stella.

'It certainly is,' said Sam Stark smiling as he walked across the reception area.

'But it looks like a real city, real people.'

'Yes it does,' said Sam smiling. 'Hi, I'm Sam Stark, CEO of Binary Cityworks. And you are?' Sam was about five foot nine with short mousy-coloured hair that was carefully styled to look unkempt. He wore faded jeans with holes in the knee, a pair of beat-up training shoes and a blue T-shirt under a puffy rust-coloured body warmer. He didn't look at all like the richest games developer in the world.

'Jack Stanton, CID.' Stanton showed his ID as he looked back at the screen.

'Hi, I'm Lisa Collier and this is Stella Robertson.' Lisa also showed her ID.

Sam moved over beside Stanton who was still looking at the monitor mounted in the wall. 'It's something isn't it?' said Sam, obviously proud of his creation. 'Over two million subscribers and counting.'

'I honestly can't believe what I'm seeing. I didn't know they could make computer games that looked this real.'

'We're actually the only people that can do it so far. But it'll not be too long until our competitors catch up. Software's a fast-moving cutthroat business.' Sam turned away from the monitor to take in all three visitors. 'So, would you like to come through to my office? We can talk there.' He extended his arm to show the way. 'Liz, could you send us in some coffee and maybe some buns from the bakery?'

'No problem, Sam.'

Sam punched a security code into a set of double doors in reception and they entered a small corridor that emerged in a large room filled with people peering at lines of text on grey screens. The software engineers were all working in near silence. Only the sound of three people talking and laughing broke the quiet hum of the dozens of computer systems.

At the other side of the room were two glass-enclosed offices. Sam Stark's office door was open and they all filed in. Sam grabbed a spare computer chair as he passed, rolling it into the office. 'Take a seat,' he motioned. Stanton allowed Lisa and Stella to sit on the comfortable looking seats in front of Sam's huge and messy desk while he took the large leather computer chair.

'So what can I do for you, Jack?' Stark wasn't big on formality.

'Well, Sam,' Stanton felt like a villain from a Bond movie as he talked from the leather chair, 'we've got a bit of a problem and it unfortunately involves *Alter Ego*.' He paused briefly as Sam nodded, his expression extremely serious. 'We're investigating a murder at the moment, a murder involving someone who was a player of *Alter Ego*. We have reason to believe that the murder is related to the game.'

'How so?' Sam asked.

'Well, we think that the perpetrator of the murder has used the game to select his victims.' Thinking of Stella, Stanton added, 'or her victims.'

'Victims?' Sam's voice was concerned.

'So far we think there might be three, although we haven't been able to locate two of them yet.'

'Wow.' A wide-eyed Stark sits back in his chair.

'We're not entirely sure what motive our killer would have for doing this, but we believe he may be systematically killing a group of individuals who play the game - in real life.'

'That's bad.' Sam's face was stony at the gravity of what was being said. 'Do you know who else is being threatened?'

'We do. All the victims belong to the group who work for the fictitious gangster overlord, Mr Janus.'

'Uh-huh.' Sam nodded. 'That would explain a lot of what's been going on in the City.' He paused briefly. 'So

Janus himself isn't real. We were wondering why he never appeared in the news.'

'So you know of the Janus group?'

'Of course we do.' Sam looked suddenly brighter. 'Employees of Mr Janus are never off the City News. They're one of the reasons the game is so successful.'

Stella smiled at the praise this game creator was indirectly showering on her. 'I'm one of the Janus group,' she said.

'No way!' It was Sam's turn to be amazed. 'Which one? Who do you play?'

'I'm Vincent,' Stella said.

Stanton swivelled his chair round to see Stella better. 'Vincent? Do you mean you play a guy?'

'Only one of the baddest dudes in the City,' Sam said excitedly standing up, his enthusiasm for this *Alter Ego* character spilling out. 'Man, I never thought you were a woman.' Sam opened his door to the room of software engineers. 'Hey guys, guess who I've got in here?' He pointed at Stella, clearly visible through the glass.

The engineers shrugged, said they didn't know, or just waited for Sam's revelation.

'It's Vincent.' Sam beamed. 'Janus's Vincent.'

Heads began to nod around the room, accompanied by replies like: "excellent", "outstanding", "righteous" and "far out". It sounded like a hippy commune.

Stella blushed at the attention.

Sam went next door to the Chief Technical Officer Andy McCormack's office. 'Hey, Andy, come through to my office.'

Andy, a bearded American hippy-sort, slowly rose from his work and bobbed through to Sam's office. He wore black jeans, Doc Martin's boots and a psychedelic T-shirt. 'What's up, dude?'

'Guess who this is?' Sam pointed to Stella excitedly.

'I don't know, man.' Sam's face was making Andy eager with anticipation. His rising excitement was displayed in slow motion.

'It's Vincent, the scourge of bad guys across the City,' Sam said elatedly his head nodding.

'Far out, man. You are, like, a hero, you know, dude?'

'Thanks.' Stella was amazed that people like this man ever managed to produce anything, never mind something like *Alter Ego*.

'You might as well stay actually, Andy,' Sam said, his voice becoming more serious again. 'Close the door over.'

'I'm Andy.' Andy introduction was accompanied by his open hand patting his chest to reinforce which one of them was Andy. He closed the door and sat down on top of a small filing cabinet. 'What's this about then, man?'

'Andy's our Chief Technical Officer,' Sam explained.

'Nice to meet you,' Lisa said. She smiled at Andy, wondering whether either of these guys would be of any use at all in finding out who Grendel was and where he was in the real world. They were doubtless passionate about their game, but that wouldn't necessarily help.

'These guys say there's been a murder, maybe even three, and that someone's hunting down the Janus group from *Alter Ego*.' Sam gave a small reassuring smile to Stella.

'Heavy,' Andy mumbled.

'Yes, anyway,' Lisa decided to try to get the ball rolling a bit faster. 'We need to know if there is any way that you can give us details on a specific character because we believe our perpetrator is also an *Alter Ego* player.'

'In theory we can,' Sam said, his facial expression pre-empting the bad news that would follow, 'but I don't know how when we have almost two million people who play regularly in the City. The good news is everyone who plays has a unique ID number. All of them had to register their details to activate the game and let them into the City, and that's when they got their number. But we'd need to give you every single player's details.'

'It's like an anti-piracy thing, man,' Andy mumbled helpfully.

'Sorry?' Stanton said to Andy.

'They register to stop the pirates, man.'

'Yes, er, thanks.' Stanton didn't know what to think of Andy. 'So is there any way we can be more specific than that or are we going to have to go through all sets of information?'

'I don't know. I don't see how else, really,' Sam replied. I mean if we knew the character was online at any given point we could dump all the active player's IDs to a file then compile a smaller list of details based on that, but that would still give you about 5,000 addresses to check out. It's slightly better odds though.' Sam made a gesture with his hands that said what do you think?

Andy was staring into space.

'It's still a lot to trawl through to try to find our man. Even considering our assumption that he comes from down in the South East. And that is purely an assumption at this point.'

'Hey, bud,' Andy began slowly, 'remember that game we did before *Alter Ego*, you know, the one we first generated the game engine for?'

'Yes, Andy. What about it?' The other three were amazed at Sam's total attention switch to what Andy was saying. Especially when it seemed so unrelated.

'Remember, like, the "digital soul" thing? You know where you grabbed the ID number from the people you killed and then cashed them in at the end of your session so we could keep score. Remember that, man?'

Sam snapped his fingers and pointed to Andy, 'I do.'

'Did we ever, like, take that code out?'

'What the hell are you talking about another game for?' Lisa asked, obviously irritated by the irrelevance. 'Don't you realise we're talking about finding a killer?'

'Hey, man, don't hit me with that negativity. I'm only trying to, like, resolve the situation.'

'Do you know what he's talking about, Sam?' Stanton said more calmly.

'I think I do. You see, when we first wrote the software engine,' Sam looked at Stanton and Lisa's blank expressions. He clarified: 'the mechanism for creating the environment for a game within a computer.' He raised his eyebrows asking if they got it now. Both nodded. 'Anyway, we first created the engine for an online deathmatch game where you fought to the death, obviously, with other players and when you killed them you pulled out their "digital soul."'

'Sounds lovely,' said Lisa.

'It was more symbolic than anything. What it did was allowed us to keep score of who were the best players, you know, in a kind of scoreboard. At the end of each session, the players would cash in all their collected digital souls, which were basically nothing more than the unique player-specific ID numbers of the people they had killed. Then we'd tally it all up and they could see who had killed the most people and who they had killed. We were using this statistical data to create emotional responses from characters. So if you met someone who you had been killed by lots of times previously, your vision would get blurry to reflect your character's fear, or your weapon would shake. Things like that.'

'I don't get what this has to do with our problem. We're talking about a player of *Alter Ego*, not a player of some deathmatch soul hunt,' Stanton said voicing his confusion.

'Well, basically the *Alter Ego* engine is an evolution of the basic deathmatch engine I just described. We just refined it. What Andy is wondering is whether the ID code is still resident in the game's software.' He looked at Andy to confirm this. Andy nodded, a wide grin stretching over his face.

'But even if it is, what use is it to know how many people someone has killed?' Stanton said. His eyes suddenly brightened, 'Or are you thinking that we could see who has the digital IDs for our dead people and then we would know who our murderer was?'

Stella spoke for only the second time, 'But the people are only sleeping in the game. They weren't killed by Grendel in the game.'

'Grendel? I take it he is our bad guy,' Sam observed.

'He is,' Stanton confirmed.

'It's a good idea, Jack,' Sam said. 'But Stella is right, we don't have bodies in the game, we have bodies in the world—potentially. Also no characters in *Alter Ego* have a means of removing the IDs from other players, so we wouldn't have a character walking around with our victims IDs anyway, even if they had been killed in the game. What Andy is thinking is that if the harvesting code is still resident in the game, we could introduce a means of extracting the ID from a player.' Sam smiled at this possible solution.

Stanton was still confused: 'Help me out here, guys.'

Sam leaned forward, his elbows on his desk, his hands clasped in front of him: 'Getting the unique ID for a character would allow us to reference the player's details, you know, the details he had to give us to activate the game. So, basically, if we can catch our bad guy within *Alter Ego* and extract his ID, we'll have the details you need about your murderer. His address and what not.' Andy's eyes opened wide as he smiled and nodded, both his hands gave a thumbs-up sign.

'That sounds like a good start anyway,' Lisa said, looking at Stella, who smiled at the thought of her tormentor being caught. 'So how do you find out if the software is still there?'

Sam jumped, 'I almost forgot about that. Too busy feeling smug about our solution.' He winked at Andy. They had been partners for over ten years and had always made the most ground when they were working together. Sam stood up quickly and opened his door then bellowed out into the main office: 'John, did we ever rip the soul harvesting code from the latest version of *Alter Ego*?'

A thin geeky-looking software engineer at the other end of the room clicked his mouse a few times and scanned down his screen. 'No, Sam, we just left it dormant. Too much hassle to take it out.' His head suddenly dropped, 'Do we need to take it out?'

'Hell no! But we do need a soul harvester for *Alter Ego*. How soon can you write us one?'

'I can probably port one in. I don't know, half a day?'

'Good enough, John.' Sam closed his door again and sat down smiling. 'We are go for launch. We'll hunt Grendel down inside *Alter Ego*.'

**25 September, 1:31pm,
Southam, Warwickshire**

The five of them sat in contemplative silence after the initial euphoria. It would be their first concrete breakthrough if they could actually catch Grendel within the game. But despite the basic simplicity of the task, everyone in the room realised that saying it and doing it were two very different things.

'Okay, what if the address he has given you is bogus?' Lisa threw the question to the rest of them.

'Well, we're not going to know that until we've got the ID and checked the address anyway,' Sam responded.

'Yes, so we'll just need to cross that particular bridge when we get to it,' said Stanton.

'Also, how are we *actually* going to do this?' Lisa said, voicing everyone's concern. 'I mean, Grendel isn't going to just take this lying down; he won't just stand there while we take out his ID. And considering so far he's managed to only let people see him when he chooses, we need to assume he's going to be one tough cookie to catch.'

'Okay,' Sam's voice took on a steely organizational quality. 'What do we know about Grendel?' Do we know where he goes? Is he findable at all within the game? Is he bumping off people he's selected without really playing the game at all himself?'

'No,' said Stella clearing her throat. 'He's only talked to me and one other of the Janus people. I don't know why.'

'So he's talked to you.' Sam focused. 'How many times?'

'Twice, although the first time he just said I would be number four; we didn't really converse. And he seems to know the game or he wouldn't have been able to find me to talk to.'

'So we're saying Vincent is the only person he will talk to right now.'

'It would seem so,' said Stanton.

'Yes, but even considering that, how do we get him to talk to Vincent? Especially when Grendel himself is the one who's called the shots so far,' Lisa noted.

'We'll need to use Vincent as some kind of bait to draw Grendel out,' Sam stated.

'Agreed,' said Stanton.

'We also have to catch him first time. Because if he has any sense, he'll stop using the ID number after the first attempt to get him. I know I would.'

They all considered the gravity of this.

'But, he doesn't know about the ID number. Only we know, man. It's not a real part of the game for him,' Andy said.

'That's true, the ID number isn't something the players need or even get a copy of, so there's no reason to assume he'd stop appearing if we didn't get him,' Sam said, a little happier.

'Maybe,' said Lisa. 'But there's also the possibility he'll stop playing the game altogether if he figures we're up to something. So we have to assume that we'll only have one crack at this.' Lisa looked at each of the others in turn. 'Stella has been told she'll be number four; and we have three people in the game who no longer wake up; and one *Alter Ego* player on a slab in the morgue.' She paused to let this sink in. She noticed Stella's eyes filling with tears. 'We can't assume anything except that Grendel will make every effort to get Stella if we can't catch him. We need to remember that this *is not* a game. We have to get this guy, and we have to get him soon.'

Stella looked deflated. In the excitement and discussion, she had almost forgotten that her life was in danger, but now her worries returned. 'I think I need to do something to draw him out, as Sam said. But that means someone else will need to go in and get him. I can probably get the other two Janus guys: Frank and Wilson.'

'One of them has gone away until this is resolved,' Stanton said. 'So we have to assume we only have one other Janus body available.'

'Away? Who's away?' Stella asked Stanton, not sure why she hadn't been told.

'The guy from Scotland. Miller? He said he was going to go away somewhere for a while where Grendel wouldn't know where he was. He figured it would be safer.'

'It would have been nice of him to tell the rest of us. As long as he's safe,' Stella said sarcastically, looking sulky.

'You didn't know?'

'No, this is the first I've heard. It's nice to know who your friends are.' Stella slumped further into her seat.

'Anyway,' said Sam, 'we can't really assume anyone who's actually being threatened by Grendel will be able to do the right thing at the right point when so much is at stake. What we need are objective professionals.'

'Yes, I agree,' said Lisa. 'But we're talking about a computer game here. Are our people going to be able to play the game and catch Grendel when he'll doubtless be more skilled at the game than they will be?'

'I don't think we should use your guys. They'd just be massacred in a game world. We need to use *our* guys,' Sam said swivelling his chair to view the computer screen that was perched at the end of his long desk. 'We need to get some professional game hunters. And I mean people who hunt in computer games.' Sam scanned his finger down the screen. 'We need to get a hold of these guys.' He swivelled back to face the group. 'We need the Action Heroes.' He smiled knowingly.

'Dude!' Andy nodded enthusiastically at Sam's suggestion—as enthusiastic as Andy ever got anyway.

'Who the hell are the Action Heroes?' said Lisa, feeling this whole situation was again not being taken seriously enough.

'They're the top team-deathmatch clan. Ever,' said Stella.

'That's right,' Sam confirmed. 'These guys have fought their way from nowhere to the top spot over the last three years in the Soul Harvester League. They are undefeated, and I mean completely. And since they already know about soul harvesting, they're ideally qualified to do this sort of work.' Sam had the same look on his face that he had when he had said they would hunt Grendel.

'Great,' said Lisa, more than a little sceptical.

In the car on the way back to Theydon Bois, little had changed to dispel Lisa's uncertainty. The Action Heroes were four guys from a database development company near Royal Victoria Dock in London. The plan was to go and see them the next day. The whole scenario seemed to Lisa not to be much like real police work.

'Are you worried about this, Jack?' she asked.

'Well, it is pretty unusual, but considering the lack of leads I don't see any alternatives.'

'I know what you mean,' Lisa conceded.

'The way I see it is that we only have possible contact with our perpetrator *in this game*, and no other leads on him at all. So it makes sense for us to pursue the only lead we have.'

'I agree,' said Stella from the back. 'We have to do something or I'll be the next one not waking up.'

Lisa felt bad for voicing her concerns in front of Stella when this was her only thread of hope. 'I know, Stella. I'm sorry. I want to see Grendel locked up as much as you do.'

'Somehow I doubt that,' Stella said as she watched the floodlit motorway whiz by.

'We'll go and see these Action Hero guys tomorrow,' said Stanton. 'That'll give us a clue how crazy this is as a plan. Let's face it, if we can catch Grendel and find out where he lives, we'll be streets ahead of where we are now.'

'I know.'

'We'll just need to wait and see.'

'As long as we can lure him out into the open,' Lisa sighed.

They drove on in silence to Stella's flat. Lisa had called ahead and the squad car was sitting outside when they arrived.

'Listen, thanks guys,' said Stella, genuinely appreciative. 'It was good to get out of my flat for a while at least. And I'm sure if we can catch Grendel in the game that you guys will find him out here.' She wasn't as sure as she sounded. But then what was the alternative? 'Goodnight. I'll talk to you tomorrow.'

Stanton and Lisa said goodnight and drove off. It was difficult for both of them. Stella was safe for now, but they knew that someone could probably still get to her if they had the will to.

The mad plan had to work.

**25 September, 8:00pm,
Theydon Bois**

Stella fed Thomas, prepared and ate a meal herself and then decided she would go online. It had been five days since she had left Vincent sleeping in the Janus building.

Vincent opens his eyes. His movements are sluggish from the prolonged inactivity. He sits up, and swings his legs to the floor. In the reclining chair in front of him he can see that Tyler has more or less withered into himself. The flaky grey-brown remains of his body have collapsed along his whole length. The sides of his rib cage and skull now act like small enclosing walls protecting the dust and flakes that are all that remain of the rest of his torso. His limbs have withered away entirely, the near-empty clothing now lying almost flat where Tyler had originally lain down.

Vincent examines the other sleepers. Boyd's body has also declined significantly. Most of his hair has fallen out and his papery skin has begun to split over the skull. His teeth are bared involuntarily and his sunken eyes are slightly open, the irises showing dull and milky.

'Oh, Niall,' Vincent says, sadly.

Swift looks better by comparison, but is sickly and fragile-looking compared to usual. Vincent looks across at his own chair realising he too has left hair behind. He winces at the realisation that he must be in a similar state to Swift. The sleeping form of Wilson contrasts with all the others in that he merely looks more artificial than usual, but that was all.

The blinds in the main room are closed, the lights off. Vincent flicks the switch as he walks in. The fire looks like it has not been lit in days. He presses a button to open the blinds, revealing twinkling lights across the City and a clear deep-blue sky filled with stars. Somewhere out there was Grendel, and they had to find some way to find him.

'Hey there Vincent, how are things?' Frank says from the door.

Vincent turns, glad to hear the familiar voice. 'Not too bad, Frank. And you?'

'All right, all things considered. I've been coming here every night to see if anyone is up and about. You know, to see if any of this has been a mistake.'

'It is a bit like a bad dream isn't it?'

'It really is. Even Wilson has stopped coming here. I've no idea why.'

'The police say he's decided to go away for a while where Grendel won't be able to find him. Did he say anything to you about doing that?'

'No, and I saw him the other night. I take it he didn't mention it to you either.'

'No, he didn't. I think it's weird, but the police went and spoke to him at his house. I guess he's just scared.'

'I suppose so.' Frank walks over so he is also looking out of the window. 'I've been emailing everyone every day, you know.'

'Has anyone written back?

'No, no one. I guess I'm just still hoping.'

There is a silence for a few seconds before Vincent speaks: 'The police found Niall's body, you know, Boyd. They said someone had cut him up pretty badly.'

'Shit. That's twisted. Have they found any of the others: Tyler, Swift?'

'No, not yet, they're having trouble tracing their addresses apparently. It seems it's difficult to find people who use Internet-based email services. It's understandable, I suppose.'

'Have they any idea who's doing this?'

'No, although they're going to try to catch Grendel using me, and probably you, as bait.'

'Hold on, that's my door bell.' Frank crosses over to the sofa and sits down. He leans all the way back and slumps as he passes out.

Vincent switches on the television, hoping to catch a news report about what has been going on these last few days. Stella knew the Janus group weren't controlling the City any more and wondered if anyone else was. *The City news is reporting on the gun battle they had seen the fragment of at Binary Cityworks.* From what she could gather this was what had been going on for the last week or so: lone gunmen running amok through the streets, taking out who they could before the police finally got them under control. People who joined the police in *Alter Ego* were usually not the best people to actually police anything; they just liked to play at being policemen. The result was lots of police and innocents being massacred every time someone went on the rampage. *This news item shows this to great effect, with inept police falling like flies as the gunman advance along Bushnell Road.* People hadn't liked the Janus organisation, but at least it kept the City relatively safe.

The newscaster rounds up the report and a chat show style program comes on. The question under discussion is whether the City is better or worse since the Janus organisation has all but disappeared. Vincent recognises the bearded man as one of the people from the Plaza he had freed from Kane's oppression what seemed like a lifetime ago.

'... I don't care what you say, at least Janus made sure people could trade here if they wanted to. The way it is now, it's just anarchy.'

A woman responds: 'Yes, that's true. But don't you think the violent way in which they controlled the City made it brutal and militaristic?'

'Have you walked the streets recently?' the man almost shouts his question. 'You're likely to get your head blown off in a second these days. Yes, brutal gangsters might have run the show under Janus, but at least they kept innocent people safe. These sorts nowadays have no respect for people who don't want a violent city. Do you know how much it costs when you lose a staff member for a fortnight, or have your shop blown to smithereens? The losses can be huge. The economic effects of the current situation are huge.'

'Well, yes, there is that,' the woman concedes, 'but it's also likely that some new stability will eventually emerge from all of this and everything will once again return to normal.'

'Yes, if everyone stays. But it also might just turn into one of those post-apocalyptic visions of the future where people do nothing but blow the crap out of each other. Then where will we be?'

Vincent looks at Frank sleeping next to him. What is taking him so long? Surely something isn't happening to him as Vincent sits helplessly watching TV.

Stella didn't realise at first when she began to say it, but as her mantra of 'no, no, please, no' continued and Vincent's face contorted to reflect her tears, she began to become aware. She was meant to be next, not Frank. She obviously didn't want that, but she also didn't want him to die while she sat there, powerless.

Vincent is shaking the sleeping form of Frank and screaming, 'NO! DON'T DIE! YOU CAN'T DIE!', when very suddenly Frank wakes up. He immediately jumps from the chair putting distance between himself and Vincent.

'What the hell are you doing?'

Vincent's face reveals his relief, a smile managing to creep over his lips. 'I'm sorry. I thought you were being murdered.'

'It was the police checking on me. Jeez, this really has got you scared, hasn't it?'

'I'm sorry, you just seemed to be away too long.'

'I'm okay, Vincent. The police have been checking on me every day about now. Don't worry about me.' Frank also figured he wasn't due to be next so had less to worry about, but he doesn't say that to Vincent.

'Listen, Frank, you need to get in contact with the people at Binary Cityworks so we can coordinate this hunt thing for Grendel. I'm going to be the main bait, but you should probably be out there too, so we have as much Janus presence as possible for Grendel.'

'That's probably a good idea. How is this going to work anyway?'

'They're going to use soul hunters from their deathmatch game.'

'Wow, mindless warmongers to the rescue, eh?'

'I guess so. Anyway, give them a call, will you?'

'I will do, Vincent. I'm going off now anyway. Take care.' Frank walks through and lies down on a reclining chair and is immediately out for the count.

'You too,' Vincent says quietly to himself.

25 September, 9:13pm, Theydon Bois

A mere thirty minutes after Frank had gone to sleep, and less than two hours since Stanton and Lisa had dropped her off at her flat, Stella sat on her living room floor with her knees pulled tightly to her chest. She cried uncontrollably, taking blasts from her inhaler when her sobs allowed.

Vincent had been shot, and it was all Stella's fault. And now they had lost their only in-game contact with Grendel, so they wouldn't be able to lure him out and catch him. Now all Grendel had to do was wait until the police got bored of watching her, and then he was going to come and kill her with a knife. Stella had been playing this revised series of future events over and over in her mind as she rocked back and forth on the floor. How could she have been so stupid?

Minutes after Frank had gone to sleep, Vincent went through his usual preparations to brave the world, strapping on a bulletproof vest and carefully hiding two machine pistols under his coat. He looked at his slightly sickly form in the mirror: his face looked taught from fear, but the machine pistols weren't visible. He had a slight wheeze to his breathing as he went downstairs. It had been a harrowing nightmare the last time he was out, and Stella hoped it wouldn't be as bad this time. *At least this time she knew the police were protecting her - although knowing you are safe doesn't make you immune to fear.*

Vincent was just about to unbolt the front gate when he heard the sound of running footsteps approaching the other side of the door. He stepped back nervously. The footsteps stopped with a thump as the runner hit the door. A few seconds passed before a fist pounded the door.

'Help us! Mr Janus! Is anyone in there? Please, we need some help.' *The young male voice was breathing heavily from the exertion of the run to the Janus building. 'Hello?' More door pounding.*

Vincent steeled himself and slid the small metal peephole back. 'What do you want?'

'I knew you people were still in here,' said the boy. 'You need to come and help us, we've got a couple of the Outlaws trapped inside a building and we need your help.'

'Why should we help you?' Vincent thought it better not to let on he was alone.

'Because "Mr Janus doesn't want scum in his City". That's what his man said on telly. You've got to come.'

Vincent slid the peephole closed and leaned against the wall.

Stella mulled over the situation: she was at home, safe, being protected from a psycho who was going to kill her. Would it really make much difference if she went and helped these people? After all, it would give Janus some credibility again if she went and helped. But then again, did that really matter when this was only a game and she was in *real* danger? Did she really care about the Janus thing now or these people? But on the other hand this would at least keep her from sitting worrying all night about what Grendel was going to do to her. This would be a good way to pass a while: play a game, lose herself in a virtual world where what she did didn't affect her real life. As long as Vincent didn't get hurt, this would be fine. She had to make sure he would still be around as bait for the hunt. Besides, he needed to spend some active time or he would be too weak to be useful as bait. This was just what was needed.

It was just before Vincent slid the bolt open that Stella admitted to herself why she really wanted to help them: it made her feel normal. It would be the first time in weeks where she would be passing her time like she enjoyed passing it: being a respected cyber gangster who ruled with an iron rod, but helped the less fortunate. Stella needed a dose of her own small highly-addictive reality. She was fed up being effectively a prisoner in her own house, scared for her life. She didn't even go to the job she hated any more because the police considered it too risky with the killer out there. What little she did have in her life was gone.

She deserved this.

Vincent took a couple of deep breaths and slid back the door's main bolt. He stepped outside. The young boy looked to be in his mid-teens and was dressed in scruffy clothes.

'We've got them in a building on Bushnell Street. You've got to come and help us.' His voice was more excited than scared.

Vincent and the boy began a brisk walk. The streets were quieter than usual, but there were still a few people around. As Vincent walked he could hear some people shouting their encouragement: 'Go on, kick their butts ... All right, Janus man ... Sort it out.'

As they walked, Vincent noticed a recurrent graffiti image that had not been around just a few days before. The logos were roughly spray-painted on a number of walls and windows. The image was of a skull with the left eye socket replaced by a cross mark, like the eye of a clown. Its bared teeth sneered. Above each skull was the word "OUTLAWS". The gang members he was going to kill belonged to this group of new hopeful heirs to the City's throne.

They reached Bushnell Road and found a group of about fifteen people in what looked like a lynching mob from old cowboy movies. Most people were holding fire torches made from makeshift poles with petrol-soaked strips of material wrapped round the ends. As Vincent and the boy walked towards the group, Vincent noticed that minute droplets of fire were falling from the torches, landing as small explosions of fire on the ground. His approach also revealed to him that the group was totally peopled by very ordinary-looking City dwellers. None were dressed the way killers tended to be dressed: in long coats that can easily hide weapons. The reality was that of this group only a handful even had firearms.

Vincent and the boy walked up and joined the group, the boy pushing through to clear a path. They arrived at the man from the television broadcast Vincent had been viewing earlier, the same bearded man he had helped by disposing of Kane.

'So we meet again,' Vincent said with a curt nod.

'Indeed we do. I was beginning to think you people were gone.'

'No, we're still here.' Vincent looked like the old Vincent: no fear, no looks of sadness, just resolve that he would do this task. Vincent was playing his part well. 'So what's the situation?'

'Well,' the bearded man began, 'six of the Outlaw gang were rampaging around town tonight so we decided to get a kind of posse together to put up a bit of a fight.'

'Who are these Outlaws people anyway?'

'They're just a gang of psychos who've emerged in the last week or so. Just the usual sort of hoodlum really, trashing the place, destroying the shops, vandalising. We tried to contact Janus, but we couldn't get a hold of anyone until you came tonight.'

'Yes, we've been pretty busy.'

'Not running the City, though.' The bearded man's face looked angry. Vincent figured it was understandable. The Janus organisation had taken on a role in the City people

had begun to rely on, and now it was all but gone. The Janus people had been unaware, but they were protecting businesses just by their very existence, even when they weren't involved in carrying out mercenary assassinations. As the most organised crime syndicate in the City they had ensured meaningless crime had been kept in check by reputation as much as action. Now the City was out of control.

Vincent responded quietly, 'I know, there's been some problems, but we're still here.'

'So how are you going to get the two we've got in here?'

'The old classic strategies are usually the best; so I guess I'll just go in and get them.' His steely voice had returned.

'One of them is on the second floor,' said the bearded man.

As if to punctuate the statement, machinegun fire from a second floor window sprayed the crowd, miraculously only hitting one unfortunate man. As the Outlaw gang-member shouted, 'Come and get us, you bastards', the stricken man clutched his throat, gurgling as he fell to the ground. Blood pumped from his neck onto the street.

'Do you know where the other is?' asked Vincent.

'Nope, sorry.'

Vincent pulled a machine pistol from his coat and ran across to the doorway of the building, his head taking a quick look into the hallway before he committed himself to entering the building. The doorway opened into a corridor with doors off to each side. The only light in the corridor came from one of the open doors. It spilled into the corridor revealing small repeat pattern wallpaper. At the far end was a stairway that turned back on itself as it led to the first floor. Vincent slowly and carefully walked forward to the stairs, checking each room as he went, his gun scanning the way forward. In the one lit room he could see a sofa, a television set and the smouldering remains of an armchair. He continued to the stairway, walking almost silently.

Looking up vertically he could see the stairs ran up to all four floors of the building. Only the third floor had light, which was good since that would mean they would be unlikely to see him coming up. Keeping close to the wall, he began to edge his way up the stairs. The silence was palpable as he reached the first floor. He checked around in case the second gang member was there, systematically and quietly opening each door, finding each time that the room was empty. He returned to the stairs and climbed slowly to the second floor.

There were four doors, two on each side of the corridor facing him. He decided to do the far end first, the street-side end, since one gunman was definitely there. He tried to gauge which room the window was in that the shots had just been fired from. He figured it would be the left hand room.

He crept over, barely making a sound, and turned the handle; it gave a slight squeak then clicked. He hoped the gunman would be preoccupied with watching the mob outside as he slowly began to open the door, but when it began to creak, he stopped. Listening, he could hear the gunman shift behind the door. Vincent wasted no time: he kicked the door open and burst into the room.

What occurred next took no more than two seconds. Vincent lined up on the gunman who was crouched by the window. The gunman's face was turned towards the door, but his gun was still coming round. Vincent squeezed out three rounds: two slammed into the gunman's chest, while the third clipped his left earlobe, splashing his skinhead with a streak of red. He slumped over, his glazed eyes staring towards Vincent as a pool of blood began to spread over the carpet.

Vincent turned back out into the corridor. Hopefully the other gang member had thought the gunfire was from his counterpart, although Vincent was aware the weapon he had used sounded sharper than the deeper reports the gunman's had produced when he fired on the street. And there had been the sound of the door being kicked open.

He opened the opposite door, quickly moving into the room. He scanned back and forth with his gun. On the wall on the left was a door that was either a cupboard or another way into the room next door. He hoped it was the latter.

Listening closely at the door he heard nothing. He turned a creaky handle and the door clicked, springing open slightly. He moved his eye to the crack that had emerged. With his limited view he could see only a desk at the far side and the door that led to the corridor. To minimise the noise, he swung the door quickly open. Papers from the desk fluttered as they were blown onto the floor. The room was empty apart from various pieces of ornate furniture. Vincent took a couple of deep breaths. This was pretty tense stuff.

He crossed to the other door, the door to the corridor, and stopped. A floorboard creaked. Footfalls right outside the door. He quickly changed magazines on his machine pistol. It was always better to have a full clip in these situations. Even three bullets could mean the difference between life and death--they had for the poor sucker lying spilled all over the other room.

Vincent edged closer to the door, stopping as he saw shadows move underneath the door. First one, then two, then four were visible.

At least two people.

He looked at the doorframe in front of him. It was only barely visible since the room was lit only by light coming in through the window, but he could just about make out the hinges. The door opened into the room, so he wouldn't be able to kick it out and maybe knock them off their stride. He considered returning to the corridor via the other room, but

167

then he'd be at the end of a corridor with nowhere to run if things turned sour. No, he had to act now, while they were walking past this door.

He grabbed the handle and yanked the door open then shoulder barged out into the corridor. He was blinded by a bright light which seemed to be pointed right in his face. He let off a quick burst of gunfire and the light went out. There seemed to be three of them from his initial impression.

'Hold on, we're from City News.'

'What the hell?' Vincent was totally distracted by the mobile news crew when the silhouetted figure began to appear down the stairs. The crew had been quick to get on the scene when they had been informed that one of Janus's men was out in the City for the first time in over a week. They were anxious for the scoop that would have everyone glued to their screens this evening and tomorrow morning as they broke the story about what had been going on with Mr Janus these last weeks.

The cameraman was pointing the camera at Vincent, while the soundman, knocked off balance by Vincent's exit from the room, was accidentally prodding him with the furry microphone on the pole as he tried to regain his feet. Abstractly Vincent realised the reporter was asking him questions: 'What's been going on with Janus lately, and why has there been no street presence of late?'

The whole thing had unfolded in a matter of seconds, and Vincent was only just becoming aware of the silhouette levelling its firearm at the group when the first muzzle flash erupted almost in slow motion.

The news reporter was blasted sideways as three slugs tore into his body. Vincent at this point began to turn and level his weapon on the figure that was now artistically lit by muzzle flash in the stairwell. Next it was the turn of the cameraman. As the hail of gunfire ripped through his body, bits of his camera flew off in every direction adding to the general maelstrom in the corridor. Vincent began to return fire in the general direction of the gunman on the stairs. He watched abstractly as the wall beside the new gunman began to explode as a line of bullet holes made its ambling path towards the figure. Then came Vincent's turn: thud, thud, thud, thud.

Black.

That had been seven minutes ago.

25 September, 9:13pm, Lisa's Flat

Lisa Collier had just settled down to eat the Chinese food she had just had delivered when the phone rang. She was still sticking chunks of chicken into her mouth as she answered it: 'Uh-huh.'

From the other end there was nothing but irregular heavy breathing. 'Bloody pervert,' she just about said through her sweet and sour chicken before she hung up.

The phone rang again.

She picked it up and was again confronted by the breathing. 'Listen, you're breathing down the wrong phone, buster. This is Detective Constable Collier from the Metropolitan Police, and if you don't get off of this phone right now, I'll have you locked up!' Lisa knew it was a fairly empty threat, which she would be struggling to enforce. But people generally feared authority figures in these situations.

Through a croaking voice the breather at the other end managed to say: 'Tstella.' This was followed by a couple of sharp intakes of breath followed by 'It's Stella.'

'Oh, sorry, Stella. It was just the breathing: I thought you were some mucky phone caller.' Lisa felt acutely embarrassed. 'Sorry,' she said again.

Stella was trying to say something, but Lisa couldn't make it out.

'Slow down, Stella. Take a few deep breaths and start again.'

'Vincent is dead, and it's my fault.' Stella managed to blurt out.

Lisa was stunned. She knew that Vincent was probably the best chance they had of getting Grendel out of the woodwork and into the real world. 'What happened? How could he have been killed?'

'I decided to go outside the Janus building in *Alter Ego* to help some people. It all happened so fast.'

'Was it Grendel?' Lisa asked, although she couldn't think why Grendel would want to kill Vincent.

'No, it was a gang member from a new gang.' Stella drew another deep breath. 'It was because of the news crew, they distracted me and Vincent got shot.' The volume of her voice rose as she sobbed, 'And now we're not going to find Grendel and he's going to come and kill me!'

'Calm down,' Lisa said, weighing up what to do. If Vincent was dead like Stella was saying, this was pretty bad. They had no other clues to catch Grendel. How on earth could this woman have been so stupid as to play with her only lifeline? Lisa made sure she didn't let on that this was how she felt because on the other end of the phone Stella sounded like the world was coming to an end. Lisa could hear Stella's breathing changing as the waves of panic washed over her. The sound of the inhaler was soon interlaced with Stella's blubbering. 'Listen, Stella, I'm coming across. Don't worry, we'll find a way to sort this.' Lisa had no idea how, but she wanted Stella to believe it.

From the other end of the phone, all Stella could manage was, 'K.'

Lisa hung up.

Stanton was watching a late evening news broadcast when Lisa called him.

'You're working a bit late tonight, aren't you?'

'Sorry,' replied Lisa. 'Stella just called me in a real state. She says Vincent has been killed in the game. So it looks like we've lost our only lead.'

'Shit! How the hell did that happen?' He muted the TV. 'Did she say what happened?'

'Just that she decided to go out and help some people. I don't know what all happened, just that Vincent seems to be dead. Listen, I'm going across to her flat. She's all over the place in a real panic. I'm not sure she should be on her own right now.'

'Okay. Do you need me to do anything?'

'No, I just wanted to make sure someone knew where I was.'

'Good thinking.' Stanton paused. 'Lisa, listen: be careful, will you?'

'I will.'

'No, seriously.' Stanton thought her reply sounded a bit too flippant. 'We've got a killer out there and Stella's his next victim, so be careful.'

'Jack, we've got uniforms watching the place round the clock. I think it's got to be pretty safe. Don't worry about it. I'll be all right.'

'Okay, I'll speak to you tomorrow.'

Lisa dressed in her warmest clothes, remembering how cold Stella's flat had been during the day. The last thing she wanted was to spend a night there feeling cold. As she walked to her car, two streets away where the parking was free, she looked like she was dressed for the great outdoors, rather than someone going to sleep in a flat. Still, she wouldn't be cold.

Her eight-year-old red Fiesta was where she had left it, nestled between two large executive cars. Her little runabout was the oldest car in the street and the fading paintwork and creeping rust in the wheel arches didn't hide the fact. She climbed into the driving seat, feeling a little constricted by her layers of clothes. The air in the car was stale; this was the first time she'd been in her car in the last month at least. She put the key in the ignition and turned it. The first three times she did this it made a click as something in the engine drained the last miniscule drops of power from the battery. After that, the key might as well have been turning in mid air for all the effect it was having.

'Bugger!' Lisa said, rifling through the glove box for details of her AA membership. At times like this she was glad she parked as far from her flat as she did. Her AA membership didn't include any sort of home start help, and since she was parked quite a distance from her house she wasn't really abusing the system – sort of. She dialled the number into her mobile and was told there would be someone there within twenty-five minutes. She considered phoning Stella, but then figured it would probably only make her more frantic. It was going to take Lisa almost half an hour to get there even when the car was going, fifteen minutes or so wouldn't matter too much. She got out of the car and walked up and down to keep warm.

At Stella's flat the squad car officers had finished their last flask of soup. It had lasted just long enough since it was now only five minutes until they would be going back to the station for the shift change.

'Thank goodness that's us done for the night,' said the driver, a middle-aged and overweight officer with a moustache. 'It's bloody freezing out here.'

'You said it.' The younger officer in the passenger seat was packing the flask into a bag. 'When are you on again?'

'Tomorrow night again,' said the fat officer. 'What about you?'

'Not for another two days. I've been lucky with it.'

'I can't wait until they catch this Grendel fella. It's a bloody nightmare watching this place. You'd think they'd just have moved her to somewhere safe.'

'I know, but then you know what the people who run the show are like.'

'Hmmph.'

The single patrolling officer made his way towards the squad car. The original plan for two officers to patrol had been abandoned after they found there weren't enough officers to police the rest of the area. Now a single officer walked the route around Stella's flat. The officer got into the car.

'Hello, boys.' He took off his leather gloves and rubbed his hands together to warm them. 'Jeez, it's like a fridge in here, isn't it?' He was glad that he got to walk about outside. At least the exercise was keeping him reasonably warm.

'Any sign of our man?' the fat officer asked.

'Nah, nothing at all.' The patrolman had removed the flask that had just been put away by the young officer and was shaking it. He looked unhappy when he couldn't hear it slosh. 'Is this done? You greedy bastards!'

'You try sitting in here for four bloody hours,' said the driver. 'Then tell me I'm greedy.'

'Make sure you get the next boys to make up some more soup before they come down here.' The patrolman said grumpily. 'When are you boys off anyway?'

'We're just about to go. So get your lazy arse out of the car and back on your beat.' The younger man, smiled cheekily.

'Oh, I'm officer greedy guts. I get to go home and you don't. Na-na-na-na-na!' the patrolman mocked the young officer in a squeaky high-pitched voice.

'See you later.'

'Just remember the soup.'

Grendel watched as the squad car pulled away. The policeman who had been previously walking round a patrol route now stood at the front door to the flat…

…which meant the back was now unprotected. Grendel stayed deep in the shadows as he skirted his way round to the back of the property, letting himself into the yard filled with old cars behind the garage. From here he could see the large rear window of Stella's flat. The curtains were drawn, and from the light pattern it looked as if she only had one light on. He moved forward towards the wall. All he had to do was carefully scale the wall, climb over the railing and he'd be on the roof. Not too difficult at all. He put one booted foot up on the front wing of half a car that had been pushed against the wall, then carefully stood up, trying to be as quiet as possible. His hands searched for a handhold to pull himself up.

Checking to the left on a ledge he found there were no good holds; moving to the right sharp pains shot across his hand tearing the surface of his skin as he reflexively pulled back. He bit his top lip as searing pain messages assaulted his brain. A large furry cat was staring down at him hissing and making a mewling sound. He struck the cat in anger and it flew from the ledge into a pile of empty oil cans. As it scrambled to get up to escape it upset more cans before knocking over some thin strips of wood as it ran off. In the quiet that was Theydon Bois, the upset seemed ten times as loud as it was. In the distance a dog began to bark.

Grendel froze as he heard the footsteps of the policeman moving to look through the front gate for the cause of the noise. Seeing nothing the officer went to the other side of the building. He pulled a long torch from his utility belt as he moved. Grendel eased himself off of the car, worried that the front wing would make a metallic pop as he stepped off. It didn't. He rubbed his injured hand and moved into the deep shadows at the back of the lot. The beam of the torch searched through the one-inch gaps in the fence, until it landed on a pair of eyes.

Thomas, still spooked from his earlier encounter with Grendel, shot off through the yard scrambling and knocking everything in his path.

The officer laughed gently. 'Only a cat.' He switched off the torch, returned it to his belt, then walked back to the front.

Grendel once more moved to the wall.

Stamping her feet to keep her circulation going, Lisa Collier was fed up. It had been a long enough day when she finally got some food and settled down for the evening. And now here she was walking around trying to keep warm, waiting for the AA to come. It had only been ten minutes.

Two drunken men came round the corner towards her. Both were large well-built men in their twenties with trendy short haircuts and large fleecy jumpers. They were laughing and joking with each other in slurred speech. As she got near them, one said: 'Well, you're certainly dressed for it.'

'I sure am,' she said, gauging the good-humoured statement for what it was.

'What's a nice girl like you doing out on a cold night like this?' The man was smiling, swaying slightly as he asked the question.

'Good line, Bob,' said the other one hitting the first weakly. 'I'm sorry, madam, but my friend here is very drunk and doesn't know he's giving you a line.'

'That's no problem,' said Lisa. 'Hey, you guys couldn't do me a favour, could you?'

'For a beautiful woman like you, anything at all.' The first drunk was still hopeful that Lisa would be wooed by his charms.

'Ah, you're too kind,' said Lisa playing him along. 'Could you give me a push in my car? I've got a flat battery.'

'We sure could,' said the drunk again. 'Can't we Michael?'

'I believe we can. Where's your car?' It sounded more like "we-zhi-ka".

'It's along here.' She led the way followed by the two hulking men, who bumped into each other like they were both walking down a narrow corridor on a ship in stormy seas.

'After we've got your car going, would you like to come for a drink with us?' The first persisted with his chat up.

'That would be really lovely, but I've got to be somewhere.' Lisa really did fancy a drink, even with these two big drunk men. Anything was better than working at this time.

'That's a real shame.'

They got to the car and Lisa got in and wound down the window. 'Okay, guys are you ready?'

'We sure are.' They began to push the car, which quickly gathered speed as the men powered it forward.

'Okay, I'm going to let up the clutch.' Lisa shouted to the men. Neither heard, so when she let up the clutch and the car suddenly slowed as its engine coughed into life, both men crashed into the back of the car then fell to the ground as the car accelerated forward. Lisa watched in the mirror as the two helped each other up. They zigzagged to the window, leaning down, smiling. 'Thanks guys, that was really good of you.'

''Sno problem at all. Are you sure about that drink? You look parched.'

'Maybe some other time, gentlemen,' Lisa said.

'Hold on.' The Romeo drunk dug in his wallet then pressed a business card into Lisa's hand. 'Some other time, yes?' He hiccupped then looked shocked at the surprise of the rogue spasm.

'Come on, Bob, let's go,' said his friend.

Lisa engaged the gear and drove off. As she looked in the mirror, Bob the Romeo drunk was waving wildly. Above the sound of the engine she could hear him shout: 'I love you, you know.' She smiled, putting his card in her glove box.

Grendel had eased his way up onto the edge of the roof where he quietly vaulted over the railing. His footfalls had sounded crunchy on the roofing felt that covered the makeshift patio, and he had taken an age to cross the five or six metres, concerned his footsteps would give away his presence. He pressed an eye to the window and looked through a small gap in the curtains. The woman was in the kitchen; her eyes were large, red and puffy. He'd soon sort that out, he mused. He slowly moved across to the door that gave access to the flat. It was more like two half-width doors, fastened with a bolt in the middle. He pushed, wondering if the doors were locked.

Lisa flicked the heater controls to the hottest setting and turned the fans to maximum. The headlamps dimmed slightly at this, before the fans suddenly died and the brightness returned. 'Great,' said Lisa. 'Just what I need tonight.' As she felt her feet getting colder she accelerated: there was no way she was dallying at the speed limit in this mobile fridge tonight, policewoman or not. She blasted through an amber light as she sped towards Stella's flat. 'I have got to get a new car,' she mumbled as she pounded along, her breath billowing from her mouth.

Grendel removed a small wallet of tools from his pocket. His prowess at lock picking learned from Internet sites wouldn't be of any use to him tonight, but the small hacksaw blade would be. He passed it through the join between the doors and began slowly sawing the bolt that blocked his path.

He stopped when the woman, *Stella*, his mind spat into his thoughts, came through for just a second and flipped off the light. If she had just glanced across she would have seen the blade poking between the doors. But she didn't and Grendel was soon back at his work.

After a few minutes he lifted the tool out and peered to see how much was still to be cut. He couldn't see anything so put it back between the doors and began to saw again. His hand hurt from the deep scratches the cat had inflicted. He wished he had been wearing the leather gloves that were in his pocket, but he wanted them to be absolutely clean when he went into the flat.

The saw blade suddenly clicked downwards as the bolt was cut through. Grendel put his tools back in the wallet and placed it in his jacket pocket and zipped it securely. He removed the black leather gloves and pulled them onto his cold hands, pressing the leather between each finger to ensure the gloves were snugly fitted. He then pushed gently at the two doors, maintaining pressure until the friction between the doors was overcome with a gentle thud.

He entered Stella's flat.

The living room was sparse, only a computer and desk, a coffee table, a television and a bookcase adorned the room. He made his way slowly across to the door. He froze as a lightly sobbing Stella walked from her bedroom and crossed the hall to the bathroom. After a few seconds she walked back, half closing the door.

Grendel walked into the kitchen. His eyes scanned for knives. There were none visible. He crossed to the only drawers in the kitchen. Stella had put on some music in the bedroom. He smiled under his balaclava: this would make getting a knife out easier. He slid open the first drawer. It was filled with papers, a plug, Sellotape and other useful household stuff. He opened the next one, the cutlery drawer. On the left he found two chopping knives. He selected the larger of the two. As he held it up and inspected it, the blade glinted.

Grendel moved towards Stella's bedroom door.

Lisa thundered along the road, the cold having crawled from her feet up to her knees. She blew alternately on her hands as she drove. 'Why did I forget my gloves?' she muttered. 'Especially when I'm practically wearing every other piece of clothing I own.' She braked hard and pulled into Stella's street. The police officer outside Stella's flat was standing stamping his feet outside the front door. 'I know how you feel, mate.' She pulled up with a screech outside the door.

Grendel stopped in the hall. Stella was moving around inside the room, and the occupant of the car outside sounded like they were coming across to the front of the flat. Grendel retreated deeper into the hall, then as Stella came out of the bedroom, he moved into the bathroom. His breathing was shallower as he felt every noise, including his breathing, was like a loudspeaker saying, "Here I am!"

Shit, he thought as Stella went down to open the door. He could hear a second woman's voice. Then it happened: the draught from the open front and back doors caused the back door to slam shut.

'What was that?' He assumed this was the new woman's voice. She sounded alarmed.

'I don't know,' said a very frightened-sounding Stella.

'Wait here,' said the first woman again, then, 'Come on.'

Grendel slid the bathroom door shut. There was just enough of a crack for him to see the other woman and the uniformed policeman race upstairs. He turned and opened the bathroom window. He could hear the people in the other room: 'Shit, he's been in, or is in.' He heard footsteps coming through into the kitchen. He looked out of the window. The drop from the window was about fourteen feet. He scrambled up onto the window ledge, knocking over shampoo bottles and smashing a bottle filled with dark liquid. The door to the bathroom was sliding open.

He looked back, his eyes wide as Lisa Collier charged into the bathroom. As Grendel began his drop Lisa miraculously managed to get a grip on his black canvas jacket. His falling weight dragged her over the edge of the bath, knocking the wind from her lungs as she slammed against the windowsill. For about two seconds Grendel hung, kicking his legs as Lisa strained to hold his weight, before, just as she was about to shout to the other officer to get outside, Grendel lashed upwards with Stella's knife. The first blow raked the stone wall, flaking off some of the aging white paint. The second sweep caught Lisa's forearm. She shrieked and let Grendel drop. Cradling her arm she saw his dark figure scramble over the fence, running quickly across the car park next door before disappearing into the night.

The officer who had already been on his way outside, soon came running round the side into the car park. Lisa shouted, 'Over there!' She pointed with her uninjured arm. The officer ran off into the shadows. Lisa was beginning to go into shock. Her arm was drenched in blood. She wrapped a towel round it and staggered out into the hall, slumping down at the top of the stairs. Halfway down sat Stella. She was as white as a sheet and so petrified she was barely even crying.

Lisa got herself to her feet again and managed to get to the telephone. She phoned for an ambulance then collapsed to the floor, pressing as hard as she could on her wounded arm.

25 September, 11:26pm, Theydon Bois

When Stanton arrived, the walls around him were flashing blue from the ambulance and the two squad cars that were there. He walked the last stretch of road, pulling his ID from his pocket. Lisa was sitting in the kitchen in the care of a paramedic. The wound to her arm had been deep but not life-threatening.

'It seems all my layers of clothes probably saved me from the worst.' Lisa said. Stanton noticed a pile of clothes with bloodstains over them.

He crouched down beside her. 'Are you all right?'

'I've been better, but yes, I am.'

'What happened? They said Grendel was here.'

'Yes, he waited for the shift change and cut his way in at the back door. I almost had him when this happened.' She lifted her arm.

'Keep still, please,' said the paramedic who was still dressing the wound.

'Did we get a better ID on him?'

'Not really, the boys are searching the area for clues and prints, but he was all balaclavaed up again.'

'How's Stella?'

'She's through there.' She nodded to the living room. 'This has shaken her a lot – understandably.'

'I'll bet.' Stanton stood up. 'I'll go and check on her.'

A female officer was comforting Stella. She was the same officer who had seen her about the stalker previously.

'How are you, Stella?' Stanton asked.

Stella was staring forward. 'He was here. In my flat.'

Stanton looked at the door that had been closed over. The small pile of metal shavings on the floor between the doors was the only sign that something had been amiss.

'Yes, I heard.' He squatted down. 'Did he touch you?'

'He was in my house; isn't that enough? Does he have to cut me up before we catch him?' Stella sounded both hard and extremely scared.

'Stella, we'll catch him, and from now on you'll have an officer in here until we have.'

'And how are we going to catch him, eh? Now that Vincent is dead?' She was still staring.

'What happened to Vincent?'

'I made a mistake and he got shot.' Stella looked at Stanton as she said the last word, and then resumed her stare. 'And now this Grendel can come into my house to kill me and we can't find him anymore.'

'How do you know he is dead?'

'I heard four shots hit him and it all went black. What do you think happened?' Her voice, although monotonous, spat out her words angrily.

'I see,' Stanton said gently. 'Listen, we'll find a way, Stella. You have to believe us.'

Stella just stared.

After Stanton had made sure that the scene was under control and that there would be an officer resident in Stella's flat until this was resolved, he drove Lisa home. She stared out of the window: it had been a long night. Detective work was proving more physical than she'd thought. Finally she spoke: 'You know, I don't know how we're going to do this now. And tonight has done nothing if it's not shown us that this psycho is willing to go to pretty extreme lengths to get Stella.'

'I know,' Stanton replied.

'I mean, we don't even know who he is or why he's doing this and tonight he was in her house. *In her house.* She'd be dead if I hadn't decided to go across – and I very nearly didn't go.'

'I know. You saved her life tonight.'

'Hah.' Lisa knew it had been more fluke than skill. She sat in silence as they drove and soon dropped into a deep sleep as her wearied body succumbed to the hypnotic hum of the engine and the warmth of the car. She woke as Stanton pulled up outside her flat.

Inside, Lisa sat heavily down on her couch. She rubbed her bandaged arm, which was now throbbing with each beat of her heart. She caught sight of the cello her father had bought her when she was a child. It sat on its stand in the corner of the room beside a foldaway music stand. A smile crept slowly over her face; a smile that soon evolved into a laugh. She giggled as tears rolled down her cheeks.

She hated playing the cello, yet every day she felt compelled to practice at least a little. It was a guilt-trip she had been forced into by her father as a child that she had never quite managed to shake off – even when she had stopped seeing him. She looked at the pleasing curves and dark wood of the polished instrument in the corner, 'Maybe being stabbed has its benefits after all.' She wouldn't be playing the cello for quite some time.

She wiped her wet cheeks and went to bed.

**26 September, 7:07am,
London, Stanton's Flat**

Stanton clawed his way from a nightmarish dream as the sound of the telephone slowly grew in his consciousness. He had been back on the moor, walking in sickly slow motion for all the world like he and the others had just gone over the top on some First World War assault. Explosions were raining down.

He burst to the surface and abruptly sat up. The phone continued to ring as he rubbed at his eyes then picked up the receiver.

'Patrick here.' Patrick's telephone voice sounded very serious, not the usual way he tended to be with Stanton. 'How are you?'

'I've been better, Patrick. I take it you heard about last night.'

'I did. Is Lisa all right?'

'She got a bad cut on her forearm, but she's fine.'

Patrick exhaled his relief. 'I'm so glad to hear that.'

'I take it you've had some joy with the addresses.'

'Yes, last night they ran an overnight search diagnostic to find the addresses for the other two; and to cut a long story short, we've got one good address. The other email account seems to have been checked from lots of different computers at lots of locations, so there is no fixed address there.'

'At least we've got one of them.' Stanton shivered. 'Which one is it anyway?'

'It's a guy called Arthur Braithwaite. He lives out near Ruislip in the West.' Patrick slowly read the address while Stanton wrote it down.

'Okay, do we know which one of the players that is?'

'I've got it written down somewhere, but I think it's the Swift one.'

'Is there any way we can check out the locations for the other account?'

'Yes, we can. But the ones I've phoned this morning are Internet cafés and places like that.'

'And do they keep a note of who's using the systems?'

'No, you just pay and play as they say.'

'Catchy. Anything else?'

'Just one other thing, Stanton: when did you say the Tyler guy went missing? You know, the other one?'

'Last Thursday. No, that was Swift. Shit, why can't they just use their own names? Tyler was weeks ago.'

'Ah,' said Patrick, 'I think someone's mixed the names up then. They told me this morning that the Tyler account had been accessed last Thursday, but they probably meant Swift. They must have the names and pseudonyms confused because it would be Swift who would have used the account most recently. I'll get onto them this morning and get them to double-check it anyway; and I'll print out the details I have and leave them with reception, okay?'

'That'll be fine, Patrick. I'll get onto Forensics and get round to Ruislip straight away. And thanks.'

'It's okay, Jack. Speak to you later.'

Stanton made a few phone calls and was soon on the road to Ruislip to meet the same people from Forensics who had checked Niall's flat. He had called the station local to Arthur Braithwaite's address who were sending a couple of uniformed officers who would be there within the hour. His final call was to Lisa. She sounded tired but chirpier. He updated her with the new developments on the case before he got on his way.

He wasn't looking forward to this.

An hour later he was sitting two streets from Braithwaite's address poring over a street map. He rolled his eyes when he realised how close he was and pulled round the last three corners and searched along for number 14. He didn't need to look too hard. The squad car and the white Transit van from Forensics were parked on the opposite side at the far end of the street. He parked in front of the Transit. Two officers emerged from the squad car and walked across. The people in the van also began to appear: two Forensics people and Lisa from the front, the photographer from the rear.

'How come you're here?' Stanton asked Lisa, pleased to see her but concerned she wasn't resting.

'I figured with your stomach for these things, I'd better drag myself down here to help,' she smiled

'Are you sure you're up to it?' Stanton was looking at the way Lisa gingerly held her bandaged arm slightly away from her body.

She lifted it: 'Yes, it's fine. Just a bit stiff.' In reality her arm was much more painful this morning. There was a deep pain all around the area of the wound. But Lisa had work to do. She wanted to see Grendel caught now more than ever. 'Anyway, let's get kitted up, because it might take me a while.'

'Sure,' said Stanton.

The five of them were soon enclosed in their paper suits, masks, gloves and glasses. While they were standing by the van dressing, they even wore blue plastic elasticated overshoes to keep their soles clean until they entered the house. Stanton felt sick just at being inside this gear again. He was glad Lisa was there.

The inside of Braithwaite's house was better decorated and had finer things than had been in Niall's flat. Although they had been equals in *Alter Ego*, in real life they were from opposite sides of the tracks. The front door was soon sealed with a polythene sheet, and after the photographer had documented the hallway, Stanton and Lisa entered. There was no smell like there had been in Niall's.

The hallway had two doors coming off of it; both were closed. Forensics dusted all the handles and door frames. Stanton walked forward and picked up a picture of a graduate in an ornate frame sitting on a small semi-circular table beside a telephone. Presumably this was Braithwaite. He was a large man; Stanton figured he was probably morbidly obese. He returned the picture.

When they entered the living room they found a large widescreen television as the focal point of the room. A huge stacking Hi-Fi system was playing an Enya CD quietly in the background. Lisa noticed it was on repeat as she examined the unit and moved to switch it off.

'Don't touch that!' Richardson from Forensics shouted from the other side of the room. 'It's not been dusted.'

'Sorry,' said Lisa, annoyed with herself for the rookie mistake. She stepped away.

The room showed no sign of disturbance at all. The connecting dining room was similarly devoid of signs that anything was wrong. Braithwaite's computer system was set up here.

The photographer had cleared a path upstairs and Stanton and Lisa went up while Richardson dusted the handrail for prints. All the upstairs rooms were open and Stanton and Lisa began their systematic search. The first bedroom window was open, the curtain moving slightly in a gentle breeze. Lisa walked over and looked at the window.

'I think this might be the point of access,' she said. 'Look, the retaining hook has been sawn through. Just like at Stella's.'

'Looks like it.'

They both moved aside as the photographer popped a few shots of the hook. Soon the whole window area was being dusted for prints.

'Where the hell's the body, though?' Lisa asked absently.

They moved through to the master bedroom, pushing open the door which was ajar. In Stanton's mind the room was going to have blood smeared on the walls, upset furniture and the hulking semi-naked body of Braithwaite lying face up on his bed in a pool of blood, his face roughly hacked off. As the door swung completely open, there was no such scene. The large King-sized bed was neatly made, and the yellow room with its expensive yet sparse furniture was completely as it should have been. Stanton breathed a stifled sigh. Maybe they'd got dressed for nothing. But then why was the window hook cut through?

The bathroom and a small box room were the only other upstairs rooms. Neither had Arthur's body in it and a check of all the upstairs cupboards also revealed nothing. They went back downstairs.

Richardson had finished the stairs and had also dusted the kitchen door that now lay open. He was now working on the small utility room handle at the back of the property. Walking round the kitchen, Stanton and Lisa were wondering whether the body was here at all.

'Maybe he took the body away?' Stanton proposed.

'But why would he mutilate one and take the other away? It doesn't make sense.'

'I don't know. I just don't get this.'

Stanton looked around the large well-kitted kitchen. 'Looks like our man liked his cooking.'

'It sure does.'

'Where does that door go?' Stanton pointed to the door in the corner beside where Lisa was standing.

'To the garage, I suppose.' She reached for the handle.

'Hold on there.' It was Richardson. 'I need to dust that.'

It took a little over five minutes before Lisa could open the door. She reached around the doorframe and flicked on a light switch. The shelves on the opposite wall of the garage stared back at her. 'Yup, looks like a garage.' She walked in, closely followed by Stanton. Half of the garage was a normal garage; the other half had been walled off. Stanton and Lisa stood and stared at the large metal wall in front of them. In the centre was a door with large hinges at one side. They were looking at a large industrial fridge that Arthur had had installed into the rear of his garage.

'Looks like he *really* liked his food,' Stanton observed, his eyebrows rising. Everyone present now had the same feeling of foreboding at the large metal room they faced.

The handle was soon dusted for prints along with the edge of the door and the surrounding area. Stanton walked forward and pulled the heavy locking mechanism. The door needed a good pull to get it moving. Once free of the frame it swung open freely.

The light from the garage spilled into the large fridge revealing the body of Arthur Braithwaite lying on his side in the middle of the fridge, his upper body half under a series of shelves to the left.

POP-WHINE.

Stanton jumped as the photographer snapped off his first shot.

With the light switched on in the fridge, the true barbarity of the scene was evident. Not only were there large cuts of meat from various animals hanging around the small metal chamber, but also half of the floor was covered in blood. The bulk of Arthur had blocked it from coming round to the front of his body, except around his head area, although that could have come from what remained of his face. It didn't look to Stanton like he had been garrotted, but then Stanton was now standing nearly seven feet away from the body.

Lisa was less fazed and was examining the corpse for wounds. She shouted out what she was seeing and Stanton wrote it down since she couldn't hold a pad and write. 'There's a lot of blood soaked into his shirt at the back. Looks like a knife wound up into the chest between the ribs from the shape of the cut in the shirt material. The autopsy will confirm that, though.' She paused. 'His face has been removed in a similar way to Niall's. It looks about just as messy a job.' She leaned over the body, having to ease herself between Arthur and the shelving to view the back of his head. She was breathing in short sharp breaths as she pointed a small torch into the shadowed area where Arthur's bulk was blocking the light. She slumped back to a sitting position. 'Yup, looks like our guy has tried to put the face onto the back of his head. His hair is covered in blood and these look like bits of skin on the floor. Looks like they've been placed on the back of the head but have slid off.'

The smell of blood was hanging in Lisa's throat as she sat and stared at the corpse. One of Arthur's eyes stared at her where she sat. His nose, which she had recognised in the small pile of tissue on the floor behind his head, had been reduced to a small piece of white bone sitting above the hole of his nasal cavity. Lisa closed her eyes. Her arm throbbed.

A half hour later, the coroner had arrived and was carrying out a similar examination. He didn't observe anything new. The autopsy would perhaps give them more clues.

Removing Arthur took the coroner, the three Forensics men and one of the uniformed officers almost twenty minutes. They had to use a rope looped under Arthur's arms to pull his bulk from the confines of the fridge since the slippy blood-soaked floor was not giving any purchase to lift him. Lisa winced as his massive form shlucked out onto the garage floor.

Stanton was safely in his vehicle on the road to meet Sam Stark in London, the dashboard fans blowing cool air onto his face.

26 September, 12:41pm,
London, Royal Victoria Dock

Stanton drove to Royal Victoria Dock and parked. He had called Sam Stark because he had to find out what they could do about Vincent being dead, and if the hunt was still a possibility somehow. He also figured Sam would be the better person to explain the ins and outs of getting the Action Heroes into *Alter Ego* than he himself would – assuming they could do something about Vincent. They had agreed to meet in a coffee house Sam knew near the Dock.

As Stanton walked to the meeting place he thought about how much this case was swinging from grim and scary to strangely compelling. He was mostly intrigued about meeting the Action Heroes, yet the juxtaposition with what had happened the previous night and this morning made this a roller-coaster ride of a case that was deeply unpleasant overall. Stanton found Sam reading a paper over a fancy-looking coffee.

'Hi, Sam. It was good of you to come.'

'That's no problem at all, Jack. It's nice to be in the city. Would you like a coffee?'

'I'll have what you've got there.'

Sam nodded to the waiter. 'Hi, another café latte, please.' Stanton sat down. 'So,' Sam continued, 'what was the problem last night then? You mentioned something about Stella and Lisa on the phone.' Stanton hadn't mentioned they'd found another body.

'Grendel got into Stella's flat last night. Luckily Lisa was on her way and managed to scare him off.'

'Shit. That's not good.'

'You're telling me.'

'Was everyone okay?' Sam asked, a small foam moustache on his lips from his latte. He licked it off.

'Lisa got a bit of a cut on her arm, but apart from that_' Stanton trailed off. 'So as you can imagine, we need to catch this Grendel guy soon, because he's wasting no time.' Stanton paused as the waiter placed his coffee on the table along with two biscuits wrapped together in clear plastic. 'Thanks.' He waited until the waiter left then continued, 'The biggest problem is that Stella says Vincent got shot last night. So we've lost our bait.'

'Actually, that's not quite true. I didn't tell you on the phone this morning because it seemed like you had a lot on the go, but Vincent is alive and well and sleeping under the supervision of some of the kindly townsfolk.' Sam smiled. Even he could hardly believe that his invention, his game, could have produced such a storyline.

'But Stella said he was shot last night, then it all went black.' Stanton stirred a couple of the roughly-shaped sugar chunks into his coffee.

'Yes, that would be right. Obviously she's never been killed in *Alter Ego* before. When you die, it doesn't go black, it goes back to the character set-up screen. It only goes black if you are rendered deeply unconscious.' Sam began to move uncomfortably in his seat as he spoke. He quickly removed his mobile from his pocket and pressed the button on top to stop its vibrations. He read the display on the unit as he listened to Stanton.

'So are you saying Vincent is unconscious now?' Stanton asked.

'Well, now he's actually just asleep as normal; all Stella needs to do is log on. I assume she hasn't tried to yet.' Sam pocketed his phone and looked back at Stanton.

'I wouldn't think so. She was pretty shaken by last night's events.'

'It's understandable,' said Sam. 'Anyway, it seems from the news footage I saw late last night at the office that

Vincent was hit four times in the chest. But he was wearing a vest at the time so was only knocked unconscious. The soundman on the scene survived the same attack, so when the cameraman got hit we still had the live report on audio. I don't know where Vincent was taken, but the soundman's commentary said the locals carried him off somewhere.'

'So why didn't the gunman finish him and the soundman off?'

'It seems Vincent was firing when he went down. So in a kind of John Woo style shootout, both men went down shooting. He was found on the stairs full of holes. A second news crew went to the scene early this morning to get some pics. From the live sound broadcast and video of the scene they shot later, you could pretty much work out what had happened.'

'Wow, that's lucky, although I still don't get why news is so big in this game. Or more than that, why it's even in the game.'

'It's for two reasons really. The first is more to do with things external to the game: we use the news reports to cut together trailers for the game, you know, to play in games shops and for people to download. It helps keep the advertising dynamic since no two trailers are the same. The second reason is internal: if you have news reports that people playing a large game can watch, then people can keep up with events that they haven't been able to actually see. You'd be amazed at how immersive this game can become.'

'I can imagine,' Stanton stated.

'Also people like the Janus organisation used the service to promote their reputation. It's a bit like modern wars: the more media coverage you can get, the better - as long as it's good coverage of course. All in all, it was something we just thought we'd try out and we found that we were getting massive in-game viewing figures so we kept it going. And as for magazines:' he whistled, 'they run a monthly news roundup that they pay a handsome sum to buy. It's all pretty cool.'

'It sounds it,' Stanton said. 'But Vincent is okay, though?'

'As I said, he was - last I heard – which was later than the last time you heard. So I'd say yes.'

Minutes later both caffeine-fuelled men were on their way to the Action Heroes' place of work. Sam called his office on the way to discuss the text he'd received. Stanton, meanwhile, wondered what to expect when they got there. If Andy and Sam were anything to go by, it could be anything.

**26 September, 1:03pm,
London, Royal Victoria Dock**

The office of Wilsco Software was a dingy and incredibly messy bunch of rooms on the second floor of a building accessed from a door on Churchill Road. They were a small software company with only eight employees. Four of them were the deathmatch clan known as the Action Heroes.

As Sam and Stanton walked up the four flights of stairs to the second floor, Sam said, 'I'm actually quite looking forward to meeting these guys. I've watched them play a few times.' He nodded, '*Very* cool.'

Stanton was just hoping they'd be able to help.

At the second floor a buzzer unit comprised of a small speaker and a red button confronted them. Sam pressed the button. The receptionist's voice thundered from the speaker, slightly distorted from the excessive amplification: 'Hello, can I help you?'

'Yes, Hi. This is Sam Stark. I'm here with the police to speak to some of your employees, the ones who are in The Action Heroes.'

'Hold on Please!' blasted out.

A few moments passed before the door clicked as it was unlocked by a switch on the other side. A spindly man with greasy black hair that sat in a heavy fringe on his brow answered the door. 'Hi. Can I help you?' His voice was slightly nasal and squeaky. He removed his heavy-rimmed spectacles and wiped them with his kipper tie as he spoke. Sam and Stanton looked at one another.

Sam's eyes were wide. Could this be one of the Action Heroes? 'Hi. We'd like to talk with the members of the Action Hero Clan. This is Detective Inspector Jack Stanton and my name's Sam Stark.'

'*The* Sam Stark?' said the man, totally ignoring Stanton.

'I suppose so.' said Sam, shooting a smile from under his own fine wire frame designer spectacles.

Stanton pulled out his ID. 'Sir, I'm afraid this is official police business. We're in the middle of a murder investigation and we need the help of the Action Heroes. Can we come in?'

'You need *our* help,' the man stated astonished. 'Wow. Yes, come in.' So he *was* one of them. They moved through into the messy office. 'If you'd like to take a seat for now, I'll go and get the other guys. I'm Reggie, by the way, Reggie Karlinski.' He cleared large piles of papers and folders off two chairs that Sam and Stanton hadn't even noticed. 'If you could just wait here.' He went to the far end of the office and through into a smaller office bumping into the corners of two desks on the journey. Stanton shook his head, his eyes pressed tightly shut.

A few moments later Reggie came out of the room and crossed to a desk by the window. He spoke to the occupant, who got up, looked across at Stanton and Sam and then went into the small office. Reggie then asked Stanton and Sam to come through as well. The name on the door said William Stevens CEO.

As Stanton and Sam walked in, the three men already in the room stood up, smiling eagerly at Sam as they mumbled their hellos. Stanton took control: 'Good morning gentleman. I'm Jack Stanton from CID.' They all took their seats again. Stanton scanned the room: all of those present must have come from the same factory that produced Reggie. The man next to Reggie wore thick-rimmed glasses repaired with insulating tape. His hair was cut short all over except the back, which hung onto the collar of his floral shirt that was only partially hidden under his striped tank top. Next to him was a blond man with large frizzy hair that was combed in a side parting. This had probably been an endeavour to tidy the hair, although the result looked like a ramp on his head. His clothing included a tight checked shirt, a pair of grey slacks and some training shoes. His top teeth sat on his bottom lip. Finally there was William Stevens. His hair was combed straight backwards where it sat in three uniform waves on his head. He wore small round spectacles and had a small bum-fluff moustache. The grey school-style shirt he was wearing was pulled tightly at each button. Stanton tried not to show it, but he had always thought that people like these only ever existed in films or books. Yet here he was confronted by four of them – in one room.

He hoped that they were as good as Sam seemed to think. He desperately needed their help, regardless of how they looked.

'The reason we're here,' he continued, 'is because we've heard you're the best people around to hunt someone within a computer game.' Stanton's eyes widened just slightly as two of the largest sets of buckteeth he had ever seen emerged from the smiles that all four now had on their faces. 'The game in question is *Alter Ego* and we're after a specific player's character within the game and we need his ID extracted.' The four looked perplexed.

'We need his digital soul,' corrected Sam.

They all bobbed, smiling and nodding.

The blond one, Ryan Worthington, sitting near to Reggie spoke as he fixed his large fringe by running his hand across his forehead, the thumb under the fringe and his fingers above it. 'But we don't have characters in *Alter Ego*.' He was wiping the palm of his hand on his grey slacks as he continued, 'We play the deathmatch game.'

Sam intervened, 'Yes, what we plan to do is temporarily port you across from your current machines, and translate you into *Alter Ego*, complete with your weaponry.'

'Uh-huh,' smiled Ryan, his bottom lip shining as his teeth protruded onto it in a smile, 'And we'll have all our weapons, you say?'

'Whatever you need.'

William Stevens looked excited. 'When is this going to happen? Is it going to be soon?'

'Well,' said Stanton, 'we'd appreciate if you could get whatever things you need together in the next hour or so. We'll arrange for a van to collect you and take you up to Binary Cityworks up in Southam.' They wowed and smiled and slapped each other on their backs with excitement. 'Sam here will help you sort out what you need to transfer the characters.' Stanton motioned to Sam. They all nodded eagerly again. 'And we'd appreciate if you could continue on the project until we have captured and got the ID for our man. We'll put you all up in a hotel for the period.' The four looked like they had won the lottery. 'So it would also be useful if you could get someone from home to mail you some clothes at Binary Cityworks.' All four men began to move uncomfortably. The atmosphere had died a sudden death.

'There's no-one at home to send me any clothes,' the last Action Hero, Donald Bailey, said looking through his thick spectacles at his fidgeting hands.

'Nor me,' said Reggie pushing his own spectacles further up his nose. The other two had similar looks.

Stanton suddenly realised these men probably didn't have wives to send them clothes, and probably all of their friends were in this one room. 'Okay,' said Stanton, 'we'll get the van to drop by each of your houses to pick up some stuff.' The party atmosphere returned with a vengeance. Stanton turned to Sam: 'Maybe you could take the characters ahead and get them into the game while they get clothes and stuff. It will save us some time.'

Sam smiled. 'Sure, Jack. No problem.'

'Good. Anyway, I have to shoot now to pick up Lisa. I'll get across to your offices this afternoon as soon as I can.'

'Sure thing, Jack. And don't worry, I've got this covered.'

'Thanks, Sam. You're a great help.'

Sam nodded and shooed Stanton out of the room with a movement of his hand.

26 September, 3:26pm, Ruislip

Stanton picked up Lisa from the scene at Ruislip, which also put them on the right side of London to easily pick up the M40 up to Southam and Binary Cityworks. They decided to go straight there. Stanton had offered to drive Lisa home first, but she was insistent that she was fine to come. They had been driving listening to the radio for the last half hour when Lisa turned down the volume: 'So I take it we can expect to find our third man in a similar state of mutilation now.'

Stanton took a deep breath, releasing it through his nose noisily. 'Looks like it, doesn't it? I can hardly believe that you managed to stop Grendel last night.'

'I know.'

'I mean we were probably just minutes from finding Stella in a similar state.'

'Don't remind me,' said Lisa rubbing her arm. It was bad that she'd been hurt, but it had been a small price to pay to save Stella. 'Do you think this hunt thing will work?'

'I don't know. Don't get me wrong, I'm sure they're very good at what they do, but I've never met a bunch of geeks quite like the Action Heroes in my life. I just hope they are better at doing things in games than in real life.' Stanton slammed on the brakes and changed lanes as an ignorant Mondeo driver cut him up. 'Arsehole!'

'What do you mean?'

'Well, one of them managed to spill a drink all over one of the others as I was leaving. It was all flailing hands and clumsiness. Not exactly inspiring.'

'Indeed.' Lisa hoped they would be able to catch Grendel. If not, she wasn't sure what they would do. 'We'll just have to see.'

They arrived a little after five o'clock and walked into reception where they were immediately shown through to Stark's office. Sam was with the four Action Heroes in the main area. They were being set up on four systems along one wall. Sam came through.

'Hi, Lisa. How's your arm?' Sam was rubbing his hands together like a man who was busy but felt he should ask the question anyway.

'Not too bad. It's getting a bit stiff now.'

'That's a shame.' He turned to Stanton. 'I meant to ask you: how's it going with the body hunting these days?'

Stanton's mind flashed back to Braithwaite lying in the giant fridge. 'We found another this morning.'

Sam made an unhappy face and a clicking sound with his cheek. 'Pretty grim?'

Stanton changed the subject, 'How's it going here?'

'Not too bad at all.' He clapped his hands. 'John's almost done on the harvester *and* we're almost set up with the Action Heroes. It'll only be a couple more hours before we can introduce them into the game. You can come through if you fancy.'

They both agreed and they all filed through. The programmers were swarming around the four database developers-cum-heroes, like technicians round Apollo moon astronauts. Various bits of computer hardware had been set up since they had last been here. The process of bringing the characters from the soul harvesting game into *Alter Ego* looked like it was a complex business.

Stanton arrived beside the desk of John, the engineer who was developing the soul harvesting unit.

'Hi,' Stanton said.

'Hello,' John smiled. 'D'you want to see?'

'Sure, why not.' Stanton sat down in a spare chair and looked at the three-dimensional object rotating on the screen. It looked like it would be worn like a knuckle-duster that fitted like a fist-shaped cup over your hand. The trigger was on the inside where your fingers gripped the device. Two serrated pointed prongs sinisterly protruded from the front.

'Yes, I was dead lucky with this. I found a rudimentary harvesting unit for *Alter Ego* already in the system, so all I've been doing is tweaking it and making it look good.'

'That's not really what we need. We just need it to work.'

'I know,' said John. 'But until these boys are ready to go, I might as well polish this little beauty.' He pulled up a window onscreen and typed in something via the keyboard. He pressed a button on some speakers. 'Watch this.' He pressed the RETURN key. A hum emanated from the speakers. The harvesting unit was glowing along the two prongs. A bolt of electricity suddenly zapped to the end of the prongs, turned bright orange and flashed with a zap sound. 'You see, you stab the person you want to harvest, then pull the trigger. Then it's just zap and Bob's your uncle.' Stanton thought it looked like a brutal weapon and was glad it was confined to a game world. But if it would help them find Grendel, then all the better.

Sam came across with Lisa. 'Listen, these guys are going to be ready to rock and roll in about an hour. How about we go and get some dinner, because we'll want to watch this from over in our other building anyway.'

'How are we going to watch it?'

'Characters all need to be introduced into the City. Basically people usually arrive on trains. It's so we keep the illusion of a virtual city alive. If we just had people popping into existence on the streets, we'd lose the realism. '

'Uh-huh,' said Stanton.

Just over an hour later the three drove into the car park of a large building in an Industrial Estate at the edge of Southam. The sign above the main door read "Binary Cityworks News Service and City Servers". Sam punched in a code to open the door and they entered an altogether more science fiction place of work.

The walls and carpet were black, as was the ceiling. Lighting was provided by up-lights fitted near the ceiling. As they walked along the main corridor they passed dimly lit rooms containing large consoles with blinking LEDs and about twenty screens mounted into the walls. Three technicians worked each large workstation, controlling the multitude of switches, lights and levers. The monitors displayed various scenes from the City as well as streams of data that were being processed and dumped to the main computer core.

Stanton and Lisa suddenly felt very out of their depth. Before they had come here, this had been an odd case that was a little hi-tech. Now they felt like they had passed into some alternate universe. Neither had been anywhere like this before.

'Take a seat in here.' Sam showed them into a small cinema-like room. Five rows of chairs were set up facing a large viewscreen. In the red light of this room, Lisa could make out speakers placed all over the walls and ceiling. She and Stanton sat down.

'This is a bit weird all of a sudden. Isn't it?' Lisa said quietly.

'You're telling me.' Stanton looked over his shoulder to the back of the room. Sam was in a booth behind a barrier of glass. He nodded at Stanton as he worked the console in front of him. Sam's voice then boomed from all around them as he spoke into a microphone.

'We'll just be five minutes more. Hold on.'

Stanton gave him a thumbs up. 'Jeez, was that loud enough?' He asked Lisa as he pressed his finger into the ear nearest the speakers.

Lisa couldn't help but smile.

'Actually,' Stanton said, 'I'm going to go and see if I can get Stella on the phone. We'd be as well to have her out in the City if these guys are going to be up and running soon.'

'Good idea.'

Stanton got up and looked for somewhere brighter to make his call. He bumped into Sam who led him back outside. 'Just buzz the door when you're done and someone will let you back in.'

'Sure. Thanks.' Stanton dialled Stella's flat. It rang about eight times.

'PC Adams.' The male voice identified itself.

'Hi, Jack Stanton here. How's it going over there? How's Stella?'

'Well, sir, it's been a hell of day. She had a bit of a hysterical fit this afternoon that turned into an extreme asthma attack.'

'That's not good.'

'No, sir. The doctor has given her something to make her sleep. Do you need her tonight?'

'Yes, well no.' Stanton's mind raced, 'We could have done with her being up and about. But I assume tomorrow will be all right.'

'I'll tell her you called, sir.'

'Thanks.' Stanton hung up. This was just what they needed. 'Shit,' he said suddenly. He had forgotten to phone and tell Stella that Vincent was alive. As he hit the redial

207

button he shook his head: he had to work on this dead body thing because it was occupying his mind constantly. Poor Stella was still under the impression that Vincent was dead and that there was now no way for them to find Grendel, while *he* had known that Vincent was alive for half the day!

'PC Adams.'

'Hi, it's Stanton again. Listen, can you do something for me?'

'Sure, sir. What is it?'

'When Stella wakes up, tell her to go online; tell her Vincent isn't dead. He's being looked after by other people from the City.' Stanton found he was pacing round the car park. 'And apologise to her for me. I forgot to phone and tell her earlier. Tell her we're back on track and we're getting the hunters into the game tonight.'

'Vincent fine, town people, apology Stanton, hunters into game tonight.' He said each word as he wrote it down. 'Okay, sir. Got it.'

'And don't worry, Adams, she'll know what all that means.'

'Alright then, sir. Goodbye.'

He pressed the buzzer.

26 September, 7:15pm, Southam, Binary Cityworks

Stanton was let back into the building by a technician who blinked at the brightness of the car park's lights. He walked back along the black corridor. This time as he walked he took a better look into each of the rooms. The rooms on the left were the ones with multiple screens, while those on the right each held three smaller workstations. On the door to each room was written "City News Crew" followed by a number. He walked into one of the rooms. The people who ran this crew were obviously not working at the moment.

He walked over and sat at one of the control consoles. It looked mainly like a standard keyboard, with a smaller hand-shaped set of keys off to the left and some kind of complex mouse on the right. The large screen in front of him was grey since it was switched off.

'Would you like a quick demo?' Stanton jumped as Sam spoke to him right by his right ear.

'No, I don't want to be any trouble.' Stanton made to get up.

'It's no trouble at all,' said Sam pushing Stanton back down into the seat. He flipped up a small plastic cover and pressed the button protected beneath it. The system in front of Stanton sprang to life. Sam typed a few things over the keyboard and a small text window popped up. He typed some more then said, 'Sit still for just a sec while it calibrates.'

Stanton sat totally still as a small camera in the console registered his facial dimensions.

'That's it,' said Sam. 'Now, put your hands on the mouse and the hand keyboard and we're ready to go.'

Stanton took the controls and was soon walking around a room. There were two men sleeping on beds at the other side of the room. He walked to the window.

'Use the mouse to grab it and open it,' said Sam.

Stanton reached forward and grabbed the window handle and opened the window.

'It's pretty intuitive to control, isn't it?' Sam said. 'It took us a while to work out the best controls, but now we actually bundle these with the software at a reduced cost to the user. It takes no time at all to get completely familiar with playing the game.'

Stanton looked out on the street. For all the world he could not tell that this was not a video camera looking out of a window.

'It's absolutely amazing.'

He looked back at the room and then walked over to what looked like a mirror on the wall. A face he did not recognise looked back at him. By this point Stanton had almost forgotten he was viewing a computer game he had become so absorbed in the onscreen image. He licked his lips unconsciously. 'Surely not,' he said quietly. The face in front of him had just licked its lips and was now moving its mouth exactly in time with Stanton's speech. He stuck out his tongue; so did the reflection. Every twitch and movement of Stanton's face was being reproduced in front of him at exactly the same time he did it. 'How can you do this?'

'It's optimised use of hardware and some pretty secret coding. If I told you I'd have to kill you.'

The onscreen face smiled.

'So what about the voice? Stella plays a man. Does he have a woman's voice?'

'No, her voice is transformed into a male voice. Each character has a randomly generated vocal tract based on the physical characteristics of their character.'

'You mean these characters have insides?'

'Yes, completely, right down to organs; although they are only there for effect, they don't function. People like their gore in games, so they really come into play in fights and the likes.' Sam shrugged. 'Anyway, the software translates the voice of the player, reinterpreting it on the basis of the vocal tract of the character in the game and the sex of the character. Here, let me show you. Put these headphones on and look at me.' Stanton put on the headphones while Sam typed into a window he had made appear over the top of the game image onscreen. When he was done, he tapped Stanton on the shoulder. Stanton turned to look at him.

Sam's mouth moved as he spoke into a small microphone and Stanton heard the words in his earphones. 'As you can see, or rather hear, the voice can be changed to whatever we want it to be.' The voice Stanton was hearing was a woman's voice. It was *exactly* in synch with Sam's lips. 'The only thing that remains is your accent, but if you're into a bit of creative role-playing, you can be entirely who you want to be in *Alter Ego*.' Sam put down the microphone.

Stanton was absolutely stunned. 'This is the most incredible thing I have ever seen,' he said removing the headphones. 'And people have this level of stuff in their houses?' He gestured at the console in front of him.

'Not this whole console, but yes. The mouse and small keypad are game specific, as is the camera.' He tapped a small lens built into the top of the screen, 'And what you've seen on this screen is exactly the quality of the whole game.'

'It's amazing.' Stanton was astonished.

'Anyway, let's get going, we're about to bring in the Action Heroes.' Sam was scribbling a small note on a yellow Post-It note as he spoke. He stuck it to the screen of the terminal before they left. It read: *Needs recalibrated. Sorry. Sam.*

26 September, 7:33pm, Southam, Binary Cityworks

Sam showed Stanton back through to the room with the screen. Lisa was looking a bit bored—and tired—and was glad to see him.

'You took your time,' she said.

'I know, sorry. Sam was just showing me the game. It really is incredible, you know. How's the arm?'

'Sore.'

Behind them in the glass booth were two technicians as well as Sam. It didn't take too long before what lights there were dimmed and Stanton and Lisa were plunged into almost total darkness.

'Ladies and Gentlemen,' a voice they didn't know began. 'Binary Cityworks is proud to present,' the voice paused, 'The Action Heroes.'

A fanfare began which Lisa recognised as the music from Rocky.

'They're going to town a bit with this, aren't they?' Sam said, feeling every bit like he was at the cinema.

Lisa couldn't help but smile. This was a welcome release from the morning's work. 'These guys make entertainment. I suppose they can't help it.'

The music had now reached the end of the fanfare intro and was in full flow. The voice spoke again, 'Put your hands together for William Stevens as Blade.' The name was stretched to "Blaaaaade".

Stanton and Lisa watched as a spotlight appeared on the screen in front of them. A circular hole appeared on the black floor and a figure began to rise up out of it. The sound of a crowd's rising cheers began. The man had short-cropped hair and had his back to the camera. He seemed to be wearing black battle-armour with the name "BLADE" emblazoned across the shoulders. He looked a little like an American football player without a jersey, although the armour plates seemed to fit better to the man's physique. As the figure was raised to about its waist, the camera began to rotate around. He was a huge hulking man and it was soon evident he was holding a huge futuristic-looking compression rifle which hung from his hand with its muzzle resting near the floor. A smaller weapon was slung over his back. His legs were similarly armoured to his upper body and he wore large boots on his slightly-oversized feet - the large feet, which ensured maximal stability, were a standard physical attribute of all deathmatch warriors. His head had been facing down, but now that he was almost at floor level he raised his head moving his face into the light. He had a chiselled jaw line and a light stubble across his face.

'Isn't that Arnold Schwarzenegger?' Lisa asked Stanton above the sound of the music and cheers which were now at fever pitch.

'You know, I believe it is.' Stanton couldn't help the huge grin which had spread across his face.

The voice continued, 'Ryan Worthington as Striker.' (Strrrraaaayker).

The camera cut to another spotlight where a second hole slid open. The top of the head of a second figure began to emerge, again facing away from the camera. A second wave of cheering began over the top of the first and the music pumped along apace. Like Blade, Striker had his name across his shoulders, shoulders that were rippled with red battle-armoured muscles. This Action Hero had slightly longer hair than Blade, with a slight curl to it. His muscle definition was also greater than Blade's, although he seemed to be slightly smaller than the first Hero because the hole he was rising from seemed bigger. The camera began to rotate around the rising figure. He was holding a large rifle with a plasma chamber mounted on the top. He gripped the barrel with his left hand. He did not have sleeves below his elbows, and his muscular forearms had prominent veins below the skin. He raised his head, the spotlight lighting his tanned face. The face had intense eyes and a mouth with its upper lip slightly raised on one side.

Stanton laughed out loud: this second Action Hero was Sylvester Stallone.

'Donald Bailey as Intruder.' (Introoooooduuuur).

Again a new spotlight appeared along with a hole in the floor. The new figure began to emerge to more cheers above the general cheers and music. The shoulders displayed his name in stencilled lettering like the others. His armour was dark blue and extremely worn-looking and his head was shaved and suntanned. He was well built, but not ridiculously so, and his battle-armour looked impressive on the physique. As the camera began to rotate around him he shuffled, moving the large rail-driver he cradled in both arms. The weapon had coils running to the front of the barrel and a video sight mounted on its top. Slung over his back was a smaller weapon, while clipped onto his utility belt was the soul harvesting unit Stanton had seen earlier. As his feet neared floor level, he lifted his head into the light and smiled. Intruder looked exactly like Bruce Willis.

Stanton shook his head and glanced at Lisa, who despite her throbbing arm was smiling at the humour of the Action Heroes.

'Reginald Karlinski as Thorium.' (Thoooreeeyuuuum).

A final spotlight, hole and rising figure appeared on the screen to yet more roars. The armoured shoulders read "THORIUM". He had short neat hair and seemed even smaller than Striker. His torso had an athletic muscular build and his armour was camouflaged like army fatigues. His sleeveless battle armour showed off his muscular arms, adorned with large tattoos running from shoulder to elbow. His hands gripped a mini-missile launcher with a huge magazine clipped onto the bottom of it. He also had a minigun slung over one shoulder with an umbilical connecting it to an ammunition satchel strapped to his back. As the camera rotated round him, he flexed his muscles and pulled an aggressive pose, his oversized feet far apart. Then suddenly he lifted his face into the light. It was Robbie Williams. He looked into the camera and winked.

The cheers were all around and the music was blaring. It was difficult not to be carried away with the atmosphere. And as the voice said, 'Ladies and Gentlemen, put your hands together for the Action Heroes,' and the music pumped and the cheers roared even louder, both Stanton and Lisa smiled and clapped. These people might just be able to help them after all. The Action Heroes were all standing together on the screen, the camera rotating round them.

To the left of the rotating screen a large door hissed and opened with a clanking grinding sound. The Action Heroes all began to jog in the direction of the door.

'Action Heroes ready for insertion. Please stand by.' The onscreen door thudded shut and the music and cheering continued before the lights slowly began to rise and all the sound slowly faded out. Sam came across from the booth.

'That was all a bit extravagant to get them into the game.' Stanton said.

'That's what we do. Besides that'll look great on trailers—' Sam was saying as Stanton cut him off.

'Hold on there, Sam.' Stanton was suddenly very serious. The Action Hero insertion had been a bit of light humour in an otherwise black series of events, and he wanted Sam to be aware of that. 'We're not making trailers for your game here. The object of this is to make sure we catch Grendel and get the ID so we can go and arrest the psycho.'

'I know.' Sam was nodding his head. 'But once you've done that, we might as well use the footage.' He shrugged.

'That's your call,' Stanton said. 'But just remember that at least two people have died and *that's* why the Action Heroes are here. If you can honestly in all good conscience use the footage, that's up to you.'

'Stanton,' said Sam. '*This* is news.' He motioned to the screen, 'News in our game. What's happened outside has affected what's going on in the City. We can't hide that. Our subscribers expect to hear about what's going on in the City, and *this* is what is going on. This is just what current games are, warts and all.'

Stanton was disappointed by Sam's attitude considering real lives were at stake. 'Look, Sam, can we have a meeting with everyone here just now? Because we need to keep this under wraps until we've got Grendel.'

'Sure. I'll just go and get everyone. But it is going to be pretty hard to keep the Action Heroes under wraps in *Alter Ego*.' Sam left and soon technicians and news crew operators began to filter into the screening room. Soon the room was full, with some people needing to stand at the back.

'Ladies and Gentlemen, thank you for coming. For those of you who don't know yet, we're from CID and we're currently involved in a murder investigation. We have a player within *Alter Ego* who has called himself Grendel, and we intend to catch and ID him using the Action Heroes - as you no doubt know. What I want you all to know is that a woman's life is at stake in this situation.' Stanton paused to let the gravity of his statement settle. 'Last night the lady in question, who plays *Alter Ego* as Vincent from the Janus organisation, had her home broken into and her life threatened by Grendel. He would have killed her if Detective Constable Collier here hadn't intervened.' He motioned to Lisa. 'As you can see she sustained an injury during this intervention, which highlights that we are not dealing with a game, but real lives which can be lost.

'For that reason, I would request that each and every one of you refrains from discussing what is going on here for as long as it takes to resolve the situation and catch Grendel. Please do not speak to newspapers or reporters, should they get wind of what is going on. Also I would ask that no reference be made to this investigation within the in-game media service. It is imperative that we do not alert Grendel to our plan in case he goes into the woodwork and disappears.

'We've seen what you can do tonight, and it certainly is a huge spectacle. But we must, I repeat *must*, keep all of this as low profile as possible in the game and out of it, until we have caught Grendel. Any questions?' There were none. 'Thank you for your time.' The people began to file out, back to their jobs. Sam came across.

'Good speech,' Sam said. 'It'll take ten minutes to get the boys into the City proper, then we're ready to rock and roll. Have you got Stella sorted out?'

'I'm afraid Stella's not available tonight,' Stanton replied. 'Last night hit her pretty hard.'

'I'm not surprised; having someone in your house, people getting stabbed. It must be a bit much. What about the other Janus guy?'

'I'll phone him just now, because some Janus presence might be useful in drawing Grendel out,' said Stanton

'You know, our plan really is pretty weak.' Lisa interrupted. 'We're just hoping he wants these guys gone and that he's going to come and tell them that again, aren't we? You do realise our whole plan hinges on the fact that he might want to come and goad Stella some more? And if he decides he doesn't, we're snookered.'

'I know,' said Stanton. 'I still think it will work, though.'

'So do I,' Sam agreed.

Stanton continued, 'If he'd just wanted to kill her in real life, he wouldn't have given her any clue that she was next in the game. I think he'll be back. I think he must be getting some kind of twisted satisfaction out of the in-game goading. I don't know.'

'Let's hope so,' said Lisa. 'Because *I* want this guy caught.'

26 September, 8:45pm,
Southam, Binary Cityworks

Stanton found Rawling was home and was only too willing to get into the *Alter Ego* City as Frank and help out. With Miller away and Stella laid up, Stanton was glad they at least had one of the Janus organisation to try to lure out Grendel. Stanton had asked Rawling to get Frank down to the station where the Action Heroes would be arriving any time. They had been given a panic button to give to Frank. The plan was simply for Frank to walk about, doing what Janus's people would normally do and hope that Grendel took the bait. When he did, all they had to do was hit the button and the Action Heroes would come - and the hunt would be on.

It all sounded extremely simple. And simple plans have less likelihood of failure than complex ones; at least that's what Stanton and Lisa were hoping. Stanton was going to stay and watch what happened for another hour and then he would go back down to London.

The plan was for Lisa to stay in the same hotel as the Action Heroes tonight; there was no need for both of them to commute back and forth while they waited for Grendel to show. Right now, though, both sat in the screening room with Sam Stark watching the action from the closed circuit system that was installed subtly round the City as well as via the headset cameras on each of the four Heroes.

Onscreen a train is on its way to the City. Two new residents look across at the four hulking Action Heroes, eyes wide. All four Heroes are breathing heavily despite their lack of activity: deathmatch games involved running almost non-stop, so the developers had done away with the fine-tuning of the character's breathing systems—instead of deathmatch characters only breathing heavily when they exercised, they breathed heavily all the time. The time constraints involved in getting them into *Alter Ego* meant this feature hadn't been removed.

And so it was that the Action Heroes stood, crammed into the small carriage with their weapons and gear, breathing heavily as the two amazed faces, mouths hanging open, watched them from the other side of the carriage. It was a sight to behold.

Frank wakes, vests up and holsters a gun inside his overcoat, then quickly makes his way down to the station. It isn't too far: just down Muzyka Street then down the Mound to Bushnell Road where the station is accessed via an entrance down some steps. He runs down since the Action Heroes are due any time.

He arrives just as the train pulls up. The electric doors open and two normal residents exit the train. They are followed by Arnold Schwarzenegger, Bruce Willis, Sylvester Stallone and Robbie Williams, all armed to the teeth and clad in battle-armour.

'You guys must be the Action Heroes,' says Frank smiling broadly. 'Hi, I'm Frank, one of Janus's men.'

'I'm Blade,' says Blade in a deep and manly voice. 'We were asked to give you this.' He hands Frank a small black box about the size of a matchbox. It has a red button on the top. 'Just press that and we'll come. We'll be tracking you anyway, but we won't act until you press the button. Give it a go now.' Frank presses the button and beepers on all four Heroes are set off. They all reset their alarms.

'Okay. Well, I suppose I'd better just go and get on', says Frank.

'We'll be nearby,' growls Blade.

'That's fine.' Frank can't hide his smile. As he walks off the Action Heroes put on interactive headsets and activate them allowing each to communicate with the others no matter where they are in the City. They also broadcast a video image from each man to a console which was displayed on the large screen in front of Stanton and Lisa.

Now they would just have to wait to see if Grendel would take the bait.

PART III - THE HUNT

26 September, 9:03pm,
Viewing Room, Binary Cityworks

The Heroes were hanging back from Frank by about a quarter of a mile. There was no way the deathmatch warriors could blend in entirely, but with a minimum of fuss they were moving reasonably surreptitiously along the streets of the City, covering their advance in a conventional military leapfrogging manner.

In the viewing room, Stanton, Lisa and Sam watched their progress. The screen was divided into four sections, with the view from each Action Hero's camera filling a quadrant, while speakers around the room were piped with the sound of their radio chatter.

'Blade, moving.' A "tchook" static sound punctuated the end of each radio message.

'10-4. Intruder following.'

'Roger that. Thorium in position.'

'Roger, Roger. Striker is watching you.'

Two of the onscreen images began to undulate regularly as Blade and Intruder began their run to the next area of cover. In the screening room, the sounds of the move came from all around: footsteps, breathing and the sounds of equipment hitting against battle-armour. The images changed as new cover was found and weapons were raised. The video sight on Intruder's rail driver showed a magnified image of Frank who was still a quarter of a mile ahead. Two green lines emerge on the sight: a horizontal one from the top and a vertical one from the left; they met on the image of Frank, a red box appeared around him accompanied by a short beep.

'Intruder, ready!'

'Blade in position.'

'Roger that. Thorium moving.'

'Striker on the move.'

Frank is aware of the Heroes' presence, but is surprised at their cat-like grace. Occasionally he glances back and catches sight of the cohesively working Heroes as they protect each other's advance. He just hopes they'll be able to pull off the job – assuming there was a job tonight!

The City is quiet and Frank is finding it hard to find anything useful to do on behalf of Janus. He thinks the best way to get Grendel out is to show everyone that Janus is still to be reckoned with, in the hope that it will incense Grendel enough for him to show himself. The problem is Frank can't just make things happen. People usually came with their problems to Janus and then Janus made the problems go away. Looking for things to do wasn't the usual and the situation was irritating.

Lisa was unhappy: 'You know, I don't get how we're going to encourage Grendel to come out if we don't use the News service in the game to publicise what Frank's doing tonight.'

'I know,' Stanton responded.

'We could send in a crew or two,' said Sam.

'The problem is that if we do that then everyone who plays this game is going to come running. And more important than that, people in the real world will realise there is a manhunt going on in *Alter Ego*,' Stanton said.

'How are they going to know there's a manhunt?' said Sam. 'I mean, as far as the normal playing public are concerned, this is just business as usual for Janus people because they use the media all the time. Why from their point of view will this be any different? And as for the Action Heroes, as long as they're not mentioned on the news, it will only be word of mouth that's promoting them. So we should be able to do this. It's not like we're broadcasting it on the six o'clock news on TV. Is it?'

'No, I suppose not,' Lisa accepted.

'We'll need to use a live broadcast and pipe it out through the game all the time, though. What do you think?' Sam asked.

'I guess we'll have to go with that. I don't see any alternatives really, especially with Vincent out of play,' Stanton said.

Lisa sighed. 'I don't see any other way right now either.'

'Okay,' Sam said. 'I'll go and get a couple of crews out there. Maybe we'll get an interview with Frank too. You know, so he can say that Janus is still around and whatnot. It might get Grendel worked up and he might appear.'

'We can only hope,' said Lisa.

Sam went through to get the news crews into the game.

'I knew this was a weak plan,' said Lisa, 'but I never really thought about just how thin this whole thing actually is.'

'I know what you mean. But it's all we've got.' Stanton thought back to Braithwaite's house. 'I mean, Braithwaite's house looked spotless, and the guys from Forensics weren't exactly finding blatantly useful stuff at the scene. My bet is it will be as sterile as the Davidson flat.'

'Hmm,' Lisa agreed. 'Anyway, we'll find out the preliminary stuff from Forensics tomorrow, and you never know. I still don't like *this*, though.' She motioned to what was on the screen.

Sam came back through. 'We'll have two mobile units across in under five.'

'Good stuff,' said Stanton.

'Then we'll see who we can draw out of the woodwork, eh?' Sam smiled.

The reporter is firing questions at Frank: 'So, does your presence out here this evening mean that Janus is back to reclaim his position as top dog in the City?'

'We've,' Frank corrects, 'He's always been top dog.' Frank looks into the camera lens. 'And anyone who thinks otherwise can come down here and I'll explain why.'

'And what about Vincent being shot last night? Doesn't that show that your guys have lost their edge?'

Frank looks a bit shocked at the question. He had assumed the media would have been sent to help them, not make them look bad. 'Vincent's shooting was nothing but an unfortunate accident. And looking at the news footage this morning, you guys seem to have contributed to it as much as anything.' And you know as well as I do that he wasn't killed, he thought.

'The power of the media, eh?' The reporter smiles.

'The stupidity of the media, more like.' Frank grabs the front lens of the camera and pushes it away. 'That's it. We're done.'

The camera moves back to the reporter, 'And that was an interview with one of Janus's junior lieutenants, Frank. He says Janus is still here, is still strong, and more importantly that he's ready to have a go with anyone who disagrees.' The reporter's voice has the usual sensational quality. 'And we'll be covering events as they unfold, so stay tuned.'

Watching on the large screen, Lisa rolled her eyes. Why couldn't they just get on with what was needed? She decided to keep quiet and just wait and see what happened. Stanton looked at his watch. It had now been two hours since he'd said he'd give himself an hour more, but he was as eager as anyone to catch Grendel so they could get out there and arrest him.

After the broadcast, a crowd of people has congregated round Frank as he moves through the City. They are eager to see some action. When Frank is attacked, it takes everyone by surprise.

A single scruffy male forces his way through the crowd, emerging to completely surprise Frank. 'You people are nothing!' he spits. 'I'll kill every last one of you and I'll kill Janus too!'

He then swings a large wooden makeshift club. It all happens so quickly that Frank is knocked to the ground by the blow before he can react. Blood pours from a wound to his temple. Through the haze of ebbing consciousness, he finds and presses the button in his pocket.

About two hundred yards away, the alarms begin to sound on the battle-armour of the Action Heroes. They move quickly towards the crowd, covering each other and scanning the surrounding area for attackers.

'Go! Go! Go!' Blade shouts into his headset.

The sounds of their breathing and movements intensifies as they cover the distance to the crowd, who are standing in awe at the approaching warriors. Frank's attacker sees them and starts to run.

'Thorium, bring down that wall. Block his exit!' Blade orders as he looks at the alleyway the attacker is running towards.

'Roger that,' Thorium says, bringing his weapon to bear on one of the walls that makes up the alleyway. His launcher spews out a stream of about fifteen small self-propelled explosives which leave smoke trails hanging in the air as they scream towards the alleyway. The multiple impacts bring about a quarter of the building down and set it ablaze. The crowd is dispersing as fast as it can since this sort of situation could leave you dead in no time. About twenty people are caught in the fireball and flying debris despite their best escape efforts.

TLEOOW-TLEOOW-TLEOOW: Striker's rifle spits bright yellow bolts of plasma. The first narrowly misses the running figure of Frank's attacker as it rips into the slabs of the pavement around him. He looks petrified.

There is a squawking sound over the radio: Intruder shouts, *'I've got him locked in. Firing!'* The rising whine as the weapon briefly powers up is suddenly replaced by the tortured sound of ripping air as the projectile is hurled at near light speed from the weapon. Frank's attacker is only saved by a second volley from Thorium's missile weapon which blows him off his feet and out of the path of the rail driver projectile at the last possible moment.

The scruffy attacker doesn't wait for the smoke to clear and immediately gets to his feet and runs again, this time for the road that will lead him to the bottom end of Muzyka Street. He leaves a light trail of smoke as he runs, now that his body has been heated almost to clothing melting point by the rain of missile explosions he has just survived.

The Heroes give chase.

'Thorium advancing.'

'Roger, Roger. Sweeping left. Where did he go?' Striker asks.

'I don't know,' replies Intruder. *'I think he must have got along that other alleyway in the smoke.'*

'Two on two, guys,' Blade barks out his order. 'We don't want this guy getting the better of us.'

'Roger, Roger.'

'Roger that.'

'Come on, Blade,' says Intruder. 'Let's move.'

Blade and Intruder run forward, finding cover in the remains of the building Thorium has all but destroyed.

'In position,' Intruder's bassy voice informs.

'10-4.' Thorium and Striker begin to sweep forward as the other two cover their advance. 'There he is!' shouts Striker as he unleashes a fresh wave of fury from his weapon. TLEOOW-TLEOOW!

The bolts slam into the house Frank's assailant is moving past in a crouched posture. But he soon decides crouching will get him killed and breaks into a more upright run as Thorium's minigun erupts with a high-pitched firing sound. The walls behind him are disintegrating into dust.

PSHOING-PSHOING: the first reports from Blade's compression rifle begin to blast huge chunks of the building into the street behind the running form of Frank's assailant. As he crosses one of the many bridges that had appeared when a second level to the City had been introduced, it is clear to see that his arm is bleeding badly. The dust covering his body is stopping it from looking wet.

'He's on my scope,' Intruder calmly observes. 'Locking him in.' There is a brief pause that ends in a beep before the weapon's rising whine is replaced by a ripping sound. This time Frank's assailant is hit on the leg and launched over the bridge's wall where he drops around twenty-five feet to the street below. 'Got him. He went over the wall.'

All four Action Heroes begin to run, checking around for other possible aggressors as they make their way to the bridge. Thorium jumps onto the wall and looks down. The figure is lying on the ground below. 'He's down.'

'10-4. I'll go and take a look.' Intruder says as he runs down to the end of the block and follows the road that leads down to the street below. Blade jogs by his side, his equipment clacking as he runs. Half a minute later they are beneath the bridge.

'Where is he?' Blade barks.

'He crawled under the bridge. Can't you see him?' Thorium responds.

'No, he's not here.'

'Hold on,' Intruder says switching the mode on the video sight of his rail driver. The screen turns to a green image of what is being viewed. The multi-coloured image of Blade's body heat glows brightly as the sight passes over him as Intruder scans the area. *'There's the trail.'* The image on the scope shows a slowly dissipating heat signature where their prey has dragged himself under the bridge and into an open doorway. Intruder and Blade walk over, their weapons shouldered in readiness for immediate action.

Frank's attacker is lying in the hallway of the building. He had been trying to make it to the stairs at the far end but has only got about half way in his badly injured state.

'Careful,' says Blade as he lines up his compression rifle on the chest of the body that has now lifted its head and eyes weakly. The assailant is only semi-conscious and is barely alive.

Intruder moves carefully forward to the prone form, removing the soul harvesting tool from his belt as he advances. Blade covers him. As he nears his prey, the physical effects of the onslaught on Frank's attacker are obvious: he is black and bloodied and his eyes blink slowly as he looks weakly at the hulking form of Intruder towering above him. Blade keeps a careful watch for any last ditch fight the injured man may have as Intruder lines up the harvesting unit which gleams in the light cast from the street *lamp that shone through the window in the stairwell. The assailant's eyes close as he is stabbed in the chest by the twin prongs of the unit; the last of his life is sucked from his body as Intruder pulls the trigger with a zap.*

They had the attacker's digital ID.

26 September, 11:17pm,
Southam, Binary Cityworks

In the Binary Cityworks building, four computer nerds were being cheered heartily. In the screening room, the cacophonous sounds were booming from the speakers as the cheers came through the microphones that Reggie and company had been using to talk to one another in the hunt. It brought a smile to everyone's face.

'I can't believe we got him,' said an astonished Stanton. 'Especially so quickly.'

'I hope it's the right guy.' Lisa was not quite so sure. 'This seemed a bit too easy.'

Sam was through at the console behind the glass panel with two technicians. He returned with a printed sheet with the identification number and the name, address and telephone details. 'Here it is!' Sam said excitedly. 'We've got him!' He handed the paper to Stanton.

'Great!' Stanton looked at the paper nodding. 'If you'll just excuse me a moment,' he said pulling out his mobile. 'I need to make a call. He went outside with the details, where he held the heavily-sprung main door open with his foot as he called the station. 'Hi, Stanton here. Get some guys round to this address to detain a Derek Armstrong for me immediately, please.' He gave the address. 'Tell them to tell him it's about *Alter Ego*. Armstrong is the prime suspect in a multiple murder case, so they should assume he is armed and very dangerous and that the situation should be handled with extreme caution. I'll be setting off in about five minutes to get there myself.' He hung up and went back inside.

'...as long as the details are correct,' Lisa was saying to Sam. 'I mean he could have falsified them.'

'I suppose so.' Sam replied as Stanton walked in. Stanton had felt a lot surer that they were onto Grendel before that particular seed of doubt had been planted in his mind. Sam pulled his phone from his belt and read its display screen.

'Is there any way we can see what this guy's been up to in *Alter Ego*, Sam?' Stanton asked. 'Because presumably we'll find some clues for a motive in the game if this Derek,' he re-checked the surname on the paper, 'Armstrong is our man.'

'Sure,' said Sam. 'We can run the ID through all the old news archives and see if his character, or characters, have been up to anything news worthy. If there is anything any of his characters have done that has attracted the news people, we'll have it stored away in the archives. All we need to do is look for it.'

'Okay, let's have a look,' said Stanton.

'Could you just give me a couple of minutes,' Sam said holding up his phone. 'I need to take this.'

'Sure.'

'Just wait through there.'

Stanton and Lisa followed Sam's pointed finger through to one of the rooms with the multiple monitors. The technicians were monitoring the multiple screens.

Sam came in. 'Can you boys pull up anything with this ID in the old news tapes?' Sam asked the technicians. Stanton gave them the sheet of paper.

'Can do,' said a tall technician with a ponytail. He typed in the ID and some text appeared on a monitor built into the desk. 'Says here he's been a player for about three and a half months, eight characters, eight deaths. It'll take a few minutes to process the information to find any appearances on the news.'

'Man, I'm really sorry about this.' Sam apologised as he again pulled out his phone.

'Don't worry,' said Stanton absently; he was more engaged by the information scrolling across the technician's screen.

Sam moved to the doorway, 'Bonjour again, Celeste! What's the problem now?' He paused, listening. 'Shit. You're kidding. And have you tried to reinitiate the protocols on the main server?' He paused again. 'Well that's just great ... okay ... okay ... no, I'll get Andy across to you guys tonight or first thing tomorrow. The last thing I need is for this thing to get screwed up just before the launch.' He shook his head and made a rolling eyes face at Lisa. She smiled supportively. 'Okay, I'll speak to you soon.' He hung up the phone. 'Dammit!'

Seconds later the computer system finished its search. 'Nothing on video except tonight's stuff,' announced the technician.

'So there's no motive within *Alter Ego*,' said Stanton. 'That's pretty odd.'

'Doesn't look like it,' said Lisa, equally perplexed.

'Well, we better get moving anyway.' He offered Sam his hand. 'Thanks for the help, Sam. We'll be back in touch if this isn't our guy.'

'No problem,' Sam smiled.

'Thanks,' said Lisa as she and Stanton walked out to the car.

'And good luck!' Sam called from the door.

Stanton drove fast through wet streets to North London and Grendel's flat. It took a little over an hour and it was almost half past midnight when they arrived. A squad car was parked outside the flat.

Stanton parked and they crossed to where one policeman wearing a large waterproof overcoat was standing at the main door to the tenements. There were heavy clouds in the sky and a light drizzle was falling.

'Hello,' said the officer as Stanton and Collier showed their IDs. 'We've got him upstairs. Two officers are in questioning him with his parents.'

'His parents?' Lisa said confusedly.

'He lives with his parents,' the officer clarified. 'He said he got the game from his friend who had got his older brother to buy it. He says he's really sorry about hitting the guy tonight. I dunno what he's on about with that. Did I hear something about him being a multiple murder suspect?'

'We'll see,' said Stanton walking into the building shaking his head.

They took the dingy and muggy stairs up to the third floor where a second officer let them into Derek's parents' flat. Derek Armstrong sat on the sofa beside his mother who was wearing a bathrobe. His father, wearing striped pyjamas, sat on an armchair set up to face the room's television. An officer was asking questions as Stanton and Lisa entered the hall of the flat. The boy looked about thirteen and had a lot of spots and long hair. He was at the gangly stage where his body had grown taller recently but hadn't had time to fill out yet, and his fading Nirvana T-shirt swamped him. He was crying quietly at the stress of it all. He didn't look the sort who usually had dealings with the police, and having them wake him and his parents up to question him about a computer game he shouldn't have been playing was proving too much for him to cope with.

'That's not him,' Lisa observed from the living room door. 'He's too young and too thin. Damn it!'

The questioning officer was grilling the boy about playing the 18-certificate game. His parents were getting flack for allowing it too.

'I knew you shouldn't have been playing those games, Derek,' his mother was saying. 'Rubbish your mind, they will. I told him, officer. You might as well take him and lock him up. It'll be the ruin of him sitting there every night at that computer. I tell him that.' She rambled on, talking over her son and the questioning officer. The father merely sat looking very red and angry. The boy would doubtless get a good hiding for having the police round to the house—especially so late.

Stanton called over the officer who was doing the questioning, 'He's not our guy.'

'How do you know?' asked the policeman.

Lisa replied: 'I had a hold of the guy we're after hanging from a window last night and he was about twice the size of this boy here. I know it's not him.'

There wasn't even any point in questioning Derek about tonight and his attack on Frank. He was just a kid who had presumably seen the interview on the news service and figured he'd have a go at being a hitman or a hero or whatever he thought the attack would make him.

'So what shall we do with him, sir?' asked the officer.

'Oh, I don't know.' Stanton opened the door to leave. 'Whatever comes to mind.'

'Er, okay. I will do, sir.'

Back in the car Stanton began to vent his frustration: 'I should have thought about this, you know. I mean, if this Armstrong kid has been playing for three and a half months and has been killed eight times, he couldn't be Grendel.'

Lisa nodded, although Stanton hardly noticed.

He continued: 'Based on what Stella was saying about getting a two week penalty when you get killed, someone who has been killed eight times and has only been playing for a *maximum* of three and half months *couldn't* be Grendel because he's had no time in the game. Shit, and here we are traipsing across the country to arrest a bloody thirteen year old kid who's illegally playing the game.'

'But we had to check it out, Jack.' Lisa tried to make Stanton feel the trip was justified. And she was right; someone did have to check Derek Armstrong out. Admittedly uniformed officers could have done it considering the unlikelihood that they had caught Grendel. But then hindsight was always a great thing.

'And nothing in the video archives except tonight's stuff.' Stanton hit the steering wheel in frustration. 'We should have known.' He wanted to catch Grendel and now he knew they had shown their hand. It was frustrating. 'And now everyone in the City knows that the Action Heroes are hunting someone – including Grendel.'

'I know,' Lisa said quietly. 'We'll just need to hope we didn't scare him off tonight. At least we know if Grendel does appear that the Action Heroes are likely to get him. I mean, they made mincemeat of young Derek.' Lisa tried to find the brighter side. 'And half of that building.' She laughed quietly.

Stanton smiled. Lisa was right: what had happened had happened. They just had to hope for tomorrow. 'Of course, young Derek was exactly that: he was young,' said Stanton. 'We'll see how they do against someone who fights back. And I'd imagine Grendel won't go down quite so easily.'

'We'll find out if and when he appears.'

Stanton pulled up outside Lisa's flat. 'I'll pick you up at eight tomorrow. I want to check in at the office before we go back up.'

'Okay, Jack. And thanks for the lift.' She got out of the car then leaned in again so Stanton could hear her, 'And Jack?'

'Yes?'

'We're going to get him.' She closed the door and walked up to the main door to her flat. She got her keys out from her bag, her arm feeling very stiff and painful as she unlocked the door. Stanton waved as she went in then drove off.

It had been another long day and it was with a weary body that Lisa stepped over the two boxes that she still hadn't put back into the hall cupboard. She peeled off her clothes and fell into bed, only stopping to pour herself a glass of water to wash down a couple of pain-killers.

Back at his own flat Stanton checked his answering machine which was flashing the number two on its small display. The first caller hung up and the second message was from his father. He sounded drunk.

'Hello, Jacky. How's it goin'? Listen I need to meet you. Gonay gee me a call and we'll meet up. I'm in a spot of bother, Jacky. And you wouldn't leave your old man in the lurch, would you? Geeza phone, that's a good lad.'

Stanton shook his head. His father only ever called him when he needed money to pay rent or buy someone a present or whatever other excuse he could come up with so he could get money for more booze or to pay off his gambling debts. It had been like that since his brother Simon had died back in 1982. And like every previous time he'd called, Stanton wouldn't be calling him back. If his dad really was in trouble *he'd* call back. More likely he'd be too drunk to remember making the call and Stanton wouldn't hear anything more. That's what usually happened.

He decided to watch some television despite the late hour. He rifled around in the cabinet under the television and soon found *The Great Escape*. 'Just the job,' he said, peeling the plastic wrapping from the tape and pushing the cassette into the player. He set it to scan forward and sat down on his favourite chair, pulled the lever on the side to swing the leg rest into place and then held both armrests as he pushed the back of the chair to a more reclined angle. His ideal viewing position was achieved just as the forwarding reached the opening titles. He pressed play.

Stanton had fallen into a fitful sleep before Steve McQueen had even been thrown into the cooler for the first time. His dreams were again filled with the walk on the moor, the explosions. Simon. Simon! SIMON! He wept uncontrollably as he held Simon's mutilated and limbless body. Then, through the tears he realised he was no longer on the moor, but now sat on the floor of Braithewaite's fridge in a pool of blood; and tonight, Simon's face was also missing.

27 September, 7:59am, Outside Collier's Flat

The next morning, a dark-eyed Stanton sat waiting outside Lisa's flat at eight o'clock sharp. An embarrassed Lisa was less on-the-ball and had given him a five more minutes gesture from her second floor window, so he was searching for a news channel on the radio while he waited. Seconds later he sat in a state of shock as the announcer talked: '… self-proclaimed murderer has given a statement by telephone to a local newspaper, confessing to a series of murders. The unidentified caller also used the call to describe how he had removed the faces of each of his victims and placed them on the backs of their heads. So far no one on the investigation team has been available to give comment on the murders the caller claims to have committed, and at present we have no further details on the man already branded "The Janus Killer"'. Stanton couldn't believe what he had heard. He switched off the radio as the announcer moved on to give the weather forecast and jumped as Lisa opened the door.

'Sorry—' Lisa began, before noticed Stanton's ashen face. 'What is it? You look as white as a sheet.'

'Grendel seems to have gone to the papers.'

'No way. How_'

'They're calling him the Janus killer.'

'Did they mention *Alter Ego*?'

'No, they just said he made a statement to a newspaper stating he had committed some murders and that he'd removed the faces of his victims and placed them on the back of their heads. Pretty graphic stuff for a Media confession.'

Lisa looking sickened. 'That's just super. And now the Media have got themselves a nice new story and a catchy name for the sick killer who's still at large. This is just great.

Do we know it was definitely Grendel who contacted the papers?'

'Well apart from you, Forensics and myself, no one knows about the mutilations except Grendel. And why would Forensics call it in?' Stanton paused. 'And even then, why the hell would Grendel do it?'

'I suppose he maybe wants the publicity,' Lisa suggested. 'You know how they always seem to think that serial killers want to be caught at some level. Maybe that's what it is.'

'But why go to such extremes to keep the crime scenes free of incriminating evidence if that's the plan?'

'I don't know. Maybe it's part of the twisted game he's playing. One thing is for sure though, the press are going to have a field day with this.' Lisa shivered again at the thought of Grendel promoting his acts in the news newspaper. 'It's sick, but the press are like moths round a candle with stuff like this. There's nothing quite like a mutilating serial killer to keep the masses reading your rag.' She shook her head.

They drove to the office, mulling over the implications of what Stanton had heard. When they had to drive towards a throng of reporters and TV crews at the main gate to their office's building, they realised exactly what the implications were: a media circus.

'Try to look unconcerned for the cameras, and don't say anything as we drive through,' said Stanton.

Flashes assaulted their eyes as photographers and reporters pressed against their car, which Stanton had slowed to a snail's pace to make sure he didn't run anyone over. They could hear the muffled questions through the windows:

'Do you have any prime suspect in this case?'

'How many Janus murders have there been?'

'Are you close to finding the killer?'

'Are all the murders local to London?'

And then the one shock question they didn't want to hear: 'Are the murders related to the Janus characters in the *Alter Ego* computer game?'

How the hell could they have made that connection already? Stanton thought.

'Was the manhunt in the game last night an attempt to identify the killer?' All questions about *Alter Ego* were from one reporter.

'Is the killer murdering people he's selected from within a computer game?' Others were now joining in now and the atmosphere was rising to fever pitch.

Shit, shit, shit! Stanton's mind raced. That reporter had somehow made the connection that the loosening of Janus's power in *Alter Ego* was related to these murders. The question was: how? There had to have been a leak. But who would have anything to gain by leaking the information? Or maybe this reporter was a player in *Alter Ego* and had witnessed the ebb of Janus's control, or maybe he was just guessing. Stanton felt increasingly frustrated, eventually revving the engine high and letting the clutch up a little for a fraction of a second. The car jumped quickly forward by about three inches, just enough to cause the reporters and news crews to push away from the car enough to enable him to speed away.

'Well that's just great, isn't it?' Lisa said. 'How could they possibly have made the connection with the game?'

'I don't know, either a lucky guess, because it was only really one guy who was asking about the game, or there's a leak. Either way, this thing is gathering a lot of momentum in not a lot of time.'

'You're not kidding.'

Stanton pulled the car up outside the office. They could see photographers with zoom lenses snapping off pictures of them before a uniformed officer moved them along. They were in their office five minutes later.

Stanton had four messages. Lisa had a pile of paperwork from admin that had to be filled in so she would be paid correctly. The only good thing was the fact that her arm wasn't up to any of it. She'd need to drop in and sort it out when she had time.

Stanton's face was stoney. He had a note from Patrick saying that Tyler *was* online the Thursday that Swift was killed; he had double-checked with the email company.

'How the hell can that be?'

'What's that?' asked Lisa.

'Patrick is saying that Tyler's email account was accessed last Thursday, the night Swift was killed.'

'But I thought Tyler was dead, you know, the guy who plays Tyler. I mean wasn't he the first person in the game whose character didn't wake up?'

'He was. At least that's what we've been told by Stella. But the details of the email account have been double-checked and it *was* accessed by somebody.'

'Were there any messages written or was it just checked?'

'It doesn't say here. I'll need to ask Patrick.'

'It doesn't make sense: if Tyler isn't dead, why has he not told any of the others? They said they've not had any replies from him?'

'You don't think Grendel has got the details of the account and is using it, do you?' Lisa's distaste for Grendel was written all over her face.

'I don't know. But we do need to find out if there have been any mails sent out, because that might be a clue. I mean, this guy might have just decided he was cutting his ties with the other Janus people and that's why he's not replying to them. He's maybe just stopped playing *Alter Ego*. I'll get

Patrick to find out if there were any emails sent recently and to mail the account and see if *we* can get a reply.'

'I suppose there's also the possibility that someone shares the account with Tyler,' Lisa said.

'Maybe, but why they didn't come to the police if they found him dead with his face cut off is a bit of a mystery then.'

'Assuming they were in the same place.'

'I suppose.' Stanton picked up the phone and dialled Patrick's lab. It rang twice.

'Patrick Bateson.'

'Hi, Patrick.'

'Hi, Jack. How are you?'

'Not wonderful.'

'Yes, I heard the news this morning and I saw all the press people outside on my way in today. I take it they were for you?'

'It would seem so. Our psycho murderer has decided to involve the press for some reason.'

'Any idea why?'

'Not yet.' Stanton got down to business: 'Patrick, do you know if any emails were sent out from the Tyler email account or was it just checked?'

'I think it was just being checked. They didn't say anything about it being used to send anything.'

'Hmm. Can you do me a favour and find out? And can you send an email to the account too, saying who you are and see if whoever is using it will reply to you.'

'I can do. What are you hoping for?'

'Well as far as we knew, the guy who uses the account is dead, so it's pretty weird that someone is now using it. But there is the possibility that he's just decided he doesn't want to play *Alter Ego* any more and that he's just not replying to

Janus emails. Hopefully that's what's happened, and maybe a simple email will mean we've got one less body to look for.'

'Okay, Stanton. I'll get onto that this morning and get back to you when I hear.'

'Thanks, Patrick.'

Stanton's second phone call was to the coroner. His stomach tightened at the thought of talking to the polite little man with Stanton's own personal worst nightmare of a job.

'Can I speak to Albert Steadman please?'

'Speaking.'

'It's Jack Stanton here.'

'I'm just returning your call about the Braithwaite murder.'

'Hold on for just one second.' Stanton, like the last time, held the phone away from his ear as Steadman shuffled and bumped around in his search of his desk for the right file. 'Here it is. Are you still there?'

'I certainly am.'

'It's fairly well the same kind of thing we encountered last time, I'm afraid. Let me see now…' He paused as he murmur-read down to the relevant area. 'Ah, yes. Here we go. His reading voice took over: '"Mr Braithwaite's body was found lying on his side in a large custom-built refrigerator in his garage. Initial examination to ascertain cause of death revealed a single puncture wound on the right side of the subject's back. The autopsy confirmed that the resultant piercing wound had a trajectory in the direction of the heart, the blade initially pierced between the third and fourth rib where it travelled to cause fatal damage to the heart. Cause of death: severe sharp trauma to the left ventricle. Death would have been almost instantaneous. The wound suggests Mr Braithwaite was stabbed from behind, probably taken by surprise.

'In a similar manner to the case of Niall Davidson (File Ref.: FR43 ... blah blah), Mr Braithwaite's face was removed post-mortem. The same level of inexperience was evident in performance of the surgery to remove the facial tissue, although in the case of Mr Braithwaite the depth of the incisions was greater, resulting in the entire face remaining relatively intact on removal. The depth of cutting also accounts for the removal of most of the left eye and nose."' He scanned down to more relevant information with a 'Dat-da-rah-dat-dat.'

'"The facial tissue appears once again to have been placed on the back of the head, evidenced in this case by small pieces of tissue and a large amount of blood in the hair of that area. The facial tissue itself was found on the floor of the fridge, where it appears to have fallen due to the body's orientation on its side."' Steadman cleared his throat, 'So, Mr Stanton, we've basically got a stabbing, followed by another face removal etcetera, etcetera, with obvious similarity to the Davidson case.'

'Was there anything like tissue under his fingernails or anything else that would link someone to this murder?'

'I'm afraid not. It would seem Mr Braithwaite was caught totally unawares and didn't get the chance to struggle with his attacker.'

'Damn it!' Would they never get a break? Stanton's mind screamed. 'Sorry, I don't mean to vent my frustration on you, Mr Steadman.'

'Don't worry, Mr Stanton. These murders are tough on everyone.'

Yes, except you seem totally unfazed by them, Stanton thought.

'Anyway,' Steadman continued, 'I'll get the report in the post to you today. And if there's anything you would like to ask about, just give me a call.'

'I will do.' Stanton hung up. 'What a fun morning,' he said to Lisa who had been listening to the calls Jack had been making for scraps of information.

'I know.' Lisa said, raising her eyebrows.

'And we've got to go and see Mayfield this morning as well. It just gets better and better.' Stanton held up the next of his messages. 'And I'm sure he's thrilled about the press camping out front.' Stanton looked down at the last message on his desk: from Forensics. He dialled.

'Richardson,' the male voice reported.

'It's Stanton. Have you found anything?' he asked hopefully.

'I'm afraid not. I'm just calling to say that all of the prints, hair and fibre samples we took from the scene belonged to Mr Braithwaite. We've still got people going through the scene with a fine-toothed comb, but we haven't turned up anything useful so far.'

'Not even a rogue print or hair or anything?'

'I'm afraid not. The smear marks we dusted from door handles and the banister have been left by someone wearing leather gloves, the sort you can buy in almost any high street clothes shop. And all the hairs are Braithwaite's. So I'm afraid we've no good news. We'll keep you informed of any progress we make.'

'Thanks,' Stanton said. 'Has the Davidson house still not turned anything up?'

'No, I'm afraid not. We've been through everything, and again we've only got evidence of Mr Davidson himself. I'm sorry.'

'It's not your fault. We've obviously just got an extremely careful killer. Anyway, keep me informed.' Stanton hung up.

'Nothing at all from either scene?' Lisa said.

Stanton nodded. 'Nothing.'

'So Grendel is still in control of this game.'

Ten minutes later Collier and Stanton were sitting in Mayfield's office.

'Why are there news reporters swarming round the front gate, Jack?'

'It seems our killer has decided to tell the press about his killings. I only heard about it on the radio this morning; they were already here when we got here.'

'And are we any closer to finding out who the killer is?' Mayfield's brow was low as he looked over his glasses, his eyes bouncing between the two detectives.

'Not so far, sir,' Stanton responded. 'Forensics haven't found anything at all at either of the crime scenes and we're still trying to catch the perpetrator within the computer game. We're hoping we will be able to coerce him out soon.'

'The computer game the victims have been selected from.' Mayfield said slowly as he sat back in his chair, turning slightly so he could glance out of the window. 'Have we nothing more concrete than trying to find some Space Invader for these heinous crimes?'

'I'm afraid not, sir,' said Lisa, a little nervous that they were defending the computer game hunt – something neither she nor Stanton really would have chosen if there had been the possibility to avoid it. 'It's our only lead, and if we manage to catch him in the game, we'll have all his details. The game is our best chance to find the killer.'

'Uh-huh.'

'And considering all of the victims belong to a group known as the Janus organisation within the *Alter Ego* game, and that the mutilations of the bodies correlate to the Janus name - each victim's face was removed and placed on the back of his head - we're sure we're on the right tracks with the investigation.'

'Janus, the god of entrances, of going in and coming out,' Mayfield said quietly.

'Indeed, sir,' said Lisa.

'And how is the Robertson girl?' Mayfield asked. 'How is she coping with the prospect of being this Janus killer's next victim?'

'She's pretty close to cracking, I'm afraid, sir,' said Stanton. 'Our perpetrator managed to get into her flat on Tuesday night.'

'Yes, I heard about that particular fiasco. Well done, Collier.' Mayfield nodded at Lisa before he continued in a stern voice, 'Although why the situation was allowed to progress that far is beyond my comprehension. I don't know what sort of police protection that was supposed to be. How is your arm anyway?' His voice softened as he asked.

'Not too bad, sir. It's a bit stiff now, but I'll be okay.'

'Good.' Mayfield pondered the whole situation for a moment as he looked at the sky out of the window. 'So what do you plan to do now?'

Stanton replied: 'We're going to press on with the plan. We're going to try to get him to show himself in the game again and try to catch him. We've got an officer in with Miss Robertson at all times now. And apart from that we'll just need to try to keep the press from getting too much information that could hurt the investigation.'

'Keep me informed, Jack. I mean it.'

'Yes, sir!' Stanton almost snapped to attention as he replied.

'And Collier.' He paused. 'Take care of yourself.' His eyes crossed to Stanton 'Both of you.'

'I will, sir. Thank you, sir.' Lisa blurted. A curt nod was Stanton's acknowledgement.

27 September, 11:53am, Theydon Bois

Stella Robertson was running as fast as she could. Behind her was a man wearing a balaclava carrying a large knife. He wasn't gaining on her, but she couldn't outrun him.

As her mind raced in the inescapable nightmare of her drug-induced sleep, her body tossed and turned, sweat slick on her face and chest. Her bedclothes were kicked down, tangled round her lower legs.

'Stella,' the voice said. 'Stella.' Her body was being shaken by her shoulders.

She pushed at the hands of the balaclaved man as he pulled at her. 'No, No, NO!' Her mumbles became a scream.

'Stella, wake up,' Lisa shook Stella harder as her eyes rolled high into her head. The lids opened quickly then slowly shut again. 'Wake up, Stella, you're having a nightmare.' Lisa wiped a cold damp cloth over Stella's brow.

'Don't cut me,' Stella mumbled. 'Please.' She was crying in her sleep.

Lisa looked at Stanton and the officer standing in the hall. 'What did the doctor give her? It's half past eleven and she still seems drugged to the eyeballs.'

'I'm not sure,' said the officer. 'I just know he gave her an injection to calm her down.'

'Come on, Stella. Wake up.' Lisa placed the cool wet towel on Stella's forehead; a trickle of water ran down past her ear to the sweat-damp pillow.

Stella could feel the cold clammy hand of the killer on her forehead as he stroked her face. The knife was being slowly scraped close to her ear. She shivered uncontrollably, her breathing becoming wheezy. 'Please don't kill me,' she pleaded. The man suddenly and quickly used the knife to slit her throat. She gasped for breath clutching her throat with her hands to try to stifle the wound.

Lisa sat back, watching Stella in her wheezing convulsion as she clawed at her throat.

Stella noticed there was no blood on her hands. She felt at the wound: there was no injury. 'No!' she screamed in a short burst aimed at the balaclavaed man as he lashed out at her again. 'No, you son of a bitch, you are *not* going to hurt me.' She fought back her breathlessness and launched herself at her assailant. 'You're not going to fucking kill me, you bastard!' she shrieked as she knocked him to the ground. Seizing the momentary advantage of the situation she quickly knelt on his arms and sat down heavily on his chest. He gasped for air. She grabbed the large kitchen knife from his grasp and paused for a few seconds looking at it. Abstractly she became aware it was her own missing knife, the one Grendel had taken when he violated her home. 'You sick fucker,' she said quietly and deliberately. The eyes peering through the holes in the balaclava opened wide as she lifted the blade high above her head in both hands. It hung momentarily before she slammed it down into his chest.

Stella's eyes shot wide open, and she sat up with a series of loud breaths. Her hand flailed out to her bedside table, grabbing instinctively for her inhaler. She barely noticed Lisa as depressed the plunger.

Stanton sat in the living room with the other officer while Lisa helped Stella sort herself out. Lisa came through. 'She's in a pretty bad way. She's just staring all the time and nodding.'

That's not so good,' Stanton said. 'Do you think she's going to be able to play Vincent?'

'Right now? I don't know. I'm hoping she's still coming out from the tranquilliser, but...' Lisa trailed off.

'Hmm. What do you think we should do?'

'Didn't you say you'd tried this game when we were up there last night?'

'Yes, Sam gave me a quick demo.'

'How hard was it to play?'

'Are you thinking you could be Vincent?'

'Well it would make the most sense. Especially when Stella is so volatile.' There was a noise from Stella's room. 'Hold on a sec.' Lisa went through to see Stella.

In the other room, Stella was now dressed in her usual fleece and sweatpants. Lisa squatted down next to her. 'Stella, Vincent is still alive. We found out that he was only unconscious. Some of the people took him away and have been looking after him.' Stella's gaze remained fixed. 'We need to get Vincent out on the streets, Stella, so we can catch Grendel.'

Stella nodded and turned her eyes and focused for the first time that day. Lisa looked into the deeply-sunken blue eyes that were probably usually quite pretty. The bloodshot whites and the slowly-moving eyelids told of the horror Stella was living. Lisa noticed that her pupils were still slightly dilated too, the hangover from the calming drugs. 'Are you staying with me?' Stella said hoarsely.

Lisa nodded, looking into Stella's eyes. 'I can, if you want me to.'

Stella's eyes visibly hardened as she whispered, 'I'd like that.' She swallowed. 'Thank you.' Her voice was clearer.

'Listen, Stella, we need Vincent out there today. Do you think you're up to it?'

Stella gave Lisa a new look that made her shiver. Lisa had never seen her like this before. Was this what people looked like when their lives were threatened and they were not prepared to lie down and accept the outcome? Lisa didn't know, but the look on Stella's face did not look like that of someone who was going to take any more of this. Stella began slowly: 'I want this bastard dead. And I'm going to do everything I can to do that. This shit has taken my life and I am not accepting it any more. So, yes, I'm ready.'

Lisa nodded slowly. 'Good.' She paused before continuing, 'There's something else you should know.' She tried to think of the best way to tell Stella what she had to say. 'Grendel has gone to the newspapers and given a graphic confession to them about the killings he's committed so far.'

Stella didn't say anything, although her face turned a little whiter. Lisa hoped she wasn't about to have another asthma attack.

She didn't.

'Stella, we didn't tell you before, but now you'll probably hear about it either on the news or from someone in *Alter Ego*, so you should hear it now.'

'Go on,' Stella's voice was hard as if whatever was going to be said would only compound her hatred for Grendel.

'Grendel has been cutting off the faces of his victims.'

Stella blinked three or four times then rubbed her eyes with two fists. When she removed the hands her eyes were wet. But she was still in control. Her breathing didn't falter at all. The tears were for Niall, her friend, who didn't deserve to die and certainly didn't deserve to be treated like that. 'Why has he been doing it? Is it a serial killer trophy thing?'

'No,' Lisa said. 'He's been putting the faces on the back of their heads at the crime scene. It seems to be a kind of trademark.'

Stella gave a single "hmf" sound then simply said, 'Janus.'

'Yes. Janus. We didn't want to have to tell you. But now he's made it public, I'd rather you found out from me than from the media or some *Alter Ego* voyeur.'

Stella wiped a single rogue tear from her cheek as she turned to look at Lisa, 'I appreciate that, Lisa. I really do.' Stella's thoughts were still on Niall. He hadn't done anyone any harm. His life shouldn't have ended so brutally. Stella decided as she sat that she sure as hell wasn't having some psycho son-of-a-bitch kill and mutilate her. Not if she could help it. She was going to take Vincent out and when Grendel showed up she was going to make him pay. And then the police would catch the sick bastard and lock him away and throw away the key.

Lisa was concerned at Stella's silence: 'Are you okay?'

'Yes,' Stella nodded. 'I am.' And she looked it.

'So is she going in as Vincent?' Stanton asked.

Lisa nodded.

'And do you think she's up to it?'

'Let's hope so.' Lisa said quietly looking through to the living room where Stella sat. 'But I'd say she is.'

'So we're back in the game.' Stanton stated.

'We are. So, you better get on your way. I'll phone ahead for you and let Sam know what's going on.'

'Okay,' said Stanton. 'I'll call you later and see how things are going.'

'All right.'

'Good luck.' Stanton left.

27 September, 1:02pm, M6 Motorway

Stanton drove along the M1 heading North on his way to Binary Cityworks in Southam. It was a little after one o'clock so he flicked on the radio for the news. The third item was the one he wanted to hear. How much had the media worked out? What were they speculating? And would they be able to get Grendel before he got Stella?

The male news announcer's voice had the standard clipped news reporting quality: 'After the shock confession from the so called Janus Killer this morning, it is now thought that the popular computer game *Alter Ego* may hold the key to the selection of the alleged victims and the reasons for the mutilations. Our Technology Editor David Stevens has been investigating.'

Another voice took over: 'It seems that over the last weeks a situation has been brewing in one of the most popular computer games ever to be released, *Alter Ego*. *Alter Ego* is one of the so-called Massive Multiplayer Online Role Playing Games where all characters in the game are in fact other players and the game world itself is persistently online. This type of game has been found to have an addiction level higher than that of crack cocaine and with subscription levels estimated to be doubling each year.

'The highly popular *Alter Ego* world is a virtual city where people become their own invented alter egos, characters of their own choosing who do whatever the player wishes. A hyper-evolution of Internet chat rooms of yesteryear, the *Alter Ego* City has inhabitants who trade, talk, drive cars and kill each other in a contemporary version of a 1920s gangster town.

'Witnesses who were playing the game last night talked of heavily armed hunters capturing someone who attacked a member of a group who work for a person called Mr Janus. Further investigation led us to discover that Janus was considered until recently to be the undisputed overlord of the *Alter Ego* City. His control was not however seen by everyone as popular, with the brutal regime adding an element to the game which some found distasteful. In recent weeks the grip of Janus has lessened, leading to the rather macabre possibility that the murders which the Janus killer confessed to this morning bear some relation to the demise of the Janus organisation within the game world.

'The god Janus from Roman history is conventionally visualised as a man with one face on the front and one on the back of his head, and the similarity of this to the mutilations described by the caller is difficult to dismiss.

'At this time we have no way to corroborate the events within the game; and with only a few eye witness accounts it is proving difficult to distinguish what is really going on from the wave of wild speculation. It is not even possible to visit the virtual city to clarify the situation since obtaining a copy of *Alter Ego* is almost impossible. All major high street shops we've visited this morning say they have sold out of the game due to a purchasing surge from people who intend to witness what will doubtless be one of the most dramatic and unusual manhunts ever undertaken by the police.

'Employees of Binary Cityworks, the game's developer, have so far declined to comment on the events happening within the game world, and the police have not yet made an official statement on the case. But we'll bring you news as and when we get it. This is David Stevens for the lunchtime news.' The first voice returned, 'The industrial tribunal looking into the...'

Stanton switched the radio off. It was worse than he thought: people flocking to the game to see the hunt and reporters flocking round Binary Cityworks. This could only make the situation worse.

He was right. As he approached the office at Pendicke Street, Stanton saw half a dozen reporters and a couple of camera crews hanging around the front door. He decided to park in the nearby supermarket car park and make his approach on foot. As he neared the front door the reporters clocked him for the detective he was.

'Are you one of the detectives working the Janus case? Would you care to comment on the investigation?'

'No comment,' Stanton replied.

'Is there going to be a second attempt to capture the suspect within the game city today?'

'No comment.'

'Are the killer's confessions about mutilating the bodies true?'

Stanton grabbed the young male reporter by his lapels and slammed him against the Cityworks office windows, which wobbled at the blunt impact. 'Listen, people have been killed by this psycho, who we're doing our utmost to catch; and others are still in extreme danger. Do you really think it will help the case if I tell you anything considering all it will do is fuel your insatiable tendencies for speculation? We will release a full statement as and when it is the correct time to do so. Until then we have no comment. Okay!' He roughly released the reporter and pushed open the door into the reception area of Cityworks, a beefy security guard made sure the reporters stayed outside.

'Nightmare,' said Stanton to no one in particular.

'Indeed, sir,' replied the guard.

'Hi. Is Sam around?' Stanton asked the receptionist.

'I'm afraid not. I've been asked to get Andy for you instead. I'll just give him a call. Your partner called about half an hour ago. Andy'll fill you in on the details.'

'Thanks.'

Two minutes later Andy walked into reception. 'Dude.' He said in welcome, extending his hand. Today he wore large denim flares and a striped shirt.

'Hi, Andy,' Stanton said shaking his hand. 'How are you?'

'I'm truckin' man. How's it hangin' with you?'

'I've been better.' Stanton gestured to the reporters visible through the glass.

'Those cats are, like, blood-suckers, man. They just look for things to peck the eyes out of, man.'

'You're not far wrong.' Stanton said as Andy punched in the code to access the back offices. 'Where's Sam today?'

'He had to go to Paris, man. I don't fly too good, and I need lots of time to prepare my mind and soul. So Sam had to go to Paris instead of me. Man was he pissed.' Andy laughed quietly in his throat, his eyes giving Stanton a crazy *but-what's-he-gonna-do* roll.

'Okay,' Stanton said slowly, smiling at just how hippy Andy could come across. Somehow it didn't surprise him that Andy didn't fly. In many ways it was odd that a figure like Andy was involved in hi-tech anything. 'So, how's it going with the Heroes?'

'We've got them locked away in one of the news reporter's flats in the City. The place is, like, teaming with people, dude. The trains have been getting busier all day.' He opened his eyes wide as his hands gestured at his words. 'I've not seen it this busy since, like, the Janus people first took power.'

'I meant did they have any problems with the press at their hotel?'

'Oh, sorry. I thought you meant, like, in the game. They all seemed swell this morning.' He was nodding. 'And they were all, like, totally here before the vultures arrived. So it's all cool.' Andy leaned in close, 'And dude?'

'Uh-huh.'

'I think, like, a couple of them stayed up last night watching those special movies at the hotel.' Andy nodded knowingly as he scratched his bearded chin.

'That's super, Andy.' Stanton nodded, humouring Andy.

They walked into the large offices. Reggie and the other Heroes were round the Coke machine in the corner. Their screens were up and running against the wall, so they were ready for action whenever they would be needed. Reggie waved at Stanton.

Stanton nodded then turned to Andy: 'Did you speak to Lisa about Stella?'

'Oh, yeah.' He nodded slowly as he smiled broadly.

'And is she up to speed?'

'Yup. I even gave her a few special tips myself.'

'Great. So we're ready to go again?'

'We are, like, totally ready,' Andy said in his drawly speech. His thumbs were up in confirmation.

27 September, 8:00pm, The City

'We were beginning to wonder when you'd come round,' says a woman's voice.

Vincent sits up stiffly, taking then releasing a long deep breath. He turns round to face the woman, 'Where am I?'

'You're in the Plaza in the back of one of the shops,' she replies, smiling. 'I'm glad you came back,' she says with a slight nod and a smile. 'I knew you guys wouldn't go down that easily. It was a shame about that other one getting knocked down by that cowardly attack last night. It just shows you how things have changed. A couple of months ago no one would have dared attack a Janus man in broad daylight. And now ... well ...'

'Do you still have my gun?' Vincent asks moving across to look through the room's one exit. He sees a shop front with gardening equipment on various stands and shelves around the room; ready for the shoppers to pick up and play with before they decide whether or not they want to purchase.

Things had come a long way in the year since Alter Ego *had gone online: websites that had previously been composed of simple lists and photos of products had swiftly become a thing of the past. Now the norm was online shops where you could go inside, virtually, and see fully-working simulated replicas of the products you might want to buy. The sub-businesses that generated the 3D models for these new online shops was a new boom industry that was making more than a few people into multi-millionaires.*

Vincent looks back at the woman who hasn't replied. 'My guns?'

'Yes, I've got them here.' She opens a cupboard and lifts the two machine pistols out and places them on a work surface that runs the length of the back wall. 'And your vest.'

She places the bulletproof vest on top of the gun then steps back.

'Thanks.' Vincent slips on the vest, fastening the Velcro at the sides to secure it; then he pulls on his shirt and his double holster. He takes the machine pistols and checks they are working correctly and have full clips of ammo before sliding them into their holsters under each arm. When he finally dons his long coat he looks like he usually does: rugged, masculine, hard-faced and remorseless. There is only one difference to usual: the four holes in the front of his clothes - a reminder in future to shoot first and ask questions later. Vincent is tooled up and ready for action. He takes another deep breath. He is ready to face Grendel.

'So are you going after the Outlaws?' the woman asks as he turns to leave.

'Sorry, how ill-mannered of me.' Vincent's face suddenly looks apologetic as he speaks. 'Thank you for taking care of me since the other night. And thank anyone else who was involved.'

'That's no problem. Just you get those guys.'

'Listen, I will. But first I've got to take care of a bit of personal business. Okay?'

'We figured you would. If someone were after me I'd want to do everything I could do to get them. I've seen all of that stuff on the news about the Janus Killer. That's one sick individual.'

'I know.' Vincent's face is extremely serious. 'Which is why I need to sort him out.'

'We understand.'

Vincent smiles and moves to the door. At the door he turns and says, 'And thanks again.'

'Good luck,' says the shopkeeper as he leaves.

He walks into the front of the shop which is on the ground floor of the Plaza where he had met with the shopkeepers previously. The lighting has all been replaced and most shops are boarded up with stickers over the boards that say, "RE-OPENING SOON". It doesn't look like the same bleak place he had been in before. There is some evidence of renewed violence in the mall, no doubt courtesy of the Outlaws, but things aren't nearly as bad as they had been when Kane was on his spree. Vincent lights up a cigarette as he walks past the large pool that has now been drained of its dark liquid. The feet of the statue he'd seen before stand to attention beside the remains of its body, shattered into different sized blue chunks on the pool bottom. The other figures are in similar scattered pieces: a head here, a part of an arm there, a torso. Vincent blows smoke into the air and sets off for the City streets.

He emerges from the entrance to the Plaza into a bright sunny mid-afternoon. There are white clouds sitting on the horizon and the sun is casting long shadows from the many residents of the City who are on the street. The place is busier than Vincent has ever seen it. He walks along Bushnell Road to the Mound then up and across Muzyka Street to the rooms the in-game media people use. He buzzes the door at the bottom.

'It's Vincent,' he says when the speaker activates. When the buzz comes he pushes the door open, letting it slam shut as he marches resolutely upstairs.

Blade opens the door for Vincent. The room looks crowded with the four Action Heroes and their equipment. Vincent nods at Blade as he enters before passing pleasantries with all of the Action Heroes. Both he and they profess their admiration for the other's group's dominant position within their game. They have never met before, but all are aware of the others' reputations.

Frank looks small beside the Heroes, his bruised face shows how effectively the boy had assaulted him the previous evening. One eye is almost closed and Vincent can see that the cut on his temple is deep where it protrudes from the large first aid patch that has been applied to it. 'How are you doing?' he asks Vincent.

'I've been better. Did you hear about what this sicko's been doing to the others?'

'I have.' Frank's head drops.

'Hey!' says Vincent lighting a fresh cigarette. 'We're going to get this guy. It might not be tonight, but we will get him.' His voice is upbeat.

'That's right, Vincent!' agrees Thorium. 'We are gonna kick this Grendel's ass and harvest his soul.'

Around the room smiles begin to break out on the faces of each of those present.

'Yeah, cos we're bad ass motherfuckers!' says Intruder standing up.

The other Action Heroes look stunned at Intruder's strong language. Vincent laughs for the first time in days, 'Yes we are. All of us!'

'Yes!' Blade says. 'We're gonna kick Grendel's sorry ass!'

They all laugh.

'Yes, we're gonna,' Striker isn't sure what to say to top the others' statements, 'waste his bastard bum.' It was a fair effort for Ryan Worthington in the Cityworks offices.

All of them are now on their feet, the smiles and enthusiasm obviously contagious. Some of those present would be playing in a game where their lives were at stake, but it doesn't seem to matter in this moment. They can do anything they want to.

In the viewing screen room Jack Stanton sat smiling. The camera that had been set up in the corner of the room clearly showed the Heroes and the Janus men. The looks of resolve and confidence were clearly visible on each face around the room. These people were the best players of two of the most popular games of all time, an incredible accolade when the numbers of people who played the games were considered. If anyone in this City could catch and kill Grendel, they could.

It didn't escape Stanton that the screen in front of him showed the common perceptions of what heroes should look like: manly, stubbled, rugged men who looked every bit like they could do just about anything. But in other rooms around the country he knew that the reality was quite different: in Theydon Bois sat an asthmatic female office worker, in Manchester a quiet unassuming bricklayer, and in Southam four database developers. For most people who would meet them, all would be considered to be a little bit odd, possibly socially not quite up to scratch, probably a bit geeky. Certainly not cool. But these were the people who would be taking the hunt to Grendel. They would never be mistaken for heroes in the streets of the real world. But in the virtual online computer worlds they were soon going to be in front of a massive viewing public in a high-stakes battle for real lives. And they were, without a doubt, elite troops for this battle.

27 September, 8:36pm,
The City

They would all be in contact through headsets this time, and Vincent and Frank would be wearing small shoulder-mounted cameras. The Heroes had a couple of each to give Vincent and Frank since they always carried spares, because there was nothing worse than breaking a piece of technology at a crucial point in a fight and losing because you couldn't tell someone else where to shoot.

The plan was a simple one: the Action Heroes would wait in the camera crew room until they knew the Janus men had definitely drawn out Grendel. That would keep the number of people who had come to the game to watch the hunt to a minimum before the action began. It would also mean there would be a delay in how long it would take the Heroes to get to Grendel, but they figured they'd be able to get to almost anywhere in the City in about ten minutes running at full tilt. And at least this way there was less chance that something would go wrong due to an excessive crowd building up round them. Only Vincent and Frank would attract crowds. They would each have a mobile unit following them broadcasting live. And this time anyone who made a move would be shot first and questioned later. There would be no repeat of the previous night's events.

They were all ready to go half an hour after Vincent had arrived.

'Okay, men, lock and load,' says Blade.

'Roger, Roger.'

'Roger that.'

'10-4.'

Vincent smiles at the Action Heroes, 'See you boys soon. We'll be in touch.'

Frank and Vincent leave the room and are met in the stairs by the two crews who will accompany them.

'Mr Vincent, do you have anything to say to the people of the City?'

'Just one thing,' Vincent looks into the camera lens: 'Grendel, we're coming for you.' His face is serious, his voice is hard and his eyes look like they are pure evil.

'Man,' says the cameraman.

They step out onto the street. The clouds which had been fluffy and white and on the horizon before are now dark and heavy and directly above them. The light gives the City a foreboding atmosphere. It is an ideal scene for a showdown. As long as Grendel decides to show.

Vincent heads down towards Bushnell Road, his assigned camera crew trailing behind him. Frank decides to head towards the west side of the City to see if he can draw Grendel out from there.

After half an hour of milling around, Grendel still hasn't appeared. Vincent's radio squawks as he begins to speak to Frank. He starts his question again: 'Hey, Frank, it's Vincent. Any joy?'

Frank's voice sounds like it is being broadcast across a radio as Vincent receives it. 'Frank to Vincent. No, it's all quiet on the western front. Over.'

Vincent smiles. 'Where are you going now? I'm going down to the waterfront.'

'I'll head across to the far side of the park then,' Frank replies.

'Okay. Keep in touch.'

'Roger, over and out.'

Frank's radio use amuses Vincent. He speaks next to the Action Heroes, 'How are you Heroes doing back there?'

Blade responds, 'We're ready to rock-and-roll whenever you are. Just say the word.'

'That's right,' Thorium says laughing. 'Just pick up the phone and dial 0800-DIAL-A-BADASS and we'll be right down.'

'Will do.' Vincent laughs. In his earpiece he can hear Frank laughing too. He looks around: there are a lot of people watching from a safe distance after the previous night's accidental deaths at the hands of the Heroes. As he makes his way to the waterfront down the Bleszinski Walkway the sheer amount of people on the streets is more than he's ever seen in the City. Word of mouth and the live news broadcasts made it impossible for anyone in the City not to be aware that the Janus men were on the prowl for someone. And from the real world news, the speculation made sure the people at least had an inkling that the reason was to find out who was behind the Janus killings. It was a compelling and tense situation for every person who stood on the street, hung from a window or watched on a television somewhere in the City. And the watchers were growing in number every minute.

Another hour passes and the clouds begin to unload their contents. In the distance lightning strikes in jagged forks, the time between the bolts and the noise of the thunder revealing it is many miles away. Vincent stands in a doorway on Bushnell Road, the expectant crowds scattered around the streets and buildings nearby. Now that the sun is down he looks every bit like a character from a noir thriller as he stands in the doorway sheltering from the rain, smoking a cigarette. The rain falls through the barley-sugar coloured light cast by the street lamp in front of him and bounces off of the street, occasionally leaving bubbles where a large drop has impacted. Where they hit the tin casing of the lamp itself, they make a plinking sound.

Lisa picked up her phone and dialled Stanton in the screening room at Cityworks.

'Hey, tell the girl she's doing good,' Stanton said into his phone.

Lisa held her hand over the mouthpiece of her mobile and Stanton could hear some muffled words. *Vincent smiles as he stands in the doorway and nods, looking into the camera.*

'So what do you think, Jack?'

'Dunno. It's a pretty dead hunt really, isn't it?' Stanton looked at the large number of people on the screen. 'Even the Outlaws aren't doing anything. The whole City seems to be just watching and waiting.'

'I know. It's amazing how people are drawn to other people's misfortune,' said Lisa.

'I know what you mean. You end up watching like some kind of addict. It's pretty sickening really.'

'So do you think we should call it a night?' Lisa asked. 'Because maybe fewer people will waste another evening tomorrow,'

'Maybe. Let's give it another half an hour, because we need Vincent and Frank to be out there if Grendel is going to show otherwise we won't know he's there at all. If only there was something more we could do to entice him out.'

'Yes, but then if we had other options, we wouldn't be walking a beat in this game in the hope our murderer would turn up. Would we?'

'I suppose not. It's frustrating though.'

'Right then. Half an hour more.' Lisa hung up.

It was eleven o'clock.

At midnight it was decided that Grendel wouldn't show tonight. Vincent was going to go to his old safe house since that's where Grendel had found him the last time they had spoken. It was a slim hope that he'd reappear there at some stage, but it was a hope nonetheless.

Vincent walks up towards the safe house trailing about a hundred people behind him two hundred yards behind. 'So it looks like you boys are off duty now,' Vincent says to the Action Heroes through his headset. Frank has already gone back to the Janus building and has just logged off.

'Looks like it,' Thorium says.

'Yes, we'll see you tomorrow.'

'Good. See you then.' Vincent quickly moves through an alleyway keeping in the shadows before he ducks into another street. He pauses and waits to see if the crowd has spotted him. He can see people looking confused through the alleyway, but no one seems to know where he is.

On Stanton's viewscreen the image had switched from the TV crew view to Vincent's camera, confirming even the crew had lost him.

Vincent slips in the back door and makes his way upstairs to the room he has used so frequently. The carpet on the landing is soaking from the rain coming in through the damaged skylight. It makes a familiar squelching sound as he walks across it.

Stanton stood up, still looking at the screen. It had been a long night and he still had to get back to London. He walked to the back of the room to where Andy was standing.

'Bummer about the hunt, man.' Andy said.

'Yes, it's a pity.' Stanton rubbed his eyes. The low light levels and the prolonged viewing had left his eyes tired. 'I can't believe so many people were out in the City to see this.'

'I know, man. Our servers are busier than they've ever been.'

Stanton shook his head at the entertainment value the Janus group's misfortune was providing to the other players, but what could he do? Out of the corner of his eye he could see Vincent enter the room. The message, "YOU WILL BE NUMBER 4, STELLA. IT WILL BE SOON!" was sprawled over the wall. No wonder Stella was so scared, Stanton thought to himself. If it was his name up there, he'd have been pretty scared too all things considered.

'Hello, Stella.' A raspy voice came over the speakers.

Stanton scanned the screen. It was so dark in the shadows he couldn't see who had spoken, but the voice sounded creepy like Stella had told him Grendel had sounded. 'Grendel,' he said.

'Grendel,' Vincent said calmly. 'I didn't think you'd have the balls to come.'

Grendel laughed.

'Andy, get on the phone *now* and get the Action Heroes online again *immediately*. They need to get across to,' Stanton looked at the screen, his hands gesturing wildly as he tried to establish where they should go. 'There!' He pointed at the screen. 'Tell them to get there *now*!' He felt totally helpless as he was then forced to just sit down and wait to see if they could catch Grendel. He was vaguely aware of Andy "dude"-ing, "hurry"-ing and "like Grendel"-ing on the phone behind him as he listened to a very calm sounding Vincent talking to Grendel. Only the choice of words revealed any emotion.

'Because you are a chicken-shit-bastard. Did you know that?' Vincent said.

'Sticks and stones, Stella. Are you not enjoying our little game?'

'They'll catch you, you shit. I hope you know that.'

In the Pendicke Street office, the Action Heroes had not yet left the building, and now, like fighter pilots being scrambled to action, they each jumped into a chair in front of their respective consoles.

In the media office in the City, first Intruder's, then Blade's and Thorium's, and finally Striker's eyes snap open. Each hero quickly jumps to his feet grabbing his gear.

'Okay, gentlemen, this is not a drill. LET'S GO!' Blade opens the door and the four Heroes pile downstairs. It will take them seven minutes to run to where Vincent is.

'The Police? The Action Heroes? We'll see,' says Grendel. His voice is totally calm and in control. 'We'll see if they can.' Grendel lights a match, showing everyone but Stella what he looks like for the first time. 'I brought along a nice little gun to play with the Action Heroes. We'll soon see if they are as good as they think they are. I've been looking forward to a little game with them.'

'They'll kill your sorry ass and the police will be round knocking on your door before you know it, you sick fuck.' Vincent's face isn't visible, but the voice is unwavering.

'We'll see, Stella. Or maybe I'll kill the Action Heroes and then come round to your lovely house – nice colour scheme in the kitchen by the way – and slice off your face and make you into another of my nice little Janus sculptures. How would that be for an end to the game?'

'You're welcome to try, you sicko. I'm ready for you. Come and face me and we'll see if you're any good when you

aren't catching people unawares.' Vincent's voice is angry, not scared.

'Anyway, Stella, it's been nice to talk to you, but I have to go now. I've got a date with destiny ... well, with the Action Heroes anyway.' Grendel launches himself quickly at Vincent and miraculously manages to deliver a good blow with the same blackjack he'd used on him before. Vincent falls to the floor. The lens on the headset camera mounted just above his right ear cracks with the force of the impact.

Stanton got on the phone to Lisa immediately as he watched Grendel's feet walk out of the view of the cracked camera. He then heard the door open and Grendel's footsteps squelch towards the stairs.

28 September, 12:22am, Theydon Bois

Lisa's phone had only begun its ring tone when she pressed the pick-up button. 'Jack,' she said before he had a chance to speak. 'Vincent's been knocked out. It'll probably take about two or three minutes for him to come round.'

'Okay, the Heroes are on their way down the hill to the park just now. How's Stella?'

'She's angry as hell and twitching to get Vincent back on his feet.'

'Shit, I hope we don't lose Grendel.' Stanton could hardly sit still as he helplessly watched the screen.

The Heroes clack and puff loudly as they run down towards the large park and the road that Vincent's safe house is on.

'Vincent, this is Blade. Do you copy?'

Nothing but static.

'This is Blade, do you read me?'

Static.

The Heroes charge through the crowd of people who had lost Vincent and are now on their way to the Janus building in search of another Janus man to follow around. About half a dozen of them are knocked off their feet as the Heroes barge through, their legs pounding their huge boots across the tarmac on the way to face Grendel.

'Sorry.'

'Excuse us.'

'Coming through.'

The crowd turns and begins to run after the Heroes: no doubt where they were going meant a bad guy was going to get it. The crowd runs hard, but the Action Heroes are fitter, stronger and faster and are pulling out a fair-sized lead as they cross the grass.

'Okay guys, switch to night-vision, heat enhancement filter overlay,' Blade orders.

The screen in front of Stanton turned speckled green as four high-pitched whines marked the activation of the relevant technology. Heat signatures were visible as multi-coloured blobs overlaid on the night-vision background. The coloured images of people became more detailed as a Hero got closer to any person he viewed.

The first sign that Grendel is going to fight is when a tree next to the advancing Heroes explodes into splinters in the middle of its trunk. A passer by is crushed as the top of the tree falls freely now it has no support.

'Break left,' Blade barks. 'Two on two. Head for the building on the far side of the road. Intruder, find me our shooter.'

'Roger, Roger.' *Intruder throws himself onto his stomach and quickly switches his viewing mode to normal so he can scan the area ahead with his video scope. He moves the weapon left and right, looking for a target to lock onto. From the corner of his eye he sees the trace of another projectile tearing through the air. It explodes behind him killing six or seven of the now-fleeing crowd. Intruder scans across to where he thinks the shot originated, but there is no sign of anyone.*

'Striker in position.'

'Roger that, Thorium on the move.'

'Blade in position. Where's our man Intruder?'

'I can't see him. Intruder moving.' *Intruder's vision switches back to green as he runs for the next piece of cover ahead of Blade and Striker. He scans the buildings for signs of heat. He finds none. Thorium is ahead of him running as fast as he can, heading for a burnt-out vehicle by the side of the road ahead. Intruder continues to the far side of the road and the protection of a low wall. He quickly switches view modes again and starts scanning. 'Intruder in position! Scanning!' he yells into his headset.*

'Acknowledged. Moving.' Blade starts to run. He is immediately blown off his feet by an explosive projectile that hit less than ten feet away. He spits out an order, 'Thorium, lay down some covering fire on the buildings on the right.'

'Roger that.' Thorium stands and leans his weapon on the car wreck's roof. He sprays out about twenty-five projectiles that whine off on their course to the buildings. The explosions boom an echo up and down the road as giant balls of fire plume into the night sky lighting up thousands of tiny droplets of rain as they fall.

Blade begins a new run, this time making it to the corner of the buildings on the left, the objective point. The fireballs are turning to smoke as he squats down and raises his rifle to provide cover for the others.

Striker is behind a small wall about a hundred yards away on the side of the road nearest the buildings. The crowd is now about quarter of a mile away, watching the battle like it is some kind of fireworks display or a school playground fight.

Vincent shakes his head, trying hard to rise out of the blackness. As his vision clears he becomes aware that there is smoke in the room. He drags himself to his feet and stumbles towards the door. The hallway is missing its roof and the stairwell is now nothing but a pile of rubble about thirty feet below. The front of the building is simply gone, as are the fronts of most of the buildings on that side of the street. Vincent looks down where the stairs once were: there is no way to descend. He will have to scale down a drainpipe. His feet splash as he runs to the back of the building.

'Any sign yet, Intruder?' Blade asks.

'Nothing. He seems to be firing and then immediately displacing. He's good - and fast.'

'We're better!' Blade says as he walks forward into the street. His battle-armour is smoking from the left shoulder where a piece of shrapnel has embedded itself during his near miss earlier. His compression rifle is at his shoulder as he looks down its barrel, scanning the windows for Grendel.

In a third floor apartment Grendel shakes his head and pushes himself to a sitting position. His weapon has been damaged in the explosion and the rail driver is now non-operational. He edges forward, looking through the scope mounted on his weapon. As the smoke blows momentarily out of his field of view he can see Blade's muscled form slowly moving forward scanning in the street below. He fires off a single shot, hitting Blade in the thigh.

Blade goes down immediately from the impact, a spray of his own blood showering him where he lands. 'Third floor, fourth building, right hand side. Thorium, suppressing fire!' he commands.

Thorium drops his rocket launcher onto the roof of the car and swings the minigun from his back. The weapon screams as the barrels revolve and it blasts hundreds of projectiles into the third floors of the buildings. As Blade moves again into cover behind a car he is showered again, this time with fragments of building. The building looks like it is vibrating into small pieces as the slugs pepper it.

'Striker, get up there!' Blade yells, as he stops the bleeding from his thigh.

Striker runs and vaults over a car parked in the street. He lands fifteen feet from where he has jumped, but doesn't stop there. He uses the momentum to propel himself up the rubble in front of the building on the corner as if it were a makeshift stairway designed to quickly get him up to the third floor. 'Moving across now,' he says. 'Make sure you don't shoot me, Thorium!'

'Roger!' Thorium shouts over the noise from his gun.

Striker jumps between rooms that would have been separate flats if the walls still existed. He is closing in on Grendel's last known position. 'Cease fire, Thorium, I'm going in.'

'Roger that.' Thorium's finger lifts off of his trigger, where it stays, hovering. Ready.

Striker jumps into the room, taking no chances at all. His plasma rifle spits bolts of plasma in an arc across the room. But as his enhanced vision clears of the resultant explosions he sees no human-sized heat traces.

Grendel was gone.

'This is Striker. Grendel's gone. He must be on his way down to the street.'

Intruder runs across so he can train his weapon on the path that Grendel would need to cross to get out onto the street. He switches his vision to view his targeting screen as he lies flat on his stomach on the street.

Thorium is walking slowly: his minigun at hip height, its barrel sweeping back and forth, his trigger finger ready. When Grendel jumps across the path, the sounds of three weapons simultaneously erupt: Intruder fires and the air rips as his launched projectile makes its way into the sky above the buildings at the top of the street; Striker's plasma rifle spits five bolts that trail Grendel's running form but don't quite catch him before he makes the doorway at the far side; and Thorium's minigun screeches its projectiles into everything in the street ahead of him when he sees the bright coloured heat signature of Grendel running across his vision. It is nothing short of a miracle that Grendel isn't hit by any of them.

'Hold your fire! Hold your fire!' Blade is shouting into his headset as the vehicle he is behind is hit by dozens of Thorium's rounds.

An eerie silence descends on the street. Smoke blows and the rain patters the cars.

28 September, 12:47am,
The City

Vincent is in the area enclosed by the backs of all the buildings in the block. He moves quickly to cover the ground to the street because it sounds like the mother of all battles is being fought. He pulls both his guns from their shoulder holsters and sprints out through an alley. It takes him twenty seconds to move to a position where he can look down the street the Action Heroes are fighting their way up. The action has just stopped. Three guns quickly train on him.

'It's Vincent!' he shouts into the microphone sitting on his cheek. His guns are held in the air.

Blade gets to his feet as Vincent walks down to where he is. He motions for Vincent to get across to the side of the road Grendel has just moved to, so that the angle would be more difficult if Grendel decided to try to shoot him. Vincent moves quickly through the rain and stands against the wall of the end building. Both machine pistols hang from his hands, the muzzles pointing at the ground. Water drips from the tips of both barrels.

Striker climbs quickly onto the roof of the building he is in, never once turning away from the buildings opposite. Thorium and Blade move quickly towards the doorway Grendel had entered, while Intruder takes up position directly opposite. The Action Heroes have switched to hand signals to communicate now the place has gone quiet. Even the crowd which has moved in closer to continue watching the hunt aren't making any noise.

Blade orders his men into the building, signalling with a fist and a variety of other gestures not dissimilar to those used by soldiers in action films. The others nod their responses and run to fulfil the orders. Striker jumps down from the roof using the rubble like platforms to jump down to. Thorium walks carefully along the path to the open front door, while Intruder and Blade cover the front of the building.

It is momentarily even quieter for Thorium as he enters the doorway and kneels down. The only sound to break the silence comes from behind him as hundreds of feet move quickly onto the rubble on the opposite, destroyed, side of the street. Camera crews are also moving with the crowd, looking for the best locations to catch any action.

Blade limps forward to the doorway as Striker crosses the street. They both enter the hallway at the same time and make a sweep of all the rooms in the lower floor. There are no rear doors to this property and all the windows are closed and intact. It is unlikely in this fight that Grendel would have taken the time to close a window after himself, so the chances were he was upstairs.

Striker and Blade stand at the foot of the stairs just outside any possible firing arcs from above. Blade makes a "tluck" sound twice with his tongue since he is in shadow and the others can't see him. Intruder and Thorium were safe to move forward.

The footsteps on the stairs, when they begin, are uneven and heavy as they make their shock descent: THUD-THUD-THUDYTHUD-THUD-THUD. It sounds like Grendel is pretty injured and is coming down to face them in his death throws. Blade and Striker brace themselves for the imminent action as the footsteps get louder and closer.

Outside, Vincent moves along the front of the building down towards the doorway the others are at. Any attempt he is making to do this with stealth is removed by the sudden rising applause of the crowd. It begins with a few people pointing and shouting, 'Go on! Get him, Vincent.' And before he has passed three doorways, it is a full applause with whistles and cheers.

He tries to ignore it and continues on his way, not wanting to be caught out like the other night with the news crew. The rain is falling faster now too, adding to the roar.

The footsteps are rounding the last corner and Grendel will be on them in less than three seconds. Blade lines up the sight of his gun where he figures Grendel will appear. To his horror, when the footsteps come round the corner, he has it totally wrong.

'GRENADES!' He dives backwards behind a small bookcase, the only available cover. Striker is already there. Thorium is half in a doorway at the far end of the corridor and Intruder is just about to enter the building from the street.

The two grenades thud down the last couple of steps of the carpeted stairs. There is a brief pause as they roll to a halt in the corridor.

Then they explode.

Vincent can't believe what is happening in front of him.

Intruder is blasted across the street through the air, where he slams into one of the cars opposite as the giant orange fireball follows him out of the doorway. The camera crew and crowd members immediately opposite the door are instantly incinerated by the conflagration. A small building fire takes their positions as the greater fireball turns to black smoke that rises high into the air. From the other side of the City, the fireball actually lights up the lower surfaces of the clouds in a pastel orange colour.

On Stanton's screen the fireball coming directly at the camera had been a horrific sight so real that it had caused him to move his head back and lift his arm. It had taken everyone by surprise. A lower quadrant of the view screen in front of Stanton now sat blank, where the image from the camera that had been hit by the fireball had sat just seconds before. It took almost twenty seconds for the technicians to find another feed.

Vincent walks slowly down to the doorway to see a blackened and smoking Thorium stagger from the door. As Vincent looks into the corridor he can make out the face down bodies of Blade and Striker, lit by the dancing light cast on the corridor by the burning wallpaper.

In the Cityworks offices, an angry William Stevens pulled off his headset and threw it at his black screen in a single fluid motion. 'Damn it!'

Ryan Worthington beside him rubbed his eyes, unable to take in what had happened. He too had a black screen. Both men knew they were only unconscious, having been saved by their battle-armour and the small cover they had managed to find. But if the fire grew out of control before they could move, then that would be that. Stevens picked up his headset and put it on again, his fingers drumming on his controls impatiently as he watched for signs of Blade coming round.

Intruder gets to his feet, his whole body smoking. He runs his hand over his blackened head. If he had had any hair to begin with, it would now have been gone.

'Intruder, okay. Call in!'

'Thorium, okay.'

'Vincent, okay.' *Vincent figures he should call in too.*

It seemed odd to Stanton that Intruder should have asked this, considering the men controlling the Heroes were all sitting next to each other in the other office. But with no time to look around and check other people's screens, a quick word was more effective. Intruder now knew there were only two of them left. And, of course, Vincent.

'Cover me, Thorium.'

Intruder dumps his guns by the doorway and runs past the now crouching Thorium. He runs to the far end of the corridor and grabs the unconscious body of Striker and drags it to the street outside. He then returns and pulls out Blade. Both men's chests heave as they lie on the wet street. The unconscious Blade is leaking a red stream of blood onto the street, which runs in the direction of the park, helped on by the rain.

Intruder grabs his weapon and charges once again into the building. Vincent doesn't wait to be asked and follows him. Thorium covers the corridor until he sees the others reach the bottom of the stairs, then he advances. Vincent squats down by the stairs and reholsters his weapons. He has found the discarded and far more powerful weapons of Blade and Striker. The plasma rifle takes his fancy and he picks up the large gun. It has almost a full tank of plasma – this would do.

Thorium runs into the stairwell and miniguns up into the stairs, in case Grendel is looking down to see what damage he's inflicted. Thorium looks like he is being snowed on as small fragments of woodwork shower onto him. 'Clear!' he shouts.

Intruder slings his rail driver on to his back and replaces it with a smaller machine gun. The one-shot power of the rail driver would be no good if he had to suppress Grendel for any period. He runs upstairs with Vincent. They quickly kick open each door on that floor and check the rooms. Meanwhile Thorium comes upstairs to cover them. The floor was clear.

Thorium sprays up into the stairwell again: 'Clear!'

Vincent takes the lead this time and charges up to the next floor. He catches a brief glimpse of light at the far end of the corridor for just a fraction of a second. It goes out as he steps into the corridor. 'Cover me! He's at the far end!'

'10-4.' Intruder runs forward, his machine gun butted into his shoulder as he advances.

Vincent kicks open the door and unleashes an arc of plasma bolts across the room. As the small explosions light up the room he can see Grendel near the street side window. He staggers as he is hit in the stomach by one of the bolts. Vincent moves further into the room and lines up on Grendel, who is silhouetted in the window. He fires of a quick burst of four shots.

The first hits the window frame which splinters and breaks the window; the second tears through Grendel's arm between the elbow and shoulder, entirely severing the lower portion which drops to the floor still holding his gun. The third and fourth bolts slam into Grendel's chest, lifting him off of his feet and propelling him backwards out of the window. He lands on the roof of a car down in the street two floors below.

Vincent looks out of the window and shouts down at Grendel who is moving weakly, 'How do you like that then? You shit!'

Intruder and Thorium are already on their way down as Vincent turns to follow. They find Grendel still lying on the roof of the car, which has been dented in and is now acting like a giant bowl as Grendel's blood runs from the shoulder stump where his arm had been blown off. Intruder unclips the harvesting unit from his belt and pulls it onto his hand. Thorium aims his minigun at Grendel in case he has any fight left in him.

Vincent is walking towards this scene as Striker finally makes it to his feet. He moves over to Blade and stifles his newly bleeding thigh wound. Blade's eyes slowly begin to open. No one says anything as Intruder lines up the harvester.

'Good game, guys,' says Grendel weakly. 'I thought I had you there for a while.'

Intruder just shakes his head and slams the harvester into Grendel's chest with a crunch. He pulls the trigger, and accompanied by a zapping sound and an arching spasm from Grendel, not dissimilar to defibrillation, he extracts Grendel's digital ID.

The crowd goes wild.

28 September, 12:59am,
Southam, Binary Cityworks

Stanton was on his feet and through at the door of the glass fronted booth as soon as Grendel was blown out of the window. He could see the kill was imminent and wanted to have every possible second in hand when they got the address details from the ID.

He watched on the view screen as Intruder extracted the ID. A technician beside him punched some keys and soon the printer was spitting out the details. Stanton hoped the address would be local. He figured it would be since the murders were local. But, theoretically at least, the address could be anywhere in Britain. Andy handed him the paper with a: 'We got him, duder!'

'We sure did,' Stanton said as he read the printed sheet. 'Ian Sanders.' The address was in Acton in London. Stanton was immediately on the phone to the station: 'I want an armed unit to this address immediately.' He gave the address. 'No one enters or leaves the building until I get there, okay? I'm leaving to get there right now.' He turned to Andy. 'Andy, I need you to run the ID through the old news archives and phone me on this number with whatever you find.'

'No problemo.' Andy took the small piece of paper with Stanton's mobile number.

'And can you patch me through to the boys at the other office from here?' Stanton asked hopefully.

'The technician said, you can use the Tannoy if you want. Everyone in all the offices will hear, but if you don't mind—'

Stanton interrupted before the technician could finish, 'That'll be fine.' The technician showed Stanton a microphone built into the console and which button to press to transmit. Stanton clicked the switch causing a brief feedback whistle. An audible hiss coming through the viewing room's speakers confirmed he was live. 'This is Detective Inspector Stanton. I'd like to thank the Action Heroes for their help. And if I can, I'd like to ask if some of you people would take them out and buy them some beer. Send the bill to Detective Chief Superintendent Mayfield.' He released the button. 'Call me,' he said to Andy.

Spinning the wheels on the wet tarmac, Stanton sped towards the motorway and London.

The Action Heroes were lapping up the praise the Cityworks workers were lavishing on them. On the view screen no one was now watching, they could be seen hobbling and helping each other through the applauding crowds on their way back to the media office. Vincent walked with them.

'Good job there,' Thorium said to Vincent.

'Thanks.' Vincent smiled as he walked through the crowd.

Stanton's phone rang and he struggled to do a right turn on a roundabout, change gear, steer and answer the phone all at once. It was Lisa.

'Tell that lady she's a hero,' said Stanton.

'I think she knows that. You should see the way the crowd are acting. It's like those shots of the allied armies liberating European towns in the Second World War. People are everywhere.'

'We've got Grendel's address. So get someone to drive you down here as quickly as you can. I've got an armed unit on the way just now. I told them to wait until we get there before they go in.'

'Good. I'll sort out a car and see you there.'

Stanton increased his speed, his windscreen wipers beating back and forth at the highest setting to keep his vision clear.

Vincent was back in the Janus building fifteen minutes later. In Theydon Bois, Lisa had left Stella online. Their conversation had been a short and congratulatory one. Stella's only sentiment was that it was now their turn to get Grendel. Lisa had reassured her they would.

Vincent walks up the stairs to the main room, a dirtier, slightly-blackened version of his former self. He crosses to the window and looks out over the City. The lights twinkle. The rain is stopping. He moves into the sleeper's room. As he looks over the decayed corpse of Boyd, he can see the black plume of smoke still rising from the scene of the battle. 'I got Grendel for you, Niall,' he says gently, looking at the husky drying body in front of him. He doesn't touch the corpse because he doesn't want the body to collapse like Tyler's, where chunks of skull lie on top of one another and his jawbone now sits over the backbone at the neck like a clamp fastening him to the chair.

Vincent lies down on his reclining seat and sleeps. His job for now is done.

Stanton's phone rang as he sped along the motorway.

'Hey, this is Andy.'

'Hi Andy. What did you find?'

'Grendel is, like, a real big player in *Alter Ego*. At least he was. We found, like, a load of video for that ID. We're taping it all for you now and we'll send someone down with the tape.'

'So do we have anything that would suggest why he has this vendetta against the Janus people?'

'Man,' Andy said, 'I think we do. We found some old newsreels where Vincent, Boyd, Wilson and Swift had a kind of gunfight at the OK Corral sort of thing. It happened about six months ago. I didn't know it was Grendel at the time, but he was, like, the boss of the City before the Janus people came. It looks like he just hasn't been happy about losing that title.'

'That sounds like it could be it. Our man must have decided to take his revenge for the loss where he felt he could better beat them. Thanks, Andy,'

'Dude, I'm not done.'

'What else is there?'

'It's creepy, but Grendel and Tyler from Janus have the same ID number. The most recent video footage from the ID before the Grendel stuff tonight, was of Tyler, the Janus dude, killing people in the City.'

'Shit, so Grendel had infiltrated the Janus organisation.'

'I think he must have, dude. It's far out.'

'That would explain why Tyler's email was being checked recently.' Stanton said absently. His mind raced. 'Bollocks. That means there's no body in the real world for Tyler, which means we've been wrong all along about the first victim and the order of the killings.' Stanton tried to think the puzzle through: if Tyler wasn't dead, but Sanders had just abandoned the character, then Boyd/Davidson was the first victim. The others all appeared at the meeting after Boyd's death according to Stella, which meant they were all alive then. Since then, Swift/Braithwaite had been killed and they'd found his body. Frank/Rowling had been online tonight and was alive, and Wilson/Miller had been checked and was okay but was in the highlands or somewhere until this was over. 'Miller,' said Stanton, his stomach suddenly tightening. Miller was most likely the third victim because he was incommunicado. Stella was fourth; they knew that absolutely since Grendel was currently and verifiably after her. Stanton needed to get someone to Miller's house as soon as possible.

'Sorry, man, I can't hear you.' Andy said loudly.

'Listen, thanks, Andy,' said Stanton.

'My pleasure.'

'Can you get the tape to us first thing tomorrow?'

'I'll get someone to drive down and drop it off as soon as it's finished tonight.'

'Thanks.' Stanton hung up and immediately called the station and told them to find the number for Sergeant Dickinson in the Lothian and Borders Police and call him back. Ten minutes later he had the number. It was two o'clock in the morning, but Stanton didn't care. He dialled Dickinson's number.

'Hi, it's Jack Stanton here.'

'It's the middle of the bloody night, Stanton!' Dickinson, unsurprisingly, had been asleep. 'Can't whatever this is wait until morning?'

'I'm afraid not. Did you ever corroborate that Miller had gone to the highlands?'

'Skye, you mean. No, I didn't. I figured since we were the only people who knew he was going there that he'd be fine.'

'I think he's probably dead already, possibly even in his own house.'

'Now why would he be dead? I spoke to him and he was fine.'

'Look, you're going to have to go and check his house.'

'Okay, I'll go tomorrow. But I'll bet he's on Skye.'

'I want you to go right now,' said Stanton firmly. 'Break the door down if you have to.'

'For goodness sake.'

'Call me on my mobile when you've checked the house, okay?'

'All right,' Dickinson sighed, swinging his legs out of bed. He hung up and began to put on his warmest clothes. He didn't bother with his uniform since it was the middle of the night. His wife snored noisily from the other side of the bed. She hadn't even stirred when the phone rang. Dickinson rolled his eyes: even if he wasn't going out, he wouldn't be getting any sleep with that snoring going on. He went downstairs and flicked through the yellow pages looking for a local emergency locksmith.

**28 September, 2:34am,
Acton, London**

Jack Stanton pulled up round the corner from Grendel's address. The street looked quite well-to-do. Each house had a small garden in front of it and the cars lining both sides of the street were of good quality. The armed unit had every exit to the house covered.

They had arrived at the scene less than fifteen minutes after Stanton's call had come in, and since then no one had entered or left the house. No lights were on and the street had the sort of quiet that accompanies the middle of a night. Stanton crossed to where the leader of the unit was crouched behind a car with Lisa.

'Any sign of Grendel?' Stanton asked as he too crouched.

'No,' Lisa whispered. 'Nothing at all. He maybe left before these guys got here.'

'Possibly, but who stops to put out all the lights when they're running?' the officer stated. 'No, I reckon there's someone in there.'

'Do you have a battering ram with you?' Stanton enquired.

'Of course. We're ready to infiltrate whenever you want.'

'Well, we might as well get the show on the road straight away.'

'Okay. You two stay right here,' he ordered. Where guns were involved, there was no point in unnecessary people being in the vicinity. Stanton and Lisa would be called when the house was secured. The armed officer clipped an earpiece and microphone that had been hanging loose on his shoulder onto his ear. 'We're ready to go. Everyone move into position.'

In the quiet of the Acton road, as Stanton explained to Lisa about Grendel and Tyler and the possibility that Miller was dead, the sound of the policemen's running footsteps echoed loudly, despite the best efforts of the unit to move quietly. There were about fifteen officers in total. Ten would be used in the frontal assault, and the remainder would enter via the back door. Each man was guided to his correct position by quiet orders to their earpieces, and soon the two groups were ready to enter Grendel's house. They were just waiting for the word. A cat mewled nearby at the intruders.

On his way to Oxton in the Scottish Borders and Miller's cottage, Dickinson was blinking frequently to make sure he didn't nod off. He knew that to keep from falling asleep, the best thing was to keep the temperature down, but he couldn't stand the cold. He occasionally had to yank on the steering wheel of his car to avoid going into the fields that lined the road as he briefly nodded off. On the third such event, he shut down the heater and wound down the window. He felt less drowsy almost straight away.

He pulled up onto the verge outside the small cottage he had visited before. There was no way he was walking anywhere tonight, even if he was half blocking the road. He got out, crossed to Miller's front door and used the knocker a few times loudly. There was no response, so he climbed back into his car and waited for the locksmith. Stanton would be paying for the locksmith, he'd decided. Mainly because calling a locksmith out at this time of night wasn't going to be cheap and why should his force pay to find out that Miller was on Skye, but also because it would be a way to punish Stanton for getting him out of his bed in the middle of the night. As he sat waiting, he pulled up his collar against the cold and soon dropped off to sleep.

With a nod, the man with the battering ram was given the go ahead. Just as he swung it back, the order to go in at the back was given: 'Back door, go.' The ram smashed the lock and the decorative glass that made up the top half of the door. Dogs barked nearby as nine men piled through the front door. The final man stood outside watching all the windows, in case anyone should try to escape.

At the rear, less than a second after the front door was opened, the back door caved in and four officers entered the kitchen, guns pulled into shoulders as they searched using torches strapped to the muzzles. The well-equipped kitchen had a large wooden table with matching chairs around it. An ornately-crafted highchair sat at one end.

'Kitchen, secured!'

'Front hall, secure!'

A small child or baby was crying upstairs and a small amount of light was spilling down from upstairs where a light had just been switched on. The front door team moved quickly upstairs, barging into the rooms on the first floor, using their torches to guide their path. The room on the right had a clothes rack and a bed that was empty. Large bookcases covered most walls. 'Clear!'

Downstairs, the back door team secured the ground floor. They entered the large living room, covering each other. It was decorated in deep red colours, the whole room coordinated with expensive furniture including two large sofas. The room was empty. The adjoining dining room had a large oak table that would have seated eight people comfortably. Six chairs sat around the table, while two others sat at either end of a matching dresser filled with fine china. This room was also empty. A further room at the front, which appeared to be a study, was also empty.

'Ground floor secure.'

'Roger.'

Upstairs, one officer entered a room to find a woman getting up from her double bed. She screamed as he aggressively ordered her to stay on the bed, 'Armed Police, ma'am. Please stay down!' He kept his gun trained on her as he said: 'Front bedroom secure.'

The woman didn't know what was going on. 'I need to get my baby! I need to get my baby!' she cried.

A large television room was next door, with two large sofas set up for ideal viewing of the television. An upright piano sat on the wall the door opened from.

The room opposite was the crying child's room. The child stood in a cot and screamed, its face red with the exertion. It looked like a little girl of almost two years old, and the officer who secured the room shouted 'Clear!' then slung his weapon over his shoulder and picked up the child, hushing her as he rocked her back and forth. But the child was inconsolable and large tears ran down her cheeks as she wriggled to push herself away from him.

'First floor secured!' He heard over his earpiece. The trampling officers had been through every room on the first floor.

Then through everyone's headphones came an alarmed statement from one of the officers. 'More stairs! More stairs!' The action that had momentarily ebbed was now back on full power. Four officers ran to where another was pointing his shouldered weapon up another set of stairs. At the top were three doors: one facing the stairs, the other two facing each other.

Three officers moved slowly up the stairs while two others stayed at the bottom. The officer nearest the top opened the left hand door and rushed in. The room was a nursery with a rocking horse and various children's toys scattered around the floor. He quickly checked the room and the cupboards at the back. 'All Clear!'

Meanwhile the second officer opened the middle door. 'Water tank,' he declared as he shut the door since there was no room for anyone to be inside. He opened the final door and charged in, knocking over a painting easel. The room was a makeshift art studio. He checked the room thoroughly and found no one. 'Second floor secured,' he said into his microphone. Then he sighed with relief that no one had shot at them and no one had been shot. His feet left yellow paint marks on the stairs as he came back down to the first floor.

Dickinson jumped. The knocking was right beside his head, which was leaning against the glass. He tried to focus, and soon saw through his misted windows that a van was now parked outside the cottage. He could just about read the "G.D. McClellan – Locksmiths. 24-Hour Service" written on the side. He pulled the handle to open his door and got out and stretched. 'How are you doing, Douglas?' he asked.

'Well not too good considering it's the middle of the night, George.'

'Ach, I know. Some bloody detective from London wants me to look in here tonight. I don't know what he's thinking.'

Douglas shook his head: 'The bloody English.'

'Aye, it wouldn't be so bad if it was an Englishman, Douglas, but the man was a Scot. Sounded from the west.' George rubbed his hands together against the cold, then blew on them. 'Anyway, you'd better get on.'

Douglas McClellan opened his van and took out his tools. Soon he was kneeling down working on the lock. The small gargoyle on the doorknocker watched his progress.

28 September, 2:36am, Oxton, Scottish Borders

If Douglas McClellan hadn't been a locksmith, he could have been a pretty effective burglar. The door clicked and he smiled to himself. He put his tools back in his bag and carried it to his van, before knocking on the window of Dickinson's car. Dickinson's head was against the window again, his eyes closed.

'That was quick, Douglas.' George Dickinson stretched disappointedly as he opened his door. 'If I didn't know you were on the level, I'd swear you were a thief.'

'Aye, George, well we'll see how on the level you think I am when your bill for this comes through.'

George laughed. 'That we will. I'll be sending it straight down to London for them to pay anyway.'

'Aye, well just make sure it does get paid.' Douglas wasn't so keen on him not knowing who to chase for his money. 'Anyway, I'll be off if you don't need me any more.'

'Well maybe you could just hold on just now,' said Dickinson. 'In case I need you to unlock any doors inside.'

'Aye, good point.' Douglas retrieved his bag and shivered: it was a cold night and in the darkness of the Scottish Borders the Milky Way filled the sky above them.

Dickinson slowly pushed open the front door, which opened with a creak. 'Hello,' he said into the cottage.

All the lights were now on in the house in Acton and Stanton was making hot sweet tea for the woman who had been scared half to death by the forced entry into her home. Grendel had been nowhere to be found and Stanton sloshed a teabag around in a cup in frustration as he impatiently waited for the tea to turn the correct colour so he could go and question the woman and find out what had happened to Ian Sanders.

In the large ground-floor living room, Lisa was sitting on a fashionable sofa beside the woman who was now holding her baby close to her. The child's eyes were getting heavier by the minute as she was rocked back and forth, while the woman's face was becoming systematically angrier now she was getting over the initial shock of what had happened. She looked to be around thirty years old and from the pictures around the room of her and the baby, she looked well-to-do. Stanton came through and gave her the sweet tea he'd made. Both he and Lisa knew there was no way this woman could have been Grendel because she was too petite.

'Yes,' said the woman. 'Like a cup of tea is going to fix my doors.' She took it roughly from his hand, spilling some on the sanded floorboards. She spread the spill around with her slippered foot.

'Madam,' said Stanton. 'We're really sorry about this, but we have this address down as the residence of a Mr Ian Sanders.' Stanton had wished he had taken the time to double check with someone, anyone, that this house was even occupied by anyone called Sanders.

'It's actually Dr Sanders.' Stanton breathed a sigh of relief. This was the right house. 'But he doesn't live here. Not anymore.'

'Are you his wife?' Lisa asked.

'Not any more. At least I won't be when the divorce is finalised.'

'Do you know where he is, Mrs Sanders?' Stanton asked.

'That's *Ms* Barnbrook,' she said declaring her maiden name. 'And no, I don't know where he is. If I did, I'd have the police round to collect the child support payments he's due for Alice here. That bastard,' she said angrily. 'Anyway, why are you kicking in my front door in the middle of the night looking for Ian? What's he done?'

'We're investigating …' Stanton paused: was there any point in telling this woman, Sanders' ex-wife, that her soon to be ex-husband was prime suspect in a multiple murder investigation? Stanton figured he had to. 'We're looking for Ian in connection with at least two murders.'

Ms Barnbrook lifted her hand to her mouth involuntarily, but recovered her spite for her ex-husband quite quickly: 'I knew he was crazy. I knew it when he hit me.'

'He beat you?' Lisa said.

'Yes, he did. I threw him out that same night. He was addicted to some stupid computer game and when he got killed in it one night and I said it was just a game, he just flipped out.'

'*Alter Ego*,' Lisa said.

'Yes, that was it.'

'When was this?' Stanton asked.

'Oh, I don't know. Maybe six months ago. I just threw him out though. I wasn't having him hitting Alice here in a rage one night. Not ever.'

'Do you know, by chance, if he ever mentioned an organisation from the game called the Janus organisation?'

Ms Barnbrook cocked her head slightly, 'That rings a bell actually. The night I threw him out he said some people had killed him and some friends he played with. I think he said they worked for someone called Mr Janus. Would that be right?'

'Yes,' said Stanton. 'That's right.' He paused. 'Ms Barnbrook, I'm afraid your ex-husband appears to be killing the players who killed him in the game that night, the people who played as the characters who worked for Mr Janus.'

'I knew he was sick. I just knew it. That's awful.' She rocked the baby agitatedly.

'Do you know where we can get in contact with Ian? Do you have an address for him?'

'No, I'm sorry, I don't. I didn't ask for one and there's a restraining order on him contacting me. I send his mail to the university. I don't know if he still works there, but that's where it goes.'

'Which university,' Lisa asked.

'King's University, London. He works in the English Department there.'

'Do you have a picture of him we could have?'

'No, I burned every picture when I threw him out.'

'Okay. Thank you, Ms Barnbrook.'

'So what's going to happen with my doors?'

'We've got someone on their way round to fix them temporarily just now. A joiner will be round tomorrow to refit them properly, or replace them if needed.'

'I *will* be contacting my solicitor about this. I'm sure this is in breach of my civil liberties!' she shouted as Stanton and Lisa filed out. They could hear the baby crying again as they left.

Some uniformed officers had been called to relieve the armed unit and they were arriving as Stanton and Lisa crossed the road to get to their cars.

'Well, no one's going to be in the university just now,' Stanton said looking at his watch. It was quarter to four. 'I think we should meet again tomorrow morning at the university.'

'Sounds like our man, though, doesn't it?' Lisa said. She looked tired.

'Yup. He's got the motive anyway, and the fact he beats his wife shows a violent tendency.'

'Although even wife-beating is pretty far removed from murdering people and cutting off their faces.'

'I know.' Stanton rubbed both his hands up and down on his face. 'Listen, we'll meet at the university tomorrow at half-eight. We'll get an armed unit to come as well. Maybe he'll be there, and if not we should at least be able to get an address for him.'

'That's fine. I'll see you tomorrow then.'

'Okay. Enjoy what little sleep you can get.'

'You too.'

As Stanton and Lisa were making their way to their respective flats, George Dickinson was doubled over, his hands on his knees, coughing the last vomit from his throat in the street outside Miller's cottage.

'What is it?' Douglas asked.

Dickinson held back more wretches, waving off the question as he vomited again. Eventually his coughing subsided and his stomach stopped its inexorable twitching. He pulled a handkerchief from his pocket and wiped his mouth. His forehead was icy cold from the sheen of sweat the vomiting had induced and now the chill of the night cut at his face.

'What's up, George?' Douglas's voice had risen slightly and he sounded obviously concerned.

'He's dead,' said Dickinson simply.

Five minutes before, Dickinson had entered the cottage, flicking on lights as he went through both of the downstairs rooms. There was nothing of any note to see downstairs, just the usual table, chairs, settee and television you would find in almost any small sitting room that also serves as a dining room. The kitchen next door was painfully small, with just enough room for a Belfast sink, a tiny surface and an old gas cooker, the sort that had a grill at the top that juts out over the burners. Everything in the kitchen looked ancient.

'I'm going upstairs,' Dickinson said from the doorway to Douglas.

'Aye, you do that George. I'll just be out here.' Douglas was feeling a sudden air of tension from George. Maybe it was something to do with that strong smell that had wafted out when the door had opened, a smell he couldn't quite place just now.

George walked up the steep stairs. He couldn't find a light switch and it gave him goose pimples as he creaked up each step. There was a smell to this house he didn't like, and it was getting stronger. He ran his hands on the walls either side of the stairs looking for a switch. These old properties never had usefully positioned electrics or switches, probably because when electricity was installed, it wasn't needed like it is today.

At the top of the stairs was a single door to the one room that was the upstairs. George pushed the door. It dragged up the carpet and jammed, half open. He felt around the wall inside the room for a light switch. He flicked it: nothing happened. He waited, allowing his eyes to adjust to the dark, then began to squeeze himself through the half-open door. He had to hold his stomach in and cursed his fondness for sandwiches as he puffed through the gap. There was a bed in the corner with a bedside table with what looked like a small lamp and a coffee mug on it. It looked like the roof was either leaking or had leaked badly as the ceiling was flaking off above the bed from what George could make out. He breathed in further. A large desk was at the far wall, with a large computer system. He looked the other way as he pushed the door to make more room. The chest of drawers he was now looking at had the usual bits and bobs you keep on such items of furniture: deodorant, hairbrush, some books. The usual.

His stomach suddenly jumped through the gap and he was in the room. He could hear scurrying from the right hand side of the room. He wished he'd brought a torch. He turned round, his nose twitching from the smell.

'Oh my dear Lord.'

In the side of the room he had been unable to see because of the door sat Miller. From the light coming in through the window, Dickinson could see he was tied to the chair he sat on. His head was forward, his chin on his chest. On his shoulder sat a medium sized rat. It chewed on the sinews of Miller's left ear. Dickinson made a swift move and the rat jumped down and scurried away, as did its companion which was journeying back to the body after retreating from George's initial entrance. At the bottom of the chair George could see dark stains. They looked black in this light. He knew the black was blood.

He walked over to see if the lamp on the bedside table was working, making sure he didn't knock over the half empty coffee mug as he moved his shaking hands under the shade to slide the switch. The lamp dimly lit the room with a yellowish light. George walked back over to the body, which he could now see wasn't tied, but had been taped with that tape you can buy in DIY superstores. The head of this poor man looked like it had been beaten to a pulp.

'Oh my dear Lord.'

He crouched down. Immediately his head began to swim and his stomach began to convulse at the site of the faceless man. He fell backwards, then staggered as he got back to his feet. He grabbed the door handle and yanked it, but the door wouldn't open. He shook it, clawing at his throat, his stomach beginning to churn in powerful ejective waves. It was a few seconds before he thought to look down, close the door and flatten the carpet down so that the door could ride over it. He stumbled down the stairs and out into the street.

It took ten minutes for George Dickinson to go back inside. In the interim, he had called the coroner up in Edinburgh who would be down as soon as possible. Forensics wouldn't be there until the morning. They had said that by the time they got everyone from where they were down to the site, it would be morning anyway.

So it was up to George just now to find out as much as he could from the scene. His stomach contents were on the street, so he knew the worst was probably over. And at least this time he knew what to expect.

'Have you got a pad and a pen, Douglas?' Douglas was back in his van.

'Aye, I do.' He rummaged around and gave George an invoice pad and a pen.

'And a torch?'

'Aye … Here you go. Are you going to need me now?'

George thought about being by himself, in the middle of nowhere to all intents and purposes, with the faceless body upstairs. 'Eh … maybe if you could just stay until someone else turns up. You can charge the time.' He nodded hopefully.

Douglas thought about it. He wouldn't like to be at a murder scene by himself. 'Okay, I'll stay out here. But I'm not coming in.'

'Thanks, Douglas.'

'And you'll owe me a drink for it.' He paused as he began to look for something, 'Actually …' Douglas rifled in his bag in the seat beside him. 'Have a swallow of this.' He pulled out a hip flask and passed it to George who took it gladly. He took a swig of the single malt Douglas kept in it then passed it back.

'You're a good man, Douglas.'

'Aye, I know that.' He wound up his window and took a swig from the flask himself.

George went back into the house, his throat and stomach warm from the whiskey. This time he found the elusive switch to light the stairs. It was in the corner behind the front door. George figured whoever had decided that would be a good place for the switch had obviously been some kind of genius. He creaked back upstairs, pushing the door at the top open slowly so it wouldn't catch the carpet.

The room didn't show any sign of a struggle. He wrote that on the invoice pad. Neither did the downstairs for that matter. He wrote that down too. He flicked on Douglas's torch. Nothing happened so he banged it with his hand a few times. It lit up. He swung the beam around the yellow room. The scene appeared confined to the area around the body. He took a few shallow breaths, to steel himself to look at the body again. They were shallow so he wouldn't need to inhale the smell too much.

His torch came to rest on the man's head. That was odd: his hair was very dark, where the Miller he had spoken to had lighter, shorter hair. This wasn't the same man. He was writing down whatever he thought might be useful when he would phone Stanton in London. The upper body of the corpse was drenched in blood. Dickinson shone the torch onto where the face once was. The teeth were clearly visible in an involuntary toothy grin. George shook his head. Who would do a thing like this? He moved round a little and felt a squelch under his foot. He looked down and saw a piece of the DIY tape had stuck to the sole of his shoe. He pulled it off and shone the torch onto it.

His breathing quickened and his heart raced as he saw a complete upper lip stuck to the tape. The gap in the dried-in bloodstain of the sticky side clearly showed that this had been stuck on the mouth and that the mouth had been opened slightly, probably in a stifled scream. George Dickinson shivered at the thought.

He walked round behind the body to view the wound to the head. 'Oh no,' he said quietly. He could clearly see that the wound was in fact not a wound but was the skin from the face. The missing lip was obvious, but the rest of the face was there albeit very bloody and cut up. George whispered, 'You poor man.'

He scanned round the room with his torch for anything else Stanton might want to know. His torch caught sight of the coffee mug on the bedside table. He hadn't noticed before as he was more concerned about the body itself, but the cup had something on the outside of it. He walked over, crouching to see what it was.

Fingerprints. Bloody fingerprints.

The cup also had small dried-in lumps of flesh embedded in the finger marks too. George realised that the killer had supped this coffee during or after he'd done those terrible things to the man in the chair. He didn't touch the cup in case he ruined any evidence, but from what he could see there were no good prints anyway. All of the marks looked the same, like maybe the person who'd made them was wearing gloves.

George wrote everything down.

28 September, 3:49am, Stanton's Flat

Jack Stanton crawled into his bed and his body relaxed as he let out a long breath. He was absolutely exhausted, but at least the case was progressing.

But his night wasn't over.

As his body got heavier, he became vaguely aware that the phone was ringing. Struggling awake he slowly sat up then went out to the hall where the phone sat on a table. He picked it up.

'Stanton.' The phone kept ringing. It was his mobile. He hung up the hall phone and staggered back into the bedroom where he rifled through the pile of clothes he had peeled into the bundle that now lay on the floor. He found the phone and clicked the button to pick up the call, but he didn't speak until he was out in the hall and had closed the door: 'Stanton.'

'Hello. It's George Dickinson.'

'Hi George. What did you find?' Stanton's tiredness began to lift quickly.

'I found a body. The coroner is here just now.'

'Damn it.' Stanton hadn't wanted to be right with this one.

'There's more,' Dickinson said. 'His face was cut off and put on the back of his head.

'Yes, I figured if there was a body that it would be like that.'

'You knew about this?'

'Yes, I didn't say because I hoped you were going to be right and that Miller was going to be somewhere on Skye. I'm sorry.'

'Hmmph.'

'Was there anything else at the scene: fingerprints, footprints?'

'There are bloody finger marks on a mug in the room where the body is. Looks like the killer had some coffee after he mutilated the victim.' George was scanning over the invoice pad. 'Oh, yes. And the body here doesn't belong to the Miller I spoke to when I first checked.'

Stanton was wide-awake now. 'Are you sure?'

'Absolutely. The person I spoke to had lighter coloured hair. The body here has dark hair that's longer and a bit curlier.'

'Shit.' Stanton's thoughts tumbled. Could Dickinson have seen the murderer? 'You must have seen our killer.'

'That's what I've been starting to think.'

'Can you describe him?'

'Yes. He was of about medium height and build, with lightly coloured short brown hair. He wore glasses and was probably about twenty-five to thirty-five years old. English accent …'

Stanton considered the description as Dickinson described their killer. It was more than they had before, but it still wasn't much. 'Do you people have police artists up there?'

'We do. In Edinburgh.'

'Well, can you get up there first thing and get someone to draw who you saw that night and then get it faxed to me as soon as you have it?'

'Good idea. Yes, I'll do that.'

'Listen, thanks for doing this tonight, George.'

'It's okay,' George said. At least now he felt this had been worthwhile because he might be able to give evidence that would catch whoever had killed the poor man upstairs.

'Goodnight.'

'Aye, what's left of it,' George said. 'Goodnight.'

Stanton returned to his bed and lay down, but this time sleep was not so quick in coming.

They would soon have an artist's impression of Grendel, the Janus Killer.

28 September, 7:31am, Lisa's Flat

Lisa felt awful. She felt more tired now than when she had gone to bed; and now her eyes were heavy and swollen from the miniscule amount of sleep she had been able to salvage. Somewhere in her mind she realised that if she hadn't wanted to be a detective that she'd still be asleep. But then these last weeks had been more interesting than all the rest of her time on the force put together. So it was worth it – and she thought she was doing pretty well, apart from the obvious run in with Grendel. And this was only her first case after all. Her arm throbbed due to her excessive tiredness. She made a half-hearted rush for the shower.

At Jack Stanton's abode the same sluggishness was evident. Stanton's alarm would be a welcome release from another dream where he walked the moor and helplessly watched his younger brother blown to pieces in front of him. As he screamed silently in the maelstrom of the machinegun and mortar fire, he noticed the slow-motion walk of Stella also crossing the moor. He began to run to her, through treacle-like slow motion. He couldn't save Simon; he had to save her.

He moaned loudly as the alarm went off and it didn't help that he knocked it to the floor when he tried to switch it off. There was no escape even in sleep these days. Stanton was exhausted.

It would take him about half an hour to get to the university to meet Lisa. He set off just before eight o'clock, switching on the radio to see what the media speculators had made of last night's events. The DJ was still chatting about the difficulties of travelling across London: the usual slightly humorous drivel morning DJs tend to chat about - enough to make you smile when you do listen, but nothing important enough to hold your attention all the time. Stanton hummed along as the final track before the news began to play. It was Dionne Warwick singing, *Do you know the way to San Jose?* Stanton liked the song, it reminded him of being in his mother's kitchen when she'd play music as she made dinner for him, Simon and their father. Good times.

The traffic was heavy and he had only made about two hundred yards in the time it took to play the song. The newscaster began his reports. Thankfully the story hadn't made the top slot; at least that meant it wasn't being driven too over-zealously. But it *was* the second story, so it was still pretty bad. Stanton listened.

'... four hunters pursued and captured a man within the *Alter Ego* game late last night. Witnesses to the events described scenes of building-to-building searches for the character that sources believe will lead the police to the Janus Killer. Inside information suggests that by capturing the character the police will now be able to trace where the killer is through a trace on his telephone.'

'Good guess, but no cigar,' said Stanton.

'Police have still rejected the opportunity to comment on the investigation, although last night's events appear to have provided a promising avenue of investigation for detectives. Detective Inspector Jack Stanton, the senior detective leading the investigation into the Janus killings, was seen leaving the offices of Binary Cityworks immediately after the in-game apprehension. Our Technology Editor, David Stevens, has been finding out more about the *Alter Ego* game itself.'

David Stevens picked up roughly from where he had ended the day before: '*Alter Ego* has only been online for just over a year, yet the revenues generated by this runaway success have propelled Binary Cityworks to a market position at present as the wealthiest entertainment software development house in the world. The *Alter Ego* world brings together a large number of successful elements from many genres of computer game including role-playing games, so called shoot-'em-ups and trading games; and all of this within a computer-generated City environment indistinguishable from conventional video. There has been some speculation that the recent spate of killings related to the game may have damaged the popularity of the game and reduced the share price of the company. However, at close of trading last night the share price reached an all-time high as investors jumped on the recent surge in popularity, which is clearly evident from the difficulty in finding a copy of *Alter Ego* in almost every city in the country.

'Witnesses to last night's hunt described large crowds of people within the *Alter Ego* City following events as they unfolded. This blatant violence voyeurism has caused many anti-violence groups to once again condemn computer game violence, citing the Janus Killer as an obvious example of the connection between such games and real violent crime. The debate on the issue has long been a contentious one, and the recent killings have done little to assuage the fears of the anti-violence lobbyists. And while the Janus Killer remains at bay, the games publishing community has refrained from making any comments on any possible correlation. This is David Stevens for the early morning news.'

Stanton pulled up in the street near the main tower of the Arts Faculty of King's University on Gower Street. Lisa was already there in the car she had borrowed the previous evening from one of the officers in Epping. There were two unmarked Transit vans filled with Armed Police parked in front of Lisa. Stanton walked across and got in the passenger side of Lisa's car. She looked over groggily. She had been there for ten minutes and was about ready to fall asleep when Stanton had pulled up.

'Man, I thought I looked tired,' Stanton said.

She laughed. 'You do. You look exhausted.' She sat up straighter to feel a little more awake. 'So what's the plan?'

'It's unlikely after last night that we'll find him here; I mean, who would come to work as usual knowing we're on his tail? I think we should go and find the department and see if we can get details about where we might find him.'

'Sounds reasonable.'

Lisa's feet were dragging a little as she tried to find the energy to walk. As they crossed over to the front of the two Transit vans she observed another possibility Stanton hadn't mentioned: 'You do realise Sanders might not even *work* here anymore? His wife wasn't exactly sure.'

'I know. It's all we've got just now though and we'll just need to cross that bridge if and when we come to it.'

'I suppose so,' Lisa said through a stifled yawn.

'Morning gentlemen,' Stanton said into the van. 'It's unlikely Sanders will be here after last night, so I don't think we're going to benefit much by scaring the life out of all of the students around here by storming the English Literature department.' The faces crammed into the van looked disappointed. Stanton continued, 'I'm thinking that Lisa and I will go up to the department and see what we can find out.'

The senior officer looked concerned. 'I understand what you are saying, sir, but what if he *is* here? Wouldn't it make sense to cover all the exits as we're here, just in case? Better to be over-cautious than get caught out. We are dealing with a multiple killer after all.'

'Makes sense,' Stanton agreed. 'Is there any way you can do it surreptitiously, though? So we don't scare anyone.'

'Also, it might be an idea to send a couple of guys into the stairs, because I think that if he is here and does decide to run he'll use the stairs rather than the lift. Because he'll probably assume we'll have someone covering the foyer outside the lifts.'

'Sounds good,' Stanton nodded.

'Give us five minutes to get in position.' He began to get out of the van. 'And if you two are going in, I want you each wearing one of these.' He handed over two bulletproof vests.

'Sure.' Lisa was happy to take the vest. She'd already had a run in with Grendel, and she didn't fancy getting any more wounded by his hand.

As they put on the vests and adjusted their clothes so they weren't too obvious, Stanton and Lisa watched the armed officers move into place. They took up unobtrusive positions around the building in less than two minutes; once they were situated they weren't that obvious – although anyone who had seen them deploy would know they were there. Stanton hoped Sanders – if he was here – hadn't.

Stanton and Collier began their walk up the steps to the automatic doors of the Arts Faculty tower. On the wall on the right as they entered through automatic doors was a floor plan for the building. The English Department was on the twelfth floor.

'These things are heavy. I'd forgotten what it was like to wear one.' Lisa hadn't had a vest on since her last training course about four months before. Stanton couldn't remember the last time he had worn a vest. In their tired states the vests weighed both of them down.

The automatic doors hummed open and they walked in, double-checking the floor for the English Department. Stanton pressed the button to call one of the two lifts. A small upward-pointing arrow appeared where he had pressed. As they stood, a few students and staff gathered on their way to the first lectures and tutorials of the day. In the four or five minutes it took for the lift to come down, visiting every floor on the way it seemed, about twenty people had gathered.

PING: the lift arrived and Collier and Stanton got in, followed by about fifteen other people.

'What floor?' someone asked everyone in the lift.

'Six.'

'Eight.'

'Two.'

'Why don't you just walk to two?'

'Why don't you just press the button?'

'Nine.'

'Twelve,' said a man standing just in front of Stanton and Lisa on the left. He looked fed up with the crammed lift already.

'Did you press eight?'

'Uh-huh, it's done.'

The lift surged and began its rise to the first stop on the second floor. The lazy student got out, saying, 'Thank you' as he left. He reminded Stanton of Andy from Cityworks.

As the lift surged upwards again, Stanton began to rifle in his jacket to get his ID out. The fed-up looking man had his back to the wall and was watching him as he did it.

'You know,' said Stanton. 'I wish we knew what this Sanders guy looked like. It would make this a lot easier.'

'I know what you mean,' Lisa replied.

The watching man looked away. The lift stopped at the sixth floor and he said, 'Excuse me' as he began to push his way out.

Stanton looked at him oddly. 'Didn't he want our floor?' he asked Lisa quietly.

'I don't know. I wasn't really listening.'

The man was at the doors now and had to push them back so he could get out as they tried to automatically close. Stanton watched as he broke into a run towards the stairway as soon as he was free of the lift. He immediately ran into a secretary who dropped a pile of photocopies she was taking to give to one of the lecturers.

'Sorry,' said the running man, not stopping.

'Good grief,' said the woman. 'There's no running in the departments, Dr Sanders!' She bent down to pick up the papers.

'Shit, that's him!' said Stanton as the door shut. 'Open the doors!' He began to push forward, but the upward surge of the lift told him it was too late. 'Press the button for the next floor.' He looked up at the floor indicator above the door. 'Press seven. Now!'

The student by the controls looked shocked and began mashing at the buttons. Soon all the buttons from four to eleven were pressed. Stanton and Lisa were pushing through to get to the door. 'Excuse us. Police.' Lisa said as a weak apology for all the shoving.

The doors opened on the seventh floor and Stanton and Lisa both piled out. Stanton was faster in his vest than Lisa and he slammed through to the stairwell. The door bounced noisily off of the wall as he barged through. He looked down: the man was running down the stairs four flights below.

'Stop, Sanders. Police!' shouted Stanton. But the man kept running. Stanton set off in pursuit, closely followed by Lisa.

They were running down the first few steps of each flight then jumping the last half and using the banister to swing round through a half turn to go down the next flight. On the fourth floor some half-sleeping student appeared in their path just in time to be knocked to the ground without even an apology.

Stanton had pulled out a two-flight lead when he ran headlong into one of the armed policemen at the bottom. 'Where is he?' Stanton said, bent almost double from the exertion, his chest feeling like it was on fire.

'No one's come past here at all.'

'Shit!' Stanton slapped his palms against the wall noisily; the sound resonated up the multiple flights of stairs. 'Shit!'

Lisa walked down the last flight when she saw that this particular chase was over.

'Don't let anyone into or out of this building, okay?' Stanton puffed at the officers. 'And I want you guys ready to go through every floor of this building in five minutes!' His orders were relayed to the rest of the group, who moved in and isolated the building from the general university populace with their short deadly looking machine guns.

Stanton and Lisa got into the other lift and went back upstairs to the twelfth floor. On the wall of the English Department was a large poster that said "THE STAFF". Stanton soon found a picture of the man from the lift: "Dr Ian Sanders, Old English Literature, Middle English Literature. Room 12.04," it said below his photograph. A rather pissed off Stanton ripped the photograph off so they could show the officers downstairs. He marched into the secretary's office.

'Hello, Jack Stanton, CID.' He showed his ID. 'Is Dr Sanders in today?'

The secretary was in her late fifties or early sixties and was shocked at how abrupt Stanton was, but he was in no mood to care. 'He should be. I've not seen him in today yet, though. We can go and have a look and see if he's in his office if you'd like.'

Stanton nodded. He'd like to know what was in the office despite the fact he knew that Sanders was hiding somewhere

319

else in the building. 'Actually, you do that, Lisa. I'll take this picture downstairs so they can start looking for him.'

'Okay, Jack.'

Stanton pressed the button for the lift as Lisa was lead along to Sander's office.

The office was of course locked and empty, but Lisa asked the secretary to let her into it anyway since it was now a crime scene and she wanted to see if there was anything of immediate relevance. The office looked like any other office in a university: walls lined with shelves which were packed with books, papers lying in piles around the room, a large table in the middle with eight chairs around it, and a computer terminal in the corner. Beside the terminal was a picture of the little girl they had seen in the small hours of the morning at Sanders' ex-wife's home. In the picture the little girl was smiling and rolling on some grass with Sanders.

The lift pinged its arrival and Stanton walked out into the foyer. He was carrying his coat and was in the process of pulling off his vest. He didn't plan to be running around looking for Sanders in this building, so he wasn't going to carry about the extra weight of the vest. He walked over to talk to two servitors who were in a large glass-fronted booth opposite the main doors. 'Can you get me twenty copies of this picture immediately, please?' he said, flashing his ID.

'Can do.' The servitor walked to the back of the booth and opened a door. A few seconds later he emerged from a door to Stanton's right. 'I'll just be a few minutes.' He ran up the stairs.

Stanton crossed to speak to the officer in charge of the armed unit again. 'Okay, we've got a picture, and we know he hasn't left the building, so it's going to be up to you guys to flush him out. He can't have been armed with anything bigger than a penknife if he's armed at all, because when we saw him he wasn't carrying anything and he's not been to his office. But obviously a lack of weapons doesn't mean he's not as dangerous as hell. If he does have a knife, he's not scared to use it.' Stanton hoped Sanders hadn't grabbed himself a hostage or worse still, hostages. He decided not to voice that particular concern.

'We'll be careful,' said the officer.

The servitor reappeared with a neat bundle of photocopies. 'I blew it up to fill the page. I figured with the photocopying, it might be difficult to see otherwise.'

'Thanks. That's good thinking.' Stanton gave a copy of the picture of Sanders to the leader and the other two officers in the foyer. Then he went out and gave one to each of the men outside watching the doors. When he returned, he gave the nod for the search to begin. He watched as the men moved from defensive to offensive postures and began to move up the stairs.

Lisa was on the phone in the secretary's office. 'I need Forensics over here right away to dust this computer … I don't care. I want them here in the next half hour.' She slammed down the phone. She might be new to this, but she was in no mood to take any hassle this morning. Her next call was to Patrick Bateson.

'Patrick. It's Lisa Collier. I need you to get along to King's University right now. I want you to find out if the computer we've got here has been used to check the Tyler email account.'

Patrick was taken aback by the fact he hadn't even had a chance to speak yet—and that he was speaking to Lisa. But from her tone he was in little doubt that the computer she wanted him to look at was crucial to catching the killer. 'Do you have an address?' Lisa gave it to him. 'I'll be on my way in five minutes.'

Lisa hung up, thanked the secretary for her help and told her to keep the door to Sanders office locked. No one was to go in unless Lisa was with them. The secretary was in a state of shock from her dealings with these two sunken-eyed detectives and she just nodded as she fanned herself daintily with a folder to calm herself. Lisa then got into the lift and went down to the foyer twelve floors below.

28 September, 9:19am, King's University, London

Stanton sat heavily into one of the chairs beside the automatic doors at the base of the tower. He had his head on the back of the chair and was rubbing his eyes roughly as the lift announced Lisa's arrival.

'Hey, you shouldn't do that, you know. It feels really good at first, but you'll only end up sore.' Lisa was dragging a chair from near the lift that she then used to jam open the doors so the lift was effectively out of action. She pressed the button to call the other lift.

'Good one. This is turning into a fine morning, isn't it?' he said sarcastically.

'You're not kidding. So much for him maybe giving himself up easily.' She dragged another chair to the door of the second lift.

'I just hope he's not going to put up too much of a fight,' said Stanton 'And if he's taken hostages ... man, I don't even want to think about that.'

The other lift arrived which Lisa also jammed open before she walked over slumped down in the chair next to Stanton's. 'We'll, just need to wait and see.'

'Indeed.' Stanton sighed.

Upstairs, the armed units were moving systematically through each room of the first floor of the tower, their guns butted stiffly into their shoulders as they scanned the various offices and the small library belonging to the Classics Department. The petrified staff and students they met were quietly told to go down to the bottom of the tower where there was a large common room. No one was permitted to leave the building, but at least if Grendel did decide to get involved in some kind of fire fight there wouldn't be too many innocents in the immediate area. In general the search was going well, although occasionally someone would scream in hysterics at being confronted by an armed policeman pointing a gun in their face.

Downstairs Stanton and Lisa watched as people began to appear in a loose procession from upstairs. One of the armed officers was guiding them into the common room. Most of those filing past looked relatively calm in what was quite a tense situation, although those who had panicked now looked as white as sheets and had to be helped across the foyer by colleagues.

'Yup, this was a great call,' Stanton said.

'Yeah, but what were we going to do? We've just been following the leads. If we could have arrested him last night we would have done.'

'Hmm.' Stanton couldn't imagine how it would feel to have your house raided by armed police in the middle of the night when you were innocent. He was pretty sure it was not a good feeling. He watched as more people walked by and decided he should make a call to get some uniforms down to the university to look after the people in the common room so that the armed units could concentrate on the search.

On the second floor, the purging operation was going well. Eight officers had systematically emptied all the offices at one side of the building. The procedure was fairly simple, kick in the door and tell everyone to get on his or her stomach. Then they would check each person against the picture they had been issued with. If you weren't Sanders then you were told to go downstairs.

'Second floor, clear!' came the squawking radio message over everyone's earpieces.

'Did we check the toilets on this floor?'

'Negative.'

'Someone check the toilet.'

'Roger.'

Two officers moved slowly to the door of the female toilets. They kicked in the front door and quickly ran in, their guns scanning the room. No one was outside the cubicles. One officer bent down to his knees then lowered his head to look under the doors of the cubicles for any ankles. They may have been raiding, but they were going to warn any toilet users before kicking in the doors. He was glad this was a female toilet: kneeling on the floor of male toilets would have been a completely different issue and would probably not have resulted in this level of good manners. There were no ankles and the two officers used the muzzles of their weapons to push the doors open to check for anyone standing on the toilet seats out of view. The bathroom was secure.

Letting down their weapons they walked back to the door.

'Tsh,' said the shorter of the two officers lifting the butt of his gun into his shoulder again. The other officer did the same.

Behind the half-open door through which the two men had entered the toilet, a door without a handle was moving slowly back and forth shakily. The front officer quietly closed the door out of the toilet. On the front of the moving door it said CLEANER'S CUPBOARD. The officers moved slowly forward. The door appeared to be being pulled into its doorframe more tightly as he advanced. The hearts in the chests of both men beat quickly and seemingly loudly from the thumping in their ears. Opening a door on a potentially armed suspect was never an easy operation in a confined space like this, but one thing was for sure, neither of them would be standing in front of the door when they swung it open.

The shorter officer took the end of the muzzle of his machine gun and used it to swing the door open. They both saw the hand that had been trying to hold the door shut pull back into the cupboard.

'Armed Police!' Both officers yelled loudly as they moved across the front of the door ready to take this character down if he looked like he was going to harm either of them.

The man's face was hidden in shadow at the back of the cupboard and his tweed jacket, shirt and tie were covered in dirty looking wet patches from where a mop head had fallen on him when he had climbed in.

'Out of the cupboard and lie face down on the floor! Now! Keep your hands plainly visible at all times! Move it!' In the tiled confines of the toilet the shouted instructions were jarringly loud.

The man began to slide out from the utility cupboard then slipped carefully onto his front as he rolled down onto the floor.

'Look at me!' said the taller officer as he pulled his photocopy of Sanders out from under his vest. The other officer kept his weapon trained on the man on the floor.

The man looked up at him. It was Sanders. He looked absolutely petrified. When he had seen Stanton and Collier in the lift they had been a couple of detectives from CID. That's what he had run from. And now he found himself dealing with highly tense and aggressive armed officers: a far worse situation. The two darkly-dressed men kept their weapons trained on his head and chest.

'We've got Sanders,' reported the shorter officer as he covered his companion who used a plastic cable-tie to bind Sander's hands tightly behind his back. Sanders was then painfully yanked onto his feet by his tied arms, causing him to emit an involuntary yelp as pain shot from his shoulders. 'We're bringing him out.'

The increasingly frustrated Stanton in the foyer was amazed when Sanders was manhandled down the stairs. He looked humiliated, angry and like he was ready to cry, all at once. Stanton and Lisa both stood up and walked to meet him.

'I'm not saying anything until I speak to my lawyer,' said Sanders.

Stanton gave Sanders his rights and concluded by saying, 'And you're going to fucking need a lawyer.'

The uniformed officers were just arriving and took over the job of detaining Sanders. Patrick arrived at the same time but waited until Sanders was on his way out the door before he approached the detectives. He looked relieved that the arrest had gone off without more injury, especially to Lisa.

'You got your man, I see,' Patrick stated.

'We did,' said Stanton. His voice was hard at having faced Grendel knowing what he had done to his three unfortunate victims. 'He's one sick man.'

'Still, you've got him now.'

Stanton looked at Patrick and nodded.

'I'll show you his computer and you can get started,' said Lisa.

'Great. Lead me to it and I'll see what our man's been up to.'

'Good stuff. I'll see you at the station.' Stanton said to Lisa. 'I want to make sure there are no hiccups in the paperwork with this guy.'

'Okay. I'll be as soon as I'm done here.'

'Right.' Stanton walked towards the automatic doors which opened with a hum and a swish. As he walked outside into the cooler air, Richardson from Forensics nodded at him and rushed past, case in hand, on his way to Sanders' office.

Richardson joined Lisa and Patrick in one of the lifts and the three of them went up to the twelfth floor where Lisa had the secretary let Richardson into Sanders' office. His priority was to lift prints off of the computer so Patrick could get on with examining it for any evidence that would connect Sanders to the Tyler email account. About twenty minutes after the print lifting was started, Richardson came through to the staff room where Patrick and Lisa were drinking coffee kindly made by the department secretary. The coffee was bitter and the powdered milk was not a good addition, but Lisa was glad of the caffeine jolt the drink was giving her.

'That's the computer done. You can come into the office now. Just don't touch anything but the computer.' The small fluffy brush and dust-covered rubber gloves were a dead giveaway that he was from Forensics.

'Did you get any good prints?' Lisa asked.

'Yes, lots. Especially from the screen. Whoever uses this computer looks like he reads with his finger. And there was a good thumb print on the picture at the side too.'

Patrick and Lisa went through to the office while the secretary offered Richardson a coffee. Patrick noticed the view over London. 'Would you look at that.' Lisa looked out. It was indeed a spectacular view from the tower. She hadn't even noticed it the first time she was in the office; she gave a slight sideways glance at the Irishman. She hadn't expected him to be so sentimental. The two silently looked out, together. Lisa liked the moment.

'You better get cracking on with this.' She blinked back to the job at hand. 'And I better get on my way too.'

'Sure thing,' Patrick said, his eyes lingering on hers as he sat down in front of the computer. 'Good luck with your man.'

'Thanks,' replied Lisa. 'If you find anything, call us straight away.'

'I will do.'

Patrick paused as his eyes followed Lisa out of the room. 'Er, Lisa?'

'Yes.' She turned, her face looked tired and strained.

Patrick shuffled slightly embarrassed in the seat. 'Eh, You wouldn't fancy coming out for a drink or, er, dinner with me when this thing is all over, would you?'

Lisa ran her fingers over her hairline, moving a couple of strands of her hair. She suddenly felt very messy and aware that she looked dreadful. Yet here was Patrick asking her for a date. She smiled. 'I'd love to, Patrick.'

'Top stuff!' Patrick grinned broadly. 'Top stuff.'

28 September, 11:44am,
London, Metropolitan Police Headquarters

Stanton had Grendel safely in a cell and had made sure every 'i' was dotted and 't' was crossed on all of the paperwork. Only then did he feel relatively secure about things. Sanders had been given a phone call to contact his lawyer, who would be there within the hour. Stanton decided to use the time to check on how the artist's impression of the killer was going with Dickinson. The line was engaged, so he gave Andy a phone at Cityworks.

'Hi Andy, did you get the tape off yet?'

'It should have been with you, like, an hour ago.'

'So it's been sent?'

'It was like Pony Expressed, man. We got one of our dudes to drive it down. And he phoned to say he's on his way back.'

'It must be down at the front desk. Listen, thanks Andy.'

'Not a problem.'

'Tell me, is Sam there? Is he back from Paris?'

'He sure is. Hold on and I'll get him.'

Stanton was put on hold. He took the opportunity to walk down to the front desk to see if the parcel was there. A brown Jiffy bag with the videotape was with the front desk. It had arrived about twenty minutes before.

'Hi, Jack,' said Sam's voice in Stanton's ear.

'Hello, Sam. How was the trip to Paris?'

'Not too bad. Busy.'

'You'll have heard we got Grendel.'

'Yes, I did. Congratulations.' Sam sounded genuinely thrilled.

'Thanks. Anyway, we've arrested the guy this morning, and I just thought I'd phone and say thanks for all the help you and your people gave us. You guys have been great.'

'That's no problem, Jack. No problem at all.'

'Listen, if you fancy we could all meet for a meal tonight to celebrate catching him. What do you say? We could take the Action Heroes out on the town.'

Sam's voice betrayed his disappointment, 'That sounds really great, Jack, but unfortunately I've got an appointment in London tonight that I can't really break. Maybe we could take a rain check on the meal.'

'Sure thing. I just figured it would be a good thank you. We can do it some other time.'

'Sounds good. Listen I have to go. I've lots to catch up with here now I'm back.'

'Okay, Sam. And thank Andy for me again.'

'I will do.'

Stanton had just put the tape into the machine and pressed play when Lisa arrived.

'How did it go?' he asked.

'Patrick's working on the machine right now and will phone whenever he finds something.' She couldn't help but smile a little as she talked of Patrick. She shook her head and continued, 'And Forensics got some good prints of Sanders. But then, I suppose, they would do in his office.'

'But at least if we find any of Sanders' prints at any of the scenes now, we'll have him.'

'Is this the tape from Cityworks for the Grendel ID?' Lisa was holding the box that Andy had kindly annotated with time references that would allow them to fast forward to specific characters the ID had been used for - namely

Grendel, Tyler and Jameson, the character who was killed by the Janus people in the big shootout.

The tape began to play and Stanton turned the sound down quite low with the remote. He was in no mood to listen to the sensational reporting if the in-game news service just now. The video showed a couple of scenes of a character Stanton and Lisa had never seen before. From the reporting they could hear the name Jameson again and again. The scenes showed the same man involved in various fights and destroying various buildings in the town. The newscaster seemed to be saying Jameson was the most dominant man in the City, which meant that at the point these video sequences were recorded he was top dog in *Alter Ego*.

After about ten minutes playing time and a bit of fast-forwarding by Stanton to a point Andy had recommended, the scene was filled by three Janus people walking up a street towards the camera. Stanton and Lisa were both glued to the screen, hoping this would provide them with a possible motive for the killings.

'Do you notice that the only Janus characters there are the Sanders' victims' characters?' Lisa observed.

'Uh-huh,' said Stanton.

'If the killings *are* related to this then that explains why Frank wasn't threatened in the game.'

Stanton nodded.

'Although why was Stella selected as well?' Lisa asked. 'Vincent isn't there.'

The scene showed two groups approaching one another on the main street of the City. The way they approached each other was like an old Western. Only one camera view was used throughout the report, so as the Jameson group walked past the camera's position, their faces moved out of view. Stanton turned up the volume on the television with the remote.

The reporter's voice faded up: '... foolishly were not at all scared at the prospect of the call out made by the new Janus organisation. This scene happened at around three o'clock this afternoon and marks the most fundamental power swing in the City's history.' The reporter stopped talking.

'So you guys think you're going to run the City?' Stanton and Lisa couldn't see which character had spoken, but assumed it was Jameson as he seemed to be the leader of the five-strong group.

Swift spoke on behalf of the Janus men as he lit a cigarette, 'Yes we are. And if you've got any sense you'll let us do it peacefully. Otherwise ...' The Janus men each removed a machinegun from an underarm holster.

Jameson's group also removed guns, their bodies tensing in readiness for action. One of them laughed. It was Jameson again, 'Nope, I think you'll need to fight us for the City. It's too big a prize to just give it away.' His group began to run for cover that would be useful in the ensuing gunfight. But before they had even got half a dozen steps, two of them were lying bleeding or dead on the ground. One had been shot in the head and had gone down immediately. The blood pumping from the hole just above his forehead formed a large puddle in front of him. The second man had managed a few staggering steps after getting hit in the chest. His body gave out by a kerb at the gardened side of Bushnell Road, where he lay staring at the sky.

The three Janus men began shooting their machine guns, catching a third running man in a hail of fire that had his body jitterbugging as the dozens of impacts shook his body, blowing off small chunks of flesh in the process. He went down in a bloody pulp after about four seconds of sustained fire.

The cameraman now moved the camera at the sudden realisation that the first shots weren't fired from machine guns. He scanned the windows at the end of Bushnell Road and then the rooftops and caught sight of a figure moving to a better firing position. The camera zoomed in on the running figure.

'Vincent,' said Lisa.

Stanton nodded as he leaned forward to make sure he took in every detail.

Vincent ran to the corner of the building and got into a new firing position. The camera turned again to the action on the street immediately in front of the camera. The Janus men were advancing forward, using a hail of bullets to keep the remaining two Jameson men pinned down. Then the situation seemed to become a stalemate as the three Janus men and the two Jameson men fired at each other from behind cover they were unable to advance from.

As the camera watched, the ground around the Jameson positions began to experience occasional impacts. And the shrapnel from the impacts moved in a different direction to the machine gun fire. The screen showed one Jameson man suddenly slump over sideways. The camera zoomed to show his glazed eyes looking directly into the camera. Blood trickled from his mouth. The only surviving member of Jameson's group now was Jameson himself.

The cameraman began to move to try to get a view of him, and the image became shaky and uneven for about ten seconds before the camera picked up Jameson crammed into a curled up shape behind the small amount of cover he had. He was looking up towards the position where Vincent was. The camera swung round and zoomed in on Vincent again.

The slight muzzle flash occurred about half a second before the sound of the shot could be heard. The camera wheeled back to where Jameson was. The body was slumped where it had sat, still looking up at where Vincent was, although the eyes now looked dead. A small rivulet of blood was running from the centre of Jameson's forehead, past his nose and mouth to finally drip off of his chin. The bullet hole was almost black.

The reporter continued, 'There's a new boss in the City tonight. His name is Mr Janus. And if we thought the last two months under Jameson and his crew was violent, this new breed of gangster already appears to be prepared to take things to a new level in the City.'

'So Jameson was the head honcho,' Stanton stated. 'And Vincent killed him after he and the other Janus people had killed the rest of Jameson's crew. A motive?'

'It seems so, although you can't get away from the fact that this,' she gestured at the screen, 'is only a game. It seems a bit excessive based on this to go and kill the people who control the characters who killed you in the game. I mean, why not just come at them in-game again?' The screen they were both watching was now showing Tyler, according to Andy's notes scribbled on the box, brutally killing someone in the streets down near the docks.

'I know, but having said that, it does fit a bit too alarmingly to ignore. First, we have a motive in that the people the Janus Killer has murdered, or wanted to murder, were all present when the old City boss was taken down.'

'In a cyber city in a computer game,' Lisa reiterated.

'Granted. But also, you said that Grendel was from some Old English poem, which our guy Sanders would know because of his job. And then there's the fact that his wife said he beat her showing his predisposition to real-world violence. And he did run when he saw my badge.' Stanton looked at Lisa. 'And probably most important, Grendel was controlled from his *Alter Ego* ID number.'

'I suppose so,' Lisa conceded. 'Still you've got to be pretty mad to decide to take revenge for something that happened in a game.'

'But then we're obviously not talking about a rational individual anyway, because how many people do you know that would cut off someone's face, never mind just kill them? He's obviously not firing on all cylinders.' Stanton paused. 'That's the other thing: this Janus mutilation aspect to the killings. If the murders weren't related to Sanders losing the City to these specific Janus players, then why are the bodies made to look like Janus?'

'Good point. You're right: too many things add up for this not to be our man. Although every single piece of evidence we have is purely circumstantial.''

'Indeed.'

'And without a confession or some good forensic evidence, he's going to walk.'

Stanton nodded silently.

There was a knock at the door and a uniformed officer's head appeared round the door, 'Sanders' lawyer is here.'

'Okay. Thanks,' said Stanton.

'We'll be through in a minute,' said Lisa.

Stanton fast-forwarded through the rest of the tape and they both watched for anything of use. After two stops that proved less relevant than they'd hoped they eventually got to the hunt for Grendel. Stanton pressed rewind on the tape and watched as the time counter ticked back to the scene of the face off. He stopped and ejected the tape. Then both he and Lisa went down to the interview room where Sanders and his lawyer were waiting.

28 September, 1:15pm,
London, Metropolitan Police Headquarters

As Stanton and Collier walked in, the tirade from Sanders' lawyer began: 'What the hell are you people doing arresting my client using armed police?' He stood up as he spoke, his chair making a honking sound as it scraped over the floor.

'Sit down, sir,' said the uniformed officer at the door.

The lawyer sat down again. 'It is totally unacceptable to arrest a man in that manner.'

Stanton and Lisa sat down.

'Sir, would you please calm down,' Lisa ordered. She looked at Sanders. Was this the man who had cut her arm?

The lawyer looked angered at Lisa's request.

Stanton started the tape recorder, stating that he and Collier were present along with Sanders' lawyer at this first interview with Sanders. He finished with the date and time before he turned to Sanders' lawyer: 'And your name is? Please speak clearly for the tape.'

'Gavin Bradley, representative for Mr Sanders,' Bradley said loudly. But he didn't stop there: 'a man who has been grossly mistreated by your officers: his wrists are bleeding from your barbaric method of binding his hands and his shoulders were almost dislocated as your ruffians hauled him around. The situation is most contemptible for a man who is being bled dry by a greedy wife using child support as her excuse. Are you aware that woman doesn't even work? And you're bound to have seen how she lives!'

'Mr Sanders,' Stanton began, 'we'd like to know where you were on the evening of Monday the 14th of October, Thursday the 18th of October and Sunday the 20th of October through until the following Monday Evening.'

Sanders looked at Bradley questioningly. Bradley looked as confused as Sanders: 'What on earth can that have to do with back payment of child support?'

'Mr Sanders, you are at present under arrest for three homicides,' Stanton stated. 'We'd like to know where you were on these dates.'

'What?' said Sanders. 'How ... what?'

Bradley seemed quite stunned at this revelation. 'And what are you basing these multiple murders allegations on Inspector Stanton?'

Stanton looked at Sanders. 'We have compelling video evidence from the game *Alter Ego* which shows your character being killed by Janus men, three of the people who played these Janus characters are now dead, and a fourth narrowly escaped with her life. We also recently spoke to your wife, who told us that around six months ago, at the same point at which you lost your dominant position in the *Alter Ego* City, that you beat her when she observed it was only a game. This aggression and your obvious displeasure at being ousted in the game has led us to conclude that you have taken it upon yourself to exact revenge for losing control of the City by killing the offending players.'

Sanders could hardly believe his ears. 'But ... what do you mean? Who am I meant to have murdered?'

'Don't say anything, Ian, I'll deal with this,' said Bradley. 'Yes, who is he supposed to have murdered? And what is all this twaddle about a computer game?'

'Mr Sanders is accused of the murders of Mr Niall Davidson, Mr Andrew Miller and Mr Arthur Braithwaite, all of whom belonged to the Janus group who killed Mr Sanders' character in *Alter Ego* and took the City from him around six months ago.' Stanton reiterated. 'We have evidence of him subsequently using a new character to infiltrate the Janus organisation in the game from where he would have been able to establish the real world whereabouts of the players, which he subsequently used to murder them.'

'What?' Sanders was stunned. 'But I haven't played *Alter Ego* for about six months.'

'Sorry?' said Lisa.

'I've not played for about six months. After I hit Linda I—'

'Don't say anything more, Ian, I'll deal with—'

'Shut up, Gavin!' Sanders snapped at Bradley. 'Don't you see, they seriously think I murdered these people. I have to explain what I know.' He looked back at Stanton and Lisa, 'Yes, I hit Emily once, and I mean one slap. It was a mistake. At that time I was playing *Alter Ego* a lot, and when the Janus people killed me, yes, I was pissed off and I got angry and slapped Emily when she said it was only a game. I was very involved in the game back then, but that doesn't mean I killed anyone.'

Stanton continued, 'Can you explain to us then why it is that the four victims selected from the Janus group were the four who killed you and your men in an incident in the City around six months ago?'

'I don't know why,' Sanders said. 'I haven't played *Alter Ego* for six months and I don't know anything about any murders.'

'Mr Sanders, we know you are lying about not playing *Alter Ego* because we have video evidence which shows that you played the game as recently as last night as a character called Grendel.'

Sanders was doing a sterling job of looking like he had no idea what they were talking about. 'Oh my God. You think I'm the Janus Killer, don't you? The one from the news. Oh my God.'

'Do you know who Grendel is?' Lisa said.

'He's a monster from *Beowulf*,' Sanders said quietly. He shook his head before continuing, 'I didn't kill anyone.'

'So where were you on the nights in question, Mr Sanders?' Stanton pushed a sheet of paper with the dates written on it across to Sanders and Bradley.

'I ... I ... don't know.' Sanders looked at the paper. This last date, I think I was maybe at the cinema.'

'And where was this cinema, Mr Sanders?' Stanton asked.

'It was in Leicester Square.'

'And can anyone corroborate you were there? Did anyone accompany you, or do you have a receipt or ticket stub that would put you at the scene, or anything else that would corroborate you were at that location on that evening?'

'No, I throw my tickets away after I've been to the cinema and I don't buy anything at the cinema because it's so expensive. How was I to know I'd need to confirm where I was that night?' He looked very confused. 'And how could I be online last night when I know I wasn't?' He was looking at the table and fidgeting with the piece of paper Stanton had given him.

'Do you have anyone who could corroborate that for us, Mr Sanders?' Lisa asked.

'No. Since Linda and I split up, I've not really had any friends. She told everyone that I beat her, you know after I slapped her once, and now none of our friends even talk to me.'

Stanton sighed, feeling this was not moving forward easily. 'Interview terminated 1:47pm.' He switched off the tape. 'Would you like a coffee, Mr Sanders?'

'Yes,' he said quietly, looking up at Stanton with bloodshot eyes.

'And you?' Stanton asked Bradley.

'No, thank you.'

'Lisa?' Stanton gestured for Lisa to come with him.

As the uniformed officer walked in and closed the door Stanton and Lisa both walked along the hall looking perplexed.

'He's not really like I thought he'd be,' Lisa said.

'Do you think he's the one who stabbed you?' Stanton asked.

'I don't know. He's about the right size. But with only his build and height to go on, I can't say for certain.'

'He seems genuinely shocked by all of this, doesn't he?'

'Yes, he does,' Lisa replied. 'But then if he's used to being someone else in *Alter Ego*, a violent someone else at that, maybe this is just a persona we're seeing.'

'Maybe.' Stanton thought for a second. 'Okay, we'll let Sanders stew for a while and I'll try and get Dickinson on the phone again to see how the artist's impression is coming along. It's likely that the man Dickinson saw *was* our killer. And if the image is of Sanders, then Dickinson becomes a witness who can put him at the scene of the Miller murder, which then means all the rest of the evidence becomes a feasible motive for the killings.'

'Okay, I'll meet you here when you're done.'

Stanton managed to get a hold of Dickinson, who sounded exhausted. 'We've got some bloody great organisation up here, Stanton. We're halfway through the thing just now. The bloody artist was on his day off and the other one is at some conference somewhere in France. It took us until an hour ago to track the first man down. So we've just got started.'

'So how long will it take?'

'If I'm not on the phone to you it will take less time.'

'Good one,' Stanton said sarcastically.

'I don't know how long, Stanton. But I'll phone you as soon as we're done and we can get the bloody thing faxed to you.'

'We've got a man under arrest just now. So the sooner we get the picture, the better.'

'I understand. It will be with you as soon as is humanly possible.'

'Thanks, Dickinson.' Stanton hung up and went to the gents' toilets. He looked at his sunken eyes in the mirror then splashed some cold water on his face. He wanted that picture.

Forty minutes later, Stanton and Lisa went back to the interview room.

'Well, you people took your time,' said Bradley

'Here's your coffee,' Lisa said passing over the polystyrene cup. Stanton started the tape again, stating the time and those present.

'Ever been to Scotland?' Stanton asked Sanders.

'Yes, I was there a couple of months back,' Sanders replied. 'Why?'

'Did you ever visit the Borders? I hear it's quite lovely.' Stanton's tone sounded as if this was almost an irrelevant conversation.

'No, I usually visit the highlands when I go to Scotland. I like the mountains and lakes.'

'Lochs,' Stanton corrected.

'Yes, the lochs.' Sanders version of the word was identical to "locks".

'So you've never been to Oxton?'

'Is that in the Highlands or in the Borders? I've never been there either way.'

'What about Ruislip? Ever been there?'

'Once. Linda and I looked for a flat there but it was too expensive. Why?'

'How are you with tools, Mr Sanders?' Lisa asked.

'I'm not very good at DIY. What's this all about?'

'Yes,' said Bradley. 'What the devil are you people driving at?'

'Why didn't you move Braithwaite?' Lisa asked. 'Don't you think he didn't look as nice when you were done with him?' She was trying to provoke some kind of response based on the scene of the crime. Did Sanders know Braithwaite was too big to move alone? Would he defend his "sculpture"?

'Move Braithwaite? What do you mean? Were the other people moved? I don't know what you mean.' Sanders was becoming visibly shaken by the questioning.

'Did you think you could take the Action Heroes? Is that why you went out to face them last night?' Stanton asked.

'Action Heroes?' Sanders was staring down. He couldn't grasp what was being asked, and yet both of these officers seemed to know a hell of a lot about whatever it was that they were driving at. Unfortunately Sanders did not.

'Why don't you just admit to being online in *Alter Ego* last night, Ian,' Stanton said gently.

'I wasn't online last night. I watched television.'

'What did you watch?' Lisa asked.

'I watched a documentary about the African savannah.'

'What channel was it on?'

'BBC2.'

'And how do we know you didn't just read the television times?'

'Look,' Sanders began, 'I haven't played *Alter Ego* for months. Yes, I was killed by the Janus people about six months ago, but then I was bumped for two weeks. And in those two weeks I was thrown out by my wife, had an injunction filed against me to stay away from her and my little girl, and when I finally was allowed back into the game I had only just managed to start letting people know I was back and was getting ready to start work on ousting the Janus people when I got zapped by some psycho with a weapon that drained all the life from me. Then the next time I logged on about two weeks later I was denied access with a message that said something about my identification being unauthorised and that my reference was already in use. It said I needed to obtain a valid authorisation key or something like that anyway. *I have not played the game since then.*' Sanders used a straightened finger pointing at the table to drum out his last words emphatically. 'I took it to be a sign that I should get my life back together and move on. Which I have done.'

Stanton and Lisa sat silently for about twenty seconds.

'I haven't played the game for about six months,' Sanders reiterated. 'You have to believe me.'

'What was the weapon like?' Lisa asked.

'Didn't you hear me? I didn't kill any of the people you are talking about. How would I know what the weapon was like that killed them?'

'What was the life draining weapon like that was used on your character after you went back to *Alter Ego* after the Janus people killed you?'

'The weapon from the game?'

'Yes, the weapon from the game.'

'I don't know it was like a glove weapon thing. I don't really remember, it all happened quite fast.'

'Just a glove or anything else?' Lisa asked.

'It had two prongs coming out from a fist-shaped glove. That's all I can remember.'

'Can I speak to you outside, please?' Lisa asked Stanton.

'Sure.'

Both of them moved outside.

'That sounds like a harvester he's talking about. Do you think it's possible someone stole Sanders' ID using a harvester and then assumed it in *Alter Ego* to cover their tracks so that when they were tracked down outside that it would lead to Sanders?'

'It's possible. But it would need to be a pretty incredible frame-up considering the amount of things that fit with Sanders actually being the killer.'

'Yes, but that would also make it an ideal cover for someone else. And the bottom line is that if Sanders is telling the truth about losing his ID, then someone else could have been Grendel. If he's telling the truth, someone else *must* have been Grendel. And let's face it, he only ran because he thought it was something to do with child support payments to his ex-wife.'

'But who else has a motive to kill these specific Janus people then?' Stanton asked. 'And how ... oh shit. That guy from Cityworks who was working on the harvesting unit said he found a unit already in the computer system.'

'So someone in Cityworks must have harvested Sanders' ID number then used it to infiltrate Janus.' Lisa could hardly believe the way this seemed to be moving. Speculation and all as it was, it made a lot of sense.

'But who in Cityworks would want to kill some of their customers?' Stanton asked, confused. 'Especially when the existence of the Janus group was one of the factors that made the game so popular.'

Stanton's mobile rang. He pressed the small green telephone button to pick up the call.

'Stanton.'

'It's Dickinson here. I've got the picture in my hand. Are you ready to get it faxed there?'

'Sure, hold on and I'll get the fax number for you.' Stanton ran though to the front desk. 'What's the number for this fax?' The desk sergeant told him and Stanton relayed the information to Dickinson in blocks of three or four numbers at a time.

'Okay. I'm faxing it through just now. Hold on. Well, this is going to tell us one way or the other if Sanders is our man,' Lisa said.

Stanton stared at the fax machine. He could read on the little display that the machine was negotiating a call. The display changed to read "RECEIVING". Jack Stanton's heart was beating at ramming speed in his chest as the shoulders and neck of the killer began to emerge. The fax machine hummed as it slowly printed its image line by line onto the page.

'Oh shit!' said Stanton as the bottom of the face became visible. 'Oh shit! Go and get the car, Lisa. Now! SHIT! And you: get an armed unit to Theydon Bois right now.' He bellowed at the officer on the front desk

The paper dropped onto the tray at the bottom. The faxed artist's impression was a passable and recognisable image of Sam Stark.

28 September, 4:22pm, London, Metropolitan Police Headquarters

Stanton's stomach was in knots. He had the worst gut feeling he had ever experienced. And it involved Sam Stark. He thought back to their earlier conversation: was Sam's appointment with Stella? Was he going to try to finish his job while the police had their backs' turned? For some reason Stanton was sure he was. He slammed his car through a junction with an amber light. His engine revs were higher than they should have been, but he was dialling his phone and couldn't change the gear.

'Jack, give me the phone. You're scaring the shit out of me with this driving.' Lisa's voice was higher than usual and she was now convinced this first case may well be her last. Stanton passed over the phone. 'Who do you want me to call?'

'Phone Stark,' said Stanton flatly. 'I want to know where he is.'

Lisa dialled, but Stark's phone didn't ring: 'The telephone you have called is not switched on. Please try again later,' said the monotonous digital voice.

'His phone isn't on.' Lisa was looking at Stanton as he swerved and bobbed the car through traffic on his way to Stella's flat.

Sam Stark turned the corner into Station Approach in Theydon Bois. Stella's flat was at the far end, he knew, but he pulled left into a side street and parked. He lifted his briefcase from the back seat and walked to the end of the street. Jumping a fence carefully, he skirted along in the direction of the Underground station. Over another fence he was soon outside the station. He waited behind a wall until the next tube arrived from London then walked down towards Stella's flat.

He walked up to the officer at the front door and smiled broadly. 'Hi, how are you? I'm here to see Stella.'

'And you are, sir?'

Stark pulled a card from his inside pocket, 'I'm Sam Stark, CEO of Binary Cityworks, the people who make the *Alter Ego* game.'

'Aah, the game Miss Robertson plays.' The officer was examining Stark's card.

'That's right. I figured now you guys have the killer that she might be looking for some light relief.' Stark tapped his brief case. 'I've brought her the newest release version of *Alter Ego*. It's got lots of new features and I figured while I was in the area I'd drop a copy off.'

The officer nodded, 'She'll probably be pleased about that. She's in good form since last night's hunt.' The officer rang the doorbell and another officer inside opened the door. The first explained why Stark was there.

Stark was shown into Stella's flat.

Stanton looked at his watch. His phone began to ring. Lisa answered it.

'Lisa? Isn't this Jack's phone?' It was Patrick.

'Yes. What is it Patrick!' Lisa used her good arm to brace herself against the dashboard.

'I've just finished with the computer at Sanders' office and I didn't find anything. It was possibly the dullest computer I've ever seen. It only had work-related academic documents. All Internet surfing was related to work or train times, and apart from that—'

'Sanders was the wrong guy, Patrick.' Lisa's hand involuntarily grabbed tighter to the dashboard as they rocketed through a junction and round a corner at high speed. Stanton was working the horn to try to clear a path.

'Sorry, we didn't have time to give you a call yet. We're on the track of the real killer right now. I'll speak to you later,' Lisa said, almost in half-scream, as she watched a bus swerve to avoid their car as Stanton drove up the wrong side of the road to get through some red lights.

'Hello, Stella, how are you?' Stark said as he walked in.

'Hi, Sam.' Stella looked up from the couch in the living room. 'Much better since we got Grendel last night. And I heard today that they've arrested the guy.'

'Yes, so they've said.' Stark watched as the policeman who had escorted him through left the room. He sat down.

'Did you watch the hunt last night?'

'Sort of, I was a bit busy with other things I had to do, but I got the gist of it. You and the Action Heroes did well. I thought for a while it would all end differently. Still not to worry.'

'Sorry ... what do you mean not to worry?' Stella asked tilting her head slightly as she smiled.

'Did I say that? I meant it all worked out well. Sorry, it's been a long couple of days.'

'Yes, I heard you were in Paris last night. How was it?'

'Fine.'

The telephone rang.

'Hold on a second, would you. I had better get that.'

'No problems.'

Stella got up, went through to the kitchen and picked up the telephone.

The car was travelling at over eighty miles an hour as Lisa talked on the mobile, occasionally gripping various bits of the car as her fear of being involved in a crash fluctuated.

'Hi, Stella. How are you?' Lisa was trying to sound calm so as not to worry Stella since at this point they were working on nothing more than a hunch from Stanton, and Stark might not be on his way to Stella's at all. So Lisa tried not to worry her.

'I'm fine. How are you?'

'Yes, good.'

'I hear you got the guy who played Grendel.'

Stop talking about trivia, Lisa thought. 'So what are you up to, Stella?'

'Sam has just popped round with the new version of *Alter Ego* for me.' Stella looked across at Sam. He wasn't watching her, so he missed her smile.

'Aah.' Inside Lisa's head her voice was screaming, but she had to make sure she didn't panic Stella or give Sam the upper hand. 'Listen, the reason I was calling was to chat with the officer there. Can I have a quick word?'

'Sure, hold on.' The mouthpiece was covered and Lisa could hear Stella distantly say, 'It's for you, Brian. It's Lisa Collier.'

Constable Brian Jones took the phone from Stella. 'Hello,' he said brightly.

'Listen to me very carefully,' Lisa began. 'The man in the house is Sam Stark and he is the Janus Killer.'

The blood was draining from the face of Jones as he looked across at Stark in the living room. Stark was watching the officer intently. Jones smiled and nodded in what he hoped was a casual way. Stark did likewise.

'We're on our way to the flat, and an armed unit is due to arrive at about the same time.'

'Uh-huh.' Jones's voice was slightly higher.

'This man is extremely dangerous, so don't try and do anything. Just make sure Stella is all right, okay?'

'Yes, ma'am. Thank you. I will do.' Jones was trying to make the call sound totally routine. He hung up, his hand shaking as he replaced the receiver.

'So Sam is there?' said Stanton as he peered out of the windscreen at the streets hurtling by.

'I'm afraid so.' Lisa could feel more acceleration than usual as Stanton went even faster.

'Damn it! Why did I have to be right with this? Chase up that armed unit. I want them across at Stella's now!'

'Look, Jack, we're on our way and there are two officers already looking after Stella. It will be almost impossible for him to hurt her. We're going to get Stark before anything happens.' Lisa felt less sure of this than she sounded, but with Stanton driving like a lunatic, *they* were both going to end up dead in some horrific car crash if *he* didn't start to believe that they were going to make it on time.

She dialled the armed unit.

Officer Jones could hear the small talk coming from the living room. He stood in the kitchen for a few seconds trying to think what to do. He decided he should inform the other officer out front; maybe he should even come in. They'd have more chance of overpowering Stark if anything were to start then. He started to move to the stairs.

'Officer?' It was Stark. 'Can you come here for a second?'

'Er ... I just need to go down and check with John outside.' He continued to move to the stairs. His face was white and his hands were shaky and clammy.

Stark walked through. 'No, I think you should come and see this for now.' He took Jones by the arm and walked him through to the living room again. Stella was booting up the computer. 'Just sit here.' Sam lifted his brief case onto the small coffee table opening it at a slight angle to the policeman. Stella was turning in her chair and smiling as she anticipated the newest version of *Alter Ego* that would soon be installed on her computer. Jones looked sick.

'Now where is it?' said Stark, rifling. 'Aah yes.' Stella had turned back to see if the system had booted, and Stark's manoeuvre was so swift and accurate it made nothing but a brief "Shlook" sound. Jones grabbed at his throat that was now sliced open. Stark blinked and wiped his eyes as blood sprayed across the room. In her chair, Stella arched her back as the warm wet droplets showered her T-Shirt.

She turned round slowly. Stark was standing up, wiping his face with one of the neatly ironed handkerchiefs that had been sitting on the mantelpiece. The large knife in his hand was Stella's own kitchen knife.

'It's you,' she said quietly. Anger welled in her and she launched herself at Stark, knocking him to the floor. He was upright faster than Stella was and it was with a slight tightening of her throat that she saw his fist swing through the air and felt it slam against her cheek.

Everything went black.

The officer outside got a fright when the door suddenly opened behind him. 'Jeez, you scared the living daylights out of me there.'

'Sorry,' said Stark. 'I should probably have made more noise coming down the stairs.'

'What's that on you shirt?' the officer asked, looking at the spots of red on Stark's shirt.

'Oh, Stella's making a tomato sauce for some pasta upstairs. I must have been too close to the pan.' He wiped absently at the red stains on his shirt. 'She's wondering if you'd like to come in for something to eat.'

'Wonderful. That would go down a treat.'

Stark turned round and began to walk upstairs. As his head reached the top, he carefully faked a stumble and picked up the kitchen knife he had left at the top of the stairs. The officer was locking and bolting the door. 'Mind your step there. I always thought these steps were a bit too steep.'

'Indeed,' said Stark. He had moved round so he was behind the wall, out of view of the officer.

'You know I'm actually starving.' The officer walked into the kitchen area. He looked puzzled when he saw nothing was cooking at all. 'What …' He caught sight of the other officer's foot in the living room. Something slick was coating his shoes, and the newspapers on the table were covered in red droplets. He walked slowly forward towards the living room. 'What the hell?' He was just beginning to see Stella unconscious on a chair in the living room, her ankles bound to the chair with silver tape and her wrists also bound with tape behind the back of the chair. The officer was just beginning to realise what was going on and was about to look and see where Stark had gone when he felt a sudden sharp burning feeling in his back. His body had no time to interpret the feeling further as the blade continued to slice into him cutting his heart almost in two. He was dead before he hit the floor.

'You know, all that stuff with Sam wanting to use the Action Heroes footage to promote *Alter Ego* is starting to make sense,' said Stanton. 'I mean, apart from that he seemed fine, but there was a real mercenary streak with this that I didn't like.'

'I know what you mea— WATCH OUT!'

It was too late and Stanton made a grinding glancing blow against a large white Volvo. Sparks showered onto the street as about twenty miles an hour were savagely ground from Stanton and Lisa's speed.

'Are you okay?' Stanton asked above the screech of tires as he accelerated again.

'Just about.' Lisa was shaking like a leaf. She was pretty sure this was the evening she was going to die.

'Stella, you're awake. I was just going to get some water to throw on your face.'

Stella blinked a few times as she tried to clear her head. She tried to move her arms, but the fractional movements this translated into would be useless for getting out of this tape. She looked left and could see the officer with his throat cut. His head was sideways where it had fallen as he died and his neck wound was gaping. Stella closed her eyes tightly for a second. How had it all come to this? How had he managed to get her tied to a chair? She had put up a fight. She didn't deserve to die like this. She attempted to speak but found her mouth was covered by tape. She hadn't felt it at first because of the pain coming from what she assumed was a broken cheekbone. She suddenly became aware that she couldn't even engage Stark in conversation.

She looked at the door. She could see the hand and forearm of the other officer. Oh, no, she thought, he's killed them both. How long will it take for Lisa, or Stanton, or someone, to get here and save me...? She became abstractly aware that her breathing was relatively all right. She didn't know why, but since the dream, her panic attacks had stopped. She was glad she didn't have that to contend with as well as this psycho.

Stark stood in front of her. He was now wearing black leather gloves and as she watched he was systematically rubbing clean anything he may have touched with a piece of cloth. She watched as he removed an industrial-sized sticky fluff remover and began to roll the areas where he had been sitting. He turned round and raised his eyebrows and smiled as he showed Stella the roller's barrel. Bits of fluff and hair were stuck to it. He tore off the dirty sheet, put it in his briefcase, then repeated the process.

'You know, Stella,' Stark began, 'it's almost a shame you have to die.'

Stella looked at him. She hoped her eyes spat her hatred enough for him to notice.

'But you do,' he stated flatly as he looked around for things to clean. The bloody knife sat on a polythene bag on the mantelpiece. Stella could see the dark shadow of the small pool of blood it held. 'Because it won't be long until they find out Sanders didn't kill the others.' Stella figured Sanders must have been the person the police originally thought was Grendel. 'And at that point, you might as well be dead too, seeing as the paying public will really be happier if there is yet another Janus Killing.' He punctuated the last words using two fingers to draw the quotation marks in the air. Stella's eyes must have looked questioning. 'It'll keep them following the news and that will keep them interested in the game. It's like a wonderful cycle!' He made a rolling motion using both hands. The fluff remover rattled.

'You're wondering why, aren't you? It must seem to you at this point a little superfluous for you to die. You probably think that since the police have Sanders and another killing is going to occur while he is in custody that the police will then be onto me. That's true, although they won't be onto me,' he smiled. 'They'll just know that someone killed people for a motive relevant only to Sanders – which is certainly a bit odd. Isn't it? Oh, by the way, Stella, Sanders was Jameson. You remember Jameson, don't you? The man you Janus people ousted to take control of the City. It's all quite beautiful really.' Stark looked wistful. He put down the cleaning tool and picked up the knife which he then used to draw in the air as he spoke: 'Wronged *Alter Ego* Player Seeks Brutal Revenge In Reality,' Blood splashed from the blade as he waved it around. He leaned in close to Stella, his hands on his knees so his face was level with hers.

'You know, Stella, Sanders and his little revenge killing spree has just been a big ruse to throw the police.' He smiled. Stella shook as Stark stared into her eyes. He looked perfectly calm. 'The killings related to *Alter Ego* are already fulfilling their function. I checked this morning, and the population of the City has almost doubled. The game hasn't seen such a popularity boost, ironically, since you guys took out Jameson's people. And now you're being taken out apparently by him, and the punters are *loving it*!' Stark stood up and walked to the other side of the room, twiddling Stella's kitchen knife. She followed his every move with her eyes. This is all about money, she thought. This sick bastard had killed Niall and the others for the money it would make him.

As if to confirm this to Stella, Stark continued: 'Do you know that thanks to you I'm worth almost twice as much as I was last week?' He laughed. 'Well, I suppose you can't take all the credit, I mean, I did go to the press and tell them about the killings, and that helped a lot. But you guys were good. You've really paid your way.' He smiled again, pushing his designer spectacles further up his nose. 'So you can at least be happy in the knowledge that you've made hundreds of millions in your last few weeks. It's a shame you won't see any of it.'

Stark walked over to behind Stella's chair. She shook as much as her bindings would allow her as he spoke close to her ear. 'The Janus Killings will go down as a series of unsolved of murders. And you're going to be part of the folklore of them. The murders provoked by a computer game, the final proof that computer games really do turn people into soulless killers. Quite a legacy, eh?'

Stella's mind screamed. If only she could talk she could at least try to negotiate with him. He had to realise his stupid plan wasn't going to work and that he was going to get caught. But the tape on her mouth was stuck fast, inhibiting her speech and turning her words into sounds that would only be interpreted as the mumblings of a very frightened woman. She shook her head unconsciously as she realised that she was powerless to stop Stark from doing to her exactly what he had done to the others.

He took some of her hair between his thumb and finger. He pulled it taught, and then cut it off. She moaned, and this time it was totally involuntary. He put the lock in front of her face then released it onto her lap like he was sprinkling salt onto food. 'Anyway, time's a wastin', as they say.' Now Stark sounded mad. 'Adios, Vincent. Unfortunately we won't be seeing you later.'

Stark stabbed down between Stella's shoulder blades.

**28 September, 5:16pm,
Theydon Bois**

CRRAACK.

Stark's head turned sharply towards the door. He looked across at the door to the living room from where the sound had emanated. He ran to the kitchen, tripping over the dead policeman as he crossed to look down the stairs. Someone was kicking the front door in. Thank goodness Stella's door had so many bolts, which thankfully the policeman at his feet had taken the time to pull across.

CRRAAACK.

It was sounding like it was ready to give at any moment. Stark didn't know where to go. He ran back through to the living room and barged past the bloody form of Stella on the chair. He knocked over the chair as he barged across to the door to the balcony, leaving Stella entangled in the feet of the dead officer on the sofa. He looked at the doors he had so painstakingly sawn through the other night. New bolts had since been added to the door, and two of them were padlocked. He shook the doors back and forth in frustration.

CRRAACK.

Sam grabbed his briefcase and threw it through the window. It made a hole right in the centre of the pane.

CRRAACKTHUMP.

The downstairs door had given and Stark could hear footsteps running up the stairs. He began to punch at the glass around the hole to make a hole large enough for him to get out of. The window broke up unevenly as he did it, his hands leaving bloody marks on the bits of glass before they broke.

'There he is!' Jack Stanton shouted as he thundered across the kitchen. He hardly even glanced at the body of the policeman on the floor. 'Stop!'

Stark had no intention of stopping and was leaning over the windowsill into his newly made hole in the glass. He had one knee on the jagged edge of the windowsill and was lifting his other leg ready to jump out to escape.

'Oh no you don't, you sick bastard!' Stanton said as he grabbed Stark and pulled him back with all his strength. There was an audible pop as Stark's kneecap was severed from its tendon by the shards of glass his knee was raked over as he was roughly dragged back into the room. Off balance and unable to support himself on his now useless leg, Stark slipped and crashed face down on the windowsill. As he turned, he made a gurgling sound.

His eyes were wide as he looked at Stanton. Sam had a large shard of glass sticking from his neck and bubbles of frothing blood were gathering at it. The foam seeped down his front. He slumped down, slipping to a seated position in front of the window. He was smiling at Stanton as he passed out.

Lisa was over at Stella as soon as she could get past Stanton. 'She's still breathing. Come here and help me.'

Stanton looked over at Stark and figured he was either dying or dead. He certainly wasn't about to come round like they do in the movies. They sat Stella up in the chair again. She looked a mess.

'Oh no,' said Lisa. 'There's blood everywhere.'

'Where's it coming from?' Stanton said urgently.

'I think just from her back, but it's hard to say because there's blood all over her hair too.'

Stanton crouched down. Stella's face was as white as it could be, but it was there. 'At least he hasn't cut her face off.'

'That'll be a small mercy if we can't stop the bleeding,' Lisa snapped. 'Give me that knife.' She pointed at the kitchen knife on the floor. Stanton picked up the bloodied weapon. Lisa quickly cut the tape that bound Stella to the chair and laid her forward on the floor by the coffee table. She cut off Stella's T-shirt and bra at the back. 'There.' She looked at the wound, which had blood seeping from it. 'Get me a towel or something,' said Lisa pressing hard on the wound, ignoring the pain in her arm as adrenalin coursed through her body. 'Then get an ambulance here.' Stanton ran through and pulled open kitchen drawers until he found a towel. He rushed it through to Lisa who folded it into a pad shape and pressed hard on the wound on Stella's back. She looked across at Grendel. The foam at his neck was still bubbling down his front.

The ambulances arrived twenty minutes later, fifteen minutes after the armed unit arrived. Stella and Stark were both taken unconscious to the Accident and Emergency department at the hospital in Harlow.

EPILOGUE

16 October, 12:31pm, Glasgow, Cardonald Cemetery

Jack Stanton stood in front of the gravestone, holding his red Parachute Regiment beret.

HERE LIE THE EARTHLY REMAINS OF
L-CPL . SIMON STANTON DCM
2ND BATTALION, PARACHUTE REGIMENT

BORN:
CATHCART, GLASGOW
14TH AUGUST 1962

DIED:
GOOSE GREEN, FALKLAND ISLANDS
28TH MAY 1982

"FALLEN IN THE CAUSE OF THE FREE"

It had been years since he'd been here, years since he'd thought of his brother—until the Janus case. The brutality had been both a blessing and a curse. It had made him pull old photos out over the last few weeks, where he found himself smiling and crying as he looked at the two fresh-faced youngsters he and his brother had been, dressed in their camouflaged combat fatigues and red berets. He had smiled at how they had looked with their moustaches, almost a trademark of a Para at the time—the object had been to make them look older, but he could see from the pictures they had just been boys

Had things been different, he would perhaps have been the one who had died and Simon would have survived. Both had been members of 2 Para; only Jack's company had been on the flank of the march across the moor towards Goose Green. Such was war, and it had been a bitter pill to swallow, one which had destroyed Jack's family.

He wiped a tear as he re-read the gravestone. A half-bottle of whiskey sat propped next to the neatly kept grave. He placed his beret on top of the stone where his brother's remains lay and shook his head solemnly.

18 October, 8:31pm,
London, Soho

Lisa nervously drank from her glass before replacing it on the slowly swelling coaster. The condensation had left her palm cold and clammy. She breathed deeply, trying to shake off her nerves, an uncomfortable feeling that made her feel like she needed to go to the bathroom. It seemed crazy to her that she could deal with criminals and take in grotesque crime scenes without too many problems, yet going on a first date made her feel like she had bladder problems. She closed her eyes tightly and shook her head, debating whether or not to do a runner. But he seemed like a nice bloke. Her shoulders slumped.

'I hope you're not dropping off on me before I even arrive.'

Lisa kept her eyes closed for a second longer as she tried to think of an excuse. 'No. Sorry. No.' She knew she sounded flustered, so offered her hand. 'How are you, Patrick?' As soon as he took her hand she knew it had been the wrong thing to do. If ever a handshake was the proverbial wet fish handshake, this was it: cold and clammy from holding her drink seconds before. 'Sorry,' she apologised again. 'I was just holding my drink.'

'Don't worry.' Patrick smiled, then using her hand to pull her closer he gently kissed her on the cheek. 'It's good to see you.'

Lisa smiled.

4 June, 1:31pm,
Broadmoor Mental Hospital

Andy McCormack walked along the sterile white corridor, a pile of magazines under his arm. They were difficult to hold because their glossy covers slid against one another. He arrived at another set of white-painted bars. The gentleman clad entirely in white squeaked past him as he withdrew the keys from his belt. The door was unlocked and Andy was motioned through. He jumped as the gate clanged shut behind him. He heard keys turn in the lock and the orderly's shoes squeak along behind him again.

Two more gates and he was finally at a large strong-looking white door with a small glass window the size of a paperback book at about head height. The orderly unlocked the door.

'Ten minutes,' he said.

'Sure.' Andy walked into the large brightly-lit room. There was a table bolted to the floor over by the window. Around it, three chairs were also bolted down. They looked too far from the table to allow it to be used comfortably. Andy crossed and put the magazines down, noticing the space where the fourth chair would have been. It looked like the chair had been ripped from the floor at some point.

Sam Stark stood entirely dressed in white across by the windows. Even his slip-on shoes were white. He was looking out at the bright summer day. The windows had bars on the outside and had criss-cross wire sheets on the inside that were secured with padlocks.

'Hey, Sam,' said Andy quietly.

Sam jolted back into reality, turned and quickly crossed to Andy. He hugged him warmly. When he spoke, his voice was different, with a croaking quality from the wound he had received when the glass had stuck in his neck. 'How are you, Andy?' He looked intensely into Andy's eyes.

'I'm not bad, Sam. How are you, man? You look ... good.'

'I've been better.' He nodded profusely. 'But I'm surviving.'

'I brought some magazines for you to read.'

'Good. Good. Thank you.'

It was the first time Andy had been allowed to see Sam since he'd left Cityworks to attack Stella. 'What happened, man?'

'I don't know, Andy. I just don't know.' Sam motioned for Andy to sit down at one of the chairs. He himself limped across and sat down. 'I mean I was doing great: we were all making a pile of money and I thought I'd thought of everything.'

'What do you mean?' Andy asked.

'Well, I had my scapegoat all sorted out and I had the media doing the running for me. It was all going well; then I had that one setback when they captured me.' Sam rubbed at the scar on his throat. 'I'm really not sure why I didn't get the chance to try again. I mean, the whole thing was almost without a hitch, and I know now what I'd do to get past the level.'

'The level? Sam, it wasn't a game. You killed people.'

Sam looked at him blankly. 'You know, if I'd killed Stella that first night, I'd have won.' He paused. 'I underestimated that Scottish policeman too. I never expected that those yokels up north would have been so on the ball. Next time I'll kill him. And *then* they'll put Sanders away for it and I'll get past it.' He glanced out of the window. 'Right now, though, I seem to be stuck on *this* level.' He looked around the room. 'I've looked everywhere for levers and buttons, but I can't find anything to let me get out. I even asked the people who are on this level, in case there are characters that have a riddle or something I'm meant to solve.' He put his palms up. 'But, nothing.'

Andy looked at the man he'd known for so long. What had happened to him?

Sam's face suddenly brightened, 'You have a key for me, don't you?' Sam clapped his hands. 'That's it, isn't it? You're going to get me off of this level.'

'No, Sam. I can't let you out of here. You need to stay until you're better.'

'But I'm fine. I just need to find the key, because I've been stuck here for ages and I can't get past it.' Sam's voice was getting more agitated.

'Dude—'

'You need to give me the key, Andy!'

Andy stood up and quickly walked across to the door.

'Andy,' Sam said quietly tugging at Andy's sleeve. 'If you're not meant to tell that you've given me it, I won't tell them that you did.' His voice started to rise again, 'Just give me it. Please! I'm stuck and need your help!'

Andy banged on the door. It opened immediately and the orderly let him out, pushing Sam back in as he closed the door.

'I can't get off of this level, Andy. I need you to give me the key!' Sam's face was pressed to the small glass window, steaming it up as he shouted.

Andy covered his ears as he stood waiting at the bars of the white gate. The orderly locked Sam's door then squeaked towards Andy who was looking back at Sam's face pressed to the glass. Even through his covered ears, he could hear the muffled shouts.

'I need the key, Andy! Help me! I'm stuck on this level!'

Stella Robertson limped off of the tube at Theydon Bois station. The severed nerves in her back had made her perfectly healthy limbs look like those of a staggering cripple. She struggled with her walking stick through the turnstile then crossed the two hundred yards to her flat. Thomas was outside waiting.

'Hello, Thomas. How are you tonight?'

He meowed his response as she unlocked the door and went in, bolting the door behind her. She slowly made her way upstairs, then abandoned her stick, changed her clothes and hobbled around making supper for herself and Thomas. In recent days, the thought of the bodies of the policemen in her flat had not instilled her usual shaking fit, and she was glad she was finally getting over the events and could get on with her life.

The new carpets had helped a lot, and the redecoration of the living room had got rid of all of the bloodstains. But then she'd never seen them since the night it had all happened anyway, since in the six weeks she was in a coma her landlord had claimed the insurance and redecorated the place. Probably because he thought she wasn't going to survive.

Stella watched briefly as Thomas purred and ate his food. She grabbed her drink and her plate of food and lurched through to the living room, only slopping her drink once on the way. She sat down on the new sofa, another addition to the room she'd been pleased to find, and switched on the TV. The news was full of the usual horror stories and bad news. Stella was just thankful that the news no longer involved her.

After her supper, she slid over and switched on her computer. It hummed as it booted up. She logged on.

Vincent's eyes pop open. He sits up quickly and smiles to no one in particular. He looks across at the sleeping forms of Frank and the two new guys they have recruited. Vincent stands, lights a cigarette and walks through to the big front room of the Janus building and presses the button to retract the blinds on the large glass wall. He looks out over the City.

It is a sunny day.

Printed in Great Britain
by Amazon